PRIMAL FEAR

A man-child, almost angelic in appearance, twenty years old at best, his teary eyes bright with fear, cowered on the floor of the confessional. His hair was matted with dried blood. His face, clothes and hands were stained red. His arms were crossed at the chest and a large, blood-streaked carving knife was clutched in his right fist.

His panicked eyes peered into the beams of three flashlights.

'Didn't do it,' he murmured in a pitiful, barely audible voice, shaking his head back and forth. 'Didn't do it, Mama. Mama, I didn't do it.'

William Diehl is the author of *Sharky's Machine*, *Chameleon*, *Hooligans*, *Thai House* and 27, all international bestsellers. Formerly a reporter, he lives on St Simon's Island, Georgia.

Also by William Diehl

Sharky's Machine
Chameleon
Hooligans
Thai Horse
27

PRIMAL FEAR

William Diehl

Mandarin

A Mandarin Paperback

PRIMAL FEAR

First published in Great Britain 1992
by William Heinemann Ltd
This edition published 1993
by Mandarin Paperbacks
an imprint of Reed Consumer Books Ltd
Michelin House, 81 Fulham Road, London SW3 6RB
and Auckland, Melbourne, Singapore and Toronto

Reprinted 1993 (twice)

A CIP catalogue record for this title
is available from the British Library
ISBN 0 7493 1091 X

Printed and bound in Great Britain by
BPCC Paperbacks Ltd
Member of BPCC Ltd

This book is for
my children, my grandchildren,
and their husbands and wives
Cathy, John, Katie, Emily, and Chelsea
Bill and Lori
Stan, Yvonne, Nicholas and Jason
Melissa, Jack and Michael
and Temple
And always for
Virginia

ACKNOWLEDGEMENTS

The author wishes to thank Dr Everett Kugler, of the Georgia Mental Health Department, for his invaluable assistance in the research of mental disorders; attorney Brett Merrill, of Swainsboro, Ga., for his guidance in law and trial procedures, and for his continued encouragement; Chip and Kathleen, and Steve Collura, for their patience; the members of Save the Beach and the Gunn Committee, for their concern and support; and author Stanley Booth, who couldn't write a bad sentence if he tried, for the inspiration of his words and for making even the darkest days a little brighter. *Salud*.

PRIMAL FEAR

'I believe in the law. I believe in the sanctity of the court-room and in the majesty of justice. I also believe that things are not always as they appear, that sometimes facts can be manipulated the way a magician manipulates an audience. He distracts you with this hand, while the other hand does the tricks. It's called misdirection. The prosecutor in this case is a magician. He has misdirected your attention from the facts of the case with flashy tricks and information that really have very little to do with my client's guilt or innocence. He has produced a body of what he calls evidence – all of it circumstantial. He says my client had motives, opportunities, desires, but produces no hard evdience connecting him directly to the crime. He says my client is immoral, that he is a liar, that he was caught cheating the victim, that he was desperate. My client does not deny these allegations – but does motive or opportunity or desire make him a murderer?

'Is he being tried for being immoral? Or for lying? Or for cheating? Will you send this man to the electric chair because he is desperate? I say in the interest of justice you must ignore the wizard's card tricks and look in his other hand – the hand where the real evidence should be because if you do, you will see that it is empty. This is a court of law, not a magic show. My client faces the death penalty.

'Can you twelve ladies and gentlemen honestly say that my opponent has proven this man guilty beyond a shadow of a doubt? The system makes mistakes because no matter how finely crafted it may be, it suffers the weakness of human fallibility. My client is human and he is fallible – but so is the magician who seeks his death. So I ask you not to be deceived by misdirection. Study the evidence carefully and when you do, I am convinced you will have no other choice than to find my client not guilty of this crime.'

MARTIN VAIL
Summation to the Jury
The State *vs* Nicholas Luma
SEPTEMBER 3, 1979

1983

*There is no crueler tyranny
than that which is perpetuated
under the shield of law
and in the name of justice.*

Montesquieu, 1742

One

When Archbishop Richard Rushman, known to Catholic, Protestant and Jew alike as 'the Saint of Lakeview Drive' because of his great charitable works, stepped out of the shower he had less than ten minutes to live. Death stood in the doorway.

The hot shower had relieved the Bishop's tension and he started to hum along with the stereo playing in the bedroom. Beethoven's 'Ode to Joy' – possibly his favourite piece of music. The majesty of the chorus never ceased to thrill him. It was so loud he did not hear the apartment's kitchen door open.

The kitchen door's unlocked. Good. The room, so spotless, so sterile-clean, stainless steel and tile, like the autopsy room at the hospital. The music. So fitting. Lovely. Overpowering. Volume all the way as usual, he won't hear a thing. In the bedroom, conducting the orchestra, eyes closed, imaginary baton in hand, humming along. So fucking predictable.

The Archbishop stood in the doorway of the bathroom, dabbing himself dry with the plush turkish towel. He was a tall handsome man, muscular and hard, with a tan line from shoulder to shoulder where his T-shirt usually ended. Dark, thick hair tumbled down over his forehead. He flexed his bicep, admiring the bulge as he dabbed under his arm. When he finished, he threw the towel on the bathroom floor and began to sway with the music as he stood naked in the middle of the room.

Chocolate for energy. Can almost feel it zooming up

3

like an electric charge, down there, too, swelling me up, preparing the big O. That's what he calls it, the big O. Don't screw up, hold your hand against the big six-foot refrigerator door so it doesn't make that little popping sound when it opens. Like that, perfect. There they are, all those little pony bottles of chocolate milk. Soldiers on the door shelf.

The intruder twisted the small bottle upside down, right side up, upside down, right side up, watching the drink turn to thick, chocolatey brown before he twisted off the top and drank it. Then instead of pressing the foot pedal on the garbage container, he lifted the cover by hand and placed the bottle silently into the plastic liner.

So neat, so clean. So fucking sterile.

The Archbishop sprinkled talc into a folded washcloth and closing his eyes, rubbed it into his body. He was lost in the music, using his voice like a bass fiddle as the brass came in. Bum bum bum bum bumbumbum buuum . . .

God, I love the way the knives feel. Light, balanced, cold. So smooth, slick, oily, like she is when she wants it, when she's ready.

The intruder slid open the hidden tray under the cabinet where the carving knives were stored, ran his fingertips lightly across the handles, so carefully rubbed with linseed after they were washed. He stopped at the largest one, the carving knife, its broad, long, stainless blade honed until the cutting edge was almost invisible. It shimmered in the soft rays of the night-light recessed under the cabinets. He removed it, ran his middle finger down the length of the blade leaving a thread of blood on its ridge from the slice in his finger. The intruder licked off the blood.

The chorus is beginning to build. And me, tightening, tingle in my belly, pulse in my temples, the spasms. Not much time left before it's time to explode.

He walked through the living room with the knife held down at his side. The bedroom door was open.

Sanctum sanctorum. Scarlet drapes and bedclothes, blood of the father. White carpeting, purity of soul. Candles glowing, clean the air. Incense . . .

And the ring, lying on the night table where he always put it when he showered afterwards.

There he is. All purity and light. His Eminence, his Holiness . . . his Crassness. Blessed saint of the city? Saint, where is thy halo? On the bedpost? In a drawer somewhere? Evil he stands and naked, conducting his imaginary symphony of angels, anointed with self-righteousness.

The music was building. The intruder walked to the table, took the ring and slipped it on his finger. His Excellency was rapt in the music, eyes closed, unaware. The intruder closed in, reached out with the knife and tapped the Bishop on the shoulder with the flat of the blade. Startled, the Bishop turned. His eyes widened with surprise. The Bishop started to smile, saw the knife. Questions floated across his face.

The intruder held out the hand with the ring on it and pointed the knife toward the floor. The Bishop was stunned, began to smile. The intruder jabbed the knife sharply towards the carpet and his Holiness slowly lowered to his knees. Fear replaced curiosity. The Bishop slowly leaned forward to kiss the ring on the hand outstretched to him.

Got to be timed perfectly so we come together. Big death, petite death . . . Forgive me father for I have sinned, forgive me father for I have sinned, forgive me father for I have . . .

'Forgive me, Father!' the intruder screamed.

Archbishop Rushman looked up in time to see the knife slashing the air a minisecond before he felt the burning under his ear . . . he screamed, a horrific mixture of terror, fright and pain like the banshees of hell howling in despair as the blade sliced through tissue and muscle, through throat, windpipe, jugular and œsophagus, nicking bone before bursting out under his other ear, a cut so clean and powerful only the bony spine kept head and body together.

Blood showered from the horrible gash.

The knife slashed again, this time across his naked belly. Then again from hip to hip. The deadly blade whipped again and again, flashing in the light, as he fell backwards sending a table and lamp half-way across the room, clutching at the wounds, feeling his hand bury into the soft mass of arteries and ruptured flesh. His head lolled, jogged to and fro like a cork in water. Pain overwhelmed him . . .

In the small park across the street from the rectory, a city mailman unleashed his dachshund, Gretchen, and watched her waddle along the row of shrubs that separated the grass from the sidewalk. He could hear the strains of classical music coming from behind the blinds in the Bishop's second-floor suite and he began to hum along with the music, a melody from his past.

He stood on the walkway letting his memory drift back, sifting through time as he picked up the tune.

Suddenly a voice cried out above the music.

'Forgive me, Father!'

He looked up at the window. There was a loud crash.

The light behind the blinds went askew and a moment later he heard a harrowing scream of terror, so wrought with horror that the dog feathered its ears and began to howl.

A streak of terror as real as a lightning bolt shot down his back. The hair rose on his arms. The puppy, crying, ran back to him and he swept it up in his arms as another scream just as harrowing, just as horrifying followed, only to be cut short by a muffled cry.

Silhouetted against the blinds he saw a figure moving

in and out of the light and the mailman ran into the
street, waving one arm at a passing car, yelling for help.

Two

Lieutenant Abel Stenner was the first detective to arrive at the scene. Ramrod straight and impeccably dressed, he was a precise and deliberate man whose stoic expression shielded any hint of emotion. His icy demeanour and complete lack of passion had long ago earned him the nickname 'Icicle', although never to his face. Two uniformed cops standing near the door to the rectory watched as he got out of his car and walked without any particular hurry towards them. One of them lifted the yellow crime scene ribbon as he approached and he ducked under it.

'Thank you,' he said without looking at them and entered the three-storey brick building that was part of the towering, gothic church.

'Jesus, don't he ever wear a coat? Must be ten degrees out.'

'What's he need a coat for?' the other answered. 'He don't have any blood.'

A grey-haired veteran with the veined nose of a drinker stood with his back to the door of the bedroom. He seemed pale and shaken as Stenner came up the stairs to the second-floor suite. With his hands clasped behind him, the lieutenant stood directly in front of the patrolman.

'What happened here?' he asked.

The patrolman stammered as he read the details from his notebook.

'Man named, uh . . . Harriman . . . Raymond Harriman . . . was, uh, walking his dog across the, uh, the street there and . . . this was about ten after ten . . . and he, uh, heard, y'know, screams, that . . .'

'Who's been inside the room?'

'Just me, sir. I checked to, y'know, make sure he was D.O.A. although it . . . really wasn't necessary considering . . .'

'Nobody else?'

'No sir. I got a man at the door, uh, in the kitchen but I'm the only one was in the, the scene itself. I turned off the tape player with my pencil, it was awful loud.'

'Very good. What have you . . . what's your name? You're Travers aren't you?'

'Travers, yes sir.'

'You all right, Travers?'

'Yeah, sure, sir. But God a'mighty, I ain't ever seen nothing like this and I been on the force for twenty-two years.'

'What's happened so far?' Stenner demanded.

'Uh, ribbons around the outside. We have patrolmen completely surrounding . . . y'know, the premises. Nobody in or out but we haven't searched the . . . the church or anything yet, because I didn't know . . .'

'You sure you're all right, Officer?'

Travers nodded uncertainly.

'Go on outside, get some air. Nobody . . . *nobody* . . . goes in or out except if they're official, understand? No press. And no . . . *no* statements yet. Pass it around. Anybody says a word about this, I'll personally hang 'em out to dry. Clear?'

'Right. Yes sir.'

Travers, glad to escape the scene, rushed down the stairs, passing Stenner's assistant, a thirty-year-old black detective named Lou Turner, who came briskly up the stairs and then reared back as he reached the bedroom doorway.

'Sweet Jesus!' he cried, abruptly turning his back on the scene. He took out a handkerchief and coughed into it. There were several bloody smears on the carpet in the hallway leading to the kitchen.

9

'You handle this, Louis?'

'Yeah, sure. Just a shock.'

'It's that, all right,' the lieutenant said.

Stenner stood in the doorway of Archbishop Rushman's bedroom and stared from behind wire-rimmed glasses at a scene straight out of *Le Grand Guignol*. His jaw tightened a few times as he slowly appraised the bloody mess inside. Otherwise, his expression did not change. Cold, efficient eyes scanned the room. A few inches from his head there was an almost perfect bloody handprint on the door jamb.

'Louis, go back downstairs. I want men around the entire perimeter. A team of four in the church, another downstairs . . .' He hesitated a moment, then added, 'and on the roof. Start the search immediately.' His voice was a flat monotone.

'Think he's still inside?'

'I doubt we're that lucky.'

'Right.'

Turner rushed back downstairs. Stenner turned abruptly and, stepping carefully, followed a bloody trail of smeared footprints back to the kitchen where they ended abruptly near the back door. A young patrolman stood beside the door, looking like a startled deer. There was another scarlet handprint on the kitchen counter.

'What's your name, son?' Stenner asked.

'Roth, sir.'

'All right, Roth,' Stenner said flatly. 'Go outside the door there and keep everybody out. I'm going to lock it behind you. Don't move around until the lab people get here, understand?'

'Yes sir.'

The young cop went outside and stood on a wooden landing, hunching his shoulders against the frigid air, and stared down a sturdy, wooden staircase to the grounds below, where men moved back and forth, their flashlights stabbing the night.

Inside the kitchen, Stenner locked the door and put the key in his pocket. He found a spool of paper towels and carried it back to the bedroom.

He stood in the doorway, his stony eyes appraising a spacious bedroom decorated in exquisite taste. The entrance was at one end of the room.

Opposite Stenner was a massive oak four-poster bed set against the centre of the wall with matching night tables on either side of it.

Facing it on the opposite wall to his left was a stereo and television set in a custom cabinet that matched both the bed and a hulking chest of drawers which was located in the corner. Except for the cabinet, the furniture was obviously antique.

A black leather sofa and coffee table were set against the wall to his right and beyond that was the door to the bathroom.

In the far corner, next to a large picture window, was a leather chair and footstool that matched the sofa.

The window was bordered on either side by thick drapes and shuttered by lavallière blinds. The drapes, bed quilt, throw rugs and blankets were all deep scarlet and the carpeting was – or had been – white. There was a large crucifix with a splash of palm leaf behind it over the bed and a sixteen by twenty photograph of the *Pietà* over the sofa.

Between the door and the sofa was the entrance to a walk-in closet.

A man who enjoyed his comforts, thought Stenner

Stenner took a notebook from his inside pocket and made a hasty sketch of the room. Then he laid the paper towel spool on the floor at the entrance to the bedroom and stepping on the end towel, rolled it into the room like a red carpet being unfolded for a dignitary. Finally he entered the scene, walking carefully along the paper path.

The walls, bed, chair and floor were splashed with

blood, as if an incarnation of Jackson Pollock had been at work in the room. As he continued towards the bed he saw a foot, then a leg, and finally the remains of the man who was considered one of the truly great men of the city.

The naked corpse lay between the bed and the windows, its head jammed against the wall and cocked crazily to one side, its eyes plucked from the sockets, its cheeks puffed and lips bulging, tongue swollen in the corner of its mouth, one hand buried to the knuckles in a straight, gaping slash that stretched just below the jawline from ear to ear. The body, legs and arms, even the toes, were sliced with dozens of deep and awesome wounds and stabbed repeatedly. The number '666' was etched with artistic precision in the stomach. Blood ran river-like from the wounds forming a soggy bed for the remains of Archbishop Richard Bernard Rushman.

As he studied the body, a sudden chill passed through Stenner. The genitals had been removed. Almost fearfully, Stenner's eyes slowly moved up the body to the gaping mouth where, he realised, the priest's private parts had been stuffed and also realised that what he had thought was a tongue was not a tongue at all.

Stenner, normally unmoved by such carnage, swallowed a sudden flood of bile that soured his throat and took several deep breaths.

Behind him, the soft southern drawl of the county's chief forensics officer, said, 'Christ, what a mess.'

Stenner turned to him.

'Mind your manners, Harvey, this is part of the church.'

'Obviously not inviolate.'

Harvey Woodside was sweating, the result of his climb up the stairs. Woodside was hemispheric, an enormous, asthmatic man whose head seemed to sprout from thick, rounded shoulders. He breathed through thick lips, a kind of steady gasp that quickly became annoying, and squinted from below fleshy eyelids, his beady, brown eyes darting in a continuous search for evidence. He wore a black sleeveless sweater over a rainbow-coloured Hawaiian shirt both of which were tucked into grey slacks that were badly in need of pressing and supported by red, white and blue braces. But his large hands seemed almost delicate and were always beautifully manicured. All in all, an unkempt and often disagreeable man – *but* when it came to forensics, unparalleled.

His three-man team climbed the steps carrying several aluminium cases which they put on the landing.

One of them said, looking in the bedroom, 'we could be here till Labour Day.'

Woodside waited until Stenner came out of the room then waddled out to the end of the stretched towel roll and peered down at the remains of Bishop Rushman.

'Well, well, well,' he said, and then, after a few moments of study, twisted his head and looked back over his shoulder at Stenner. 'You got yourself a first-class nut-house mouse here, Abel.'

'So it would appear.'

'Any idea when this happened?'

'Probably about ten-ten, I think we have a witness, at least an earball witness,' Stenner said, looking at his watch. 'That would be less than thirty minutes ago.'

'That's a help. Nice to get a break early on. Okay, let's go to work, boys. Complete wash, floor to ceiling. Bathroom, hall, where's that door down there lead to?'

'Kitchen.'

'And kitchen. Shoot it, print it, dust it, vacuum it, swatch it, don't miss a Goddamn thing. This one's gonna shake up the environs.'

Stenner's walkie-talkie suddenly snapped to life. It was Turner.

'Better get down here on the double, Lieutenant,' he said. 'In the church.'

Stenner went back down to the vestibule at the foot

of the stairs. A cop opened a door at the rear of the large entrance room and Stenner went through it and down a long passageway that ended in a small waiting room beside the altar. Under the towering apse and across sweeping rows of pews, Turner and four police officers were standing in front of a confessional, guns drawn.

Stenner hurried across the church and down one row, brushed the cops aside and stared into the cubicle.

A man-child, almost angelic in appearance, twenty years old at best, his teary eyes bright with fear, cowered on the floor of the confessional. His hair was matted with dried blood. His face, clothes and hands were stained red. His arms were crossed at the chest and a large, blood-streaked carving knife was clutched in his right fist.

His panicked eyes peered into the beams of three flashlights.

'Didn't do it,' he murmured in a pitiful, barely audible voice, shaking his head back and forth. 'Didn't do it, Mama. Mama, I didn't do it.'

Three

Everyone on the el was riveted to the morning paper and the banner headline:

'Archbishop RUSHMAN MURDERED!'

And the subhead:

'Youth Arrested In Mutilation Slaying.'

But Martin Vail was more interested in the copy of *City Magazine* he had bought at the corner news-stand. He checked the table of contents, flipped to page thirty-two and settled back to read the story.

Vail of Innocents

A blood-letting at the City's Expense
By
JACK CONNERMAN

'The jury's been out for an hour and a half, it's eight o'clock on a Thursday eve with only seven shopping days left until Christmas, and the court-room, which is still crowded, is as tense as a hospital waiting room. There is a lot of aimless conversation but most eyes are on the door through which the jury will eventually return. After sitting through twelve days of testimony so incendiary that at one point the Judge suggested calling in the fire department, nobody's going to leave now. Not with the last act about to go on.

' "What he is, he's the *assassin* of the legal game in this town. A vampire is what he is. Sits there in court, shit you can almost see his fuckin fangs drippin blood. He's a big game hunter, comes in with that old-fashioned doctor's bag of his, his motor's runnin, can't wait for it to happen, know what I mean? Prosecutors? Shiiit. Has 'em for breakfast, lunch and dinner, goes home, snacks on judges before he hits the sack. You're a prosecutor and he's sittin' on the other side of the room? Pack up. Take your writs and legal pads, depositions, all that legal shit, throw 'em away, go home, take a Jacuzzi. Read a book. Suck on some chocolates. Just save your juice, pal, 'cause you're already dead. You might's well be hangin' on a hook in the fuckin' slaughterhouse."

'A bailiff is talking, a red-eyed, bag-bellied old timer with bad breath and what's left of a toothpick lingering in the corner of his mouth. He's seen twenty-two years worth of barristers come and go in this town. Knows all the tricks. Could probably spout more law than any five hundred dollars an hour Philadelphia lawyer.

' "Marty Vail. Walkin' death," the bailiff says and strolls away.

'The year is staggering towards a close this December evening in Superior Court-room six – where Clarence Darrow once chewed up a hot-shot local lawyer so bad he quit and became a law professor – as the crowded court-room roots in place, waiting for the verdict in the case of Joe Pinero versus The City.

'Vail is sitting on a window-sill ignoring what's going on around him, looking out over a city ablaze with Christmas lights. He's so calm he could be in a coma. Smoking is prohibited in the room but Vail absently lights one off the other, dropping ashes and butts in a plastic coffee container. Nobody tells him to stop.

'What's on Vail's mind?

'He's probably thinking that when the jury returns, he'll own a small piece of the real estate he's looking down at, a hunk of the city which for a year he has casually stomped into dust.

'His client, a local triggerman and three-time loser named Joe Pinero, is sitting at the defendant's desk. His fingers are doing a soft shoe to some imaginary tune. If he's worried about his future, you'd never know it. But then, why should he be? Marty Vail has just done a High Noon on the best the city had to offer, Albert Silverman, an attorney of high repute, who is at this moment down in the john, puking his guts out. That's how the city's case has gone for him.

' "If Vail was a big league pitcher, he'd be king of the change-up," a sports writer friend of mine once said. "He doesn't go in just to win, man. Every game's gotta be a no-hitter."

'Charlene Crowder, tough as a stevedore after spending the better part of her life recording trials, swears this actually happened:

' "This is in his early days – six, seven years ago, okay? – he's defending a small-time stickup man. A key piece of evidence is this hat, supposedly owned by the defendant. So Vail kneecaps the prosecutor, proves the hat can't possibly belong to his client, and tucks the case in his pocket. Then when it's over, Vail walks over to the property man and says, 'My client wants his hat back.' "

'Vail says now he was kidding – but he took the hat.

'Vail, in seven years, has become a legend. He never gives interviews, carries printed business cards which say, "No comment", comes to court in suits that haven't been pressed since Elvis was in grade school. He maybe gets a haircut when the seasons change. Ties hang at half mast like a loose noose around his neck. His shoes have never heard the crack of a shineman's rag.

'He's a sleep walker, strolling around the court-room as if he's dropped an idea on the floor and can't find it. Then he's a jack-in-the-box, roaring out of his chair like a volcano going off. Then he's a charmer – smiling, soothing, patronising – before suddenly turning into an asp, striking at the jugular of an unsuspecting witness. Sometimes he smiles, sometimes he looks worried, sometimes he looks bored. But those grey eyes never change. Look in those eyes, you're staring straight at sudden death. It's take no prisoners. He is the merciless executioner, destroying opponents as casually as if he were dunking doughnuts at the corner coffee house.

'Marty Vail at thirty-two: legal *enfant terrible* for the upcoming eighties. In his hands, the law is a juggler's ball.

'Joe Pinero, known to friend and foe as Shades because he wears his sunglasses *every*where – probably sleeps in them – is a mobster, a street soldier whose sheet includes convictions for assault, attempted murder and manslaughter. The first time he gets two to five for using a sawed-off baseball bat on a shoe clerk who owes a bookie forty dollars. He's out in nine months. The second time around he shoots another hood in a territorial argument, a gang killing reduced to manslaughter because the prosecutor's case is weak. He walks in six months. A year and a half ago, Pinero and three other gangsters go at it on a crowded down-town street in a shoot-out reminiscent of World War II. When the smoke clears, two are dead and Pinero has three holes in him. Witnesses vanish, nobody can figure out who did what to who and Pinero plea-bargains to manslaughter and takes another hike. Needless to say, he is not a popular figure in law enforcement circles.

'Cut to last New Year's Eve. Pinero is on his way home from a party. Two cops fall in behind him – one is a county cop, the other a state john who is off duty, just out for the night with his pal – who, it turns out, is his brother. The county cop recognises Pinero and they pull him over and decide to hassle him, make him walk a line, touch his finger to his nose, the DUI trip. What they don't realise is that they had crossed the line into the city. Along comes a city cop and joins the party. They shake down the car and find a loaded revolver in the trunk. Pinero starts screaming about his rights, about county and state cops pulling him over in the city, one thing leads to another and next thing you know, all three policemen are beating on Pinero like he's the bass drum in a high school band.

'He ends up in the hospital with two broken ribs, crushed cheek-bone, concussion, multiple bruises and contusions, and charges of DUI, resisting arrest, concealed weapon. Then up pops the devil. Pinero it turns out, has clocked a .06 on the breatholater. He was legally sober. Rumours are rampant – the most popular being that the powers-that-be are up the river, frantically looking for a paddle.

'Enter Marty Vail with a civil suit for twenty-five mil. He ends up in a legal brawl with the state, the county, *and* the city. There is a lot of smirking over at the Lawyer's Club, where jealousy spreads like the plague. The odds are running about a thousand to one that Vail has finally bitten off the big one.

'But over the next ten months, Vail tears the city, county and state to pieces. He pits state and county cops against city cops. The in-fighting gets so vicious the three governments are threatening to sue each other. Vail sits back and clips his fingernails – before he's through he agrees to drop the charges against county and state, subpoenas both cops, and they turn on their city brother like a couple of pit bulls.

'Before it goes to trial, the odds are running even – with the smart money on Vail.

'Now Vail is contemplating the blinking lights on the county Christmas tree, his client is as cool as a draft beer in a frosted glass, the county prosecutor turned defence counsel is on his knees in the men's room, and seven men and five women are off in the jury room trying to figure out who did what to whom and how much it's going to cost.

'The jury's been out two hours when I wander over and lean on the window-sill beside Vail. He has taken off his yellow tie and stuffed it in the breast pocket of a tweed suit that looks like he's been sleeping in it for a week. He is badly in need of a shave. Early in the trial, Judge Harry Shoat, a fanatical conservative known in legal circles as Hangin' Harry and who, comparatively speaking, makes Attila the Hun look like a social reformer, admonishes Vail about his dress code.

' "With all due respect, Your Honour," Vail replies, "I came here to practise law, not audition for the cover of *Gentleman's Quarterly*."

'That sets the tone for a trial during which Vail is twice fined a thousand dollars for contempt. The only reason he does not spend ten days or so in the local hoosegow is fear of a mis-trial. Nobody wants to go through this massacre again.

' "So whadda ya think?" I ask Vail.

' "I think blinking lights on Christmas trees are the epitome of bad taste," he says, staring down at the tree in front of the court-house which looks like a red and green caution light. "Looks like a damn neon sign."

' "How long do you think they'll be out?"

' "Until they decide how much we get."

' "You think it's that simple?"

' "Yep." He lights another Vantage and drops the old one in the cup, where it sizzles out.

' "When did you figure it was in the bag?" I ask.

' "The day I took the case," Vail answers.

'Self confidence and that look, that's what nails them. It never occurs to Vail that he will lose, only how big he'll win.

'The jury is out for two hours and forty minutes. Verdict: 7.6 million dollars for ex-gunman suddenly turned millionaire Joe Pinero. The court-room goes crazy. Silverman heads back to the men's john. And Martin Vail has just earned himself a cool two and a half mil.

20

'The Judge stares balefully down from on high. "Perhaps," he says to Vail, "you can afford a new suit now, Counsellor."

'Martin Vail smiles up at the judge. "A possibility," he answers.

'Two days later, the city files an appeal.

'And the beat goes on.

'It promises to be a fun year.'

Vail shivered against the frigid breeze reaming the el car and huddled deeper inside his sheepskin jacket as he read the *City Magazine* article for the second time. *Not bad*, he thought. *Not bad at all*. The photograph was fine. It showed a hard-eyed young man with a cocky smile leaning against a judge's bench with his hands in his trouser pockets, a sheaf of writs stuffed in his jacket pocket, staring straight into the camera with a battered medicine bag at his feet. The caption was a killer:

Martin Vail
Prosecutors Benedict for breakfast

Vail chuckled. He owed Connerman drinks and dinner for this one. He slipped the magazine into his bag as the train stopped at the edge of the el loop and rushed out of the car, turning his collar up against the wet snow drizzle lashed by a hard breeze off the lake, four blocks away. Vail hated this time of year. The damp north wind blew down across the lake and slashed the flat midwestern city like a razor, knifing through Vail's thickest coat and freezing his face. He half ran the two blocks and took the wide, granite steps two at a time. Once inside, he flipped dampness off his collar and lit a cigarette. Across the broad marble and brass lobby, Bobby, the newsman, waved a copy of the magazine at him.

'Mr V,' he yelled. 'It's a killer.'

Vail strolled across the marble and brass lobby, took

the magazine, picked up a bag of shelled peanuts and dropped a five in Bobby's hand.

'Keep the change,' he said, rushing off.

'G'bless ya,' Bobby called after him.

He walked to the second floor, avoiding the crowded elevators. It was five after nine. He would be five minutes late. Fashionable. Vail had taken an hour that morning to mentally prepare himself for the meeting. Valerie Main, who had been secretary to a succession of city attorneys for about a century, glared at him as he entered the office.

'You're late,' she snapped.

'It's the weather,' he said and smiled, shucking his jacket and throwing it over a chair. He was wearing a ski sweater, no shirt, corduroy pants and thick-soled clodhoppers.

'You're in for it,' she said cryptically as he entered the inner office.

Four

The players surprised Vail. The room was bloated with old time politicos – the muscle – instead of quick, clever, young hitmen eager to slice a deal. It threw him for a minute. There was the city attorney, Arnold Flederman, who had been around since Mrs O'Leary's cow kicked the oil lamp that started the city's fire; Otis Burnside, the city council man, the masterful puppeteer who pulled the strings of the down-town first ward; and Johnny Malloway, the malevolent ex-FBI agent, now police commissioner, who knew just what pressure points to push if he wanted to stop blood from flowing to the brain.

And there was Roy Shaughnessey.

Jesus, Judge, what the hell's going on here? Vail wondered.

They all looked with disdain at his clothes. The big office was dressed out in mahogany and brass with burly furniture and expensive appointments. Steam heat made the room oppressively warm. A single hard-backed chair sat in front of the desk that dominated the room. In a semi-circle behind it were Burnside, Flederman and Malloway. Roy Shaughnessey sat off to one side.

All they need to complete the third degree is a spotlight over the chair, Vail thought.

'Mornin, Mister Vail,' Flederman drawled, nodding towards the chair.

He let his gaze wander around the room, settling momentarily on each one before he sat without speaking.

'We're all here to help you off the hook,' Malloway started. He was a lean, pale man who still dressed in the anonymous grey drab of the Bureau. 'You're on very thin ice, laddie.'

'There isn't a judge in this town wouldn't dance on your goddamn grave,' Flederman pitched in. He leaned over and let a dollop of tobacco juice gravitate into the gold spittoon beside his chair.

Vail just smiled a cock-eyed Irish smile.

'You got a problem the size of Lake Michigan here,' Burnside offered, his eyes glittering momentarily under warty lids. 'We just wanna make it easy on ya. You got a pretty good reputation hereabouts. Don't push it under.'

Everybody was interested in his welfare. Vail said nothing.

Shaughnessey, the old timer from the attorney general's office, said nothing either. He rocked slowly in an oversized leather chair, a heavy man, his bulk wrapped in a fifteen hundred dollar three-piece suit, a splash of coloured silk in its breast pocket. He had a fleshy face and his cholesterol lips were curled contemptuously in what the unsuspecting might have mistaken for a smile. His hooded eyes were keen and deadly and his massive fingers were locked and folded over his chest, the thumbs rubbing almost imperceptibly. He was a listener, Shaughnessey was, and he was also the state's high priest who with a mere nod could bring pestilence and plague down on anyone who threatened to disquiet the political seas of the state house. Vail had met him once, ten years ago. He knew Shaughnessey to be a masterful politician who had weathered thirty years and four administrations. Governors feared him and presidential aspirants sought his advice. Compared to him, the other three were gandy dancers.

What the hell was he doing here?

Vail considered the possibilities. He locked his gaze on Shaughnessey's, ignoring Flederman who droned on, dropping threats, hot air, and coarse slurs like sheep droppings, while Burnside and Malloway occasionally jumped in with veiled threats. Snow chattered against the window. The radiator hissed subtly in the corner. Neither man broke the staring contest.

'See what I mean?' Flederman concluded.

It was Shaughnessey who broke the staring contest first. He looked over at Flederman and Vail followed his lead.

'No,' Vail said.

'*No?*' Flederman said.

'Whadda ya mean, no?' Burnside asked.

'No, I don't see what you mean,' Vail answered.

'Jesus,' Flederman said and this time he spat into the spittoon. 'Yer not fuckin' stupid.'

'He wasn't listening to you,' Shaughnessey said in a harsh voice so low it was barely audible in the room.

'Whadda ya mean, wasn't listening?' Flederman stammered. 'What the hell'm I doin', talkin' t'hear m'self talk?'

'Probably,' Shaughnessey said. He turned towards Vail. 'You have something in mind?'

'I thought I'd listen to their offer first,' Vail said quietly, separating Shaughnessey from the pack. He was taking a gamble that Shaughnessey had come to the meeting without offering any stand. Shaughnessey the listener.

Shaughnessey chuckled. Not much of a chuckle, but a chuckle nonetheless. 'You learn well, Mister Vail.'

'Thanks.'

'Learn? Learn what?' Flederman asked.

Shaughnessey looked at Vail. 'Play chess, do you?' he asked.

Vail nodded. 'Used to. Not much any more, too busy.'

'Old rule,' Shaughnessey said to Flederman. 'He who moves first loses.'

Flederman looked confused. He stared back and forth between Shaughnessey and Vail, then turned to Burnside.

'God dammit, say something, Otis,' he snapped.

'What the fuck d'ya mean, *offer?*' Burnside said to

Vail. His face reddened and his voice rose almost to a scream. 'We're not offering, we're *telling*.'

Shaughnessey flicked an imaginary speck of dust off his trousers.

'Quiet down, Otis,' he said softly.

'Well, Jesus!'

'Does he think we're here to compromise?' Commissioner Malloway said.

'Not compromise,' said Vail. 'Negotiate. In a compromise everybody loses. In a negotiation, everybody wins.'

Shaughnessey chuckled again.

'What's so Goddamn funny, Roy?' Burnside asked.

'Education.'

'What the hell's that supposed to mean?'

Shaughnessey stared at him for several seconds, then said, 'Did you hear what he said?'

''Bout what?' Flederman asked.

'About negotiating and compromise.' He turned back to Vail. 'Why don't you explain it to them, Mister Vail.'

Vail nodded. 'If you go in thinking compromise, you assume you're going to give up something. If you go in thinking negotiation, you decide what you want and what you don't give a damn about. That way, you get what you want and give up what doesn't matter. Cuts through the bullshit.'

Malloway's eyes narrowed. 'Suppose we just tell you what's going to happen?' he said harshly.

'I think it would be a mistake,' Vail told him.

'Oh you do, do you,' Malloway said.

'Yes, I do.'

'And why's that?' Flederman said, adjusting the chew from one cheek to the other.

Shaughnessey answered the question. 'Because you're going to end up in court, Arnold. And Mister Vail knows nobody wants that.'

'Well . . .' Burnside hesitated. 'Who the hell's side are you on, anyway, Roy?'

'Just listening, Otis, just listening,' Shaughnessey answered. He looked across the room at Vail and said, 'I really came to mediate this event since the state is involved. I would appreciate it, Mister Vail, if you would analyse the situation as you see it. I think the first move has already been made here.'

Vail stood up. He always talked better on his feet, thinking of himself as addressing a jury. He opened the bag of peanuts and offered them around but got only glares. He ate a couple, lit a cigarette, walked to the far side of the room and leaned against the wall.

'This trial cost the taxpayers about . . . seven hundred thousand dollars so far, right?' Nobody answered. 'The appeal will cost another seven, maybe more. People in the city are going to get a little pissed over that . . .'

'You think you got everybody in this town in your fuckin' pocket,' Flederman yelled.

'Immaterial. You're going to *hit* them in the pocket if you go back at it. You've already burned up Silverman, so you also need a new attorney . . .'

'I'll take you on,' Flederman said, narrowing his eyes.

'Why? Pride? You don't even have good grounds for appeal. If you get thrown out, you look foolish to the taxpayers. If you go into a new trial, it's a gamble.'

'I'll whip yer young ass,' Flederman said.

'Easy, Arnold,' Shaughnessey said. 'Listen to the man. You're wasting your time getting into a pissing match with him.'

'Why's that?'

'Because he doesn't give a damn, do you, Mister Vail?'

Vail smiled. A wise old owl. 'No, sir,' he said.

'I don't get it,' Burnside said to Shaughnessey. 'We can make life miserable for this little son-bitch and you know it.'

'I'm not so sure,' Shaughnessey said.

'I am,' Malloway said. 'We're gonna nail Pinero for a concealed weapon. That's a felony and he's gone down three times already. He'll do twenty to life. By the time he gets out he'll be too old to enjoy whatever he gets in the appeal.'

He leaned back in his chair and smiled. Shaughnessey raised his eyebrows and looked back at Vail.

'Okay,' Vail said, snuffing out his cigarette. 'See you in court.'

The smile vanished from Malloway's face. Flederman leaned forward and glared at Vail.

Shaughnessey looked down at the floor. 'Tell them,' he said.

'You don't have a concealed weapon case.'

'Whaddya mean?'

'It was an illegal arrest. My client was not DUI, therefore the search was a violation of his rights. The court has already ruled that he didn't provoke the attack by the officers. Even if you win a depressed judgement, say half, a new jury won't reverse. So you end up owing Pinero four mil, it costs you another seven hundred to go through the process, and all you end up with is a lot of irate citizens. It's a bad call, Mister Malloway.'

Dead silence fell on the room. Shaughnessey leaned back in his chair and wrapped his fingers over his chest again.

'You have something in mind?' he asked.

'Yes sir.'

'Let's hear it.'

'Drop the appeal. The gun case is a dead issue. For the good of the community, we'll take a reduced judgement of a million-six. City pays half, county and state cough up four hundred thou apiece. We all smile sweetly and Pinero agrees to leave the city forever. He wants to move to California anyway.'

'I'll be a son-bitch,' Flederman said and spat the rest of his tobacco in the brass urn at his feet. Malloway and Burnside stared at Vail open-mouthed. Shaughnessey continued to rub his thumbs together.

'Why don't you think about it?' Vail said. 'Get back to me.'

'Oh, why not just settle it right now,' Shaughnessey suggested softly. 'Before anybody has a chance to screw it up. I'll take one of those peanuts now, son.'

After Vail left, Arnold Flederman stood up, his face flushed, and slapped his hand on the desk.

'That arrogant little prick,' he snapped. 'What was all that shit about goin' first and losin' and negotiating and compromising? What the fuck's he talkin' about?'

'He was quoting me,' Shaughnessey said with a wry smile. 'A lecture I gave about ten years ago when he was a law student.'

'Yer kiddin',' Flederman said.

Shaughnessey didn't answer. He picked up the phone and punched out a number, waited for it to answer.

'This is Roy Shaughnessey for the Judge . . . well tell him to take a recess, I need to talk to him *now*. I'll hold.' He drummed his fingertips on the desk while he waited.

'What's this about?' Burnside asked.

'Pay up time,' said Shaughnessey. 'Mister Vail is about to get a lesson in politics . . . Hello, Harry. Okay, he took us for a million-six . . . no, there wasn't any argument, he could have gone for more . . . Look, he's a smart kid, Harry, just needs some humility. It's all yours. Kick his ass.'

Five

Butterfly Higdon's. Ten thirty a.m.

Most of the breakfast crowd had drifted out by now. At the circular bar in front, Burt Sheflin, who had long ago drowned a great singing career in rye whisky, was having his first of the day, lifting a shot glass with both hands to trembling lips. The bartender, Pins, a baby-faced former professional wrestler, if wrestlers are ever professionals, nodded as Vail walked towards the rear.

Two paralegal types, stripped to their shirt-sleeves, were shooting eight ball on the single table beside the bar. One of them knelt, sighted his shot, stood, aimed carefully, and dropped the two balls as he walked past.

'You're late!' Butterfly Higdon, who was probably the best cook in the state – although at 250 pounds a butter-fly she definitely was not – yelled over her shoulder as she scraped the grill with a spatula and Tad and Fana polished tables in the restaurant section.

'The usual,' Vail yelled back.

'I'm cleaning the grill.'

'So . . . ?'

'Jeez,' she said, 'you'd think you own the Goddamn place.'

In fact, Vail did own a small piece of the bar and grill, as did a dozen other lawyers, judges, cops and newsmen, all of whom had chipped in to buy it when a greedy developer had tried to squeeze her out a year or so back. Vail took his cup from among two dozen on hooks in the corner and poured himself a cup of coffee, then went to a large round booth in the back.

The Judge sat at his usual place in the booth reserved for the regulars. Half a dozen newspapers littered the table, as did two copies of *City Magazine*, one still open to the Vail story. He sipped his coffee and perused the morning paper through pince-nez glasses which he held in place with one hand while he held the paper out in front of him with the other. A blueberry muffin lay forgotten on a plate in front of him, a pad of butter melting on the knife which lay across the plate. Vail shucked his jacket and threw it on a chair, sitting across from the elder statesman of the Higdon Gang.

'You're late,' the Judge said without looking at him. 'And I see you are now immortalised in ink.' He nodded towards the article.

Vail ignored the sarcastic compliment and laid four silver dollars in a tight row on the table. The Judge stared past the paper at them, finished the story he was reading, then put the paper carefully to one side.

'Four of them, eh?'

Vail nodded.

'Four on one. Hardly what I would call reasonable odds.'

'It worked out.'

The Judge leaned back in his chair and put his glasses in his jacket pocket. Jack Spalding was a tall, gaunt man, hollow-cheeked, his handsome face seamed with the battle scars of forty-five years in the court-room. Wisps of brown and white hair were combed carefully back from an Alpine forehead, twinkling pale blue eyes were alert to any challenge. He was, as always, dressed to perfection in tweeds, red and blue striped tie, and pale blue shirt with a fresh red carnation, picked from the nearby city park, carefully placed in his lapel.

Spalding was a man of rare distinction who had stepped down from the bench, disenchanted by courts that were degraded by millionaire drug dealers in their twenties, Uzi-wielding teenagers and lawyers who went through their daily litany with about as much passion as Division Street hookers. He now held court each morning for a handful of promising young lawyers who rehearsed their cases before him, quoting law, trying out lines, challenging his wisdom with tricks and chicanery. He always caught them, of course, although sometimes he let them get by on the theory that a good lacing in court was sometimes more educational than sage advice.

Marty Vail represented his proudest moment. This was the son he had never had. The protégé who had surpassed the master. And he accepted the young man's arrogance and conceit as the flaws of a mind so focused and disciplined that losing a court case was simply incomprehensible to him.

The Judge squinted his eyes and stared at the four silver cart-wheels.

'Four on one,' he mused. 'I would have to conclude that they threw the heavyweights at you, consequently I will rule out negotiation which therefore rules out the young sharpies. Had to be a power play.'

'Okay so far.'

'City, county and state?'

'I'll give you that, too. No more clues.'

The Judge squinted his eyes at the ceiling for a few minutes, then said, 'Two from the city, since they got the bill, one each from county and state. So . . . I make it City Attorney Flederman, it's basically his problem.'

Vail slid one of the dollars across the table and the Judge trapped it with a slap of the hand.

'Otis, he'd be the city whip.'

Vail slid a second dollar towards him.

The Judge stared hard at Vail who put on his best poker face.

'For the county . . . guessing, I'd say the meanest man they've got. That would have to be Johnny Malloway.'

'Brilliant,' Vail said, sliding him another dollar piece. 'One to go.'

'Now who would they throw at you from the state? Someone from the governor's staff maybe? Or the attorney general's office . . . or even the House. Probably somebody with a greased tongue, one of those oily bastards to balance Flederman, Burnside and Malloway, since they're all steamrollers. Uh huh . . . uh huh. And who's the greasiest one in the bunch?' He chuckled. 'Have to be Mister slick himself. Woodrow P. Carlisle.'

Vail smiled and slowly shook his head. The Judge looked surprised. 'Well I'll be damned,' he said, and slid one dollar back to Vail. 'Okay, I capitulate, sir. Who was the state's mystery man?'

'Roy Shaughnessey.'

Spalding was obviously shocked. 'You're kidding!'

'Not on your life.' Tad brought him his usual breakfast – two soft poached eggs on white toast, home fries and sausage. He attacked the meal hungrily, talking as he ate. 'Now here's the kicker – he was playing my game.'

'What do you mean?'

'My offer was a million-six and Pinero leaves the state forever. Shaughnessey told them to take it, no arguments. The whole thing didn't last thirty minutes.'

'They rolled over, just like that?'

'Just like that. I didn't even give 'em the options. I never had to put a card on the table.'

'Seems to me you may have a little problem with your client. How's he going to feel when you tell him he just had to eat six and a half million dollars?'

'He gets a million, one. I take five hundred thou.'

'How're you going to explain that? Pinero has the scruples of a hyena. I remind you, he's buried at least four people . . . that we know about.'

'I'll scare him to death,' Vail said.

'Hah! With what?'

'Twenty to life upstate.'

The Judge thought for a moment and nodded. 'Well, that's a pretty good scare card.'

'Hell, Pinero's never seen a million dollars, he can barely count to ten. With any luck at all, he'll end up in a bridge somewhere before he sorts it all out. I just hope the little hot head doesn't get his brains blown out before we get the cheque.'

The Judge redressed the morning meeting. 'Getting back to the subject at hand,' he said. 'There is something definitely not kosher here, my friend.'

'Hey, it's a very reasonable deal. The city will probably pick up eight hundred thou and the state and county each kick in four hundred. Nobody gets hurt too badly and the whole thing goes away.'

'Yes, but this wasn't litigation, Martin m'boy, it was politics and politics is never logical. What's their agenda? What are they really after?'

'I think you're being a little paranoid.'

'Oh yes, absolutely. I agree it was a reasonable deal for them, but to agree hands down? Something doesn't smell just right here. And you say Roy was on *your* side?'

'He told them to take it, in so many words. Do the deal, he said.'

'Then you owe him one, Marty. That's the way that game plays. He's going to call in a favour on you.'

'Aw c'mon. Besides, what can I do for Roy Shaughnessey?'

'Oh,' said the Judge, 'I'm sure he's got something in mind. When it's pay-off time, you'll know. And there won't be any argument. That's the way it's done, Shaughnessey style.'

Martin Vail turned back to his breakfast and ate quietly for a minute or two. Then the Judge tapped on the table with his finger.

'Here comes another problem, Counsellor.'

Vail looked towards the entrance. Joey Pinero had just entered Butterfly's. Pinero, who was also known in some circles as 'Heyhey' because of a peculiar speech pattern, was a mass of tics. He snapped his fingers when he talked, as if to hurry himself along. And he shrugged his right shoulder, like he was shucking off a fly. He came across the room very fast. Pinero always walked very fast.

'Heyhey, Couns,' he said, snapping his fingers, 'did we fuckin' have that sit down? How we fuckin' do?'

He slid into the booth beside the Judge.

'We had the sit down Joey and we did just fine,' Vail said, wiping his mouth and tossing his napkin beside his plate.

'Heyhey, what we fuckin' end up with. How fuckin' much they fuckin' nick us for anyways? Half a mil? A fuckin' *mil* maybe?' He was talking himself into a panic.

'You get a million, one, and you have to leave the state the day we get the cheque.'

'Heyhey, what! What the fuck are you saying, Couns? Am I fuckin' believin' these two fuckin' ears? You fuckin' caved in for all that loot?'

'No appeal, no problem, just take the money and run.'

'Heyhey, whada fuck, man,' he whined angrily, snapping his fingers and hitching his shoulder as he spoke. 'You tellin' me I gotta fuckin' *eat* uh . . . uh . . . whatever fuckin' million goddam dollars that is? That what you fuckin' telling me?'

'I'm telling you you're walking out with a million, one, Joey. Count your blessings.'

Pinero slammed his hand on the table, spilling Vail's coffee.

'Heyhey, count my fuckin' blessings my ass. That's your fuckin' story, Couns, it was my fuckin' head they danced on, y'know, I come off with the fuckin' black and blues, you take home a half a fuckin' million tomatoes I'm supposed to be fuckin' grateful, hey?'

Vail stood up suddenly. He walked slowly around the booth, refilled his coffee cup and came back. He stood over Joey Pinero and gave him the toughest look he had, the one he saved for when he could tell a witness was about to lose it. The killer stare he saved for expert witnesses. Pinero looked at him quizzically. Something

35

was happening but he wasn't sure what. He just knew Vail had all of a sudden done a one-eighty on him.

Vail said softly, 'Play the other side of the record, Joey. Without me, you'd be upstate doing ten to life. You'd be rubbing nickels together hoping they'd mate so you could buy cigarettes.'

'Heyhey, there's other fuckin' lawyers, y'know, other fuckin' lawyers. I gotta fuckin' take this? I can't fuckin' tell that scumbag D.A. it's no fuckin' dice, hey, we see you in fuckin' court?'

'No.'

'Heyhey, no? *No!* Just like that, fuckin' *NO!*'

'Heyhey, my ass. The deal's a wrap. Now you take your million and one and head to California. You don't? They'll make life so miserable for you, you'll *wish* you were in Rock Island State. Hey fuckin' hey.'

'Heyhey, shit, a fuckin' fuckin' from my own goddam Couns, I'm supposed to do a little fuckin' dance here, hey? What a-fuckin'-bout that, Judge?'

'I'm retired,' Spalding said diplomatically.

'Joey, before you have a conniption, listen to me. We go back in on appeal, the state, county and city are all going to be so far up your ass they'll see daylight. You're looking at a felony rap for the gun, a depressed judgement from the appeals court, and shit city for the duration. Understand what I'm telling you? Now we've got a cheque coming for one million, six hundred thousand dollars. I'm taking half a mil for my work, you're dancing out of state with the rest and that's the bottom line. Do you even *know* how many zeroes there are in a million dollars?'

'Zeroes?' Pinero stared at him and thought about that, hitching his shoulder a couple of times.

'Heyhey, who the fuck cares?' he said defensively, then suddenly he started to laugh. 'A fuckin' million dollars,' he said. 'That's more fuckin' pussy and horses than I can count either, hey. What a fuck, I got a little fuckin' bent outa shape there, Couns, okay? Okay?'

'Okay, Joey.'

He smiled at the Judge. 'Heyhey, pretty fuckin' good Couns, right Y'Honour?'

'Oh yes,' the Judge said. 'Excellent fucking Couns.'

'Heyhey. Fuckin' L.A., huh? Fuckin' La La land, maybe I'll even get in the fuckin' movies, right? Maybe I'll fuckin' *buy* myself a fuckin' movie.'

He jerked his shoulder a couple of times and leaned back and looked important, snapped his fingers, then leaned over to Vail and said very confidentially, 'Heyhey, Couns, how many fuckin' zeroes *are* there in a million bucks?'

Six

The snow had turned to a freezing drizzle. Vail half ran, half slid the two blocks from the el station to the two-storey frame house he owned. The house was located on the near northside, ten minutes by elevated from downtown, a perfect location for Vail, who did not like to drive and had never replaced his car after it was stolen two years before. Developers had reclaimed the section, restoring the old two-storey frame houses to modest turn-of-the-century splendour. It was a pleasant, upscale eight-block square community unto itself, quiet and unassuming, peopled mostly by college teachers, musicians, young professional people on the come and retired aesthetics. In deference to the historical feel of the place, Vail did not hang out his shingle. A brass plaque on the front door said simply, 'M. Vail, Lawyer.'

Sliding glass doors separated both the den to the left of the entrance, and the living room to its right, from the large vestibule which was now the bailiwick of Naomi Chance, the secretary, receptionist, organiser, researcher and aspiring paralegal of Vail's domain. The den had become Vail's office. A large rambling room with alcoves and built-in bookcases and an open fireplace. It was dominated by an enormous, hulking oak table which Vail used as a desk. Ten or twelve stacks of letters, case files, and books had encroached on him and confined the lawyer to a small working area in the centre of the table. His high-backed leather chair was on wheels so he could spin around the room – to bookshelves or file cabinets – when necessary. There was an old black leather couch in front of the fireplace for more intimate conversations with clients.

The living room became a waiting room and the second floor his private suite, its four bedrooms, each with its own bath, reduced to three after he turned the largest into a sitting room. So he could accommodate two guests if necessary although he rarely had visitors. On rare occasions he, or a friend, cooked in the kitchen adjacent to his office.

'You're late,' Naomi said as he came through the door, stamping his feet and shaking the chill from his shoulders. He took off his jacket and tossed it over the hat tree near the door.

'Yeah, yeah, yeah,' he said, heading into the office. 'How old's the coffee?'

'Thirty minutes.'

'Good.' He went to the old-fashioned ten-gallon urn he had taken as part payment for handling a restaurant bankruptcy, poured himself a mug of coffee and stared at Naomi, who was standing in the doorway to the office with a package in her hand. She was a tall, ramrod straight woman the colour of milk chocolate, almost Egyptian-looking with high cheek-bones and wide brown eyes. Her black hair was done in corn rows and tipped with different coloured African beads. A gorgeous creature who, at forty, had the wisdom of a sixty-year-old and a twenty-year-old body. There was absolutely nothing one could criticise about Naomi Chance.

'This came for you 'bout an hour ago,' she said. 'I've been dying to open it.'

'Then open it. Hell, don't stand on ceremony. Who's it from?'

She pulled the taped card off the package, took out the note and read it aloud.

'Thanks for all your help. Hope the story offends you.
CONNERMAN'

Inside were six copies of the magazine and an original print of the photograph set in an old-fashioned wooden frame. Vail stroked the wood with his thumb and laughed to himself. Connerman was being sarcastic, of course, about helping. Vail had hardly spoken to the writer while Connerman was working on the article. He never talked about himself. He wasn't particularly modest, he just figured the less people knew about his private life and his past, the better.

'File the copies,' Vail said and put the photograph on a bookshelf.

'Don't you want to read it?'

'Already did.'

'Well why didn't you say something?'

'Forgot.'

'Crap, Marty. Is it any good?'

'Usual Connerman gonzo bullshit. Go ahead and read it. And write him a note for me. Tell him I'm suing him for thirty-five dollars – every cent he has in the world.'

'That's nasty.'

'He wouldn't have it any other way.'

'Well . . . what happened this morning?'

'Oh,' Vail said with a shrug. 'All taken care of. No appeal. Heyhey gets 1.1 mil, we get five hundred thou, he leaves town forever. Case closed.'

'That's great! But how's Mister Pinero going to take it?'

'He already took it. I told him. He had a little fit. Now he's happy.'

'God, what a day, and it isn't even noon yet. Why don't you go take a nap?'

'Very funny.'

'Have you seen this?' she asked. She spread-eagled the morning *Times* between outstretched arms.

'Read it on the el.'

'A terrible thing,' she said. 'What do you think?'

'I think the Archbishop's dead and they've got a suspect in custody.'

He sat down, pulled off his shoes, put his feet on the

desk and leaning over, began rubbing them vigorously. 'Must be zero out there,' he said.

'Want me to run upstairs and get you some dry socks?'

'I couldn't ask you to do that,' he said, looking up at her. 'I mean, that could be construed as extremely chauvinistic. You are a legal assistant, not a valet.'

'I'll be right back,' she said. As she walked towards the door, she said, 'They say this kid who did it . . .'

'This kid they *allege* did it . . .'

She stopped and turned back towards him, leaning on the door jamb.

'Allege, okay? *Allege* . . . but according to the story, they caught him hiding in the church with the weapon.'

'Repeat with me . . .'

She rolled her eyes and mimed his words as he spoke. 'Innocent until proven guilty.'

He smiled patronisingly. 'Very good. Just remember, right now, as we speak, this kid . . . what's his name . . . ?'

'Aaron Stampler.'

'This kid, Aaron Stampler, is innocent. And don't believe everything you read. You know what they say about the newspapers, the first time they print an error, it's a mistake. The second time they print it, it's a fact. And don't believe everything you hear, either. The first day of law school my professor came into class and said, "From this day forward, when your mother says she loves you . . ."'

She finished the sentence for him: ' " . . . you'll seek a second opinion." I know, and the second thing he said was, "Always ask why".'

'Very good, you're learning.'

'Why not? I hear it every damn morning.' She went up the stairs.

Although Naomi knew very little about the law, she was a quick learner and a voracious digger. When pointed in the right direction, she gnawed through red

41

tape, digging out information from the devious and suspicious minions in charge of public records, and tracking names and details through labyrinths of newspaper microfilms. Give her a name, she'd come back with a biography. Ask for a date, she'd produce a calendar. Ask for a report, she'd generate a file. She was unmarried, could type 100 words a minute, take shorthand, and occasionally, when he was buried in law books, could rustle up a pretty good meal in the kitchen. What more could Vail ask except that with time, perhaps, he might mould her into a pretty good paralegal.

She came back and dropped a pair of wool socks in his lap.

'Thanks,' he said. 'Okay, let's run the list.'

She sat down across from him and flipped open her book. But he was not listening. He was engrossed in Naomi.

There were times, and this was one of them, when Vail wanted to just sweep Naomi off her feet and carry her up the stairs, Rhett Butler style. But they had a deal, Naomi Chance and Martin Vail. Business not pleasure. The sexual attraction had been there from the beginning, from the day she answered his ad in the local weekly. There had been one night, two months after she came to work for him, when the barrier had fallen. And what a night it was.

They had been working late on a brief that was due in the morning, finishing at midnight. The office floor was piled with books and notes, scraps of papers. A mess. Naomi was stretched out on the couch in front of the fire.

'We deserve a little party,' Vail said. He went into the kitchen and came back with a bottle of Dom Perignon and two glasses.

'I've been saving this for a year,' he said. 'And I've been wanting to drink it for two months.'

He popped the cork, filled both glasses and leaned over the sofa. They tapped glasses.

'Here's to us,' he said. 'A pretty good team.'

'I'll drink to that,' she said.

By the third glass, Vail was seated on the sofa, rubbing her feet. The sexual tension in the room was electric, both of them trying to avoid the inevitable. His hands moved up to her calves, then her thighs.

'Marty,' she said slowly.

'Just relax.'

His hand moved up higher, caressed the smooth sheen of her stockings, his fingers barely touching her.

'Oh my God,' she sighed. She rose to meet his exploring fingertips, pressed against his hand and, stroking her, he lay down beside her, kissing her mouth, then her ears, the small place in her throat and she responded by putting her hand behind his head and moving it ever so diplomatically down to her breasts. Months of pent-up denial exploded and they began frantically undressing each other without ever losing the cadence of the mutual seduction. Undressed, she loomed above him in the light from the fire, straddled him, settled down on him, moving in soft, wet circles while he touched every pore of her. Finally she rose slightly and guided him into her, leaning forward, trapping his cries with her mouth.

Hypnotised, they made love, stopped, held back, trembling, until they could not resist the demand of their senses and so, started again until the tension was no longer bearable and it ended in mutual release.

'Oh God,' she had cried, falling down across him and stretching out her long legs, tightening them and keeping him trapped while they kissed until, finally, it passed. He lay under her, arms enfolding her, lightly scratching her back as they regained their breath, napped, awoke, and then in frenzied reprise, made love again.

It was four a.m. when she suddenly lifted herself off him and jumped off the sofa.

'Oh my God,' she stammered as she began dressing.

'What are you doing?' Vail asked.

'What does it look like? I'm getting dressed.'

'Just stay here for the night. Why're you going home now, for Christ sakes? It's four in the morning.'

'You crazy? Everybody in the neighbourhood'll know I stayed here. Besides, I've got to go home and change my clothes. And I don't have my toothbrush. This was very . . . unexpected.'

'Fuck everybody in the neighbourhood. Hell, I don't even *know* everybody in the neighbourhood.'

'It's the principle of the thing.'

Vail said. 'Shit.' He lit a cigarette, propped some pillows on the back of the sofa, and sat up smoking and watching her as she finished dressing. 'Why don't you take a cab over to your place, pick up some clothes and a toothbrush . . .'

'Martin! Just stop it.' She pulled on her jacket, kissed him on the cheek and started out but turned at the door with a deep sigh.

'Look, that was just great, Marty. You don't know what that did for this old carcass and ego. But we can't ever do it again.'

'What do you mean!'

She came back and sat on the edge of the couch.

'It would change the whole working relationship.'

'What!' He looked at her with disbelief for a moment and laughed. 'You're very strange, Naom. You are a very strange lady.' He started to reach out to her but she pulled back.

'No, I'm almost forty years old and I'm getting practical in my old age. I just don't want to start wondering on my way to work every morning whether I'm gonna be humping or helping.'

'C'mon. It wouldn't be that way.'

'Oh yeah, sooner or later. Sure it would. We'd be sneaking upstairs for quickies between depositions. Next

thing you know I'd have a couple of outfits over here —
in case I decided to stay over. I like my job, Marty. I
love my boss, I get paid real well and on time. I love the
neighbourhood. Let's not screw it up, okay?'

'It was awful damn good, Naom.'

'It's *always* awful damn good, Marty.'

'That's an old wives' tale.'

'And I'm an old ex-wife.' She reached out and stroked
his cheek.'Okay?'

He shrugged. What could he say. Who argues at four
in the morning?

'Okay?' she repeated, somewhat ruefully.

'Yeah, sure. Okay.'

'Course,' she said with a smile as she got up to leave,
'that doesn't mean we can't keep an open mind on the
subject.'

So the tension was still there. Nothing had gone away,
it was just put on hold.

'You look absolutely devastating this morning, Naom,'
Vail said. 'I just want you to know that before we get
started.'

'Don't you start.'

'I'm not starting anything. I can't give you a compliment?'

She closed her eyes and gritted her teeth and made a
little growling sound. Then she said, 'You must be horny.
Get stood up last night?'

'I went to the Silver Screen last night, alone. Two of
my all time favourites, *Out of the Past* and *The Stranger*.
Beautiful prints. No scratches, sound track like
crystal . . .'

'You'll get mugged, going down there to that old
dump.'

'Been going to that old dump since I moved to this
freezing frigging city. So . . .'

'So, there's no list to run. You're clear today. You

thought you were going to be working on the appeal, remember? However, you do have Leroy penciled in with a question mark.'

'Ahh, Leroy. Okay, run the nitty on Leroy, short version.' He lit a cigarette, laid his head back and closed his eyes. She was great at reducing all the aggravating details of a file down into a nice, concise, chronological, detailed synopsis.

'Leroy Nelson,' she began. 'Ugly boy. White, male, twenty-six. Works at the Ames Foundry, lives with his mother on Railroad Avenue – he was divorced about six months ago. Two priors. The first, simple battery, fight in a bar, he was convicted, paid a five hundred dollar fine. The second was possession of stolen property. Caught with a hot TV and stereo, copped to possession of stolen goods, no jail time, did six prob. That was eighteen months ago. Been clean ever since.'

'No big deal,' Vail said.

'Okay. November twenty-fifth, the day after Thanksgiving, Leroy is having left-overs with Mommy. Seven at night, a guy wearing a ski mask holds up a filling station. This is four blocks from his mother's place. A police cruiser comes by, the thief panics, the filling station attendant gets in a fight with him, pulls off the mask and the thief runs out the back door, dropping his gun as he flees the premises. Based on the artist's sketch and the attendant's description, the cops stop by Mommy's house and Leroy is picked up. In the process, they find two ounces of marijuana in his zipper bag. Now Leroy has two problems, attempted armed robbery and possession of an illegal substance. Leroy claims mistaken identity and his sweet old mother gives him an alibi. That's where we came in.'

'Three weeks later, we turn over the whole card,' said Vail.

'Right. Turns out Leroy bought the gun from a pawn shop over on Elander about a year ago. His story to the cops is that he sold it to a guy a couple months before the robbery.'

'So now we got the gun to put up with,' Vail sighed. 'Did he sell it or not?'

'No receipt, no buyer so far,' she answered.

'Enter Captain Video,' said Vail.

'Ah . . . the infernal machine,' said Naomi.

'Ever read *In Cold Blood* by Truman Capote?' Vail asked as he wheeled his chair across the hardwood floor to the bookshelf where his VCR was hooked up.

'No.'

As he spoke, he rustled through the tapes, looking at the labels.

'You should,' he said. 'Great book. You could almost use it as a textbook on interrogation techniques.'

'Interrogation techniques? Truman Capote?'

'Yeah.' He found one of the tapes he was looking for and set it aside. 'Capote describes how he managed to piece together all the details of this family massacre out in Kansas. The perps were a couple of ne'er do wells named Perry Smith and Dick Hickock. Smith had a crush on Capote, Hickock never had much to say. So Capote would talk to Smith, whom he knew was a pathological liar, then he'd take the story to Hickock and Hickock, who was honest but psychotic as hell, would say, "No, it didn't happen that way, this is the way it happened." So by playing both off each other, Capote ultimately was able to write a very detailed book on the crime. Ah, here's tape number two.'

He put it with the first tape.

'What's that got to do with Leroy Nelson and that machine of yours?' Naomi asked.

'The camera is my Dick Hickock. Eventually by playing Leroy and the camera off each other, we'll get to the truth. Y'see, Naomi, people never remember exactly what they say. They may think they do, but they really don't. I can quote from a page of notes to a witness, paraphrase the quote, and most people will swear that's exactly what they said, word for word, because they think I have it written down and I'm reading it to them word for word.

'So, I tape Leroy three times. Ah, here's the other one. Three times I ask him what happened, three times he tells the story, makes a few minor errors in detail, but that's normal. Except one. This is tape one.'

He turned on the TV monitor and punched the play button. Leroy Nelson appeared in close-up, a tall, gaunt man, who looked twice his age. His faded brown hair was wispy and uncut and when he spoke, he usually ended his sentences with a question mark, as if apologising for something. He had tired, beaten eyes, his adam's apple looked like a bobbing cork in his long, slender neck, and he had foundry skin which was really no longer skin but more like toughened animal hide.

VAIL: Tell me about the gun.
NELSON: Well, I had pretty much forgot about that?
VAIL: Why didn't you tell me about it?
NELSON: Well, like I say, it got stole a couple months ago so I wasn't thinking about the gun.
VAIL: So you haven't seen the gun for several months?
NELSON: Right. Since it got stole.
VAIL: Why did you have a gun?
NELSON: Don't everybody?

Vail snapped the tape off and replaced it with another.

'So, okay, on tape he tells me the gun was stolen a month before the robbery but he never got around to reporting it. Tape two, a week later, I don't ask him about the gun and he doesn't bring it up. Now here's tape three, this is ten days later, okay? And I throw a little curve at him. You can't see me but I'm reading off my notes.

VAIL: Okay, let's talk about this gun again. This

48

is very damaging, Leroy, pegging this gun
to you.

NELSON: I told yuh, I sold it a guy I met at the
health club but I don't know him. It was
just this guy looking to buy a pistol and I
needed the money.

Vail stopped the recorder and turned to Naomi.

'See,' he said. 'Leroy *thinks* I'm looking at my notes.
He forgot he told me the gun was stolen. What he was
repeating to me is the story he told the cops.'

'So we assume Leroy's lying about it?'

'He lied to somebody . . .'

'Now what do we do?'

'I've got to get straight with him about the gun.'

'Do you think he did it, Marty?'

'The jury will let us know.'

'Are we sticking with the "not guilty" plea?'

'As of so far.'

'You'll probably get him off.'

'Ah. Listen to that tone of voice. You've already made
up your mind, haven't you. Guilty, right?'

'Maybe. But you don't even care. You're going to
defend him whether he is or not.'

'That's what we do here, Naomi. In case you haven't
noticed in the last seven months, we defend people who
are usually presumed to be guilty.'

'I haven't been able to get used to that yet. I mean, I
always feel like, uh, you know, seems to me you'd have
some kind of . . . shit, Marty, you know . . . moral problem with that?'

'I am a lawyer, not a fucking moralist.'

'But isn't that what the law's all about?'

'The law, dear Naomi, has nothing to do with morality. Look, let's say you get arrested for possession of pot,
okay? It's not the business of the court to rule on whether
you should smoke pot or not, or whether it's good or

49

bad for you. The court rules *only* on the question of possession because that's what you were charged with. Morality doesn't enter into it.'

'In other words, it's okay to smoke it but it's against the law to have it.'

'Precisely.'

'Sounds like a stupid law to me.'

'Very true. There are a lot of stupid laws and a lot of bad laws . . . not our problem. What we do, we figure out the best way to use the law — good, bad, stupid, whatever — to our client's best advantage.'

'So how about the pot?'

'We'll trash that. Illegal search. They come without a warrant, say they want to talk to Leroy down-town. They come in the house, snooped around a little, see the blue zipper bag and take a look inside. Bingo, two ounces of grass. He hadn't been charged with anything. He was being cooperative. The bag was lying on the floor, they snooped. No reason to.'

'Okay, so how about a summary on Nelson?' she asked.

'Summary? We have to defuse the gun: It's all they've got.'

The phone started buzzing and Vail turned back to the tapes as she went to answer it. Perhaps, he thought, there was something in these interviews he had overlooked. Some little something that might help him at this point.

Naomi came back in the room.

'You've got a call.'

'Take a message, I'm thinking.'

'I don't think so.'

'What do you mean, you don't think so?'

'I think maybe you want to take this call. It's Judge Shoat's office.'

Seven

What the *hell* could Shoat want? Vail wondered as the cab edged cautiously along the sleet-slick street and slipped up to the kerb in front of the court-house. Was he angry at the settlement? Was he pissed that Vail had taken the city, county and state to their knees? Had Shoat remembered some insult or arrogance from the trial? Maybe he was going to try to slap Vail with another citation for contempt out of spite. The *only* thing Vail was sure of was that it definitely would not be a pleasant meeting.

As he entered the building, Bobby the newsman yelled to him, 'Hey, Mister V, we sold out. Hottest issue they ever had.'

'Great,' Vail answered as he entered the elevator.

The court-room was on the fourth floor. As Vail entered the almost empty room, Shoat was shaking his hand and head simultaneously.

'No, no, no,' he snapped. 'Overruled, overruled. Just get on with it, I'd like to finish this procedure today if it is at all possible, gentlemen.'

Hangin' Harry Shoat presided over his court-room with dictatorial fervour. He was the lord of his domain, a Calvinistic moralist who saw the sin rather than the sinner and who dispensed justice without regard for circumstances or situation. A glowering, tense, humourless man, he had the air of a Viennese businessman: stern, formal, suspicious. His moustache was precisely trimmed and his black hair was combed straight back and tight to his skull. He was a man who seemed perpetually impatient with the process he was sworn to uphold and thus the gavel became an extension of his arm and he used it to bludgeon the court into submission.

As the first Republican judge elected in twelve years, Shoat considered the victory over his Democratic opponent as a mandate for his ultra-conservative agenda. He could barely conceal a harsh, almost prejudicial attitude towards defendants, whom he secretly believed were guilty until proven innocent – otherwise why should they be in his court in the first place? He had little time for abortionists, knee-jerkers who believed capital punishment was barbaric, or those who looked for cause and effect among the social ruins of the city.

But Hangin' Harry knew law. A former prosecutor, he had the kind of mind which instantly could recall a staggering number of legal precedents by name, date, region and subject. And although he was sometimes capable of astoundingly profound and unpredictable judgements, he was a rigid 'max-out' judge, coldly uninterested in the social circumstances of crime and perpetrator. Crime was crime. Punishment was punishment. Compassion had no place in the justice system. The only time he smiled was when he passed sentence. Once, when a youthful offender had arrogantly suggested perhaps he and his probation officer might have a meeting with the judge before sentence was passed, Shoat had smiled almost gleefully, looked down at the young man and explained, 'Son, your probation officer hasn't been born yet . . . thirty years.' Vail had always suspected that Shoat constantly had to suppress a mad desire to leap up and shout, 'Off with their heads!' like the Queen of Hearts in Wonderland.

Before Vail could take a seat, the judge saw him and pointed sharply at the door to his chambers. When Vail pointed to himself and formed the word 'Me?', Shoat nodded vigorously. So Vail walked quietly down the outside of the room and went through the door in the corner.

The small room was spotless and dustless and in perfect order. The desk was empty except for an ashtray, the telephone and a marble holder and pen. The books in the bookshelves behind the desk were lined up perfectly, as if a ruler had been used to justify each binding. The wet bar in the corner was dry of even a single drop of water. Everything in the room seemed symmetrical: the desk with its sharp edges; the straight-backed chairs which looked harmfully uncomfortable; the Waterford lamps with severe six-sided shades; the magazines on the coffee table which were stacked precisely so that the name of each was underlined by the top border of the one on top of it and placed at precisely the right angle in the corner of the table. Would anyone possibly disturb that stack to read one of the periodicals?

Precise. That was the word. The perfect description for Superior Court Judge Harry Madison Shoat. This was a very precise man. And a frustrated one – for Shoat was a man who demanded order in a netherworld that years ago had lost all sense of order.

Vail opted against making a dent in the sofa cushions and instead walked over to the recessed window which concealed the heater outlet. Hot air moved soundlessly up into the room, clouding the cold window with steam. He wiped a small circle in it and looked down at the street. Near the corner, two black, official-looking cars were involved in a fender bender. People walked with their hands out at their sides to keep their balance as they crept along the glassy pavement. One hell of a day for a spur of the moment command performance.

Shoat entered the room with a kind of snobbish sense of proprietorship. It was his place, his sanctum, and his dead eyes danced from one part of the room to the other to see if anything had been disturbed or moved out of place.

'Good to see you again, Counsellor,' he said, offering a soft, fleshy hand. 'It was kind of you to come on such short notice – and such shit weather.'

53

The epithet surprised Vail. Profanity seemed out of character for Shoat. The judge pulled his robe slowly over his head, opened a closet near the wet bar, and hung it carefully on a padded clothes hanger, slipping it in between the other clothes on the rack, all of them an inch apart so they did not touch. He put his suit coat on, smoothing it out, shooting his cuffs, and buttoning the middle button.

Sleeps in pyjamas, Vail thought, *buttons all the buttons, even the top one, slides into bed from the top so he doesn't undo the covers, probably sleeps flat on his back with his hands across his chest like a corpse, so he doesn't muss up the bed.*

'I've recessed for the day so we have plenty of time,' Shoat said. 'Care for a drink? Bourbon, scotch?'

'Got any beer?'

'No,' Shoat said and looked as if he had smelt something dead.

'Bourbon'll be fine, a little ice, maybe an inch or so of water.'

The liquor was in pebbled bottles with small brass tags around the necks. Shoat took down two glasses, lined them up carefully beside each other on the bar. He took out two ice cubes, dropped them in one glass and ran an inch or so of water over them. He held the glass up, studied the amount of water, and added another spurt. Then he filled the rest of the glass with bourbon and handed it to Vail. He filled his own glass with scotch, no rocks, knocked down half of it in his first sip, and sighed with satisfaction.

'One can always use a scotch at the end of the day,' he said. 'Particularly in this jungle.'

He sat down, appraised his desk for a moment, then moved the marble pen holder half an inch to the left. He smiled to himself, brushed imaginary dust from his desk, took a linen napkin from his desk drawer, carefully lined it up with the edge of the desk and put his drink on it. He looked over at Vail.

'I have a little favour to ask,' he said.

'Okay,' Vail said. 'What is it?'

'I have a case I want you to handle. A pro bono. That shouldn't be a problem, should it? I understand your end of the recent taxpayers' skinning is half a million dollars.'

'Joe Pinero was the one who got skinned – literally – according to the jury. If that matters.'

Shoat looked annoyed. He closed his eyes and said, 'Don't get obstinate with me, Mister Vail.'

'Just stating the facts, Your Honour.'

'And poor old Al Silverman. You really did a number on him, didn't you? The man spent three weeks in a hospital and now I understand he's applied for a teaching job at City University.'

'Why are we suddenly feeling sorry for poor old Al, Your Honour? He got his ass whipped. It happens.'

'Not to you, though. Not in the last ... what is it, four years since you lost a case?'

'There were some plea bargains in there, if I remember correctly.'

'As you know, I don't look kindly on plea bargaining,' Shoat said almost viciously. 'I say go to the bar with it, make or break, that's what courts are for.'

'Yes sir, I know your predisposition on that question. As for Al Silverman, he's a damn fine lawyer. He just got hung by a bad case.'

'A gangster, Mister Vail? Everybody knows Pinero is a hit man for . . .' he waved his hand vaguely, 'whoever.'

'Which has nothing whatsoever to do with the fact that three cops used him as their personal punching bag. Is that what this is about? Chewing me out for winning a case?'

'I told you what this is about. What this is about, sir, is that I am asking you to take on this pro bono as a personal favour.'

One did not deny a superior court judge a personal favour.

'I was hoping I could get away for about two weeks, do some fishing down in the Keys,' Vail said. 'You know, recharge my batteries. I assume this can wait for a couple of weeks . . .'

'No, no, no,' Shoat said sharply. 'The hearing's tomorrow and I hope to be able to go to court in, oh, sixty days maximum.'

'What's the charge?'

'First degree murder.'

'Murder one! You want to go to trial on a murder one in sixty days? Who's the client?'

Shoat leaned forward and smiled.

'Aaron Stampler,' he said.

'Aaron . . .' Vail started to say and then remembered the name. *My God*! He stared across the desk at Shoat for several seconds. 'The Rushman thing,' he said.

'Yes, Mister Vail. The Rushman thing.'

Aaron Stampler was the kid they nailed for killing Archbishop Rushman.

Shoat reached in a desk drawer, took out a slender dark cigar, unwrapped it and carefully snipped off the end. Vail took out a cigarette.

'Do you mind?' Shoat said.'I really detest the smell of cigarettes.' Vail put the pack back as Shoat lit the cigar with a gold lighter, twisting the stogie slowly to make sure the end was evenly fired. Then he leaned back and blew the smoke towards the ceiling.

'Preliminary tomorrow at nine. I'll set the date then. I was thinking perhaps . . . oh, the first week in April.'

'That isn't even 60 days.'

'What's the difference, Counsellor? We're going to fry him anyway.'

Vail's shocked expression drew an immediate response from the judge.

'Just so it's all on the table, I have it on excellent

authority that this little monster knew the good Bishop, was caught with the murder weapon in hand, and his bloody fingerprints are spread from the rectory to the confessional.'

'You seem to know a lot about the case. Are you trying it?'

'What I just told you is *all* I know sir, and yes, I am trying it. And I sure as hell don't expect any problem from you on that score.'

'I see. Well, if it's that open and shut, maybe we'll just plead him guilty and throw ourselves on the mercy of the court.'

'There's not going to be any mercy in this court, Mister Vail. Archbishop Rushman was the closest thing to a living saint this city has ever seen. Even the knee-jerkers are going to look the other way if Stampler gets the chair. And he will. He'll be the most despised defendant since Charles Manson. Even if you plead him guilty, he'll get the bloody chair.'

So that was it. This was the pay-off for the Pinero win. Make him try an open and shut case, turn public opinion against him, and break his back. Let's bring Vail to his knees, that's what it was all about.

Vail said, 'The first thing we'll do is file for change of venue. There's no way . . .'

'Absolutely not. No change. You don't get it, do you Counsellor? Go out on the streets, in the restaurants, ask people what they think. People are outraged, as well they should be. They deserve satisfaction, Mister Vail. They demand requital. They require that release.'

'Why don't we just string him up in front of the church. There's a nice big oak tree up there.'

'I warned you . . .'

'Warned me what? You sit there, tell me to try this case when you've already picked out his death cell. You tell me the city's on fire over this but I can't change venue . . .'

'Vail, this is a conversation strictly between you and me,' Shoat said quietly. 'If push comes to shove, it never happened.'

'Good, then I can tell you what I think of . . .'

'I am not in the slightest interested in your opinion, so save your breath. I know some of you young hot-shots call me Hangin' Harry. That doesn't bother me one damn bit. In fact, if hanging were still in vogue I'd be the first one to pull the handle on the trap door.'

'Maybe they'll let you throw the switch on Stampler.'

Shoat leaned forward slightly. 'There will be a very long line for that. We'll probably have to raffle off the privilege. Perhaps divide the proceeds up among the dozens of charities His Eminence started and supported in this community.'

Vail stood up and walked back to the window. He needed a cigarette to balance out the foul smell of Shoat's cigar. He took a long swig of his drink.

'What if I say no.'

'I don't think even you would be that arrogant,' Shoat said. 'Besides, you know what the city would think of you, turning down a pro bono after winning yourself a half million dollar settlement.'

'Tell you the truth, Your Honour, I really don't give a big shit what the city thinks. If I wanted to be popular I'd have a sex change operation and enter the Miss America contest.'

'You don't turn down a judge's request, Vail, and you know it. That would be suicidal. Turn me down and you'll insult every judge on this circuit. They'd eat you alive every time you walked in a court-room. Care for another drink?'

'No thanks, it's a little early for me. But I'm going to have a cigarette. You want me to step outside?'

'Oh, go ahead,' Shoat said irritably, getting up and pouring himself another scotch.

Vail lit up and watched a wrecker hook up one of the

two cars in the fender bender. He leaned forward and looked up and down the street. There wasn't a pedestrian in sight. It was a very strange sight, particularly in mid-afternoon. As the wrecker towed the black car away, Shoat walked to the window behind his desk and also looked out.

'Still sleeting?' he asked.

'No. But it's below freezing so it's not going to melt. Better drive carefully on the way home.'

'I don't have to drive, Mister Vail, one of the perks of the job. I have a car and a driver. Quite an impressive fellow, actually. Quite well read for a coloured. Keeps up on things. I sometimes try out my written decisions on him. Get their side of the picture.'

'*Their* side?'

'Coloureds, Spanish, I like to be fair and open. Hear their side of the story.'

'That's very commendable. Ever pay any attention to them?'

Shoat did not answer. He just glared at Vail. Then the sneer crept back. He took another long pull of scotch and clamped his teeth round the cigar.

'This is generating a lot of national attention,' he said, his eyes as lifeless and cold as pebbles. 'The Bishop was well known all over the world. That means the national press will be here in force. I want this Stampler to have the best defence possible. When we burn him, I don't want anybody saying he didn't get the fairest possible trial. And I'm going to give you a lot of leeway, just so there's no criticism of the justice system here.'

'Sixty days to prepare his trial is no leeway at all. Who's prosecuting?'

'I have no idea.'

'Yancey doesn't have a good prosecutor left. Jane Venable's leaving this month to go into private practice with, you know, Winken, Binken and Nod or whoever.'

'I assume he'll find somebody equal to the task.'

Vail walked across the room and back. He had no choice.

'Slam-dunk and I'm in the basket,' he said to himself.

'I beg your pardon?'

'Nothing,' Vail said. 'Look, I haven't even met this kid yet. All I know about the case is what I read in this morning's paper. I want ninety days. I want the preliminary hearing postponed until Friday so I can spend all day tomorrow with my client. I want a subpoena so I can get into the scene of the crime without any hassle. And I want the D.A. out of my hair for the next thirty-six hours – he's been working this case since last night. I want the same consideration. And I want full disclosures from the D.A.'s office, I don't want any bullshit about that.'

'Sixty days, Vail. That's all you get. We have to get this over with. However, I concede your other points, they're all reasonable requests.'

'Also I get court expenses, that's standard.'

'Court expenses yes. Personal expenses, expert witnesses, travel, all your problem.'

Vail finished his cigarette and ground it out in the ashtray.

'Double feature, huh?' he said finally. 'Society gets a human sacrifice and you bust my balls at the same time.'

Shoat puffed on his cigar and thought about that for a moment before nodding.

'I like that, Counsellor. That's quite an accurate appraisal of the situation. Double feature – punishment and retribution. My two favourite subjects.'

Outside, it had begun to sleet again. A county worker was sprinkling salt on the icy steps and Vail went down them slowly, hanging on to the brass railing. The fender bender had been cleaned up but a dark blue limo was now parked in front of the court-house. Some big shot working late, Vail thought. Maybe it's Shoat's car? But

60

as Vail reached the bottom step a face appeared for a moment in the rear window, then moved back into the shadows. It was Roy Shaughnessey. The driver got out, scurried around the car and opened the door.

Vail peered in at Shaughnessey.

'There's not a cab running in town,' Shaughnessey said. 'Get in, I'll run you home.'

Vail got in. The limo driver got in the front seat and turned back towards Shaughnessey.

'One-O-two Fraser,' Shaughnessey said. 'It's out in The Yards.' He turned to Vail. 'How about a brandy?'

'Oh, what the hell. Why not?'

Shaughnessey opened a compartment in the back of the front seat. It revealed a small bar stocked with three-ounce airline bottles of liquor. Shaughnessey opened two of them and emptied the contents into old fashioned glasses.

'Sorry I don't have snifters,' he said. 'Always thought that was a lot of bunk anyway, swirling it around in those glasses and sniffing it.' He held up his glass. 'Here's to you, Martin, okay if I call you Martin?'

'Sure, Roy.'

'You're one helluva piece of work,' the old war horse said, clinking Vail's glass. 'Ever thought about moving up in the world?'

'Up to where?' Vail asked.

'Look, son, you're tighter than a nun's pussy when it comes to talkin' about yourself. I know you come from down-state. No credentials. No family to speak of. Some bad breaks along the line. I pulled the package on you. Hard pull up by your own bootstraps. All that crap.'

'What's your point?'

'Time to let it out. You're Robin Hood right now. Start capitalising on that hard road up. Self-made man, overcoming the odds, it'll sell, know what I mean?'

'I don't have anything to sell right now.'

'C'mon son, you know how hard it is to break into

61

these platinum law firms without a pedigree. You're the best lawyer in the state. Nobody wants to go up against you.'

'Is this some kind of an offer?'

'Let's just say it's part of your continuing education. You've got to slick up a little.'

Vail laughed. 'You mean go legit?'

Shaughnessey laughed harder. 'That's exactly what I mean,' he said. 'Go legit.'

'Why bother?'

'Because you want to move to the other side of town. You want what everybody wants, bow and scrape, tip their hat, call you Mister and mean it. You don't want to cop pleas for gunsels the rest of your life. Ten, twelve years from now you'll have the bank account but you'll be sick of having scum for clients. You still won't be legit, as you put it.'

'Is that why you dumped this Rushman case on me?'

Shaughnessey laughed. 'Don't give it a thought. You need a little humility, Martin. Besides, they want a monkey show out of that trial and you'll give it to them. You'll make them work for that conviction.'

'So that's what it's all about, getting a good show and teaching me a little humility?'

'It's the way the process works. You don't go anywhere without help, Martin. You can't do it alone, you need friends.'

'Oh, so this was a friendly gesture?'

'You're getting a favour and doing a favour at the same time. Now's a good time to start planning your future.'

'And how do you suggest I do that?'

'Jane Venable's moving out. The D.A.'s office is wide open.'

'C'mon, you think Jack Yancey and I could spend more than ten minutes together without killing each other?'

'Yancey needs you. He's lazy. And he's lost all his

gunslingers. Jack's balls're hanging out. Hell, he never did have the stones for that job. He's a politician in a job that calls for an iceman. He has to do something fast before everybody finds out how incompetent he is. What he wants is to make judge – eight, nine years down the line – and live off the sleeve for the rest of his time. To do that, he needs to rebuild his reputation because you've been making him look like Little Orphan Annie. Twice in one year on headline cases and burned up his two best prosecutors to boot. Silverman's still in a coma from the Pinero case and Venable's on her way to Platinum City. He needs you, son.'

'I can't afford to work for an assistant D.A.'s salary. This case alone could cost me seventy-five, a hundred thousand.'

'C'mon, son, you made a half million off Pinero and you live like a hermit.'

'My nest egg.'

'I have some people who can turn your nest egg into a portfolio worth a million, million and a half over the next few years. That's where it counts.'

'All of a sudden everybody wants to do me favours.'

'That's because you're a winner. You take your beating on this Rushman thing, just shows you're human.'

'Why is everybody in such a hurry to convict this kid?'

'Because it's bad for the community, bad for the state. A thing like this? The sooner it's behind us, the better. Anyway, you see Yancey's going to get his robes. Then who knows? You play the other side of the street for a while – hell, you might like prosecuting, don't know unless you try, right? – three, four years from now who knows where it could end? You want to be doing pro bonos when you're fifty?'

He looked out the car window. 'Hell, you want to be a man of the people, do it where it counts. Let them pick up the tab.'

'What the hell's in it for you?' Vail asked.

'I don't like to fight people I can't beat,' Shaughnessey answered.

Eight

Charlie Shackelford watched from his cubicle in the rear of the big room as Jane Venable burst out of the elevator. She was huddled in a navy pea jacket, a blue knit cap pulled down over her forehead, a bulky turtle neck pulled up around her ears, galoshes flopping at her feet. As she entered the sprawling, noisy office, she swept the knit cap off her head loosing a forest of red hair and stuck a Virginia Slim in her mouth which she lit as she wove her way through the jungle of paralegal desks and file cabinets, nodding to the staff as though she were royalty and they were her subjects. Charlie sighed. She was gorgeous. She was brilliant. She was everything in the world Charlie wanted and knew was beyond his reach. She reminded him of one of those models on TV who demonstrate furs in the international fashion shows. Tall, distant, untouchable, classy, arrogant, self-confident. She had it all. Venable had been her own Pygmalion, turning liabilities into assets and capitalising on what other women might consider physical drawbacks. Her nose, which was too long, became part of an equine mystique that added to her haughty allure. Her neck, which was too slender, was masked in turtle necks and high lace collars that became the trademark of her classy appeal. She was almost six feet tall, with irreverent splashes of red hair and a stunning figure she usually disguised inside bulky sweaters and loose-fitting jackets.

Except, of course, in court.

Charlie looked forward to those days when she would perform before the bench in outrageously expensive tailor made suits designed to show off every perfect parabola of her body — from her broad, swimmer's shoulders to the tight melons of her rear. She would pull her hair back into a tight bun to accent her professionalism. She would slash the air with designer glasses to make her point. Contact lenses would enhance her piercing green eyes. A year in speech school had fine-tuned her voice into a husky, authoritative alto. The men in the jury simply salivated, while the women secretly yearned for just a touch of her poise and taste. Devastating packaging. Shackelford adored her from afar, hiding his attraction behind sardonic, passionless sarcasm.

She came back to the office a little before three, collapsed at her desk and peeled off her overshoes, then she spent five minutes rooting around one of them in search of a stuck shoe.

'Charlie!' she yelled. A moment later, the short, chubby, somewhat joyless little paralegal appeared in the doorway.

'I hate to ask, Charlie, but I can't walk, my feet are burning up. Will you get me a quick fix?'

'Sure. How'd the affidavit go?'

'Three hours with a sixty-nine-year-old woman dying of cancer, she's wandering in and out of morphine city the whole time, while I'm trying to get a sane statement out of her. Think about the possibilities.'

'Will the affidavit hold up?'

'She'll be dead before we ever get to court. It'll be okay as a posthumous admission.'

'I mean, you know, slipping in and out of this narcotic-induced coma . . .'

'Don't put it that way, that's inflammatory. She was napping and I had to wait until she woke up to talk to her. Don't be telling people the woman was in a dope-induced stupor.'

'I was thinking devil's advocate.'

'Yeah, sure. You were bugging me, Charlie. Anyway, her doctor was witnessing most of the time, he'll testify she was lucid – when I needed her to be lucid. It's all corroborative, no big thing. But it was a bitch.'

Charlie made her a cup of hot beef bouillon and brought it back to her. 'When you finish that, the old man wants to see you.'

'About what?'

'I don't know, Janie, he doesn't confide in me. He comes down and says to me, "Tell Venable to come in to my office the minute she gets back, okay?" and I say, "Yeah, sure." That was the total conversation. I figure after being out in that weather you need a bouillon fix before you face the Pillsbury Doughboy.'

'Thanks, Charlie, what would I do without you?'

'You're gonna find out soon enough,' he said and left the room.

She slouched over her desk, rubbing one foot with the other, and unwound as she drank the warm soup. Then she smoked a cigarette. And finally she sighed, 'Shit,' and taking her shoes in hand, she limped down the hall towards Jack's office.

The blinds were pulled down over the windows in the glass-enclosed office, which usually meant Yancey was hard at work perfecting his putt. She knocked and walked in. Surprise. Pillsbury Doughboy was sitting behind his desk, stripped to his shirt-sleeves, reading a slender file. He kept reading as he waved her in. Yancey was an unctuous, smooth-talking con man with wavy white hair and a perpetual smile. He had been a dark horse candidate for D.A. eight years before, supported half-heartedly by the Democrats who didn't think he could win. But Yancey, who turned out to be the ultimate bureaucrat, had capitalised on his soapy charm and a natural talent for speaking and overcame a prosaic legal background to win. Once in office he had become the perfect man for the job, pliable as putty in the hands of the king-makers and shakers of the state.

Jane Venable had no respect for Yancey as an administrator but liked him personally. What wasn't to like? His popularity had grown through the years even though he was not a litigator and never had been. He had no stomach for the rigours of court-room battle and years of plea bargaining had left him a talker rather than a fighter. Instead, Yancey had surrounded himself with a small cadre of tough prosecutors who made him look good. And since Venable was the best of the bunch, she had pretty much called the shots for the six years she had been assistant D.A. It had been an acceptable compromise until recently. As long as he had Venable, Silverman and Torres to keep him afloat, Yancey was in the driver's seat. But Torres had left earlier that year and Vail had destroyed Silverman. A month ago, Venable also had escaped the crumbling empire, seduced by the promise of a corner office on the twenty-eighth floor, a six figure salary, and a senior partnership in one of the city's platinum law firms.

Most of the rest of Yancey's bunch didn't know a writ from a birthday card, so he was in trouble and looking at another election eighteen months hence. But if he was worried about his future, he didn't act like it. He was his usual smiling self. He waved to a chair and Venable sat down across from him, crossed one leg over the other, and massaged an aching foot with her hands.

'Listen, so you'll know,' she said, 'I just spent the morning in a hospice talking to a dying woman, it's about twenty degrees outside, the city's turned into an ice-skating rink, and my feet are killing me. I'm not in a real good mood so whatever's on your mind better be good news.'

'Oh . . . well, maybe we can wait until later when you . . .'

'No, no, Jack. Don't give me that. You started, you can't stop now.'

'I really didn't start yet.'

'Of course you did, when you invited me down here for this intimate little chat, so just spit it out. What's on your mind?'

'A little favour.'

Venable eyed Yancey suspiciously. After six years, she knew him too well.

'I don't think so.'

'Don't think *what*?'

'I don't think I'm granting any favours today.'

'I haven't said anything yet!'

'I know, but I don't really have to hear any more to know the answer is "No!" You know why? Because I don't trust you, Jack. You'd lie to yourself if it was expedient. So whatever you're going to ask, if it requires this little sit down, the answer is definitely no. N-fucking-O. Now if you'll excuse me, I've got work to do. I'm out of here in twenty-eight days and I have a lot of cleaning up to do.'

'It's the case of a lifetime.'

'Case? *Case!* I don't have time for any *case*. In twenty-nine days I will be in my own corner office on the twenty-eighth floor, making a vast sum of money as a partner in . . .'

'I've already talked to Warren.'

'Warren? You talked to Warren Langton? About what?'

'Just listen to me. I'll farm off all your other cases. Forget them. I want you to concentrate on just one thing until you leave.'

'Which is . . . ?'

'The Rushman case.'

'The Rushman case? What Rushman case?'

'You haven't read the morning papers?'

'I saw about two minutes on TV. Rushman murdered, suspect in tow.'

'It's yours. It's your only problem. Get it done and you leave with my blessing.'

'Archbishop Rushman. You're giving *me* the Rushman . . . damn it, I have a job to go to in less than a month! That thing could go on forever. For Christ sake, the poor man just got done in last night. He hasn't even been buried and you've got me in court already.'

'This case is going to trial as fast as the judge can get it on the calendar. Everybody wants it over and done with.'

She jumped angrily to her feet.

'I'm sorry,' she bellowed. 'I can't do it. You can't do it to me. I'm on notice. You've got me for twenty-eight more days, period. Then I am out of here, Jack.'

'Look, Blanding, Langton, et cetera, et cetera, will eat this up. You go in a hero. Lots of publicity for the firm . . . national publicity . . . this is a headline-maker, Janie. Hell, I thought you'd be delighted.'

'I don't have time!'

'Sure you do, Janie . . .'

'And lay off that Janie soft-talk.'

'Warren and I are in perfect agreement. This case is too important for you to pass up. You don't start with them until it's done.'

'God *damn* you! Did it occur to anyone to talk to me about this? It's my career you're screwing around with.'

'You're mine until the jury brings in the guilty verdict, my dear. May as well get used to it.'

'You did this to get even with me for leaving.'

'Look, it's open and shut – we just can't afford to take any chances. We cannot screw this one up in any way, shape or form.' He paused for a minute, then added, 'And I did it, as you tenderly put it, because you're the best prosecutor I've got . . . and I wanna be damn sure we gift wrap this little son of a bitch up and strap him in the hot spot, understand? Hell, you ought to be flattered I picked you for the job.'

'Flattered hell, you don't have anybody else. Thanks

forever, Jack. All I know about Archbishop Rushman is the two minutes I saw on Channel 4 this morning.'

'We've got the suspect cold. But you know how the public can be. They want blood. An eye for an eye, so to speak.' He chuckled at the cruel joke although Venable was not yet aware that the Archbishop's eyes had been plucked out during the attack.

'Ah hell,' said Venable, 'he'll probably plead guilty anyway.'

'Won't happen. The public wants this guy charbroiled. We won't buy a plea. He burns no matter what.'

'If his lawyer decides to plead him there's nothing we can do about it.'

'Sure there is. Our stand is, he goes to the chair, period. If his lawyer pleads him guilty, we still want the max. Unless his counsel's a devout idiot, he'll go to the wall with us. He's got nothing to lose.'

'Does he have a lawyer yet?'

'I don't know. Shoat's appointing one.'

'Is Shoat hearing the case?'

'Probably. There's going to be a lot of ink in this so he'll probably run with it. Look, everybody wants it to be over as soon as possible. The hearing's tomorrow, I'd say we go to trial in sixty days. So you lose what? A month before you move? Here, read this.'

He slid the afternoon paper across the desk to her and she reluctantly sat down and read the story.

'A 19-year-old ex-resident of Saviour House and one of Archbishop Rushman's favourite "rehabs" was arrested early today and charged with the mutilation murder of the Catholic prelate, police reports said.

'Police named Aaron Stampler, of a Region Street address, as the "Butcherboy", which police have nicknamed the brutal killer. Police said he will be charged with premeditated murder.

'An unnamed source in the police department

reported that Archbishop Rushman, known as "the Saint of Lakeview Drive", was "sliced up like a piece of meat" with his own carving knife in the bedroom of the rectory at St. Catherine's Cathedral. According to Lt. Abel Stenner, the murder occurred about ten p.m. Monday. Stenner declined further comment.

' "In twenty years on the force I never seen anything like it," the source told a *Times* reporter. "It was horrifying and disgusting . . ." '

The rest of the story was mostly a bio of the victim. She threw the paper back across the desk.

'Is it really as cut and dried as it sounds? I mean, if it's that easy there's no glory in it. Jack, I could be construed as a bully before it's over.'

'There's plenty of juice there, darlin'. Besides, this crazy kid claims he's innocent.'

'Really?'

'Yeah.'

'I thought you had him cold.'

'We do, but he still says he didn't do it.'

'What's happened so far?'

'Stenner and his team have been on it since last night. Ask him, he's on his way up. Then make up your mind.'

Venable had always found Stenner a very uncomfortable man to be around. He was a great cop but working with him was like working with a robot.

'He gives me the chills,' she said. 'I mean, he's a nice man and all but . . . he gives me the chills.'

'He's the best damn cop in the city.'

'I don't care. I like people with a little blood in their veins.'

'Here he comes now.'

The stern-faced Stenner tapped on the door, then strode into the room carrying a cheap imitation leather briefcase. He nodded to Yancey and Venable and, adjusting his wire rim glasses, got straight to business. He put the case on the corner of Yancey's desk and snapped it open.

'I have copies of the initial report and a follow-up — more detailed — which I did,' he started off, taking each folder out as he spoke about it. 'First draft of the forensic findings which is fairly basic, we really need to wait for the final on that which should be Friday, maybe Monday . . . A sketch of the scene and the grounds around it . . . A mug shot of the alleged, Aaron Stampler, white, male, 19. Stampler was close to the victim and lived at Saviour House until just before Christmas when he got a one-bedroom with kitchen and bath at 2175 Region Street. A sixteen-year-old named Linda also left Saviour House at the same time and moved in with him. Apparently she moved out on him about two weeks ago. We haven't turned her up yet but I don't believe she's on the run, we just haven't connected . . . I have preliminary interviews with several of the residents at the House who know Stampler — nothing significant there, so far . . . Also fingerprint samples from the scene and a match with the accused and footprint matches. I also have two-and-a-half hours of taped recordings of our interviews with him.'

Finally he took a brown manila envelope out of the case. 'These are the pictures. Be prepared, they're not very pretty. Oh yes, the autopsy is due in about an hour.'

'You've been very busy in the last . . .' Venable looked at her watch, 'fourteen hours,' she said.

'I was told this is P.O.,' Stenner said.

'What do you think?' she asked.

'I think the boy did it. He's very scared, making up things, but . . . one of us will break him down. Only a matter of time. We've got more physical evidence than we usually gather in a month. The weapon, prints, footprints, the Bishop's ring . . .'

'The Bishop's ring?'

'He was wearing the Bishop's ring.'

'You think robbery was the motive?'

Stenner pondered that for several seconds. 'No.'

'Oh?'

'Not the way he did it. I don't like to speculate . . .'

'Oh, go ahead just this once. Speculate.'

'I'd say it was some kind of . . . religious motive. Maybe this boy, Stampler, is mixed up in Satanism or some kind of cult. It has that feel to it. You'll understand when you look at the shots. Incidentally, we haven't released any of this information so far. I'm holding on to the reports so they don't leak out.'

'Good idea,' Venable said and turned to Yancey. 'So what's the problem here, Jack? Sounds like even you could win this one.'

'Cute,' Yancey chuckled. 'I want a star. I want fireworks. I want you to go in and over*whelm* the jury with facts. Treat it like the Priority One it is, not like an open and shut case. When this kid burns I want his mother — if he has one — to be out there cheering the executioner.'

'Well, I congratulate you on what you've done so far,' Venable said to Stenner. 'But then we've come to expect that of you, Abel. The price you pay for being the best. Everybody expects the impossible.'

'Thank you,' he said. 'I'll try to keep giving it to you.'

'Modest, too,' she said, sweetly, after he left the room.

The phone rang and Yancey snatched it up. 'Yeah, this is Jack . . . you're kidding! Well I'll be damned, maybe there is justice in the world after all . . . Oh yeah, I think Jane's going to handle the case for the city.'

She shook her head frantically and stood up.

'Thanks for calling,' Yancey said and hung up.

'You're so damned sure of yourself,' she snapped. 'I'm not sure I want to be a part of this Circus Maximus.'

'You're not worried, are you?' he said, playing against her vanity. He got up, got his putter and tapped some balls out on the carpet.

'Come on, Jack, that's beneath even you. From the way it sounds, we could sleep through this one and win.'

He practised a few long putts, sending the balls into a waste-basket which, for that purpose, lay on its side in the corner.

'Might be a little tougher than that,' he said.

'Why the sudden change of heart?'

'Because I just found out who's representing the Stampler kid.'

'Really? Surprise me.'

'I probably will.' He looked up from his putter. 'Martin Vail.'

She was stunned by the news. 'Martin Vail?' she echoed.

'That was the good judge who just called.'

'And Vail took the case?'

'I don't think he had a lot of choice. He could hardly plead poverty after the Pinero settlement.'

'So he got stuck with it,' she said.

'That would be my appraisal.'

She had only faced Vail twice in court. The first time the jury had emerged after two days of sequester and announced it was hopelessly deadlocked. The case went into mis-trial. Two years later it died of attrition; a natural demise, one that could be blamed on the system, and so it ended in a draw, nobody got hurt.

The second trial was a disaster.

For three months, the county's elite Narcotics Enforcement Unit had been running a track on a Colombian named Raul Castillo, one of the city's main suppliers of cocaine. A dozen cops had taken part in the investigation. They had wire taps, film, photographs, paper trails, UC buys, and witnesses who had turned on Castillo to protect their own hides.

Their star witness was Miko Rodriguez, a boyhood friend of Castillo turned undercover cop. He had infiltrated the gang, providing the strings that tied one piece of evidence to the next, helped to close the loopholes, and enabled Venable to develop a powerful case against Castillo. She made only one mistake – she fell in love with Miko. Like most lovers, she trusted him, confided in him and, nestled in his arms in the sanctity of the bed they shared, she revealed to him the most damaging threads of her case. Finally the trap was sprung. Castillo was brought to heel.

All of her other assets faded into the woodwork when Venable hit the court-room. This was her element, the perfect showcase for her brains, beauty and élan, a chance to put everything to work at once. She was a tiger shark, possibly the best litigator the D.A.'s office ever had. Quick, immaculately prepared, deadly, always the predator waiting for her opponent to make a slip before slamming in for the kill. Venable was the ultimate jugular artist. There was no margin for error when doing battle with her.

She was just like Vail – no prisoners.

Vail became her opponent and eventually her worst nightmare.

The trial had lasted six weeks. In the beginning it had been a toe-to-toe brawl. A few rounds went to her, a few rounds to Vail. Then it began to unravel. Vail destroyed the credibility of her witnesses, branded the cops as corrupt liars and perjurers. Wire taps were thrown out of court, one drug buy after another was quashed because of the entrapment, witnesses failed to appear, Vail discredited photographs as immaterial and inconsequential, and slowly turned her carefully constructed case into a jumble of non-sequiturs. In the end only Miko Rodriguez remained to sew together the tattered rags of her case.

Rodriguez was on the stand for two days. On the second day, he began to fall apart as Vail, using some of the prosecution's own tapes, implied that Rodriguez had manufactured evidence, perjured himself, and used inside information to get rid of Castillo so he himself could assume leadership of the cocaine ring. It was a daring ploy but it worked. Castillo walked out of the court-room and vanished into the jungles of Colombia. A month after the trial, Miko Rodriguez was found floating in the lake with six bullet holes in his back. It was Venable's most humiliating defeat and it almost brought down Yancey's regime. Luckily, it had come during the D.A.'s second term and by election time, Venable, Torres and Silverman had amassed such a string of convictions that the Castillo case was forgotten. Forgotten by everyone but Venable.

There remained only two mysteries from the Castillo event. Was Miko Rodriguez really using her to manoeuvre Castillo for a fall so he could take over? His murder gave credence to Vail's scenario. Even more curious, Vail had spared Venable one final humiliation. He had never revealed, either in or out of court, that some of the inside information used by Rodriguez to set up Castillo had been gathered in Venable's bed. Was that a sign of weakness? Something she could use against him? Or was it simply immaterial to him? Whatever, the Castillo case still haunted her and she was unsure whether Yancey had given the Pinero case to Silverman because she was too busy to handle it, or because Yancey wouldn't chance pitting her against Vail again.

'How many times have you two gone at it?' Yancey asked innocently.

'You know damn well how many times. And I remind you, the first one was a draw.'

'Yeah, but that second time around that almost sank the whole department.'

She leaned across the desk and showed her fangs.

'Jack,' she hissed, 'you've been sinking this department since the day you were elected.'

His face squinched up in mock pain. 'Aw, don't get nasty. I'm just reminding you, you owe him.'

So Yancey needed her and she had one last shot at

Vail and this time his back was hard against the wall. It was an ambush, but it would make headlines.

'The press'll have a field day,' she said. 'The whole Castillo case will come up again. Grudge match. Battle of the sexes. They'll eat it up with a spoon.'

'So . . . are you in?'

She said, 'I feel like I'm cheating, playing against him with a stacked deck.'

'What's the difference?' Yancey said. 'You owe the son of a bitch one, right?'

She thought for a moment and nodded slowly. 'Yes,' she said. 'I owe the son of a bitch one.'

Nine

Vail and the guard took the elevator to the bottom of the shaft, passed through a steel door and went down another flight of stone stairs. They had to be four stories underground. The cell block was carved out of rock with one inch thick steel doors on each of its ten cells. Two screened overhead lights provided the only illumination. The floor and walls were damp and slimy and the place smelt of urine, faeces, and vomit.

'I've never been down here before,' Vail said with disgust. 'How come you're not wearing a mask and leather tights and carrying a whip? Where's the rack?'

'Very funny. You really gonna defend the Butcherboy?'

'Where'd you hear that?'

'What, that you were defending him?'

'No, that Butcherboy routine?'

'That's what everybody calls him.'

'You mean everybody in this cell block or everybody in the police or everybody in the world? Define everybody for me.'

'Y'know – everybody. It was in the papers.'

'Well, that certainly makes it official, doesn't it?'

'Here we are,' the guard said. He slid open a peephole and Vail peered in at a room no more than six by four feet. There was a canvas cot against one wall and a bucket in the corner. Vaguely Vail could make out a huddled shape on the end of the cot. The walls were the colour of mud.

'There's no light in there.'

'He don't need no light.'

'What the fuck is this? This isn't a jail, it's a goddamn dark ages dungeon. I want my client out of there. *Now!*

I want him in a cell with a toilet and lights and hopefully a sink so he can brush his teeth and I want him to have a shower.'

'You know what that little bastard did . . . ?'

'I don't give a shit if he set the Pope on fire and cooked marshmallows over him . . .'

'Who the fuck . . .'

'If you're about to ask me who the fuck I am, I'll save you the trouble. I'm Martin Vail, I'm his attorney. I'm also the guy who just took the city for five fucking million dollars. Would you like me to try for ten? Would you like that? Because either he gets moved upstairs where you don't have to pipe in the fucking air so he can breathe, or I'm going to sue you, the city, the country and every pot-bellied asshole that works around here. The key word here is *Now*!'

Half an hour later, Stampler had been showered, given a grey prison jump suit, and was reassigned to a white cell that was clean, had a toilet and sink, and smelt of disinfectant. It did not have a window, but it did have lights. Vail was waiting in the cell when they brought him in. He could hear the familiar shuffling gait and the clack of chains as Stampler approached with the guard. They stopped in front of the cell.

Stampler was shackled at the ankles and his wrists were handcuffed to a heavy leather belt around his waist. Vail looked at him with a combination of shock and surprise. Aaron Stampler was five-eight or five-nine, average build, weighed maybe 120 pounds. There was nothing special about him except his face. He had soft, aesthetic features, high cheek-bones, a straight nose, a small heart-shaped mouth, and his skin was cream-coloured and flawless. He had soft blue eyes that were as gentle as those of a fawn. A shock of lemon-blond hair tumbled down over his forehead. The youth seemed more confused than scared.

My God, Vail thought, *he's absolutely angelic looking.*

'Take all that crap off him,' Vail said.

The guard removed the shackles from Stampler's ankles, unlocked the handcuffs and, with a hand against his back, gently urged Stampler into the cell.

'Gonna have to lock this, Marty,' said the corrections officer who was an old-timer and did not take crimes of any kind seriously. 'Wanna come outside, talk to him through the bars?'

'Just lock it, Tim. I'll yell when I'm through.'

The guard shrugged, slid the steel door shut. The lock clanged. The guard walked down the long row of cells.

'Aaron, my name's Martin Vail. You can call me Martin or Marty, I come to either one.'

The boy smiled.

'The court has appointed me your attorney. I am going to defend you against whatever charges are brought against you at the arraignment Friday. I will be doing this pro bono. That means it won't cost you anything.'

'Gosh a'mighty,' the boy said. 'Thankee, I be grateful to ye. And thankee for gettin' me moved up hair.'

He spoke with the kind of Biblical early-English patois that is peculiar to the Appalachians, and with a kind of simple directness for which mountain people are known. His voice was high alto, as if it had never changed all the way and his innocent and almost childish response stunned Vail. *Was this kid for real?*

'I want you to understand that you can refuse to have me represent you,' Vail went on. 'What I mean, you can turn me down for any reason whatever. If we don't get along, if you don't trust me, if you don't think I can do the job . . .'

'I don't even know ye,' he said.

'That's why I'm here, Aaron, so we can get to know each other.'

''kay.'

'You have to do me one favour.'

'Yes suh.'

'Always tell me the truth. Don't lie to me. I have a lot better chance of saving you if I know what happened than if I *think* I know what happened and I turn out to be wrong. Anything you tell me is privileged – that means I can't repeat it or they'll kick me out of the law business.'

The boy smiled and nodded.

'Do you know why you're here?'

He nodded slowly and stared at Vail with his pale, saucer-like eyes. 'Say I kilt Bishop Richard.'

'That's what you called him, Bishop Richard?'

'Yes suh.'

'You don't have to call me sir, I don't work here.'

'Okay,' he said, and looked over Vail's shoulder at the cell door. Vail turned and looked into Abel Stenner's stony, wire-framed eyes. He got up and walked to the cell door.

'Do you mind?' Vail said.

'I've got rights here, too, Counsellor.'

'The judge and I have a deal, Stenner,' Vail said. 'No more cops until Friday morning at the arraignment. He's all mine now.'

'Nobody told me that,' Stenner said flatly.

'Then you must not be in the loop, Lieutenant. Maybe you better go ask your boss, and if he doesn't know about it yet, tell him to call Judge Shoat's office. By the way, were you responsible for putting my client down in that cesspool?'

'I'm not the booking sergeant, Vail,' Stenner said softly. 'I think the normal procedure in a case like . . .'

'I'll remind you, Lieutenant,' Vail cut him off, 'that at this moment, that's an innocent man sitting over there. And he's going to be treated the same as any other innocent man awaiting trial, regardless of what you might think.'

'. . . is to put them in maximum security,' Stenner completed his thought.

'And don't dignify that shit-hole by calling it maximum security. Maximum security, my ass. Only a sadist would put somebody down there.'

'As I told you . . .'

Vail interrupted him again. 'You've been interrogating him off and on for almost twenty-four hours. You could have let him take a goddamn shower, at least. He still had dried blood in his hair, for Christ sake.'

'I just told you, I'm not responsible for what goes on in here. I'm investigating a murder case. That's my responsibility.'

'Well you're not going to do it here or now.'

'Always have to play hardball, don't you?'

'Is there any other way to play?'

Stenner turned abruptly and left the cell block.

Vail turned back towards the boy and sat down beside him on the cot.

'That's Stenner. He's the man who's investigating your case. He's one tough cop, Aaron. They call him The Icicle.'

'Ah kin understaind thet,' Aaron said, 'I doubt he's got an ounce of blood in his whole body. Were playin' games with me.'

'Who was playing games with you?'

'Mister Stenner and his partner, uh . . . Turner. A black fella who was right friendly. That Stenner, he would look at me with his hard eyes and try to talk scary. Then he'd go out fer coffee or go to the toilet, Mister Turner would set t'sweet talkin' me.'

'That's very perceptive, Aaron,' Vail said.

'Ah finally told them both, "Look hair," I said, "I tole you all I know. I don't know what else I kin do 'cept maybe start making thaings up. Thet what y'want me t'do?" They left after thet and didn't come back again.'

Vail stifled a chuckle. He could understand how Stenner and Turner would find it difficult to handle the bald truth.

83

'Ah do sompin' wrong?' Aaron asked.

'You did just fine,' Vail said. 'I'm sure you remember my name.'

'A'course. Mister Vail.'

'Good. Let's start over. Give me your full name.'

'Aaron Luke Stampler.'

'Where you from, Aaron?'

'Kentucky.'

'Where in Kentucky?'

Aaron chuckled. 'You're gon' laugh. Crikside.'

'Crikside? How do you spell that?'

'Just arey it sounds. Crik, c-r-i-k, side, s-i-d-e. Town's about the size of ye're hand, Mister Vail. Sits aside Morgan's Crik, that's why they callin' it Crikside.'

Vail chuckled. 'And how many people live in Crikside, Aaron?'

'I dunno, two hundred, there'bouts.'

'How long you been in the city?'

'Two year next month.'

'Ever been arrested?'

'No, suh.'

'Ever been charged with a crime?'

The boy shook his head.

'How far'd you go in school?'

'Finished high school. Took two quarters of college, y'know, by mail.'

'You're pretty smart, are you?'

'Well, suh, I know enough to come inside when it be rainin'.'

Vail laughed heartily. 'Least you still got your sense of humour. Let me ask you, were you a friend of Bishop Richard's?'

'Yes, suh.'

'For how long?'

'Met him 'bout a week after I come up. Billy Jordan taken me to Saviour House and Bishop Richard were there. Tole me I could move in and I were most grateful, not havin' much money and all.'

'How long did you live there?'

'Until past December, a year and nine months. Yer suppose t'move out when yer eighteen, but he let me stay on for almost a year. I helped around the church and such. Then in December me and Linda got us a place over on Region Street.'

'So he didn't make you move?'

'Oh no, suh. Fact is, ah think he woulda preferred for us t'stay on at the House but . . . t'were time t'move on.'

'Why?'

'We, Linda and me, we be sleepin' together. Y'know, sneakin' inta the dorm after lights out and, uh . . .'

'Did you get caught?'

'No suh, but we sure would of.'

'So you didn't exactly leave with his blessing?'

'Well, he tole us we always be welcome at the House. There weren't no hard feelin's 'bout it, if that what ye be askin'.

'You didn't have any kind of fight . . . or argument . . . with the Archbishop.'

Aaron shook his head. 'Never did.'

'How about Linda?'

'Not that I know of.'

'Is she still living there? On Region Street?'

'No suh. She moved.'

'Where to?'

'Ohio. Went back home. Weren't easy, y'know. I had this job at the library, cleanin' up. Three dollar an hour. But she couldn't get a job. One mornin' she just up and left. Wrote me a note g'bye.'

'Pretty tough.'

He shrugged. 'Guess it were time. T'wasn't there was hard feelin's, just hard times.'

'But you weren't particularly bent out of shape over her leaving?'

'No suh. Y'know, I been missin' her some.'

'Did you kill Bishop Richard, Aaron?'

He shook his head emphatically. 'No, suh.'

'Did you see it happen?'

Aaron looked at him with his wide, saucer eyes and said nothing.

'Were you there when it happened?'

Aaron slowly nodded.

'But you didn't actually *see* it happen, is that what you're saying?'

The young man looked down at the floor and picked at a fingernail.

'Guess so,' he said.

'Do you know who did it?'

Stampler still did not answer.

'All right, let's try this? Are you afraid of the person who killed the Archbishop?'

Aaron looked up and nodded.

'So you do know who did it?'

Aaron did not answer.

The cab inched down the street, its driver bitching every foot of the way, and stopped in front of the church. In the back seat, Vail finished reading the story in the afternoon paper for the third time.

'Shoulda never let you con me into this,' the driver said. 'Like drivin' on fuckin' ice, it is man.'

'You *are* driving on ice,' Vail said. 'And I didn't con you into anything, I offered you a twenty-dollar tip.'

'Look, you gonna pray, pray we get home. Looks like it's gonna start again.' The driver nervously scanned the dark clouds that swept over the city.

'I'll only be a few minutes,' Vail said. 'Wait.'

The Cathedral of Saint Catherine of the Lake was the oldest church in the city. Archbishop Rushman, a purist, refused to allow any changes in its structure. It was still the same huge brick manse it had been when it was built

145 years before. The steeple towered above the trees on Lakeview Drive and was visible from far out on the lake, a reminder to the crews of the pigboats and barges as they lumbered into port that the Roman way was the best way.

Vail looked up at the spire and suddenly remembered his granny, doing the thing with her fingers entwined in a pyramid: 'Here is the church, here is the steeple, open the doors . . .' and flipping her hands over and wiggling her fingers, 'and here are the people.'

He walked cautiously across the ice-draped yard to the rectory, a stark, stern-looking addendum to the cathedral, and entered the rectory office. One side of the large room was a staircase leading to the second floor, on the other the doorway to the office. There was also a back door directly in front of him and a corridor in the corner that he assumed led to the church.

A nun sat at a desk in the centre of the room.

'Hello, Sister,' the lawyer said. 'My name's Martin Vail.'

'Mister Vail,' she nodded. 'I'm Sister Mary Alice.'

She was young, late twenties, and had a rather mischievous look in her eye. There was that sense of innocence and compassion one sees in the faces of most nuns, but something else, a spin on the look, something a little devilish.

'I'm here to, uh . . . I don't know just how to put it . . .'

'Examine the scene of the crime,' she offered.

'Exactly.'

'Top of the stairs,' she said.

'Thanks.'

It struck him that she did not seem overly upset by the demise of the late Archbishop. Perhaps she was putting up a good front. He went up the stairs. A uniformed cop was sitting beside the doorway into the Bishop's suite. Vail peered around the corner so he could see the bedroom. The grotesque blood stains on the wall and carpet had turned brown. *My God*, he thought, *somebody really did butcher Rushman.*

'Who're you?' the cop asked.

'Insurance man,' Vail answered.

'Lieutenant!' the cop yelled.

Stenner entered the hallway from the kitchen. He stopped for just an instant when he saw Vail, then stalked down the hall to the door.

'We're turning into an item,' Vail said.

'What are you doing here?' Stenner asked absently, as if he really didn't expect or want an answer.

'Scene of the crime, Lieutenant. I'm here in the interest of my client, which is our privilege. Unless Jack Yancey's changed the law in the last couple of hours.'

'We're still working here,' Stenner said brusquely. 'You'll have your chance when we're out.'

Vail stared at the stained wall. 'They really did a job on him, didn't they?' he said.

'Yes. You'll see when you get the pictures. The package you ordered will be on the sergeant's desk, first precinct, first thing in the morning. That includes the autopsy, which just came back.'

'Thanks.'

Vail watched as a technician finished cutting a swatch from the carpet and dropped it in a baggy.

'I hope there's something left to examine when you finish,' Vail said. 'We're going to be missing some titbits here and there, I assume you're going to share.'

'Don't be difficult,' Stenner said looking back into the room.

'I've got a subpoena here, Lieutenant . . .'

'When we're through we'll let you know, Counsellor. Now do you mind?' He pointed towards the door.

Vail went back downstairs. Sister Mary Alice was gone. He walked across to the office and looked in.

Standing alone on a small table facing the desk was a small bronze sculpture of Pope Paul VI, his arms extended as if to enfold the world, his head tilted in an expression of compassion. Hanging on the wall behind the desk – like a stern and resolute guardian of the premises – was a photograph of the only man to whom Bishop Rushman had been responsible, Pope John Paul II.

The desk was a large, heavy mahogany piece, as were the three chairs arranged in a semi-circle before it. It was a cold, austere room except for an easy chair in one corner with several books and periodicals piled beside it, and well-stocked, built-in bookcases on the two side walls of the room which added warmth to the otherwise stark interior.

Vail entered the office, walking down beside the bookshelves. They were jammed with an eclectic mixture; religious periodicals, a leather-bound code of canon law, and religious tracts; foreign language editions of novels by Dante, Dostoevsky, and other great writers; the works of Rousseau, Locke, Hobbes, and Darwin as well as studies of the psyche by Freud, Kant and Schopenhauer.

His desk was tidy. Telephone, Rolodex, two letter trays and an appointment book, still open to the day of the murder. Vail leafed through it. Meetings, writing deadlines, dinners, and consultations were entered on every line, sometimes only fifteen minutes apart. For the fateful evening, he had scribbled in, 'Altar boy critique' and 'tape sermon' followed by 'Subject – Descartes: I think therefore I am. Ergo, if all problems can be solved by human reason, does God become obsolete. Explain.'

It was an interesting thesis and Vail jotted it down in his notebook, more out of curiosity than because he thought it might be relevant to the case. Then he tried the drawers. The one on the upper left was locked. He took a paper clip from the centre drawer, bent it double and slipped it into the keyhole, twisting it, sensing the tumblers, then feeling it catch and twist the lock open. He slid open the drawer. Inside was a small leather journal. The front half was an address book, the back half was marked 'Personal appointments.'

He checked the appointment pages randomly. On March 9, Rushman had penciled in, 'Linda: 568–4527.' There were very few other notations. It would seem the Archbishop had little time for personal endeavours. Vail scribbled the information down in his own notebook, and closed and relocked the drawer. He got up and looked at the titles of other books on the shelves but was interrupted by a soft Irish accent.

'Excuse me, Detective, may I help you?'

The priest who had entered the room was in his fifties, portly, with pure white hair and a pleasant, almost cherubic face. But his features seemed to sag from the weight of the past few days and his eyes were bloodshot, either from lack of sleep or from crying. He wore a black band on his left sleeve.

'I'm sorry, I don't mean to intrude. I'm not a policeman, Father, I'm an attorney.' Vail hesitated a moment before adding, 'I represent Aaron Stampler.'

'I see,' the priest said, apparently neither shocked nor upset by the admission. 'I'm Father Augustus Delaney,' he said and held out his hand.

'Vail. Martin Vail.'

'Poor Aaron,' he said. 'God bless the lad. I pray for his forgiveness.'

'Did you know him?'

'Oh yes. A pleasant lad, y'know. God knows what terrible demons captured his soul that he should commit such an act.'

Vail decided against his usual sermon on the quality of innocence.

'It's an irony, isn't it?' Father Delaney said softly. 'The Bishop is not only the victim, but his privacy is violated even in death. What a shame the dear man can't rest in peace.'

'I agree,' Vail said. 'Look, Father, this is probably a very dumb question, but what exactly does a bishop do?'

The priest smiled and walked around the desk to check the mail. 'Why, he runs the show, Mister Vail,' he said, leafing through the letters. 'The Holy See – the archdiocese.' He returned the unread sheaf of paper to the letter tray and turned the pages of the appointment book until it was current.

'There are fifty-three hundred square miles in this See,' he went on, running his finger down the list of appointments as he spoke. 'Seven colleges and universities, several hundred elementary and high schools, twelve hospitals, three hundred and twelve parishes and missions, over a thousand priests, over a hundred brothers and approximately three thousand nuns. Also thousands of deacons and lay workers.' He looked up and smiled. 'Impressive territory, wouldn't you say?'

'Very,' Vail answered.

Delaney leaned against the corner of the desk with his hands folded together and said, 'Bishops are the bond between parishioners and priests and the Vatican. "Teachers of doctrine, priests of sacred worship, and ministers of governance", that's the job description by canon law. An immense job, sir, the stress of it has destroyed more than one good priest.'

'And how did the Archbishop handle it?'

'He thrived on it. His schedule was full from morning till night, there were always delegations, meetings, and of course Saviour House and the Bishop's Fund, which finances all his other charity works. In addition to everything else, the Archbishop writes ... wrote ... articles on theology for the *Catholic Digest* and several national lay publications, answered the mail from parishioners and priests and wrote a weekly column for the *Tribune*. Then there were sermons, of course, and responses to the nuncio.'

'Nuncio?'

'Papal correspondence. Bishops are accountable only to the Pope, Mister Vail, they have great discretionary power.'

'Oh. How long was he bishop?'

'Appointed by Paul the Sixth. That was in 1975. They were great friends. He was not that close to Pope John Paul.'

'Why is that?'

Delaney shrugged. 'Perhaps he was too . . . outspoken.'

'About what?'

'Come along,' he said, 'I have to check the altar.' The priest motioned him to follow and, as they continued the conversation, led him down the corridor towards the church. 'Understand, Mister Vail, this is a difficult time for all American bishops. They're pulled one way, then another. There's the liberal element – they want the Church to change its attitude about everything from birth control and abortion to celibacy and the ordination of women. Then there are the traditionalists – no change at all is too much for them. A very stressful situation exists throughout the Church. Several bishops have taken extended leaves of absence because of the stress.'

'And Archbishop Rushman took stands on these issues?'

'He tried to . . . ameliorate . . . the differences within his See. To make it a matter of the individual's own conscience. The Vatican takes a more rigid stand.'

'That get him in trouble with Rome?'

'No, not trouble. Suspect, perhaps. The Holy Father is quite conservative.'

'Did the Bishop have a fairly set routine?'

'Oh yes,' he said. 'He was usually downstairs in the common room by seven-ten, seven-fifteen. We would have morning prayers. Then he would prepare for the first mass. He did everything himself. The mass was his joy – you could almost call it an obsession. He turned on the lights himself, lit the altar candles, got the hosts, refilled the cruets with wine and water. Read morning mass without an altar boy. After mass he ate breakfast and read the newspapers – the *Tribune*, *New York Times* and *Wall Street Journal*. Then he would do his writing and mail. Afternoons were for meetings.'

'Evenings?'

'Dinners, banquets, speeches. Tuesday night was reserved for preparing his sermon. He taped them on a video camera, y'know, studied them, made sure they were perfect. He also taped the altar boys at mass and critiqued them.'

'A perfectionist?' Vail offered as they reached the apse and stopped. Several nuns were draping the altar with black bunting and lilies. Half a dozen people were in the church praying. Somewhere near the rear of the church, there was the sound of a man's soft sobbing.

'In some things. Don't misunderstand me, Mister Vail, he was quite human. I will miss him greatly.'

'I'm sorry.'

'Not your problem, sir. Well, if you'll excuse me, I must get back to work.'

'Thanks for your help,' Vail said as the priest walked away, genuflected in front of the altar, and went into the sacristy. Vail went back down the corridor to the rectory to the rear door and stepped outside. He was standing below the Bishop's apartment.

What was it the paper said? He ran out the kitchen door and a patrol car in the alley spooked him.

To his left was a heavy wooden staircase leading from the back of the apartment. He walked a few feet into the yard and scanned the ancient L-shaped brick building, walked to the corner and checked it out. The small windows on each side of the corner told him he was probably standing below the bathroom. He went back inside, walked down the long hall to the church and stood for several minutes, staring at the confessionals on both sides of the apse.

That's the way he came. Out the kitchen door, down the back stairs. Then the patrol car scared him so he ran back inside. Came down this corridor and hid in one of these confessionals.

Why? If he didn't do it, why did he take the knife and run for it?

And where did the real murderer go?

'He was in the first one, over there on the other side,' a voice behind him said and he turned to face Sister Mary Alice.

'That one,' he asked, pointing across the church.

'Yes,' she answered.

'Strange place to hide.'

'Not at all. It's like a closet. Children love to hide in closets.'

'Children? Aaron hardly qualifies as a child.'

'Man-child,' she said. 'Have you met him yet?'

'Yes.'

'Beautiful boy, isn't he?'

'Yes, I'd say that. He's also nineteen. In this state, you're considered a man when you're sixteen.'

'Which means?'

'Which means they can electrocute him.'

'Can you save him from that, Mister Vail?'

'So you know why I'm here?'

'Of course. We do read the newspapers – and watch TV.'

'I'm representing Aaron.'

'I assumed that.'

'How well do you know him?'

'As well as anyone, I suppose,' she said warmly. 'We all know him.'

'What's he like?'

'A very hard worker. Thoughtful. Sharing. A very sweet boy.'

'Did he have any reason to murder the Archbishop?'

'Is there ever any reason for murder, Mister Vail?'

Ten

Vail burst into the house as if he had been blown through the door by the wind. He was talking as he came in and he stormed into his office without even taking off his coat.

'Call Wall Eye McGinty's, tell the Judge I need him. If he gives you any static about it being post time out in California someplace, tell him I said tough shit. I want him here *now*! Then call Checker and send a cab downtown for him. And I need Tommy Goodman's phone number, I never can remember . . .'

'It's 441–4411. Real easy. What the hell's going on?'

He talked as he dialed. 'The Heinrich Himmler of King's County just blind-sided us.'

'Shoat?'

'Who else?'

'What happened?'

'He dropped the pro bono bomb of the decade in our lap.'

'You've got a pro bono already. His name is Leroy . . .'

'Try Aaron Stampler.'

Her mouth dropped open two inches. 'Oh my Ga-a-a-hd,' she said.

'That's putting it mildly. We've got sixty days to put a case together and I just met the defendant for the first time. Hello, Tommy . . . damn it, I know you're there, pick up the phone, it's me . . . Screw that answering machine, this is important.'

'So is my piece of mind,' Goodman said as he picked up the receiver. He had the hard, nasal voice of an ex-fighter.

'What're you doing?'

95

'This is the end of the quarter. I got finals in two days. Orals, man.'

'I need you over here right now.'

'Goodbye,' he said and hung up.

'Damn it,' Vail yelled and redialed. Naomi stuck her head around the door. 'Judge says it's post time at Santa Anita in ten minutes, then he'll be over.'

'Christ, I . . . hello, Tommy, it's me again. Now listen to me, I got something very, very hot on my hands. I'm going to need you for sixty days. I'll pay you twenty grand, ten a month.'

Goodman picked up.

'Twenty grand for two months!'

'That's enough to put you through the rest of law school and set you up in practice – if you don't come to work for me. But I need you, body and soul, night and day for the next two months. You'll have to drop out of school next quarter. If it's a problem, I can call Dean Markowitz . . .'

'It won't be a problem, I just hate to lose a quarter this close to the end. And I got this oral in two days, on fucking torts.'

'Torts, hell,' Vail said. 'You're going to be a litigator, not a Goddamn real estate attorney. Anyway, the Judge'll coach you all day tomorrow. The cab'll be there in ten minutes.' And this time it was Vail who hung up. He yelled to Naomi, 'You got the cab yet?'

'I got Maxie. Nobody else would come. He's thinking it over.'

Vail punched the button and grabbed up the phone. 'Max?'

'Hey, Mister Vail. Look, man, have you seen . . .'

'Max, I don't want any shit. Get in your fucking cab, go by Wall Eye's place and pick up the Judge, then swing over to Sutton and get Tommy. Go by Ike's and get enough deli for ten or twelve sandwiches, some drinks, beat it back here, pronto.'

'You can't even use chains in this shit.'
'A hundred bucks, Max.'
'Who'd you say I pick up first?'

Tommy Goodman was ready to go and waiting for the cab in five minutes. It was always that way when Marty called. Funny how Vail could get Goodman's adrenalin pumping with a two-minute phone call. Goodman could stare at the answering machine, listen to Vail rave and rant, try to ignore him, but in the end could not resist that hypnotic voice, the grifter's promise of excitement on the shady side, and so finally he would succumb, knowing that the master conman of the court would lure him away from whatever he was doing with the easy charm of a snake luring a rabbit into its jaws.

It had all started that unfortunate night eight years ago in the old Arena on Twelfth Street. Twelfth Street . . . Christ, how he missed it. The drab old barn had been replaced by a gigantic domed stadium affectionately known as The Tit, with fake grass, air-conditioning, fast food pits, and a brand new football team bought and paid for by the bankers, lawyers, hotel keepers and business entrepreneurs to whom it was just another peg in the cribbage board, that image barometer of growth and progress used to lure conventioneers, tourists, and big-time spenders into the fold. Out of town bucks was the prize, that greedy infusion of green blood pumping into the city's heart which kept its financial circulation pounding, made the rich richer, the poor poorer and kept the great middle masses marching in place. Boxing, that neanderthal blood-letting, now was relegated to seedy little rinks in the mill town satellites of the city, out of sight and sound of the grandeur of say, professional football, which took much longer to separate knees, destroy shoulders, ruin ankles, pulverise the bones, and scramble the brains of its six and seven figure steroid gladiators. The string-pullers of course enjoyed an antiseptic view of the game. Sitting far above the masses in their plush club rooms, the king-makers were spared the real sounds of gridiron battle – the thunder of bodies slamming together, the cries of pain, the snap of bones, all the true epithets of glory. What it was all about is what it's always about – money in the bank.

But five years ago, on Friday nights, one could still travel down to the Twelfth Street Gym, smell the real smells – sweat, bay rum, resin, alcohol, beer, alum, cigar smoke – and watch from ringside as pros went one-on-one, practising an art that even the effete and artsy Greeks recognised as a true test of skill, beauty and power.

Goodman was a dark-haired and handsome man despite the scars of battle he so proudly wore: a slightly flattened nose, scar-tissue eyebrows, a bent ear, a right hand so weakened by broken bones that he could barely pet a cat without wincing, and the permanently septum-deviated nasal passages indigenous to prize-fighters. He spoke like a man with a perpetual cold, yet when the occasion demanded, he could call up his 132 I.Q. points and orate as eloquently as any aspiring young barrister. He was two years younger than Martin Vail and three quarters of law school and the bar exam away from realising his dream. It might never have happened had it not been for Marty Vail.

Goodman had grown up fuelled by two passions, boxing and the law, professions not that disassociated. He was as entranced by the eloquence of the court-room as he was by the vulgarity of the ring; his heroes were legends, Clarence Darrow, William O. Douglas, Muhammad Ali and Sugar Ray Leonard. A meagre and bored college student, he depended on the sport – which had provided him hero status in high school and a scholarship to the state university – to get by. Once graduated, he turned pro in the belief that he could box his way through law school. His idol became Martin Vail, who had already carved himself a little niche in local posterity with a half dozen spectacular court wins. When he could, Goodman sat in the front row, watching Vail perform legal magic and Vail, a boxing fan, spotted the young fighter in the court-room. They became friends and Vail became mentor to the pugilistic law student.

February 3, 1975. He was matched against a slow, slough-footed, lumbering, musclebound ox named George Trujillo, who called himself the Tampa Nugget and who had the grace of an ostrich. The true joys of punch and feint, footwork, speed and agility, all had passed Trujillo by; he had moved up the card on brute force alone. He could hit like a hammer and he had an iron jaw.

Goodman withstood both for ten rounds and by a miracle was still standing when the final bell rang. For six rounds he had battered Trujillo with his powerful right hand, sneaking inside the roundhouse punches, slashing at the Mexican's nose and jaw. It was like hitting a steam engine. In the seventh, Goodman came out fast, determined to get inside and send the Nugget back to Tampa on a stretcher. The first punch drove one of his knuckles back almost to the wrist. Pain became an infection for the rest of the fight. He kept hitting, each powerful blow shattering another bone in the ruined hand, until finally he had only his left to counter and hit with. Raw pride kept him on his feet. When the last bell rang, he reeled back to his corner and collapsed on his stool.

'What the fuck happened?' his trainer, Elie Pincus, asked around a mouthful of Q-tips as he shrank Goodman's gaping cuts with the fire of alum.

'I think I broke my right,' Goodman gasped.

Indeed.

Later, sitting on the edge of the table in the dismal dressing room, he and Vail watched as Pincus cut away the glove to reveal a mauled and bloody mass. Two splintered bones protruded from swollen flesh. Blood seeped from jagged tears in the once mighty right. Vail turned away at the sight.

'I'll wait outside,' he said, to be joined a few minutes later by Sawbones Watson, the arena's resident G.P.

'He's gotta go to the Pavilion, Marty. Two of his knucks are shoved all the way back to his fuckin' elbow. But he says he won't go. I think he's afraid they'll cut his hand off or somethin'.'

'Just call the ambulance. Tell them to lay off the siren. They can sneak up on him.'

'He's through, y'know,' Sawbones said. 'Won't be able to hit a loaf of bread with that paw without he'll bust a couple bones. Damn shame, too. Very promising middle-weight, Tommy was. Fast, smart – always nice to see a college kid in the game, gives us some class. But it's all over for him, Tommy's gotta know that.'

'I'll talk to him.'

'Yea, well, stand back when you do, he can still hit with his left.'

Vail had returned to the dressing room, where Saw-bones had bound the fist, now the size of a honeydew, in bandages and given Goodman some painkillers.

'So it's a wake, huh?' Goodman said, slurring his words slightly as the Demerol started to set in.

'Sawbones says your right's in the growler.'

'Wha's he know? He was any kinda doc, wouldn't be makin' a living here.'

Goodman ran his fingers lightly over the bandaged hand and winced. 'Shit, s'long law school,' he groaned.

'Maybe not,' said Vail. 'Maybe I could use you.'

'Doing what?'

'Investigating. Most of these local bohunks can't find their hat unless they're wearing it.'

'Wha me t'*snoop*?'

'I want you to head my investigating team.'

'Sure. How many y'got on the . . . Marty Vail Bureau of Invest'gation?'

'You'll be the first.'

'Lawyers,' Goodman said, shaking his head.

'You can pick up two, two-fifty a day and expenses — when you're working.'

'Two-fifty a day?'

'Two, two-fifty.'

'Which is't? Two . . . two-fifty?'

'You start at two. If you're as good as I think you'll be, we'll push it to two-fifty.'

'Lawyers.'

'What've you got to lose, Tommy? Give it a shot. You can always quit.'

The Demerol had kicked in and Goodman lay back on the table staring at the ceiling and mumbling incoherently until the ambulance arrived. 'Don't wanna be sleazy P.I. f'rest my life, takin' pictures some sleazy slob shacked up in a sleazy motel . . .'

'I don't do divorces,' Vail said. 'Most of my clients are people with big trouble and lots of money.'

'S'I heard.'

'Examine the contents, not the bottle, okay?' Vail said. 'In Cicero's words, "justice renders to everyone his due."'

'B'shit. Marty Vail's ona case, ain' no justice . . .' He laughed as the Demerol evaporated the pain. 'W'shit, s'Clarence Darrow once said, "No such thing as justice — in or outta court."'

'Who's Clarence Darrow?' Vail answered.

It had taken four hours to rearrange the shattered bones in Goodman's hand and plaster it up. When it was over, Vail paid the bill. Two months later, Tommy Goodman became head of the Marty Vail Bureau of Investigation — and it's only member. He was better than good, he was a natural. His first year he made thirty-five thousand dollars, pretty good money. By 1978 he was clearing fifty and was well on his way through law school. Only it took a little longer than he expected. There were always those phone calls, always the seduction in the master's voice, always another mountain to kick over. What the hell, he probably learned more law spending fifteen minutes with Vail and the Judge than he would ever learn in school.

The Judge sat in one of the thick chairs at the back of Wall Eye McGinty's horse parlour, legs crossed, legendary black book in his lap, twirling his Mont Blanc pen in his fingers. He watched the electronic tote board as he considered his next move.

'Look at the old bastard,' said McGinty, who had lost his oesophagus to cancer three years earlier and now talked through a voice box that made him sound like he was gargling. 'Him and that fuckin' book. He could make us all rich in a week.'

'That or put us outa business,' answered Larry the Limp, who was reckless with guns and had blown his foot off while hunting deer in Pennsylvania.

'Anybody ever grabs that book and makes a run for it, kill him on the spot,' Wall Eye said.

The book!

Judge Jack Spalding had, as his twilight years approached, been devastated by two tragedies. His beloved Jenny, a soft-spoken and demure lady of the South who adored his crusty nature and to whom he had been married for thirty-seven years, had been cruelly injured in a car wreck and had lingered comatose for almost a month before dying. The second tragedy was of his own making. Never much of a drinker, the Judge had succumbed to a life-long, but until then controlled, addiction to playing the ponies. In a wild spree after Jenny died, he had lost thirty thousand dollars to bookmakers in a single month. His reputation and his place on the bench were threatened and a distinguished career dangled from the fingers of the bookies.

Spalding had been saved by the devotion of defence

counsels, prosecutors, cops, newspaper reporters, law clerks, librarians, and politicians, all of whom respected his fairness and his wisdom on the bench and who understood his madness. At a closed benefit dinner, they handed the Judge an envelope with the necessary pay-off in cash – and then, after he had settled his debts, his friends in the vice squad had busted all the bookies who had taken advantage of the revered jurist in his dark hours.

The Judge had quit cold turkey and, since that night had never placed a dime on the steeds. Instead, he placed imaginary bets each day, keeping elaborate records on every race, track, jockey and horse in the circuit. Without the pressure of the wager, he became a seer of the tracks, a man who collaborated wisdom, insight and a staggering knowledge of statistics into a ten-year winning streak. He dutifully recorded all the information in a thick leather journal, a book so feared by the bookmakers that they had once banded together and offered him six figures if he would burn it. He, of course, refused but assured them he would neither give tips nor impart his vast knowledge of the game to anyone else. In ten years, the Judge had gathered an imaginary fortune of over a million dollars, all of it on paper.

He had three joys in life: the morning seminars at Butterfly's, where he challenged the minds and hearts of young lawyers; his afternoons at Wall Eye McGinty's, where he practised his hobby among the side-talking fringe elements of society, spoke the speak of the trade, enjoyed the vitality of post time, the exhilaration of the stretch, and the jubilation of winning. He always sat in the back of McGinty's lavish suite over a garage on Wildcat Street. A lush emporium for horse players, it looked like the office of an up-town brokerage. A travelling neon board kept the players appraised of changing odds, scratches, and the other bits of information that would be foreign language to most humans. A bar in the corner provided free drinks to the heavy hitters. Softly cushioned easy chairs offered comfort to those who watched and listened as the ponies did their stuff.

His third joy was matching wits with Marty Vail, for this was more than a challenge, it was a test of his forty-five years on both sides of the bar. His forays and collaborations with Vail provided a euphoria unmatched by his other enterprises. The call from Naomi promised exciting days afoot.

But first things first. He had fifty imaginary bucks across the board on a three-year-old mare named Wishful Thinking who was running in the last heat at Santa Anita and who proved better than her name. A long shot, she came in second, paid eight dollars eighty to place, and provided the Judge with a 3,426 dollars overall day which he dutifully entered in his log before going downstairs to the waiting cab.

Vail took a single silver dollar out of his pocket and spun it like a top on the desk. The Judge immediately accepted the challenge.

'Ah hah. Well, now, let's see, you've got the entire Gashouse Gang here in the freezing cold, on the spur of the moment . . . the roads virtually impassable . . . so obviously we are dealing with a matter of more than ordinary import.'

'Uh huh,' Vail said.

'We have a new client.'

'I'll give you that,' Vail agreed.

'Hmm.' The Judge walked from one side of the desk to the other, staring at the coin. 'A new client,' he said to himself. He looked back at Vail.

'Did you see anybody after we had breakfast?'

Vail nodded and held up a finger.

'So you visited someone – unexpectedly or you would have mentioned it at breakfast – and as a result of that visit, we have a new client. So, was this person you visited

104

the client? Or did he represent the client? Obviously, since you threw down the silver gauntlet, it would have to be someone I know, or something I know about. A new client, someone I know about . . .'

He walked to the window and stared out at the icy landscape, pulled on his lips, mumbled to himself, walked around the room. It was quite a performance. He walked back to the edge of the desk, stared hard-eyed at Vail, and said, 'Aaron Stampler.'

'Amazing,' Goodman said as Vail slid the coin into the Judge's waiting hand.

'Elementary,' Vail said. 'When you think about it, who else could it be but Aaron.'

'Are we really defending the kid who did in His Eminence?' Goodman asked.

'*Suspected* of doing in His Eminence,' Vail corrected.

'Didn't wait long to extract their pound of flesh, did they?' said the Judge. 'Fate provided the perfect set-up.'

'What do you mean?' Naomi asked.

'Pay-off time,' Vail said. 'Their way of getting even for the settlement. Hand us a case we can't win with a client everybody thinks makes Manson look like Little Bo Peep. Well, let's kick some ass.'

'And how do you plan to do that?' Naomi asked.

'With the power of righteousness!' the Judge laughed.

'Oh shit, here we go again,' Goodman moaned.

While they were making sandwiches, the phone rang. Naomi went in the other room, mumbled into the mouthpiece, hung up and came back.

'Want to know who your opponent is?' she asked grandly.

They all looked at her expectantly.

'Jane Venable.'

'Impossible,' Vail said. 'She's going to work at one of the prestige firms at the end of this month. She's already given notice!'

'Well apparently she ungave it. That was my inside man. It's gospel.'

'They haven't missed a trick,' the Judge said. 'Everybody's getting even on this one.'

'Son of a bitch,' Vail said with a tight-lipped smile.

They gathered around the big table. Vail ignored food, striding around the room using a ruler as rapier and slashing the air with it as he spoke. He had peeled off the sweater and was wearing a Grateful Dead T-shirt which was tucked half in and half out of his jeans.

'Well, they need one thing to tie their case up and they don't have it yet,' he said.

'What's that?' Naomi asked.

'Motive. They may have the hardware, they may have the prints and Aaron's bloody little body on film and that scene in the confessional, but they need a motive to clinch this case.'

'Why? If they can put the knife in his hand, put him in the room, put him in the confessional . . .'

'Nature of the crime, Tommy,' said Vail. 'It's too nasty. The jury's gonna want to know *why*. When they see this kid up there, they're going to want to know why he committed such an act. You can bet your VW that Venable's got Stenner and his whole bunch working overtime on that one.'

The Judge said nothing. He sat quietly in his chair, eating a pastrami on rye and sipping a cream soda, watching as Vail started developing his case.

'What if they don't find one?'

'Then they'll manufacture one.'

'So what do we do about it?' Goodman asked.

'We find it before they do,' said Vail. 'So we can figure out how to tear it apart in court. Right, Judge?'

'Without a viable motive, I don't think they'll burn him. Life maybe, but not the hot seat. So, Martin, tell us about our client.'

'You're not gonna believe me,' he said.

106

'Is he nuts?' Tommy asked.

'He acts as normal as anybody in this room.'

'Which is not really saying a lot,' the Judge threw in.

'I'm telling you, this is the sweetest kid you'd ever want to meet. Looks like a choirboy. If he was six years old he could pass for Shirley Temple.'

'Does he have a halo?' the Judge asked sarcastically.

'Swear to God, he could pass for an angel. I talked to one of the sisters at St. Catherine's, you know how she described him? Generous, thoughtful, helpful . . .'

'Thrifty, brave, clean and reverent . . . that's the Boy Scout creed,' said Tommy. 'Maybe he's got a merit badge in carving.'

'Not funny. You want to hear or not?'

'Testy, testy,' Naomi said.

'I spent twenty, thirty minutes with the kid. I'm giving you first impressions, okay? He's from someplace in Kentucky called Crikside.'

'*Crikside*?' the Judge said.

'Crikside. That's because it's beside a crik.'

'Great,' Goodman groaned. 'This is gonna be mine, I can feel it.'

'You're right, Tommy. It's about an hour's drive south of Lexington near a place called Drip Rock.'

'Oh, Drip Rock. Why didn't you say so?'

'Kid says it's not even on the map, but he says anybody in Drip Rock can tell you how to get there.'

'Who's gonna tell me how to get to Drip Rock?'

Naomi came back in the room with a large road atlas. She flopped it on the table and traced the highway south from Lexington. 'Hey,' she said. 'Here's Drip Rock. It's just north of Kerby Knob and south of Zion Mountain.'

'Beautiful,' said Goodman, 'and probably buried under about ten feet of snow this time of year. What do I do, parachute in?'

'You'll think of something,' said Vail. 'I want to know everything there is to know about Aaron Stampler, from the day he was born until they found him in that confessional. I want to know where he grew up, what his parents were like, what he did in school, who his friends were, what he read, what kind of music he liked, did he play sports, when did he get laid first, who his friends are here. I want to know what he thinks, why he thinks it, what makes him mad, what gives him a hard-on . . . I want to know it all. That's you, Tommy. The kid's yours. Chapter and verse. Fly to Lexington, rent a car, get down there as soon as possible. That's where it starts. But first I want you to check him out locally. Go to Saviour House and also his place – it's on Region Street.'

'Great!'

'Check 'em both, then head for Crikside after the arraignment.

'Judge, the law's your problem. We need to get case histories on murder by mutilation, murder by stabbing, murder by religion, including sex, denomination, and age. And murder by insanity. I want to throw law at Shoat so fast and hard he'll fall off the bench trying to catch it. *Anything* that might apply. I want to know what kind of people commit this kind of crime – and why. Shit, I don't have to tell you. Naom, check your insurance sources on this. They have statistics on everything, just maybe you'll turn up something we can use.'

'That's my job?' Naomi said.

'Also files, reports, autopsies, rumours, *progress*, that's you. The old tracker back at work. Shoat's giving us a lot of headroom on this because of the time element. All their reports are ours, without having to go through discovery – although we'll probably do that, too. We want to know everything they're up to. Stenner and Venable will give you only what's required, so snoop around, keep your ears open, anything you hear could be important. And background on Rushman, everything you can find out about him as far back as possible. Check newspaper microfilm, magazines, anyplace you might pick up something. Tommy, here's a subpoena. That'll get you into the Archbishop's apartment where it all happened. Stenner was still in there this afternoon, playing cut and paste. Wait until you get back from Kentucky to do the search. By that time we should have access to their reports and a shot at the physical evidence.'

Vail shoved letters and files into a pile and cleared a place on his desk. He threw a legal pad down and made a rough sketch showing the layout.

'The apartment's on the second floor,' he said, pointing out features as he mentioned them. 'This is the bedroom. Bath here. Hallway here and the kitchen here in the corner. This must be a living room beside it. Stairs leading down from the kitchen. This is the back door of the rectory, here's a corridor to the church.'

'Okay, so what does Shirley Temple say happened.'

Vail took a deep breath. 'Now let's assume that he's innocent for the moment. Agreed?' They all nodded.

'Here's Aaron's story,' Vail started. 'He says he was in the room when the Bishop was hit but didn't actually see it happen. There was a lot of action, things breaking, lamps overturning. The next thing he remembers is seeing Rushman dead on the floor and his ring and the knife lying beside the body. So he puts the ring on, grabs the knife and starts out . . .'

'He put the ring on?' Naomi said.

'Let me finish.' Vail took a pencil and traced Stampler's movements on his sketch. 'He starts out and he hears somebody downstairs, so he goes out the back way, down these wooden steps to ground level. There's a patrol car coming down the alley, over here, so he dodges back through the door here, runs into the church, down this corridor, and hides in one of the confessionals.'

Goodman started to laugh. 'That's absolute horse-shit, Marty. That's a horse-shit story, pardon my French, if I ever heard one!'

'And that's an understatement,' the Judge said. 'It's

ludicrous! Why did he pick up the knife? Why did he put the ring on? How did he get covered with blood? Why did he do *anything*? Why didn't he just call the police?'

'He was scared. He panicked.'

'Shit,' said Tommy. 'Shoat'll throw his gavel at you, you go into court with that story.'

'He's a smart kid. Why would he make up a dumb story like that unless it's true?' Vail asked.

'Because that's the way it happened,' said the Judge. 'Except for one minor detail – *he* chopped up His Eminence.'

'We're assuming he's innocent, remember?' Vail said.

'Not anymore,' said Goodman.

'Is there any motive here?' Naomi asked.

'Not so far. He says he and the Bishop were friends.'

'Well if he didn't do it and he was there, who the hell did?' the Judge asked.

'He won't say.'

'Why the hell not?'

'He says he's afraid of the real killer.'

Tommy shook his head emphatically. 'His story's still for shit,' he said.

'But it's his story,' the Judge said, staring at the ceiling.

'What's that mean?' said Tommy.

'That means we're stuck with it until we either break it or find a better one,' Vail answered. 'And that's my problem. I've got to get under his skin and to do that he's got to trust me. I've got to find out what happened that night. And then we have to put it all together and make it work for us. And we need one more thing.'

'A shrink,' the Judge said.

'Right, Judge, we need a shrink,' Vail said. 'Not one of those jaded old farts from up in Daisyland, that's who they'll use for the psychiatric evaluation.'

'What if they don't do a P.E.?' Naomi said.

'We'll demand it in the arraignment. And we want him

moved up to Daisyland, keep him out of the public eye and mind for a while. "No comment" the press to death and hope Venable and company are too busy to manufacture news. Maybe the public'll cool down.'

'Unlikely,' the Judge said, 'although I agree we should keep him out of sight for a while.'

Vail was pacing again, slapping a ruler into the flat of one hand. 'We need somebody young. Real sharp. Somebody with a fresh approach. New ideas. We need to hit them from the side, knock 'em off balance. They're going to do everything but dig up Freud to prove Stampler's sane.'

'We're saying he's not?' said Naomi.

'We're saying maybe. Between us? The best chance we've got right now is an insanity plea and they know it, so they're going to try to step on that one early in the game.'

'Let me find the shrink for you,' the Judge offered. 'I have good friends up at the University. I'll check it out, see if they can recommend somebody good, somebody who can find the mental loopholes while I work on the legal ones.'

'Somebody who can prove this kid's crazier than a Mexican jumping bean,' Tommy said.

The Judge smiled. 'Of course, that too,' he said.

Eleven

Before dawn, the weather turned warmer and by nine in the morning the icy streets had turned to brown slush. Cars still moved cautiously, their chains clanging on the street and banging against their fenders. It was a familiar winter sound. Vail dodged splashes of dirty mush as he jumped between puddles on his way from the police station to the court-house.

Vail had picked up the package from Precinct One and he went across the street to the court-house, peeking in doors until he found an empty court-room he could use for a few minutes. He knew this room well for he had argued a dozen cases within its oak-panelled confines. He went to the defendant's table and eagerly opened the thick manila envelope Stenner had left for him.

The autopsy report was frightening enough but the photographs were devastating. He went through them slowly, his mouth growing drier as he studied each one before laying it face down in a stack. There were two dozen of them. Like all graphic police studies of violence, they lacked both art and composition, depicting the stark and sanguinary climate of the crime and the mindless indignity to which the human body was exposed. Porno-graphic in detail and obscene in content, they were cata-logued and gathered in groups; long establishing shots showing the nauseating ambience of the scene, full length studies, finally the chilling close-ups and extreme close-ups. He could see the jury now, staring in open-mouthed horror as each picture made its way down the row.

When he finished he put them back in the manila envelope and leafed through the transcript of one of two interrogations by Stenner and Turner. It had lasted from

11:41 p.m. until 1:26 a.m. on the night of the crime. The second, between 6:04 a.m. and 7:12 a.m. the following morning, had not yet been transcribed but there were copies of the tapes of both interviews included in the package. There were also preliminary fingerprint and forensics reports stamped 'Initial report, more to come.' All in all, it was an impressive assemblage for such a short period of time. The transcript told him that Aaron Stampler had repeated the same story to the two detectives as he had told Vail, on two different occasions for a total of two hours and fifty-three minutes. By now everyone in the D.A.'s office would be laughing about that.

To get his mind off the images of death, Vail stalked the empty court-room. To Vail, the law was both a religion and a contest and the court-room was his church, his Roman Colosseum, the arena where all his knowledge and cunning were adrenalised. It was here he really came alive, his energy and brain fuelled by the challenge of law; to attack its canons, dogma, precepts, its very structure, as he invoked the jury to accept his concept of truth. The legal dominion was sacred to Vail but he also felt it had to be defied and challenged constantly if it were to endure.

The door to the court-room opened and Goodman peeked inside. Vail was lost in his own cosmos, appraising an imaginary jury, formulating some ingenious argument. Vail walked past the empty jury box, sliding a finger along the polished rail that separated the sanctioned twelve from the rabble of the court-room, remembering phrases from past oratories: 'Ladies and gentlemen of the jury, you have heard the evidence . . .' Evidence? Call it evidence, or conjecture, or guesswork, insinuation, circumstance, lies, whatever, it was all constructed for one purpose, to define the crime and hopefully help the jury to separate fact from fiction – Vail's fact, the prosecutor's fiction. And so, as he speculated on the D.A.'s initial evidence against Aaron Stampler, he subconsciously practised the demands of his sport the way a long distance runner practises stride, timing and breathing.

His mind strayed back to Aaron Stampler. Could this quiet, almost pretty, mountain boy have committed such a crime? Stampler just didn't fit the mould. He was quick and articulate but also blunt and unsophisticated. There was a mountain boy's naturalness about him, yet he was not naive. And he seemed strangely apathetic to the charges against him. Stampler was well aware that he was accused of an absolutely unspeakable crime, but it did not seem to concern him, which was one of Vail's tests of innocence: Lack of fear. In Aaron's mind, there could be no punishment because he had committed no crime, therefore he was apathetic to any threat of consequence.

What the *hell* happened that night? Vail wondered. Is it possible that it happened the way Stampler described it? And if so, how would Vail ever prove it?

'Hey, what's going on?' Goodman asked.

Vail looked up, startled by the intruder, then shrugged.

'A moment of prayer,' he answered. 'Enter the arena.'

'I brought coffee,' Goodman said, putting a sack with three cups of coffee and three doughnuts on the table beside the D.A.'s package.

'Great. Take a good swig and sit down before you look at the pictures.'

'Bad?'

'Invent a darker word.'

Vail sat on the corner of the desk dunking a doughnut and sipping coffee, watching Goodman flip slowly through the catalogue of savagery, uttering an occasional 'Whew', or 'Good God.' When Tommy was finished, he leaned back in his chair and breathed a silent whistle through pursed cheeks.

'When the jury sees these, Stampler's a dead man,' Goodman said.

'Maybe, maybe not,' Vail answered.

'They're prejudicial they're so inflammatory. How the hell could you possibly make these work for us?'

'Do you think a sane person could have done that?' asked Vail.

'We going for insanity?' Goodman asked.

'If it's all we've got.'

'Then you're assuming Stampler's guilty,' Goodman said.

'Not necessarily. But if we can't prove he's innocent, insanity could be the only way to keep him off the fryer.'

'So how do we plead him tomorrow morning?'

'Not guilty.'

Tommy Goodman headed his battered VW out the Crosstown Boulevard to Lakeview and turned towards the cathedral. As he drove out the wide boulevard with its tree-lined divider, he could see Saviour House off to his right. He turned and took Banner Street down to the old high school building and parked. He sat staring at the house with the motor running. The street was deserted except for a couple of teenagers who were working on an old Chevy sitting on cinder blocks half a block away. They tinkered with the engine, stopping frequently to warm their hands over a garbage can filled with burning refuse.

As he sat there, fragments from the past seeped into his memory. Franklin Roosevelt High. Graduation day, 1973. He had been one of those 'Goddamn long-haired hippies' the Mayor had condemned, refusing to give them their diplomas if they didn't get haircuts. And so thirty-two of them had stood during the entire ceremony, capped and gowned, with their hair tucked up under tassled mortar boards and their hands over their lips, while a legless Vietnam veteran named Robbie DeHaviland, an alumnus of the school, had delivered the graduation address.

About half way through the speech and to everyone's shock, DeHaviland had suddenly unloaded on the Mayor, the school principal and just about everyone in the city, the state and the U.S. government.

'What has happened to freedom in this country?' he roared in anger. 'I didn't leave half my body in that Godforsaken garbage dump to come back here and have our elected officials walking all over our rights as citizens. What has happened to freedom of speech? Freedom of expression? What the *hell* are we fighting for? If you hate this war as much as I do, speak out! And if growing your hair down to your *ass* is your way to express your feelings, then I say grow it. You who are about to graduate and go into the adult world today earned your diplomas. And if the Mayor and the principal of this high school don't give them to you, I say they should get down on their knees in the nearest veteran's cemetery and eat every Goddamn one of them!'

The crowd had gone berserk and principal Joe Leady had indeed given out every diploma. And as each protester had mounted the platform and received his diploma, he had whipped off his cap, let his hair tumble down around his shoulders, and thrown his mortar board to the winds.

June 2, 1973. What a great fucking day that was.

Later they discovered that DeHaviland was so stoned when he made the speech he didn't remember what he said until the next day. No one could have known that the school would be closed before the war in Vietnam ended, a victim of old age and disregard.

Goodman sadly regarded the wonderful old building, now dressed in luminous rainbow colours, with its vital organs renovated, the field where they once played touch football lathered with concrete. Another one of Cardinal Rushman's great achievements, raising the money to clean up the place and turn it into a boarding school for runaways and rehabs. But what the hell, you had to give

116

the Saint of Lakeview Drive credit for pulling off such a grand project.

Well, it might be Saviour House to the late, great Cardinal Rushman, but it was still FDR High to him. *His* high school, by God, and nothing would ever change that.

He got out of the car, crossed the playground, went in through the back door and strolled down the hall. The place seemed strangely subdued and sterile. No yelling, no scuffling, no kids running to class. The lockers were gone. The old-fashioned pebbled glass doors had been replaced. Walls had been torn down to make room for dormitories and recreation rooms. The old physics lab was now the TV room. And the Winners Case was gone.

He still remembered the pride he had felt each morning when he passed it, always gazing sideways at the trophy he had brought back from the state boxing finals with the brass bust of John L. Sullivan above the plate on its base:

'Thomas Goodman, State Welterweight Champion, 1968 – 1969.'

In its place was the framed front page of the *Daily News* with Rushman in his shirt-sleeves, hands raised over his head, surrounded by cheering kids, the headline below the photograph: 'Saviour House Becomes A Reality.'

He stood with his hands in his pockets, staring at the wall, lost in time, when a young girl walked up to him.

'Can I do something for you?' she asked.

He turned and looked at her. Fifteen, maybe sixteen, a cute little thing, just beginning to bud, her hair pulled back in a pony-tail.

'I went to high school here,' he said.

'I didn't know it was ever a high school,' she answered. 'I guess I never thought about it being anything before it was the House.'

'Well, it was a great high school in its day,' Goodman

said. 'Guess we ought to be thankful they found a use for it. Better than tearing the old girl down.'

'Never heard a school called an old girl before.' She laughed, then said, 'So, you just visiting or do you want to see somebody?'

'I guess I need to talk to whoever's in charge.'

'The sisters are at vespers but maybe I can help you, I'm a hall monitor. My name's Maggie.'

'Hall monitor, huh,' he chuckled. 'Well, it's nice to know some things never change. Maggie, do you know Aaron Stampler?'

The question shocked her. She moved back a step, stood with her feet together and suddenly looked over her shoulder, as if she thought someone might be sneaking up on her.

'You're not the police,' she said, suspiciously. 'They've already been here.'

Good old Stenner, right on top of things.

'No,' he said. 'I work for the lawyer who's going to defend Aaron. I'd like to talk to some of his friends, find out what he was really like.'

'Well, we all knew him. Everybody knows everybody here.'

'*Knew* him?'

'Oh, what I meant is, uh . . .'

'It's okay,' he said and smiled. 'I know what you meant. The whole thing's a terrible shock for all of us.'

'Aaron was okay,' she said, still speaking in the past tense. 'Real smart, y'know. Kinda quiet. He moved out a couple of months ago.'

'Oh? Where did he go?'

'He was shacked up . . . uh, living . . . with Linda. Some place on the west side.'

'Linda? Linda who?'

'We don't ever use last names here, okay? I mean, it isn't cool, asking about last names.'

'Thanks for telling me. I wouldn't want to be uncool.'

She laughed again, then said, 'Well, c'mon. You can meet some of the gang. If they don't want to talk to you they'll just walk away – or tell you to drop dead.'

He did not learn much during the next half hour. There were twenty or so kids in the dining room, all of them professing to be shocked by the crime. The consensus was that Aaron was smart and friendly. Had a temper just like everybody else. Liked good music, movies, and had a girlfriend named Linda who had moved in with him when he left Saviour House. Goodman, using a singular kind of shorthand he had developed through the years, jotted down notes in a small black notebook that had become his Bible.

Why did he leave?

Everybody left sooner or later.

Where was Linda now?

Nobody has seen her since the murder.

Did they think Stampler killed the Bishop?

That's what the papers said.

Why did he do it?

Nobody had a clue.

Did he and the Bishop get along?

Everyone agreed that Aaron was his favourite in this community of lost children.

Who were his closest friends?

He really didn't have any close friends. He was kind of a loner.

'I guess maybe Billy Jordan is as close to a *close* friend as he had,' Maggie said. 'He and the other guys who were altar boys.'

'Aaron was an altar boy?'

'Not really,' one of the boys said. 'He was kind of, you know, studying for it. But the Bishop included him in with the others anyway.'

'The others?'

'The other altar boys,' the boy, who was short and had skin tormented by acne, said somewhat jealously. 'It

119

was like this private club, y'know. The Bishop used to tape the services on his television camera, then play it back to them on TV, so they could see what they were doing wrong.'

'Him too, huh?'

'Beg your pardon?'

'The guy I work for is a video nut, too. Me? I depend on the good old little black notebook.'

'Afraid we weren't much help,' Maggie said. 'Come back in the evening. Most of the kids are here then. Maybe some of the others know more about him.'

'I'll do that, and soon,' he said.

When he left, he stood outside in the playground for a while, huddled against the cold, remembering crisp fall days when they played touch out here, but only a few names came back to him – Sean Fitzhugh and Solly Friedman and a nasty little kid named Donny something-or-other who used to spit on the ball when he screwed up. Goodman had grown into manhood here and now it was a place for runaways and druggies and family rejects and despite the cheery colours and the sense of family it provided, there was about the old girl a climate of melancholy that saddened him.

He did not see the huddled figure, watching through fearful eyes from a window on the third floor of the old building, as Goodman left the place of his youth.

Jane Venable looked up with surprise when Vail walked out of the elevator and into the madhouse outer sanctum of the D.A.'s office. She assumed he was going to see Yancey but realised quickly, as he threaded his way towards her glass cubicle, that he was coming to her office. He stood outside the door, tapped on the wooden door jamb and she waved him in.

'My God,' she said. 'Is no place sacred?'

'Just a friendly courtesy call, Counsellor,' Vail said.

'Oh sure. Where are the poison darts?'

'I thought maybe we could handle this one in a civilised way.'

'You don't know a civilised way, Vail.'

He looked outside her window, at the mass of jammed-up desks, copy machines, telephones, file cabinets, and people – the paraphernalia of justice. 'It lifts my heart to see the bureaucracy at work,' he said. 'I have one person who can do in one day what that mob out there would take a week to screw up.'

'They're very good,' she said, defensively. 'We don't go in for a lot of show here.'

'You don't go in for any show at all.'

'I'm busy,' she sighed. 'Just what brings you to the lion's den, anyway?'

'Lioness,' he said.

'Uh huh. Let me tell you something, Vail, I don't trust you. It makes me nervous when you're in the *building*, let alone my office.'

He sat on the corner of her desk in the absence of an invitation to take a chair and leafed amiably through a stack of correspondence.

'What do you want?' she demanded, ripping the stack away from under his hand and moving it to the other side of the desk. 'Are you just here to harass me?'

'There's a devious mind at work,' he said. 'I drop by for a little pre-hearing sit down and what do I get? Verbal abuse. I came to make sure we both knew what the rules are.'

'Shoat sets the rules.'

'Well, it always helps for the opposing sides to make sure they have everything clear.'

'Come on, what do you really want?'

'I got on this case *yesterday*, okay? I just thought we could talk things over.'

Her eyes narrowed and she leaned back in her chair and chewed on the eraser of her pencil. Then she nodded. 'Okay, I'll tell you what the rules are. No plea bargaining.

No insanity plea. No change in venue and no reduced sentence for *any* reason. We're going to max the kid out. Any questions?'

'That seems to cover the landscape.'

Her eyes took on a vicious twinkle. 'Seen the pictures?' she asked, almost demurely.

'Inflammatory, immaterial . . .'

'Inflammatory my ass.'

'And a lovely ass . . .'

'They're admissible across the board,' she snapped, cutting him off. 'They show the heinous nature of the crime. The brutality . . .'

'Don't use heinous,' he said, wiggling a finger at her. 'Half the jury won't know what you're talking about.'

She waved her hands at him and rolled her eyes. 'Okay, okay, you want to fight over the pictures? Fine. We'll do it when the time comes.'

'Actually the pictures could make a pretty argument for insanity. Nobody in their right mind would . . .'

She cut him off again. 'I talked to Stampler for an hour before you cut us off.'

'And you really think he did that?'

'I *know* he did it,' she scoffed. 'He's as sane as you and I.'

'Which is not saying a hell of a lot. Anyway, it could have been temporary.'

'I'm not discussing this case with you, Vail. Not until we're in court and in front of the judge, got it? Not another word. You have access to anything that's public record. Other than that, I'm not telling you a damn thing.'

'I'm not here to snoop.'

'No, you have that pretty lady from your office to do that. What's her name?'

'Naomi Chance.'

'Where did she work before you hired her, the C.I.A.?'

'She wants to make sure we have everything we're entitled to.'

'I wouldn't dare deprive you, Counsellor. There's no way you're going into court and yelling foul.'

'Shoat gave me fifty-eight days to prepare this case. You think that isn't foul?'

'That's between you and his honour.'

'Hell, it'll probably take a month just to seat the jury.'

'Well, then, we'll just take a month. It's going down *here*, period. I told you, no deals. No change of venue. No nothing! Your boy's as guilty as Judas.'

'Christ forgave Judas,' Vail said with a smile.

'Unfortunately for you, Shoat isn't Christ. Forgiveness is not on his top ten list.'

'So it's no holds barred, that it?' he asked.

'Give me a break. When did you *ever* bar a hold of any kind?'

'Hardball all the way?'

She smiled sweetly.

'No prisoners,' she purred.

When he left Venable's office, Vail stopped at one of the desks in the outer office and dialed his number. The service answered. Naomi was obviously out on the range, rounding up stray bits of gossip.

'Miss Chance left you a message,' the operator said cheerfully. It says, "The Judge called. We got us a shrink. Name: Dr M.B. Arrington, due to arrive tomorrow. Great credentials. Spent the last three years working with what the Judge calls aberrational behaviour subjects. See you later. Naomi." Does all that make sense?'

'I guess,' Vail said. 'Thanks.' He hung up.

Dr M. B. Arrington, he thought to himself. Now there's a nice wholesome American name. Why couldn't the Judge have found someone named Steiner or Freudmetz – something German or Viennese. Foreign types always impressed juries more than home-grown pyschiatrists.

Well, perhaps – Vail hoped – he would turn out to be

a grey-haired, cantankerous old curmudgeon, set in his ways, arrogant to the prosecutor's prodding. Hopefully old doc Arrington would withstand the assaults of that merciless inquisitor, Jane Venable.

Squat, steel tankers and lumbering barges, laden with kraft paper from the big mills of Minnesota and Wisconsin, lumber from the forest of northern Michigan, and chemicals, pig iron and coal from New York and Pennsylvania, all skirmished winter blizzards and summer squalls to deliver their goods to the expanse of docks and warehouses known as The Region. Actually Region Street was a block removed from the lakefront but the clang and clamour of cranes, front loaders, and derricks as they dipped the cargo from the holds of the steamships, created a constant din day and night. It was a muscular, noisy community of warehouses and storage bins, not a place where one would choose to live.

But on the east end of The Region, four three-storey high warehouses lay fallow and neglected like a buffer between waterfront and city. Abandoned by their owners and ignored by the banks which had ultimately inherited them, they had long ago been condemned by the city. But the wrecking balls and bulldozers of progress were busy elsewhere and so these grim, characterless squares of brick had become flophouses for the homeless and indigent. Within the windowless walls, which its denizens called 'The Hollows', many of the city's disenfranchised erected their own peculiar domiciles, usually large wooden crates gathered together like rooms to form unstructured apartments known as 'standers' to the inhabitants. The concrete floors and brick walls compromised protection from wind and snow with a damp and frigid milieu, whatever warmth was conceived in these confines soared up through the perpetual darkness and dissipated in the eaves. Since no garbage collection or sanitation was provided, the bleak and airless Hollows smelled of rotten food, unwashed bodies and faeces. Echoing through the airless cavities were the sounds of human misery – coughing, sneezing, retching – and the diatribes of lonely, desolate souls venting their fury at the fates which had delivered them to this unsavoury madhouse. What it must be like in the summertime was beyond Goodman's comprehension.

He wandered through the scattered standers with a flashlight, hoping to find some clue to Stampler's abode. The first Hollow had produced nothing. As he entered the second, his flashlight beam pointing into the darkness like a slender finger of light, a man stepped out of the gloom, startling him. The light beam revealed a bent and decrepit human wreck, his face a vista of cracks and wrinkles, a grey scraggle of a beard masking his jawline, his eyes ravaged by failure and abuse.

'Whatcha want?' he demanded in a voice cracked with age and misuse, his breath in foul concert with the environment.

'I'm looking for a stander,' Goodman said.

'Whose?'

'Name's Aaron. Aaron Stampler. Young boy, nineteen, twenty. Pleasant looking . . .'

'Shit, I know *him*, I know all about *him*,' he said, emphasising *him* each time he said it.

'What about *him*?' Goodman demanded, surprised that he was reacting so defensively.

'Killed that priest. Ev'body knows about it. Stander's been picked clean. Got his radio, blankets, ev'thing. Word travels fast in The Hollows.' His croak was supposed to pass for a laugh.

'Which one is it?' Goodman asked. 'I'll just take a look.'

'You kin to him?'

'I'm his uncle,' Goodman lied.

'Shit.'

Goodman took out a five-dollar bill and held it under the flashlight beam.

'Which one?' he asked again.

The old derelict eyed the bill, his lips working as if he were trying to swallow something stuck in his throat. He reached out for it with trembling, dirt-encrusted fingers that protruded through the ravelled ends of an old pair of gloves. Goodman flicked the bill back into his fist.

'Show me first,' he said.

'Shit.'

The old man lurched crab-like through stunted canyons of crate and cardboard to a stander near the rear of The Hollow. It was built of sheets of plywood and had about it a sense of form, a symmetry that showed it had been structured with care and at least a conscious sense of design. A flimsy door stood shattered, its lock lying broken on the floor of the warehouse.

'Didn't take long,' Goodman said.

'He killed a priest,' the derelict snarled.

'Here,' Goodman said, shoving the five dollars into his hand. 'Go buy yourself a Cadillac.'

'Asshole,' the old man said and vanished into the darkness.

Goodman entered the stander. It had been demolished. Clothes, blankets, mattress, candles, all the basics for life in The Hollow, were gone. There was litter strewn around. A few things that had been passed over by the scavengers. Actually there were two rooms in Aaron Stampler's dreary home. The second, constructed of three refrigerator crates, was like a closet. A dowel was fastened a few inches from the top of the small room, obviously for hanging clothes. Goodman could tell Aaron had built this pitiful dwelling with as much pride as possible though it had obviously taken but a few minutes to strip it clean.

Goodman let his light roam the walls of the main room and then the closet. There were half a dozen paperback

126

books strewn on the floor – whoever had scavenged the stander was not interested in reading. Engrossed, he was unaware of the presence behind him, a mere movement of air in the darkness. As Goodman started to read the titles of the books, he heard a sound – a footfall on concrete perhaps or a subtle breath disturbing the silence – and he whirled towards it. As he spun around, he was hit on the side of the jaw. It was a glancing blow, misdirected by the darkness and Goodman's sudden turn but it knocked Goodman off his feet. He tried to swing the flashlight up but a hand knocked it loose and it went spinning across the stander and came to rest against the wall, its light reflecting dimly off the plasterboard wall. His assailant scrambled in the semi-darkness, picking up books and throwing them down. Goodman jumped up and dived across the room, wrapping both arms around the attacker. Goodman swung him around, shoved him away and socked him but his punch missed the mark in the dark. As he started to swing again the obscure figure dived head first into Goodman's midriff. Goodman's wind whooshed out of him as a shoulder slammed into his stomach. The two surged backwards, hit the flimsy wall of the stander and crashed through it, vaulting into the darkness of The Hollow. Goodman floundered in total darkness, reached out in random desperation and grabbed an ear, felt an ear-ring dangling from its lobe and, locking his fingers around the bauble, ripped it free. His attacker screamed with pain and rolled away. Goodman got his feet under him and stood unsteadily. He was as disoriented as a blind man, crouching, his hands probing the air in front of him. He stood dead still, waiting. Then he heard footsteps echoing away from him and his adversary was absorbed in the black heart of The Hollow.

He groped his way back into Aàron's stander, found his flashlight and looked at his hand. Lying in his bloody palm was an inch-long silver ear-ring shaped like a tear-drop, a bit of flesh still clinging to the clasp.

He gathered up the paperback books and headed out into the world of the living.

Twelve

The unmarked black sedan moved slowly through the traffic on Division Street and turned right at Court-house Square. A block away, a dozen members of the press shuffled impatiently at the foot of the steps to the court-house, waiting for the notorious prisoner to arrive. There were four television remote trucks, including CNN. Stampler sat in the back seat, his hands cuffed to a thick leather belt and his feet shackled with a foot-long length of chain. He was wearing a dark blue suit, a white shirt, a wine-coloured tie with tiny yellow squares, and penny loafers which were half a size too big, a problem Aaron had solved by stuffing newspaper in the toes. Vail was permitted to drive with him. Stampler sat in the middle between his attorney and a city marshall. There were two other marshalls in front, including the driver.

'Sure drew yourself a crowd, kid,' said the marshall in the back seat.

'Circus day,' said Vail, contemptuously. 'Okay, Aaron, this is what's going to happen . . .'

'I know what an arraignment is, Mister Vail. That mains we go int'court and the pros'cutor for the State'll make the charge agin me.'

'That's right. She's going to charge you with murder in the first degree.'

'Yes suh.'

'That means they'll seek the death penalty.'

'Guard told me.'

'First with the good news, huh?'

Aaron smiled. 'Reckon so.'

'I want you to understand, we could have gone in the back way, avoided the circus in front of the court-house.

129

But it's time the press got a look at you. I'm sure they're expecting the Wolfman or Dracula. We'll give them a little surprise.'

'I thank'ee for the new suit, shoes, n'all.'

'I had to guess at the trouser length.'

'They're perfect. Never owned a suit this good afore.'

'You look nice, Aaron,' said Vail. 'I want you to be pleasant but don't go in there smiling like you just finished a twenty-dollar t-bone. They're going to mob you, stick microphones in your face, yell questions at you. Ignore them, don't say a word. Not a thing. We'll get you through the circus.'

'Yes suh.'

'You won't be asked to testify to anything at the arraignment. If the judge does ask you any questions. I'll answer them.'

'I don't say nary to him?'

'Not a word. As far as this hearing goes, you're dumb as a brick wall.'

Vail had spent the previous evening in the city law library, seeking out cases to justify the motions he planned to make at the arraignment. One of his motions would attempt to subvert the use of the coroner's photographs, which would most certainly provoke the jury and torch an emotional firestorm among its members. But knowing Shoat, that probably would be futile. At breakfast, he had run his strategy past the Judge.

'It's your strategy, Martin,' the Judge had responded.

'What the hell's that mean?' Vail had asked.

'It means exactly that — it's your strategy. I have no intention of suggesting you alter your approach in any way.'

'But you have reservations?'

'As you well know for every problem there are a dozen solutions. One of the reasons I respect you is that you make decisions instinctively and you go at it with passion. What scares your opponents, and to some extent judges, is that you go in with the attitude of a big league pitcher – it's a contest and you are indomitable. You're a warrior who has great ardour for all his causes and the instinct to win – and that, sir, is a very scary combination. You also happen to be a great lawyer. So, while I occasionally might disagree with you on points of law, I would never deign to criticise your style.'

With that, he had given Martin two invaluable law references which would become part of Vail's tactics. Strategy and tactics, this was the way Vail approached his job. The strategy was to present to the public a likeable, pleasant young man and then raise two questions: Could he have done such a thing? And if so, why? His tactics would raise *not* the question of whether or not Aaron was innocent but rather whether or not he was guilty and do it so powerfully that the jurors' innate prejudice against Aaron hopefully would be nullified.

'I'm sure you'll give Shoat something to stew about,' the Judge had said. Then he laughed. He harboured little respect for Hangin' Harry Shoat, considering him a cold-blooded politician in a job that called for compassion, understanding and empathy. The Judge believed one should be a statesman of the law, not its executioner.

'Do you know the judge?' Aaron asked, breaking Martin's train of thought.

'Oh yeah, I know the judge,' he said. 'And don't worry about him. The judge is like a traffic cop – he keeps order and he rules on what is legally permissible and what isn't. The jury is who you have to worry about. Their job is to decide what evidence to believe, which witnesses are credible, and the biggie – whether they think you're guilty or not. Right now, your life is in the hands of twelve people – and they haven't even been picked for the job yet.'

'Kinda scary,' said Aaron.

'It doesn't get any scarier,' Vail agreed.

They fought their way up the stairs through the horde

of reporters with their *mélange* of hardware – microphones, TV cameras, tape recorders, still cameras – and their sometimes inane questions, one of which was, 'Did you do it?'

Did you do it? Vail said incredulously to himself. *Who in hell asked that one?*

The three marshalls cleared the way and Vail drew up the rear of the human buttress, handing out his business card to all who addressed him. His name was embossed in the left-hand corner and across the centre was printed, 'No comment.' The circus followed them into the courtroom and jockeyed for seats in a section reserved for the press. Jack Connerman was one of them. He had stood back and watched the hysteria of his peers as Stampler and Vail made their entrance. Now he was seated next to E.J. Odum, a particularly cynical, old-time court-house man for the *Trib*. Connerman was a short, red-faced Irishman with the beginning of a beer belly. He had been nominated for a Pulitzer Prize two years earlier and when he did not win, had left his job with the newspaper to join *City Magazine*, where he earned more money and could write with more subjectivity. He had a following; his pieces sold magazines.

'What do you think?' he asked Odum.

'Shit, it's a goddamn arraignment, for God's sake, not *Anatomy of a Murder*. The prosecutor's gonna charge him and Vail's gonna plead not guilty because he doesn't have a choice. So what the hell's all the fuss about?'

'It's Vail, E. J. You never know,' Connerman said.

'It's a goddamn arraignment,' Odum repeated.

Harry Shoat stood at the door of his chambers, squinting out at the crowd, waiting until the room was full before making his entrance. The night before, Roy Shaughnessey had taken him to dinner and imparted some cogent advice.

'Listen, Harry, you want to be a supreme court judge,

132

right? Well, you have to loosen up a little. This Hangin'
Harry crap is hurting your image.'

'What do you expect me to do, tell jokes?'

'For Christ sake, I'm not suggesting you go out in
black face and sing 'Mammy'. I'm just telling you, this
Hangin' Harry stuff is hurting you. We've got Vail by
the balls, so you can afford to be . . . gracious.'

'Gracious?'

'Yeah.' Pause. 'Gracious.'

Gracious! This was an arraignment. A cut and dried
procedure. What was there to be gracious about?

Alvin McCurdy, the bailiff, was watching the door.
The room was full. Well, give the devil his due – Vail
did draw a roomful. He opened the door and strode out.

'All rise!' McCurdy ordered and rambled off the cus-
tomary salutation. 'Hear ye, hear ye, hear ye . . .' as Shoat
took his seat and immediately began arranging everything
on the bench in precise order – his legal pad, two fresh
yellow Ticonderoga pencils, the water thermos and glass,
and his favourite instrument in the world, the gavel with
its little hardstand. He also had a twelve-inch stainless
steel ruler which he placed exactly parallel to the pad
and two pencils. He very specifically placed the wire
stems of his bifocals over each ear and adjusted his
glasses. He finished this meticulous ritual just as the bailiff finished his introduction.

'Call the first case,' he said.

'State versus Aaron Stampler.'

'Is everyone present?' Shoat asked.

'Yes sir,' McCurdy answered.

Shoat looked out over his glasses. Venable, as always,
was stunning. She wore a tailored dark grey suit and her
hair was pulled back in a bun. Vail was dressed almost
haphazardly. He had on a tweed jacket, denim pants,
tennis shoes, a nondescript tie and bright red braces.

'I see, Mister Vail, you haven't made it to the barber
since our last meeting.'

'I've got bids out,' Vail answered with a smile.

'Hopefully you'll get them back in and make your decision before the trial starts. Ready to proceed?'

'Yes, Your Honour.'

'Madam Prosecutor?'

'Yes, Judge. The State charges the prisoner, Aaron Stampler, with the crime of murder in the first degree, to wit, that on February 26, 1983, at approximately ten p.m., said Stampler did, in this county and this city, with premeditation and with malice aforethought, murder by stabbing the Reverend Archbishop Richard Rushman. Furthermore due to the nature of the crime, Your Honour, we request that bail be denied.'

'How does your client plead, Counsellor?' Shoat said to Vail.

'Your Honour,' said Vail. 'If it please the court, I would like to make a motion that my client be remanded to the state mental hospital at Daisyland for psychiatric evaluation *before* any charges are brought against him.'

'Murder one, Your Honour. No bond,' Venable snapped back. 'We have more than enough hard evidence to warrant the allegations.'

'Yes, I agree,' Shoat said. 'There's certainly ample provocation here for a charge of murder in the first. It will be up to the grand jury, of course, to substantiate the charge. Do you understand the charges brought against you, Mister Stampler?'

The youth looked at Vail, who said, 'Your Honour, my client refuses to answer on the grounds that his response may tend to incriminate him.'

Both the judge and Venable looked perplexed.

'The defendant is taking the fifth on whether or not he understands the charges?' Shoat said with surprise.

'Yes sir. Until we have a complete psychological work-up, he will take the fifth on any and all questions posed to him.'

'Well that's a new one on me,' Shoat said, shaking his

head. 'How about bond? Am I correct in assuming that you are not seeking bond, Mister Vail?'

'You are correct,' Vail said. 'However, because of the inordinate amount of publicity my client has already received and the nature of the crime with which he is being charged, we would like to formally request a change in venue at this time.'

'Denied,' Shoat snapped almost before Vail finished.

'Exception.'

'Noted. Anything else?'

'Your Honour, Mister Stampler underwent several hours of interrogation by the police and members of the District Attorney's Office *before* I was even assigned to the case. I feel, therefore, that his rights have been denied to him.'

'Was he advised of his rights?' Shoat asked Venable.

'Yes, Your Honour,' she answered. 'He was interviewed three times and was Mirandised all three times.'

'And did he waive his rights?'

'Yes, Your Honour. We have three statements signed by the prisoner agreeing to speak to the officers without an attorney present.'

'He still . . .' Vail started but Shoat cut him off.

'Mister Vail, it appears he was fully advised and he did waive his rights. If you'd like we can swear in the arresting officers and have them verify . . .'

'Not necessary, sir. My client does not deny waiving. Our objection is that he underwent several hours of interrogation before he even *had* an attorney.'

'Counsellor, you agreed to take this case the morning after the event took place . . .'

'And he was interrogated twice . . . *twice* . . . before that,' said Vail, holding up two fingers. He sat on the edge of his desk, feet crossed at the ankles, his thumbs hooked in flamingo-red braces.

Shoat sighed. 'I think we're splitting hairs here, Counsellor. I don't see any violation of rights.'

'A man's life is at stake, Judge. I think that's worth splitting a few hairs over.'

'I'm sure you do, sir.' Shoat was beginning to show his exasperation.

'Your Honour, I have the transcripts and tapes of the interviews here,' said Venable. 'If there's no objection, we would like to present them . . .'

'Objection, Your Honour!' Vail bellowed. 'I move that all the interviews conducted prior to counsel be suppressed.'

'Grounds?' Shoat asked.

Vail grabbed a book and moved away from his desk into the arena before the bench. He held a thick code book open in one hand and held it towards the judge.

'If I may, sir, I will call your attention to the State of Nebraska versus Flannery, Supreme Court, Volume Forty-three, page 685. I have the book right here. The court ruled, and was upheld in appeal, that Miss Flannery was denied her rights even though she had waived because she asked for an attorney at the time of her arrest and was not provided one for a period of eighteen hours during which, under great duress, she broke down in an interrogation and confessed to the crime. The courts ruled that the investigating officers violated her rights to fair representation because she requested a lawyer at the time she was Mirandised and she should have been so granted *before* any further interrogation.

'We would argue,' Vail went on, 'that once the request for legal representation is made, no further action can be taken until the lawyer has been retained and is present. If I had been representing Aaron at the time of these interviews I would have advised him to take the fifth across the board. Among other things, my client cannot adequately answer the question of cognisance – I believe that will be for the psychiatric team to determine. The fact is, there is nothing really incriminating in these interviews, anyway – it's strictly a matter of principle.'

'Oh please,' Venable said with disgust. 'Principle? What principle? He was Mirandised three times, assigned one of the best lawyers in the state . . .'

'Why thank you, Counsellor,' Vail intervened.

She glared at him and went on, '. . . and it is obvious from these interviews that Stampler understands the charges. He knew . . .'

Vail returned to his desk and picked up a copy of the transcript. He walked back and forth, one hand hooked to his braces, the other brandishing the stapled report.

'Your Honour,' Vail said, cutting her off again, 'you will note that my client stated eight times, including once when he was first arrested, and consistently thereafter, that he is innocent of the crime. Furthermore, on page one of the prosecutor's transcript, after Lieutenant Stenner read my client his rights, we see the following exchange:

STENNER: 'Do you have an attorney?'
STAMPLER: 'No, sir.'
STENNER: 'Do you wish the court to appoint you an attorney at no expense?'
STAMPLER: 'Yes sir, that would be most kind.'

'There you have it, Judge. Nebraska versus Flannery. They should have stopped right there until Stampler had proper representation. And I have an objection before the bench, Your Honour.'

'The defendant signed three – *three!* – waivers,' Venable insisted.

'*If* he knew what he was signing. Your Honour . . .' Vail started but Shoat held up his hand. He looked down at Jane Venable. 'Madam Prosecutor,' he said, 'I mean no disrespect towards your investigators nor am I implying that they – in any way – violated the defendant's rights. However, there does appear to be precedent here and there could be a grey line and I think justice may best be served if you and Mister Vail start off even-steven, so to speak. So I am going to sustain Mister Vail's objection. The transcripts are out, Miss Venable.'

'Exception,' she snapped.

'Exception noted,' Shoat said, nodding to the clerk. 'Anything else?'

'I would request that the court have my client transferred to Daisyland during the period before the trial for the purpose of a complete psychiatric evaluation by the state.'

'That can be done here, Your Honour,' Venable said quickly. 'No need to send him up-state. Daisyland's a two-hour drive from here.'

'I assume then, that prosecution has no objection to the psychological evaluation?' said Vail.

'None,' said Venable. 'We do object to moving Stampler to Daisyland.'

'That's another reason we request relocation, Judge,' Vail countered. 'As you know, this crime has generated a great deal of publicity. In fairness to Mister Stampler, I feel we need to move him out of the city, away from the limelight. Since we can't change venue, the next best option is to sequester him in Daisyland until just before the trial.'

'Well, sir,' the Judge said, 'I don't see that locking him up at Daisyland is going to reduce the public's attention any more than if he stays here. Conversely, if we are going to evaluate your client, it would seem that Daisyland would be the proper place to do it.'

'We would like easier access to the prisoner,' said Venable.

'Why?' said Vail. 'He's not going to say anything to you. He'll take the fifth if you ask him his full name.'

'Can we save the squabbling for the trial, please,' Shoat said, trying hard to be gracious.

'The State objects to moving the accused to the state facility,' Venable said.

'Overruled, Counsellor,' Shoat said. 'I see no possible

138

reason *not* to move Stampler up there. If you want to hear him take the fifth you can drive two hours to do it. The court hereby orders that Aaron Stampler be transmitted to the criminal section at Daisyland State Hospital and that he be evaluated by the staff there.'

'I would also like to request that my staff and I be given unlimited visitation rights,' Vail said.

Shoat nodded. 'Yes, yes, Mister Vail, contingent with the rules of the hospital, of course.' He stared over his glasses at the lawyer. 'I wouldn't expect you to be dropping in at two or three in the morning.'

'No sir.' Vail smiled, then added, 'Unless, of course, it's an emergency.'

Shoat glared down at him but said nothing. He turned to his book and leafed through the pages.

'Anything else?' Shoat asked, leaning hard on the 'else'.

'Yes sir,' Vail said.

Shoat groaned. 'Let's hear it, Mister Vail.'

'Defence would like to move at this time for suppression of the photographs taken by the coroner at the scene of the crime.'

Venable was back on her feet but Shoat, holding up his hand like a traffic cop, stopped her before she could speak.

In the press box, Jack Connerman laughed. He leaned over to Odum and said, 'Christ, Vail's throwing everything at them. He's trying the case at the fuckin' arraignment.'

'He's gonna piss Shoat off,' Odum replied.

'Hell,' said Connerman, 'he's been doing that for years.'

'Excuse me, Miss Venable,' Shoat said. 'I'm sure you object to the motion about the pictures. Let's let Mister Vail explain himself. Counsellor?'

'The photographs will only inflame the jury, Your Honour,' said Vail. 'We will not deny murder was done, nor vill we object to the introduction of the coroner's findings or the autopsy report. But the introduction of these pictures, particularly to a lay jury, would be both shocking and prejudicial. We would agree to perhaps a single long shot, to establish the environment. But the photographs themselves have nothing to do with my client's guilt or innocence.'

Shoat looked at Venable for a response.

'Your Honour, they identify the heinous . . .' and she looked at Vail and smirked, '. . . nature of the crime. This is not just a murder case, this is a case of mutilation, possible torture, emasculation . . . all integral to the State's case. The jury has a right to perceive the brutality of the crime. If counsel for the defence admits the crime was done, then he should have no objections to the official pictures of the scene and the victim.'

'I repeat, Your Honour, to pass a dozen gruesome pictures among the unsophisticated men and women on the jury is prurient,' said Vail. 'It smacks of a kind of sick voyeurism.'

'It shows it the way it was,' Venable said, flatly. 'Part and parcel of the crime, Your Honour. Next he'll be objecting if we introduce the murder weapon.'

'I wouldn't give him any ideas, Counsellor,' Shoat said with what amounted to a grin. 'As for the photographs, Mister Vail, I'll take your motion under advisement. I would appreciate your cooperation on that score. Will you withdraw your objection and re-enter it at the time of trial?'

'Well, sir,' Vail said. 'We would like a ruling before the case goes before the grand jury. We would like the photographs suppressed before that time.'

'I see,' Shoat said and glowered down at Vail. 'I'll do my best, Counsellor. Now is there anything *else*?'

'Your Honour,' Vail said. 'I would call your attention to the 1978 Georgia Reports, State versus Appleby, volume 156, page 978, in which the court ruled and was upheld by the state Supreme Court, that Mister Appleby was improperly arraigned for the crime of rape because he was mentally retarded and therefore did not understand the charges brought against him. We contend that Mister Stampler cannot be charged with any crime until the psychiatric board rules on his competence to understand the charges.'

'Oh really!' Venable wailed. 'What do you want us to do, Counsellor, let him go?'

'No, I am saying that he will voluntarily enter the criminal section of the state facility for the purpose of psychological evaluation. The board will determine whether he is capable of standing trial.'

'Judge . . .' Venable started.

Vail shrugged. 'Georgia code, Judge. State versus Appleby.'

Shoat read the section Vail had cited. He pulled his spectacles off and leaned back in his chair and chewed on the stem of the glasses.

'Well, he's got a point, Counsellor,' he said to Venable with a tone of resignation.

'He's *voluntarily* submitting?' Venable growled.

'I understand your consternation, Miss Venable. I would suggest that you proceed with the grand jury and get an indictment as quickly as possible so that we may proceed in the event Mister Stampler is deemed adequate to stand trial. Meantime, we can go ahead and set a trial date for April twenty-sixth,' he smiled at both of them. 'Bright and early.'

'Your Honour,' said Vail. 'We respectfully ask the court for at least ninety days to prepare our case.'

'Tuesay, April twenty-sixth, nine a.m., Mister Vail. Ample time.'

'In that case Your Honour, we object.'

'To what?' Shoat demanded.

'Setting the trial date.'

'On what grounds, sir?' Shoat exploded.

'On the grounds, Your Honour, that Mister Stampler

is not charged with a crime so you can't possibly set a date to try him.'

In the press box, Connerman threw back his head and laughed. 'Beautiful,' he said.

Shoat glared at Vail. Venable stood to challenge the objection but realised Vail was correct. The judge could hardly arrange to try someone who was not officially charged with anything. 'Why don't we just let him loose,' she spat at Vail. 'Maybe he can get a cardinal or even the Pope next time!'

'How about a prosecutor? Really do the world a favour,' Vail shot back with a smile.

Shoat lost it. He put his fist on the end of the flexible ruler, raised the other end and let it smack hard on the bench. Both Vail and Venable were startled by the sharp report that sounded like a pistol shot. The judge stood up and leaned forward towards the two lawyers. 'That will be quite enough, both of you!' Shoat yelled. 'If you have something to say, you will address the bench, is that perfectly clear? This trial – if we ever get around to it – is not going to turn into a cat-and-dog fight.' He shook his head angrily. 'I hereby remand Mister Stampler to the officials of the state hospital for a complete psychological evaluation. I also order the District Attorney's office to expediently seek a formal indictment from the grand jury on these charges. Any information gathered from Mister Stampler prior to the time Mister Vail was retained as his counsel is inadmissable to the grand jury and the court. Any further questions? Good. Bailiff, call the next case.'

Connerman settled back on the bench and stretched his arms out and shook his head.

'The son of a bitch did it again,' he said.

'Did what,' E.J. Odum said.

'Well, right now the State doesn't even have Stampler in custody, the state hospital does. The interviews have been suppressed, the pictures probably will be, Stampler hasn't been charged with anything and Shoat can't even set a trial date until Stampler gets evaluated, which could take a couple of weeks.'

'So?' Odum said with a shrug. 'Vail gets his ninety days. Big deal.'

'Think about this, E.J. Suppose the shrinks up at Daisyland rule that Stampler's incompetent to stand trial? He'll end up in the funny farm. That keeps Stampler out of the chair – which is exactly what Vail wants.'

'What happens now?' Aaron asked as the press began to surge forward.

'We get out of here,' said Vail, motioning to the marshall, who escorted Aaron out of the room. Vail motioned to Goodman who was sitting behind him in the first row of the court-room. They both followed Stampler and the marshall into the holding room.

'Aaron, this is Tom Goodman, my investigator. He's working on your case with me.'

'Yes suh,' the boy said and shook hands.

'You understand they're going to move you up to Daisyland.'

'Yes suh.'

'Have you heard of Daisyland?'

'That's the insane asylum.'

'Well, they're a little more generous than that, Aaron. They call it the state mental health institute. Thing is, you'll be comfortable there. You'll get proper attention. And you'll be treated as a patient rather than a prisoner.'

'Well, I guess it sounds okay.'

'Trust me,' said Vail. 'It's all part of the plan.'

'Plan?'

'Don't worry about it. I'll find out when they're moving you. We'll talk some more before you go. We have our own psychiatrist coming in. His name is Dr Arrington. He'll be testing you as well as the state's doctors.'

'You com'ng up thair . . . ?'

'Bet on it,' Vail said, and winked reassuringly. 'Before

we leave, Tom has a question or two to ask you.' Vail held out his hand with the ear-ring in his palm.

'Aaron, have you ever seen an ear-ring like this before?' Goodman asked.

Aaron looked at it for a minute and shook his head.

'You don't know anybody wears ear-rings like this?'

'No suh. Wair'd y'get it?'

'I pulled it out of somebody's ear. In your stander.'

'In my place?'

'That's right. He jumped me when I was checking the place out. Why would somebody attack me in there? Is there something of value hidden in the stander?'

Aaron shrugged. 'I had a radio n'some books.'

'I got the books but by the time I got there the place had been ransacked. Wasn't much left.'

'Weren't much thair t'start with,' Aaron said with a sad smile.

'We'll hang on to the books for you,' Vail said.

'No reason to. I read 'em. It was just nice t'have books around, y'know?'

'I'm sure they have a library at Daisyland,' Vail said. 'Hopefully you'll have some time to yourself.'

The boy beamed innocently. 'I'm plaised t'hear that, sir.'

Vail sat at his desk and stared bleakly at the photographs of the murder which he had attached with push-pins to a bulletin board that rested against the bookshelves. Now, over a cup of coffee and a cigarette, he was contemplating the visual impact of the photographs. He felt sure Shoat would rule against him on the motion to suppress the photos.

And there were other questions to be answered. Motive. What could possibly have been Stampler's motive for committing this crime, if in fact he did it. Perhaps Tommy's trip to Kentucky would shed light in a lot of dark corners.

Lost in contemplation, he did not see the taxi pull up outside nor the figure carrying two suitcases and a briefcase under one arm, jump out and scamper up to the house. The doorbell startled him but before he could get up he heard the door open then close and a woman appeared in the office doorway. She was bundled in a black greatcoat and was wearing earmuffs – a pleasant-looking woman who appeared to be in her late twenties, red-faced from the cold. She snapped the earmuffs off.

'Mister Vail?' she said in a timid voice.

'Yes?'

'I'm Molly Arrington.'

It did not sink in. 'What can I do for you?' he asked, looking at his watch.

She looked a little confused. 'Judge Spalding sent for me,' she said. 'I'm Doctor Molly Arrington from the Justine Clinic.'

Thirteen

Vail looked thunderstruck. The woman stood in the doorway with a somewhat bemused expression.

'I assumed he told you I was coming,' she said, almost reticently.

Vail said, 'Of course. I, uh, I guess I wasn't expecting you this late.' He jumped up and smiled. 'Take off your coat and stay a while.'

She took off her coat to reveal a tiny woman, perhaps five-two at best, who carried herself delicately as she hung the coat on the hat tree and, with both hands, pressed out the wrinkled skirt of a plain, charcoal-grey suit.

'Sorry it's so late,' she said, shyly. 'The bus was almost an hour late getting into Indianapolis. I missed my plane.'

'Bus?'

'It's the only way to get *anywhere* from Winthrop, Indiana. That's where the Justine Clinic is. I guess you've never heard of it.' She had lovely unblemished skin and bright blue eyes and her ash brown hair was cut just above shoulder length. She was so soft-spoken her voice was barely above a whisper.

'No, but that doesn't mean anything,' Vail said. 'I don't know much about the psychiatry business.'

'That makes us even,' she said. 'I don't know anything about the law.'

Great, he thought. *A shy amateur – just what we need.*

'This all happened so fast I didn't think about a place to stay,' she said, her tone still tinged with embarrassment. 'When Judge Spalding called and said it was urgent, the Board had an emergency meeting – immediately – to approve my leave of absence. Oh, it wasn't a problem. Actually they were quite excited with the idea. This will be excellent experience . . .'

'Well, I really needed . . .' he started but stopped in mid-sentence.

'Someone with more experience?' she offered.

Vail was embarrassed and showed it. He stood and walked to the coffee urn and got two cups from the cabinet.

'Let's start over, okay?' he said. 'How about a cup of coffee? Freshly made. Or would you like something stronger?'

'Coffee's fine,' she told him.

'This is a tough one. Okay if I call you Molly? I'm Martin or Marty, which ever you prefer,' he said, as he filled the two cups.

'Molly's fine,' she said. 'And I'm sorry I haven't had any experience in the court-room.'

'Hell, I've been in private practice for almost ten years, before that two in the army,' Vail said. 'In all that time, I've never had to deal with a psychiatrist. Never had an involved mental case like this in my life. I'll make you a deal. You teach me about crazy people, I'll teach you about the law.'

He handed her the coffee. And although extremely shy, she was forthright when she spoke. 'Well, I can understand it if you want someone else. To be frank, I've never even been *in* a court-room before. But I do know a lot about disoriented behaviour, Mister Vail. As a psychologist, a psychiatrist, and an epidemiologist. I've worked with over a hundred people with mental disorders. Incidentally, I'd prefer that you avoid referring to them as crazy.'

'Fair enough. What do we call them?'

'Mentally disordered. Mentally disturbed . . .'

'Is there one word that covers it?'

She stared at him for several seconds, took a sip of coffee, and said, 'How about nuts?'

147

He stared back, not sure whether she was serious or not and then, unable to hold back, broke out in a hearty laugh and she joined in, although less boisterously.

'I shouldn't have said that,' she muttered.

'Molly, in the presence of the Judge, my assistant, Naomi Chance, our investigator, Tom Goodman, and me, you may say anything you want about anybody or anything at any time. That's how we operate. I think the question is, do you want to work with us? This is a very nasty case.'

'The newspaper articles I read were not very informative.'

'The cops are being coy. So's the prosecutor. They mean to burn this kid – send him to the electric chair – unless we can stop them.'

'How bad is it?' she asked.

Vail did not answer. Instead he went to the desk and tilted the lamp so the light fell across the bulletin board of photographs. Her reaction was unemotional, which surprised him. She squinted at the board for a minute, then walked over, knelt down and studied the photographs, one by one.

'If the jury sees those, he's cooked – pardon the pun,' Vail said.

'The pictures say a lot,' she said as she stood back up but she did not explain her hurried analysis and Vail did not ask. 'When can I meet him?' she wanted to know.

'He was transferred to Daisyland earlier today. I'd like you to go up tomorrow. The sooner you go to work, the better. We don't have much time.'

'How much?'

'Less than two months.'

She closed her eyes and blew a silent whistle.

'I've spent two months trying to get a patient to say good morning to me,' she said with a sad smile.

'Oh, he'll say good morning to you. That's the least of our worries,' Vail said.

He sat down at his desk, leaning back in his chair and balancing himself so his toes were barely touching the floor.

'How'd you like to meet him right now?'

'Now?'

'I taped an interview with him this afternoon,' he said, and pointed towards the television set. 'We can watch it if you're not too tired.'

'Uh . . . ,' she stammered, somewhat flustered. 'You see, I have my bags here. I left in such a hurry, I didn't make any reservations. I think I better call one of the hotels down-town . . .'

'Well, you can do that' he said casually, still balancing himself in his chair. 'Or . . . you can stay here. I have two guest bedrooms upstairs. Take your pick. They each have their own bath and you can lock them from the inside. The kitchen is common ground and the coffee urn's always full. We'll worry about finding you a place in the morning.'

'I hate to put you out . . .'

'You're not putting me out at all,' he said.

'Well,' she said quietly, 'that would be lovely.'

'C'mon, I'll take your things up for you. I'm sure you're exhausted. We can watch the tape tomorrow.'

'No, I'll just throw some water on my face, put on my slippers,' she said. 'I'd like to see the film. And, uh . . . perhaps you have a little bourbon?'

'We need a motive,' Vail said. 'That's something I'd like you to work on – before they do. Hopefully they can't come up with one. If they can't, we have the start of a case for insanity. If they can, then we're in trouble. So first, before anything, I'd like you to figure out if Aaron had a motivation for killing Bishop Rushman, *if* he killed him.'

She sat very straight in her chair, her feet flat on the

floor and sipped her bourbon. 'Do you think he did it?' she asked.

'Yes,' he said, lighting a cigarette.

'And you're still defending him?'

'First commandment, Molly, the defendant is innocent until proven guilty. *Proven* guilty. Not what I think or you think, what the jury thinks. Of course, I don't operate on that wave length. In the beginning, I always assume my client is guilty.'

'Why?'

'Because that's why they come to me.'

'That's very cynical.'

He shook his head. 'Practical,' he said. 'If I can prove to *my* satisfaction that Aaron Stampler didn't kill the Bishop, then I can convince the court.'

'And if you can't?'

He shrugged. 'Everyone assumes Stampler's guilty. So my job – our job – is to disprove the prosecutor's case, which means I have to anticipate what their case is going to be . . . *and* prove mine at the same time. That's where you come in.'

'I don't understand.'

'The D.A. is being very tough on this one and the prosecutor is a real barracuda.'

'What's his name?'

'Her name is Jane Venable. She's very good. And she's got a personal motive. I whaled her in a case a couple years ago so she's looking to put a notch in her gun at my expense. The judge doesn't like me. The city, county, and state all want my hide nailed to the court-house door.'

'I know,' she said. 'I read the article about you in *City Magazine*.'

Vail smiled. 'Don't believe everything you read,' he said.

'I thought it was very flattering, professionally, I mean. It didn't give much insight into you as a person.'

'I prefer it that way.'

'Why?'

He thought for a moment, wondering whether she was already beginning to psychoanalyse him.

'I like to keep the focus on the client and the facts.'

'Pretty hard to do. You're so . . . flamboyant.'

'Flamboyant?'

She seemed a bit embarrassed when he questioned her use of the word. 'Well, the article makes you appear that way.'

'I better be *something*. Everybody in the city not only assumes Aaron's guilty, they want to see him fry. Other than that . . .'

'You think that will happen?' she asked. 'I mean, that they'll execute him?'

'Sure. What we want is justice, what the public wants is revenge. When a person is accused of a crime, particularly a capital offence, and you look across to the other side of the court-room — where the prosecutor sits? — there's always the victim's wife, girlfriend, mother, father, sister, brother, right behind him, demanding that old Biblical eye for an eye. A court-room is a Roman lion pit. Our job is to keep the defendant out of the pit.'

'That's how you see your clients, as human sacrifices?'

'Molly, I know the law very well. I'm damn good at this, but I'm also pragmatic as hell.'

'And aggressive . . .'

'Absolutely.'

'Single-minded . . .'

'I call it focused.'

'Cynical . . .'

'That's absolutely essential. Don't believe anyone, don't believe anything. Don't believe what you see, what you hear, what you read. And for God's sake, don't trust a soul.'

'It all sounds . . . I don't know, so . . .'

'Tawdry's a good word,' Vail interrupted her. His tone

was very matter-of-fact, almost casual. 'The law is tawdry. Murder is tawdry. Robbery, rape, assault, embezzlement, divorce, all tawdry business. Get used to it. Don't try to make a science of it. Don't look for ethics, just be grateful when you find them. Don't look for justice, just pray you get a little.' He poured a shot of bourbon in his coffee. 'What it is, you're fighting for a man's life when half the jurors are nodding off and the judge is day-dreaming about shooting two under par at the end of the day and the only person listening to you is your client. It's a gutter fight. Don't elevate it to something noble. Let the writers do that.'

'I guess I do have a lot to learn,' she said.

'You worry about Aaron,' he said with a reassuring smile. 'Let me worry about the judge and jury. In the eyes of the court, crimes are divided into two categories, *malum en se* and *malum prohibita*. The most serious is *malum en se*, which means "wrong in themselves". Inherently evil. Homicide. Rape. Mayhem. *Malum prohibita* is just about everything else, from burglary to embezzlement.' He walked in front of the board of photographs. 'What we've got here, Doctor, is *malum en se* to the max.' He pointed to the photographs. 'The State will ask for the punishment to fit the crime.'

'Electrocution,' she said.

Vail nodded. 'No prisoners, as they say. Unless we can prove he's innocent – or was mad as a hatter when he did it – the people will have their big pay-off.'

'Is there a possibility he's innocent?'

'He says so.'

'He says he didn't kill the Bishop?'

'Why don't we let him tell you,' Vail said, slipping the videotape in the machine. 'This is a short interview. They were getting ready to move him up to Daisyland. Incidentally, I videotape every interview and I want you to do the same. You'll be surprised what you can learn from watching the tapes.'

'I have some experience with videotape,' she said. 'We use it to a limited degree.'

'That's good. The equipment is light, easy to operate. This was recorded at the city prison about noon today. Isn't much to it, but at least it'll introduce you to your patient.'

He pressed the play button. It was a shot of Aaron from the waist up, sitting on a cot in a prison cell. He was leaning forward, his elbows braced on his knees. Vail was not in the picture, only his voice could be heard.

VAIL: State your full name, Aaron.

STAMPLER: Aaron Luke Stampler.

VAIL: Where are you from?

STAMPLER: Crikside, Kentucky.

VAIL: How long have you lived in the city?

STAMPLER: Fer two yairs. Come hair in March in 1981.

VAIL: Where did you go to school?

STAMPLER: Crikside school till high school. Then I went to high school in Lordsville, which air twenty miles or so from Crikside.

VAIL: Are your parents still living?

STAMPLER: No suh. Paw died of the black lung 'bout four yairs ago. M'maw died last yair. M'brother, Samuel, died in a car accident.

VAIL: Any other immediate family?

STAMPLER: No suh.

VAIL: Did you graduate from high school?

STAMPLER: Yes suh.

VAIL: What kind of grades did you make?

STAMPLER: (Proudly) I was an A student 'cept for math. Never did take a likin' t'math but I paissed okay.

VAIL: When did you first meet Bishop Rushman?

153

STAMPLER:	When I first caim to the city. Met a fella named Billy Jordan and he brought me t'the Saviour House. That's where I met Bishop Rushman.
VAIL:	And you were friends? I mean, Bishop Rushman was kind to you?
STAMPLER:	Y'suh. He took me in t'the House, let me do odd jobs 'round the church t'earn some money. Also he helped me t'get into the college extension.
VAIL:	Extension courses?
STAMPLER:	Y'suh, I were studying by mail.
VAIL:	What were you studying?
STAMPLER:	Y'know, startin' courses.
VAIL:	Like freshman courses. English, things like that?
STAMPLER:	(Nods)
VAIL:	When did you start taking these courses?
STAMPLER:	Last fall. Th'Bishop said it were a waste, not f'r me to go on with m'studies.
VAIL:	Do you like school?
STAMPLER:	Y'suh. L'arnin is my favourite thaing. Course m'accent always has made folks laugh.
VAIL:	Is that why you were in extension?
STAMPLER:	N'suh . . . cheaper. N'I always had some kinda job t'do. So I couldn't rightly go t'regular college.
VAIL:	What kind of jobs?
STAMPLER:	Right now I'm workin' at the library, cleanin' up n'all. Leastways I was, 'til this happened.
VAIL:	Aaron, did you and Bishop Rushman have *any* problems, personal or otherwise?
STAMPLER:	N'suh. He wanted me to join the

154

	Church and I were studyin' about it. Watchin' tapes of th'services, n'th altar boys, like that.
VAIL:	Aren't you a little old to be an altar boy?
STAMPLER:	Were a good way t'learn. 'Bout the church, I main.
VAIL:	Did you discuss it with the Bishop?
STAMPLER:	Y'suh. And I read books. Bishop lets me borra books from his library whenever I want.
VAIL:	What books?
STAMPLER:	All of 'em. Any I wanted t'borra. Read ever'thing.
VAIL:	But these discussions with the Bishop, they weren't angry talks, right? I mean, they were friendly discussions?
STAMPLER:	(Nods) Y'suh. We' talked 'bout different ways people believe.
VAIL:	So you weren't brought up a Catholic?
STAMPLER:	N'suh.
VAIL:	Did you go to church?
STAMPLER:	(Hesitates. His eyes look away) Y'suh. Went t'th Church of Jaisus Christ and Everlastin' Penance.
VAIL:	That was the name of the church? I don't think I've heard of that before.
STAMPLER:	Was jest a local preacherman, M'ster Vail.
VAIL:	So, to sum it up, Bishop Rushman helped you get into the college extension, helped you get into Saviour House, helped you find a job, and talked with you about becoming a Catholic and maybe even an altar boy. Is that pretty much the way it was?
STAMPLER:	(Nods) Y'suh.

VAIL: And you two never had a fight or serious disagreement?

STAMPLER: N'suh.

VAIL: Even when you left Saviour House?

STAMPLER: N'suh. He understood it were time.

VAIL: Aaron, do you understand why you're here?

STAMPLER: Y'suh, they say I killed Bishop Richard.

VAIL: Do you know what's going to happen now?

STAMPLER: Y'suh. Goin' t'Daisyland and they're gonna decide if I'm crazy r'not afore they gimme a trial.

VAIL: And you understand the seriousness of all this?

STAMPLER: A'course. They mean to execute me.

VAIL: Tell me about the night the Bishop was killed. You were in his apartment, right?

STAMPLER: Y'suh. The altar boys went up thair. We looked at the tape. Then we had some refreshments – Cokes and cookies – and talked about, y'know, bein' a Catholic, n'all.

VAIL: What time was that?

STAMPLER: Well, I cain't be positive cause I don't have a watch. Seems t'me we went up thair'bout . . . eight er so. We were thair about an hour and a half. So I reckon we left some'airs 'bout nine-thirty.

VAIL: And who all was there, Aaron?

STAMPLER: Peter, John, Billy, Sid and me. And the Bishop.

VAIL: Do they all live at Saviour House?

STAMPLER: 'Cept fer Billy and me.

VAIL: What are their last names?

STAMPLER: Don't use last names at t'House, Mister Vail.

VAIL:	You don't *know* their last names?
STAMPLER:	(Shakes his head) 'Cept for Billy Jordan.
VAIL:	Where does he live?
STAMPLER:	Has a stander down in The Hollers, jes' like me.
VAIL:	All right, so you left the Bishop's place 'bout nine-thirty. Why did you go back?
STAMPLER:	I din't. Went downstairs to the office to borra a book.
VAIL:	How long were you there?
STAMPLER:	(Hesitating) I'm . . . uh, not rail sure.
VAIL:	Why aren't you sure?
STAMPLER:	(He gets uncomfortable, restless) 'Cause . . . I jest don't remember, not havin' a watch. I were reading – it were *Poor Richard's Almanac* by Benjamin Franklin. And I haird som'thin' upstairs so I went out to the stairs and I called up but there were nary answer. I went up the stairs, callin' out t'th Bishop. When I got t'his door I could hear his stereo playin' real loud. So I knocked on th'door and cracked it open and . . . and . . .
VAIL:	And what?
STAMPLER:	I don't rememb'r.
VAIL:	You don't remember what happened next?
STAMPLER:	Next thing I know, I was standin' thair and I had that knife in m'hand and the ring . . . and . . . and the Bishop were . . . they was blood all over the place and on me and the Bishop were on . . . the floor . . . n'he was bleeding in the worst way.
VAIL:	Then what did you do?

157

STAMPLER: I guess . . . I guess I kinda panicked and I started t'run out only there was some-body downstairs and so I run out through the kitchen and thair was a police car comin' down the alley so I ducked back into the church and . . . uh . . .

VAIL: That's when you hid in the con-fessional?

STAMPLER: (Nods.)

VAIL: And that's all you remember.

STAMPLER: I swear t'you, Mist'r Vail, that's all I rememb'r.

VAIL: Why didn't you throw down the knife and call the police?

STAMPLER: Because I were scair'd, reckon. I were scair'd so. And th'Bishop were all cut up . . . I don't know why. Jes' ran.

VAIL: Aaron, who else was there in the room, when you went back upstairs?

STAMPLER: (Looks down and shakes his head.) Don't know.

VAIL: You told me last time we talked that you were afraid of that person.

STAMPLER: Y'suh.

VAIL: But you won't tell me who it is?

STAMPLER: Don't know.

VAIL: You don't *know* who it was?

STAMPLER: (Shakes his head.)

VAIL: But you're afraid of him?

STAMPLER: (Looking up) Wouldn't you be, Mist'r Vail?

Vail snapped off the machine.

'There you have it, Doctor. That's the young man they claim did that.' He pointed to the pictures. Molly shifted slightly in her seat. She put the empty bourbon glass on the corner of Vail's desk but said nothing.

'One question,' Vail said. 'Is it possible his story is true? I mean, could it have happened that way?'

She stared at the pictures for a moment longer and nodded.

'Yes. He could have gone into a fugue state for three or four minutes.'

'What's a fugue state?'

'It's like temporary amnesia. An epileptic who has a seizure goes into a fugue state. A drunk who can't remember what he did the night before was in what we call chemically-induced fugue. In this case, Aaron could have been so shocked by what he saw that he withdrew into a fugue.'

'How long does it usually last?'

'Usually fairly short term. Five minutes would be average, I'd say. But I know of cases where subjects have gone into fugue for as long as six months.'

'Six months!'

'Yes. It's a manifestation of certain types of personality disorders. I could go on for hours about this.'

'In time. The point is, you're saying Aaron Stampler could be telling the truth?'

'Absolutely.'

Fourteen

Goodman stopped the car at the top of the hill, got out and looked around. Ahead of him, the road dropped sharply down between pine-laden walls that defined a narrow valley. Cramped into its confined floor was a single street half a mile long bordered on one side by a dark, thundering stream, and a narrow gauge railroad track and on the other by the natural wall of the steep ravine. Houses and stores lined the bleak roadway. Company stores and company shanties – sixty or seventy aged, frame houses, Goodman estimated, before the valley curved and the settlement followed along. Years of black dust had obliterated paint and trim, and yet there was about the small settlement a look of neatness, a reflection of pride.

And something else. At first he could not put his finger on it. Then he realised the place seemed somehow out of place in time. Yeah, that was it. No television aerials. No neon, no billboards. It was if he had driven over the crest of the hill into another century.

There was a kind of sad, yet serene beauty here. It was hard to imagine that under these green, rolling hills and deep ravines, coal mines dipped deep into the earth, manufacturing deadly gasses and black lung dust. Truly heaven and hell, thought Goodman, and he was abruptly swept back in time for a moment. To Gary, Indiana, 23 years ago, a place different from this place in size and accent, and yet strangely like it. Dominated by smoke stacks instead of hills, its colours black and grey instead of green, Gary nevertheless had the same grim, redundant sense about it. In Gary, they boiled steel in giant furnaces; here they dug coal from pits in the earth. In both places, danger was a persistent partner. Goodman's father had died under a scalding cauldron of molten steel. Broken, body and spirit, by years of physical punishment, he just couldn't move fast enough. When he died, Goodman, then nine, and his mother had moved to the city. They had never owned anything. Everything belonged to the company. What pride they had, they left behind for it was an emotion manufactured by the company and manifested by bowling teams and football games, high school bands and Fourth of July picnics.

So Goodman knew what to expect. Gaunt, suspicious of strangers, the people would be leather-hard from a lifetime of fighting weather, poverty and geography. They would be simple people, their vision confined by mountains, fog and fear of the outside; their dreams trapped in airless, lightless, anthracite tombs; their tenuous job security in itself a death sentence. Cave-ins, explosions, disease, and climate were the Four Horsemen of their existence. And yet he knew they would be ferociously patriotic, God-fearing, loyal people, their faith nurtured in the fundamentalist church, their fervour in the flag, their loyalty in a company that would exploit them to their grave. Salt of the earth.

He also knew there would be one talker down there. There's a talker even in the smallest town.

'Crikside, Kentucky. Population 212,' the small white sign said, the number painted over and reduced several times. Sign of the times – kids leaving to find a better life outside. Aaron Stampler had been one of them.

This is what Stampler had escaped. An oddball kid, probably. Smart, frustrated, driven by a vision born in his imagination until he finally crossed the mountain into the real world. Maybe it was too much for him. Had something unleashed repressed rage inside him? Sometime, somewhere – between his forlorn valley and Archbishop Rushman's blood-drenched bedroom – had

161

something terrifying and obscene exploded inside Aaron Stampler?

The answer would start here.

He drove slowly into the hollow. The road ran between the railroad and Morgan's Creek for a hundred yards or so then curved over the tracks and curved back to become the main street of Crikside.

The hardware store was a long, squat building with a tin roof and a dim interior and pickaxes, oil lamps and harnesses displayed on a sagging porch that ran the length of the building. There followed Walenski's drugstore, the city hall − a narrow, two-storey wooden structure with a spire that looked more like a church than the political centre of Crikside. There was a rambling grocery store; a dry goods shop called 'Miranda's Emporium', and three old buildings that leaned on each other for support − a small restaurant in the centre with a bar on one side and a liquor store on the other, and a sign that read 'Early Simpson's Cafe and Bar.' There was also a frame house with a sign in front that said, 'Avery Daggett Legal Advice and Office Supplies', although Goodman wondered what a lawyer would do in this tiny hamlet. Draw up wills for folks who had nothing? Divorces? Unlikely. Suits against the company? Hell, the company probably owned Daggett and everything else in sight.

A town where a game of checkers could cause gossip.

He decided to start at the drug store but it was empty and the proprietor, a severe woman who did not look at him, had nothing to say when he tried to start a conversation. A small brass plaque beside the front door said simply, 'Leased from KC&M.' The same thing happened at Miranda's Emporium. There were two women in plain wool dresses who stood in the rear of the place and stared at him from between the shelves. The owner, a large woman with her hair in rollers, was pleasant but turned to ice when he mentioned Aaron's name. She shook her head and walked back to her customers. He left, stared for a moment at a similar brass plaque and stood with his shoulders hunched against a chill wind that whined through the sluice. He walked across the street to the grocer. Same brass plaque. KC&M owned the town all right. Everything was leased. Nobody owned anything. Anybody causes trouble, they are banished forthwith and empty-handed.

Maybe the grocer was the gathering place for the town elders. He entered a dismal, large, crowded room, manned by one man who was placing canned goods on a shelf. Goodman strolled to the back to a large soft-drink chest. The storekeeper eyed him and finally walked over. He was a rail of a man with a grey beard and dull eyes and the pasty complexion of a man who did not spend much time outside. He wore a red flannel shirt and thick wool trousers, held up by black galluses and protected by a clean, starched apron. His hand was so thin Goodman could count the veins and sinews criss-crossing through the back of it and the skin was stretched tight over long, bony fingers. He appraised Goodman with the fierce eyes of an evangelist, his expression never changing.

'Got a cold coke in that box?' Goodman asked cheerfully.

'Royal Crown's all. Jerome supposed to be hair yest'-day, didn't make er.'

'Royal Crown's fine.'

He spoke in the quaint, peculiar, lyric patois of the Appalachians – a kind of mixture of old English and Davy Crockett in which TV would become 'tay vay', hair became 'h'ar', and year would be 'yair'. There would be very little slang spoken among the elders and superfluous letters would fall by the wayside.

The storekeeper popped the top on an opener attached to the side of the chest and wiped the rim of the bottle with his apron before he handed it to Goodman.

'How much?'

'Fifty cents. Jes' went up a week ago.'

Goodman handed him a dollar. There was an open mouthed jar on the counter next to the soft drink box with what appeared to be a section of a polaroid photo cut out and scotch-taped to it. It was a picture of a rather burly-looking man with a cautious smile. A handwritten note was attached below the picture: 'For Zachariah Donald's funeral Died Monday Feb 14 Heart attack'. No commas or full-stops. A simple statement of fact. The jar was nearly full of coins of every kind and a half dozen bills of different denominations, one a ten. Goodman dropped his change in the jar.

'Know Zach did ye?' the storekeeper asked.

'Never had the pleasure.'

'Well that's ray't gen'rous of ye, then, trav'ler.'

'Least a person can do.'

'I s'pose. Not many strangers's would, don't reck'n.' He spoke in a flat monotone. No inflections, no emotion. Just words.

'You get many strangers through here?'

'Yer the third since the yair chang'd. All lost their way. Had to p'int 'em back towards Kreb's Knob er up to Zion. You lost?'

'Nope.' Goodman took a deep swig from the bottle. The storekeeper moseyed about making work, whistling an aimless ditty to himself. As he straightened things out on a shelf, he said, 'Zach farmed, din't work the mines. Up 'airs on Sackett's ridge. Ye'll pass his place, ye go south. Kept a nice place, he did.'

'Must be pretty tough farming, hereabouts,' Goodman said.

'True 'nuff. Old man Donald – that be Zach's grand-addy – he star'd the place. Couldn't braith down in The Hole, s'what they say. A'fore my time.'

'Uh huh.'

'Want somp'in' t'go with that? Cheese crack'rs, somp'n?'

'Crackers might be good.'

'Got malt with peanut butter er round uns n'cheese.'

'Peanut butter'll be fine.'

The keeper snapped a package of crackers from a display and laid them in front of Goodman.

'Be 'nother forty saints.'

Goodman gave him another dollar and once again put the change in the jar.

'You stay long 'nuff, trav'ler, we might kin bury old Zach t'morra,' he said without humour.

'How much is it going to take? For the funeral, I mean?'

'Don' rightf'ly know. This time o' yair, Charlie Koswalski, who does our undertakerin', gets ice offa Hoppy's Pond, up on th' flat. That's what he got Zach packed in over t'the fun'ral parlour. Reck'n when the ice melts round ol' Zach, Charlie'll gather up these here jars – they's all over town – that'll be what't takes t'bury him.'

'Very practical,' Goodman said.

'Well, Charlie sure's hell cain't keep Zach over 'air much longer. Been gone four days a'ready.'

'Good point.'

The storekeeper nodded down the street. 'Near'st roomin' house be next holla over – Morgan's Crik. They got th' name afore we did.' He smiled, which was probably as close to a laugh as he would ever get.

'I'm not looking for a rooming house. I was hoping to talk to Misses Stampler. Guess you know her?'

'Yess'ree,' he said, nodding, then after a moment or two, 'ye'r a mite late.'

'What do you mean?'

'She pass'd. Were, le'see, March . . . ? Yep, 'most a yair ago. Ain't kept in very good touch, air ye?'

'Afraid not.'

'She were al'ays a strange woman. Al'ays mumbling,

like she were arguing with herself. Couldn't buy an apple without she'd argue with herself about it.'

'Truth is, I wanted to talk to her about her son.'

'Samuel or Aaron?'

'Aaron.'

'Ah.' He nodded. 'Ye're hair 'bout that trouble then?'

Goodman nodded. 'Do you know him?'

''course. Been livin' in Crikside fifty-four yair. Know ev'body – here, gone . . . and goin'.'

'What was he like?'

'Aaron? Different from most the young 'uns.'

'How so?'

The storekeeper pulled up a straight-back wooden chair, sat down and leaned back against the wall, motioning to Goodman to sit on the drink box.

'Never satisfied,' he went on. 'Always tryin' sompin' new. Want'd t'be a doctor, then a actor, gonna write po'try. Too smart fer his britches. Prob'ly Miss Rebecca's doin'.'

'Miss Rebecca his mother?'

The storekeeper shook his head. 'Teacher up't the school. Always were partial to Aaron. Even worked with 'im when he went to high school over t'Lordsville. But, give 'im his due, good worker, he were. Did fer me couple yairs, work'd for the Doc. Always on time, not a complainer.'

'Did he have a bad temper?'

'Temper?' the storekeeper said, surprised. He thought a minute and shook his head. 'N'more'n anybody else. Ev'body gets riled up now and ag'in, ain't that so?'

Goodman nodded and listened.

'Aaron was a thinkin' boy. When he were no bigger'n a piss ant, he come in, stand thair in fronta th' candy tray – sometime five, ten minutes – makin' his mind up. Same with readin'. Hell, he'd hang 'round back thair a hour at a time, trying t'decide which book t'take home.'

Goodman looked to the back of the store at several

four-foot high stacks of paperback books, some scotch-taped together to keep from falling apart, accompanied by a sign. 'Books for borrow. Ten cents a day.'

'Big reader was he?'

'Could read a book in a day. Two, t'were a thin one.'

'Sounds industrious enough.'

'In some whys, reckon. Wouldn't go in Th' Hole, though. His daddy near wore 'im out, but he was stead-fast. Weren't no miner, that boy.'

'His father still alive?'

'No, no. Hole got 'im. Black lung. 'Bout four yair ago. Then his brother was kilt, le'see that would be in 1976.'

'In the mines?'

The storekeeper shook his head. 'Car accident.'

'Bad luck family.'

'So t'would appair, travel'r. Ol' Sackett's Ridge got th' h'ants, now.'

'H'ants?'

'Ghosts. Spir'ts. Were up thair a couple yairs back, in the summer? Come up over the hill with m'dogs, they all a sudd'n set up a bayin', running around in little circles, got cold like th' frost man were breathin' on me. Hell, them dogs, they was scair't silly. Then I realis'd it was right thair, right where they found the car. Ain't been back and I ain't the only one's had bad times up 'air.'

'Sackett's Ridge, huh,' Goodman said. 'Guess I'll stay away from there.'

'Good idee, trav'ler.'

'Well, thanks for the hospitality,' Goodman said.

'Ye paid fer it,' the storekeeper answered, nodding as he left.

Goodman drove two blocks to what amounted to the edge of town. Beyond its limits, defined only by the last of the commercial places, rows of narrow, two-storey houses stretched on up the road a half-mile or so and around the bend in the valley. On his right was a severe-looking two-storey square building with a foreboding sign that announced, 'Dr Charles Koswalski, General Medicine and Funerals'.

What was it the storekeeper said? *He wanted to be a doctor*, and *he worked for the doc*. The house had two doors, one marked 'doctor', the other marked 'parlour'. He tossed a mental coin and went into the doctor's side. A bell jangled over the door as he entered and found himself in a small waiting room with a broken-down sofa and a couple of old easy chairs. There was a large, wooden sliding door at the rear of the room which smelt like a doctor's office always smells – of iodine, vitamins, and antiseptic. And there was something else. It was a minute or two before Goodman detected it – the nauseating odour of formaldehyde, which apparently wafted in from the undertaking side. The big door rolled back and a short, chubby man, bald as a paper weight, looked in the room.

'Hep ye?' he said.

'If you're Doctor Koswalski.'

'That I am.'

'My name's Goodman, Doctor.' He showed Koswalski his licence. 'I'm asking around about Aaron Stampler.'

'Oh? Asking what?'

'Just trying to get a fix on the boy. What he was like.'

'If he done showed homicidal tendencies?'

The question took Goodman by surprise. He smiled. 'Well, that too,' he said.

'Damn shame, what that boy done,' said the doctor, who had a cherubic face, no neck, and thick, pudgy hands that looked like they would probably swallow a scalpel. He wore a white shirt with a turned collar that was frayed and ingrained with old dirt; his food-stained tie, which hung a quarter-inch from the top button of his shirt, was twisted so the cloth lining in the back showed. He wore a black suit, hardly an encouraging sign for those who visited this side of the establishment.

'Well, we're not sure he did it yet, sir,' Goodman said.

'Lexin'ton paper said so.'

'He worked for you, didn't he?'

'A mite, now and ag'in. Smart boy. Wouldn't a thought he'd a done that. Course he run off and left his maw alone. Truth be told, t'was a blessing when she went. Crazy as a full moon dog, she was, that last yair. N'air once left the house! Used t'look out from behind her curt'ins, talk at herself. Yell at folks.'

'Did she have mental problems before he left?'

'Well, she were always a mite strainge, but she were crazy as a bat there at the end.'

'Did you treat her?'

'Nothin t'treat. Din't hurt nary. Nobody here'bouts wanted to put her away.'

'Did he have a bad temper?'

'Aaron? N'more'n anybody else. Had his bad days. Come in, be kinda quiet, mumble t'himself. Feisty n'angry-like. But we all have a bad day now and agin, ain't it th'truth?'

'I'd have to agree.'

'Probably got a lickin' the night afore, was pissed off 'bout it.'

'He get a lot of lickings, did he?'

'All boys get lickin's, Mister Goodman. It's a natural thaing twixt a boy and his paw. Aaron just din't take t'kindly to it.'

'The other boys took their whippings but he didn't, that it?'

'Honour yer father and mother, says the Bible. Yuh don't stand agin yer father, t'aint done. Here'bouts, least. Why, I can remember when the boy was only ten, eleven yair old, he pushed old Gabe Stampler over a chair, run outta the house, n'hid out in my garage all night.'

'What did Aaron do for you?' Goodman asked, changing the subject.

'Cleaned up. Sometimes hepped me in operations. Gonna be a doctor, onc't, for 'while anyways. Wanted t'be a lotta things. Had a contrary notion 'bout his future.'

'He assisted you in operations?' Goodman asked with surprise.

'Well, not 'fficially a'course. Held a light fer me, hand me m'tools.'

'Kind of like a nurse?'

'Might say.'

'And he cleaned up after operations?'

'Yep. Little blood din't bother 'im. Y'know, I coulda used old Aaron. Woulda made a damn fine un'taker, would've. Weren't interested, though. Too busy studyin', dreamin' big dreams.'

'So he worked both sides, huh?'

'Yes'ir. Had the right att'tude, din't let it bother 'im. Funny, when his brother Sam and Mary Lafferty died up ona hill? He hepped bring 'em in, was like he never met 'em.'

'That was the car wreck?'

'Hell, weren't no car wreck. Them two was up on the ridge, screwin' in his daddy's old Ford. Bein' winter and all, they had the car runnin'. Carbon mo-nox-ide did 'em both.' He leaned closer to Goodman and whispered. 'Din't have a stitch on, n'ither one of em. Fact, Sam was still layin' atop a her. Never knew what hit em. Not a bad way t'go, eh?' He tapped Goodman with his elbow and chuckled, a phlegmy laugh that sounded like a hen clucking.

'And he helped you with the autopsy?'

'Sure 'nuff. Hell, old Aaron, he could watch a autopsy, eat a candy bar at t'same time. Din't bother him a'tall.'

The two-room schoolhouse, a simple, one-storey white frame building with a peaked roof, was across the street. It sat hard against the cliff-side with wide wooden steps leading up the hill from the road and looked like it had been recently painted. The windows were trimmed in bright red, a departure from the colour scheme of the surroundings. Goodman walked up the stairs to the front door. The brass plaque beside it was a little more formal:

Donated to the town of Crikside
by the KC&M Company

He considered waiting until school was out but changed his mind and entered the building. It was a single, large room, with twelve students gathered into three groups, each with half a dozen chair-desks bunched in rather haphazard order around them. One of the groups had only two students, both of whom appeared to be in their early teens. The back of the room had three doors and no windows, probably rest rooms and the cloak closet.

The teacher, a tall wisp of a woman who looked to be in her late thirties, scowled at him and said, sternly, 'Yes?'

'Nothing at all, teacher.' Goodman flashed a smile, trying to be charming. 'I just thought I'd sit in for a few minutes. Maybe I'll learn something.'

She stared at him quizzically for a moment, looked away, then her pale green eyes flicked back at him.

'Huh,' she snorted and turned back to her students.

But he didn't listen to her, he watched her. She was dressed straight out of the Sixties. She wore a denim jacket over a flowered shirt, an ankle-length applique skirt and black boots. Her thick, flaming red hair was streaked with grey and was pulled back in a tight ponytail. She wore no jewellery or make-up. And although her features, charmed with freckles – a small nose, square chin, etched cheek-bones – were delicate, she had a bold look about her, a defiant look, which, he decided, made her appear older than she probably was.

When school was over, the students filed out, each glancing sideways at him as they left, probably wondering if he was the school marm's new boyfriend. She crossed the room very resolutely, her hands jammed in the pockets of her jacket, and stood a few inches from him, her eyes locked on his.

'Now, just what're you up to?' she demanded in a voice that was resolute and had no recognisable accent.

'My name's Goodman,' he said, brusquely. 'I work for the lawyer who's going to defend Aaron Stampler for murder.'

She stepped back, shocked.

'Oh,' she said. Her shoulders seemed to square a little more and she lifted her chin slightly. 'And what d'you do for this lawyer who's going to defend Aaron Stampler?'

'I'm an investigator. I do the same thing the police do only for the other side.'

'Do you know Aaron?' she commanded, her eyes scrutinising him.

'No, not yet. I had to leave early this morning.'

'And you're going to help defend him?'

'I have to start someplace.'

She liked the answer and her tone became less recalcitrant.

'Do you think he did that?'

'The evidence against him is very strong.'

'I didn't ask you that.'

'At this point, he's presumed innocent.'

'You still didn't answer my question.'

'That's why I'm here, Miss . . . your name's Rebecca, isn't it?'

She continued to stare at him but did not answer.

'Look, teacher, I told you, I'm on his side. I need to find out as much as I can about him. Can we do that? Talk about Aaron?'

She went back to her desk, stacked up several text books and put them in a tall locker in the corner which she secured with an old-fashioned Yale lock. He moved the desks around as she began to sweep the floor.

Suddenly she said, 'Sometimes one, just one, can make it worthwhile.'

'Like Aaron?'

She stopped, leaned her chin on the end of the broom-stick and stroked the handle absently with one hand. 'Yes. He was the best student I ever had. Difficult. Most genius I.Q.s are . . .'

'He has a genius I.Q.?'

'Yes. Always a step or two ahead of you, you know? Always wanting to know more.' She returned to her sweeping. 'Hard when you're trying to teach fifteen or twenty others at the same time.'

'How was he difficult? In what way?'

She thought for a moment. 'Well, demanding I guess would be more accurate. It was like . . . like trying to fill a bottle with a straw in it. He sipped it out as fast I put it in.'

He held the dustpan for her and he gazed up and caught her studying him but her glance darted quickly away and she swept the pencil shavings, balled up papers, and gum wrappers into it, then took it from him and poured the refuse in a barrel in the corner.

'Reading,' she said, almost to herself. 'Aaron read everything. Shakespeare, Thomas Paine, the Rover Boys, Freud, Hemingway, oh God, he read every book he could get his hands on. Do you know he could read Latin? He could read Latin quite well.'

'What kind of person was he?'

'It was like . . . like he was starving to death and knowledge was food.' She shrugged. 'He was loveable, arrogant.' She stopped for a moment, searching for the right words. 'Sometimes frustrated, then cheerful, then moody. He was different from the rest, Mister Goodman. For one thing he refused to go down The Hole. His daddy used to whale about that. Took his belt to him, but he wouldn't go down there. Hopefully I had something to do with that. Determined not to be a miner like everybody else hereabouts. He's quite a beautiful boy, y'know. Didn't have many friends. The others picked on him, made fun of him.'

'I'm looking for clues, Rebecca – not fingerprints or needles in the carpet – not things like that. Clues about him. Could he have done it? Why? Could something have made him that angry?'

'You really do think he's guilty, don't you?'

'Like I told you, the evidence against him is very, very strong. We may have to go for an insanity plea.'

'He's not crazy, Mister Goodman.'

'When's the last time you saw him?'

'Two years ago. The day he left. His mother fought it. It would have been a tragedy for him to stay here.'

'It was a tragedy that he left.'

She looked up sharply. Her expression dissolved slowly into sadness. Her body seemed to shrink and lose its resilience. She sat down at one of the chair-desks, her back very straight, and stared out the window as if in shock. Finally she motioned vaguely around the room with one hand and said, 'I teach eight grades here, Mister Goodman. One to three over there; four, five and six there; seven and eight here. You know what that's like? I feel I've accomplished something if I just get them into high school. If they don't make it by the time they're fourteen, fifteen, the boys end up in the mines. The girls get married.'

'At *fourteen*?'

She nodded.

'Did you talk Aaron into leaving?' he asked.

'I told you,' she said. 'I'd like to think I had something to do with it.'

'Listen to me, Rebecca, I'm not here because I want him to end up in a madhouse. What I want to do is keep him out of the electric chair.'

The profound nature of Aaron Stampler's dilemma suddenly overwhelmed her. She put her hand over her mouth, closed her eyes and tears squeezed out and seeped down her cheeks. She tried to stifle her sobs. 'All that knowledge,' she mumbled through her hand. 'All those years.' Then in a tiny, pitiful voice, she murmured, 'What a waste, what an awful . . . Goddamn waste. He could have been anything, he just needed . . .'

'Needed what?'

'Oh . . . I don't know. Encouragement, approval. He dreaded loneliness. I think he feared being alone more than . . .'

She stopped, unable to go on, the tears flowing down her face.

'I guess we all do,' he said. 'I'm sorry, I'm really very sorry.'

She shook her head. 'No, *I'm* sorry,' she sobbed.

He walked over and put his hand gently on her shoulder, felt her stiffen at his touch but left it there until he felt her body begin to loosen. He rubbed her shoulder very gently and after a while she moved her head slightly and her hair whisked the back of his hand. He raised it slowly, cupping her cheek in his palm and she moved her face against his hand, turning slightly until he could feel her breath on his fingers, then the brush of her lips. He put the other hand on the back of her head and gently urged her head against his side. Her tears crept under his fingertips. She finally relaxed and wept without shame.

He held her for several minutes until her sobs turned to little gasps and finally she pulled away from him and turned her head.

'I'm very sorry,' she said.

'What for? I'm glad I was here. Sounded like you needed to do that.'

She didn't answer and finally he said, 'Look, I'm sorry I bothered you. I'll go over to the restaurant, ask around, maybe . . .'

'No,' she said. 'Don't do that. The men are coming in from The Hole. They'll be drinking. They don't like strangers, particularly ones who ask questions about their people. Even if they didn't like Aaron, they'd take offence. It's the way they are.'

'But I'm here to help him.'

'They won't believe you.'

She turned back to him and looked up at him, her features softened from crying.

'You come to my place. It's just up the road, back in the woods. I'll fix you something to eat and we can talk about Aaron Stampler.'

Fifteen

She turned off the main highway and followed the signs that led to a pleasant group of incompatible buildings surrounded by a brick wall. There was a modest office building at the front gate and a small brass plaque that identified the complex:

The Stevenson Mental Health Institute
FOUNDED 1924.

The guard, who wore khaki pants and a dark blue shirt and did not look like a guard, came out and when she identified herself, he told her pleasantly to follow the road to the main building. Then he went inside to throw the switch that would open the large iron gates. Molly sat quietly and waited for the adventure to begin.

Molly Arrington was a junior at Iowa State pursuing her dream of becoming a marine biologist when a single, shattering event altered forever the course of her life's journey.

Her father, Walter, was a devout farmer who adored the rich, black Iowa soil and all the creatures on earth who derived life from it and who shared with his children, Bobby and Molly, an abiding love affair with nature and the earth. He refused to use pesticides, preferring instead to plant an extra acre 'to take care of the critters,' raised no creatures for slaughter – cows for milk, chickens for eggs, two steers for breeding calves – and took in every stray dog and cat that passed their door. Eight dogs of every size and breed and half a dozen alley cats shared the two-storey farmhouse with them.

The first time Walter Arrington witnessed, through the miracle of television, napalm bombs engulf and devour a verdant Vietnamese forest, he got physically ill. He was so appalled by the nightly display of human misery and earthly destruction that he refused to watch television reports from the embattled land, even during the year his son served over there.

Athena Arrington had died at the age of thirty-six and not unexpectedly. Walter Arrington had married her knowing there was a time bomb in her chest – a congenitally malformed heart – and death would be persistent and always a heartbeat away. But he adored her and was devoted to making her life as happy and full as possible. When Athena died, her three loving survivors walked the tilled rows in the moonlight and sprinkled her ashes by hand over the farm she loved. Molly was twelve and Bobby was fifteen at the time. It was a memory Molly cherished for the field had become a living, nurtured memorial to her mother.

Walter, Molly and Bobby were an uncommonly loving family, demonstrative and open and dependent on each other for support, encouragement and sanctuary. They shared their triumphs and disappointments fervently, wept on proper occasions, trusted each other without qualification, and were bound together by such fierce loyalty that when Cy Wright, Bobby Arrington's best friend, ungraciously jilted Molly to pursue the most nubile of all the high school cheerleaders, Bobby had invited him out under the football stand and walloped him soundly. They had never spoken to each other again even though Molly had tried her best to heal the rift.

She had just finished her freshman year when Bobby graduated from grad school as an architect and went off to Vietnam. She was a beginning junior when he returned. But it was not Bobby Arrington who came back to The World – it was a hollow shell of a man, uncommunicative, morose, his fear-struck eyes mirroring the horrors that had possessed him in that far away land. He abandoned architecture and returned to the farm, tortured by memories he would not or could not share. Conversation became so painful for him, he spoke only in short, sometimes cryptic phrases and lost his temper when he was misunderstood. He was an insomniac, preferring to lie awake in bed rather than risk the nightmares that stalked his dreams. Molly dropped out of school for a semester, then another, and for a year she and her father watched helplessly as Bobby slowly but steadily withdrew from reality, seeking solace from his pain in a world of his own making.

The awful event that climaxed that dreadful year occurred on a warm day in early June. She was at a baby shower when she was summoned to the phone.

It was her father and he was sobbing.

'Papa what is it?' she cried.

'He shot the dogs, Molly. He shot all the dogs.'

She raced home to find Walter Arrington sitting on the porch swing, weeping inconsolably. She wrapped her arms around him, staring over his shoulder at Bobby, who was sitting at the edge of a cornfield, his forearms resting on his knees and the gun dangling from one hand. Eight dogs lay in a semi-circle around him.

'He went out there with a bag of food,' Walter sobbed, 'and he called the pups out. Hell, I thought he was going to play with them. Next thing I heard the gun go off. Bang, bang, bang, over and over, and I ran out there and he just looked at me and you know what he said? He said, "I had to do it, they were in pain. The ground was burning their feet." God, Molly, what did he mean? What's happened to our Bobby?'

She went out to him and sat down next to him and carefully took the gun out of his hand and laid it beside her in the dirt and he looked over at her and said, 'Somebody, please help me,' and Molly put her arms around him and rocked him gently as tears flooded her cheeks.

After a while, he said, 'Come with me, Mama' and that was the last thing he ever said. They sat like that for a long time until she felt the tension ease from his body and he slumped against her and fell asleep.

He never woke up, not in the real world, anyway. Bobby Arrington had been comatose for ten years. And Molly Arrington had abandoned her dream of swimming with dolphins to pursue a darker but no less defined goal.

The gate to the Stevenson Institute, cruelly known as Daisyland because that was the name of the town, swung open and she drove through, heading up a gravel road bordered on either side by knee-high winter shrubs. Every mental institution presented Molly Arrington with a vast acreage of potential knowledge. She regarded the communities of catatonic and inarticulate souls – slouched in chairs, regarding the world without cognisance – as captives waiting for her to strip away the veils of numbed thought that entrapped them in perpetual and stupefied twilight. She yearned to repair their disabled brains and urge them back to the shores of the living and, by so doing, unearth the secrets that had bound them in that uncharted and nebulous terrain where thought and recollection were suspended. Secretly she craved to invade those perilous realms, to roam their undefined regions in search of mist-bound souls like Bobby whose own fears, paranoia, torment, and anguish, had lured them into self-imposed exile in unplotted sanctuaries they themselves created.

For a time she had experimented with hallucinogenics, hoping to pierce the shroud and enter those forbidden and camouflaged precincts, but to no avail. She had even once tried electric shock therapy in order to understand its effect on the human mind but the pain was so literal, so massive and overwhelming, that she forbade her own patients from submitting to the treatment. Because the disorders that crippled the mind were so inexorably linked to suffering, pain in any form became unacceptable to her. Ultimately her experiments had side effects. She had created her own singular cosmos where pain and pleasure were so closely fused that one begot the other and because pleasure and pain were twins, she avoided both, rejecting even the ecstacy of orgasm as an unfair prize in the delicate struggle between joy and sorrow. And so she was a daring innovator who took copious notes on her own experiences, for she was well aware that negotiating the rim of that abyss was a perilous inquest. She carefully catalogued her own neuroses knowing full well that a mis-step could plunge her over the side into her own unmapped and perhaps inescapable netherworld. The clues she left behind might help one of her peers lure her back to reality. And so she approached each new patient with both exhilaration and apprehension, wondering how close the next journey would take her to the edge.

Aaron Stampler was different. He was conscious of the world around him and if he had created another country which she was not yet aware of, perhaps she could follow him into it. It was an exciting thought, one she felt was abundant with promise.

Harcourt Bascott, the director of the Stevenson Institute, was away but had left instructions for the staff to fully cooperate with her. A young black man named Clyde, who had a pleasant smile and a casual manner, carried her video case for her as he led her across the yard to what was known as New Wing. It was a three-storey building with a peaked atrium, its slanted sides constructed of large glass squares. The windows were not barred but were made of thick, bullet-proof glass. All in all, a pleasant-looking structure, and obviously built with a sense of humanity towards the inmates.

The maximum security section was at one end of the New Wing, sealed off with a wall and a single sliding steel door. Its security officer, dressed in khaki and blue as was the guard at the front gate, sat at a desk beside the door. There were no firearms in view. He smiled as Clyde and Molly approached and offered her a sign-in sheet.

Inside the steel entrance was a wide hallway, well-lit from the glass-panelled roof, with rooms on both sides. The guard led them into the first room on the right. It was large and had a small desk, a wooden chair, a cot, and a window that was at least six feet above floor level. The walls, furniture, and floor were painted pure white. The guard unscrewed a fixture over the electrical outlet on one wall so she could plug in the video equipment and left to get Aaron Stampler.

She was not prepared for his youth, his openness, for the irrepressible aura of innocence that seemed to encompass him. He was dressed in pale blue pants and shirt, soft, cotton shoes and white socks and he regarded her with surprise when he was led into the room. She was pleased to see he was not shackled.

'Aaron, I'm Doctor Molly Arrington. I think Martin Vail told you I was coming up here.'

'Oh, yes m'am. But I weren't expecting a lady.'

'I know. I think Martin was a little surprised, too.' She turned to the guard. 'Please wait outside,' she said.

The guard flicked a look back and forth between Molly and Aaron. 'You sure?' he said.

'We'll be fine,' she answered. He left the room a bit reluctantly.

'Martin says you have no objection to the video camera.'

'No m'am.'

She smiled and motioned to the cot while she tried to adjust the camera. She had trouble focusing it.

'Want me t'do thet, m'am,' Aaron asked. 'You kin jest sit down thair and I'll get it in focus fer yuh.'

'Well, thank you,' she said. She sat in the chair and he fiddled with the camera for a minute and tightened the tripod head.

182

'All ready,' he said. 'Just push this button to start er up.'

'Where did you learn about video cameras?' she asked.

'From Bishop Richard,' he said. He lay back on the cot and stretched out with his feet crossed at the ankles and his arms folded across his chest. He seemed energised, animated, his eyes bright with anticipation. Perhaps it was just having company in the cell and the temporary comfort she provided from the awful loneliness that chaperons anyone banished to solitary isolation.

'Are you comfortable?' Molly asked.

'Yes'm.'

'I don't want to talk about the Bishop, Aaron, not yet at least,' Molly said.

'Well thair's a relief. I told that story so many times. Don't know what more I can say.'

'I'd like to talk about when you were growing up.'

'Uh huh. Not very interestin', though.'

'Tell me about your hometown.'

'Called Crikside.'

'And that's in Kentucky?'

'Uh huh. Friend a mine once said if yair lookin' fer Crikside, you got t'go to lost and found.'

'That's very funny.'

'Yes m'am. But Crikside's not s'funny.'

'What do you mean, not so funny?'

'It's a dirty little town. Hardly big as this place is. Nothin' t'do thair. Don't even have a library. Work, go to church, n'die, that's what m'maw used to say.'

'Did you agree with your mother when she said that?'

'Well, long's you stayed thair, there was nary to disagree with.'

'What did you want to do? When you were growing up, I mean?'

Aaron seemed open and responsive to her questions. He was candid, never emotional, and at times so objective it was as if he was talking about someone else.

183

'I don't know. Seems like I tried ev'rything. Worked fer Avery Daggett, the lawyer, and Doc Koswalski and Mister Boise who owns the groc'ry store. Cut the grass at the city hall one summer. Mainly I wanted t'learn.'

'Learn what?'

'Ev'rything. Read everything I could find. Readin' was like . . . like takin' a trip somewhere. It was a way to get out of that place. And Rebecca – Miss Rebecca – our school teacher? She had a lot of books which she lent me and then she'ud ask questions, t'see if I knew what they meant. When I got t'high school it was better. That was in Lordsville – which was 'bout twenty miles over the mountain, we went by bus – and they had a good library thair.'

'What kind of books did you read?'

'Ev'ry kinda book they was. History books and geography, n'books 'bout philosophy and science. Law books n'medical books and books of poems and books that're fiction. Adventure books. Every kind of book you can imagine.'

'Was Miss Rebecca important to you?'

'She was the one helped me t'learn. She came thair when I were nine yairs old. Yes m'am, she were most important t'me.'

'As important as your mother?'

'Well, m'maw was . . . uh, kind of . . . well, she were of a single mind, m'maw was, and it was that all men were born t'work in The Hole.'

'The Hole?'

'Uh huh. Was like, there was no other way but that, y'know? You were a man, you went to The Hole. That was it. She knew I feared The Hole but it never made any diff'rence t'her.'

'You feared it?'

'Yes. I feared The Hole most.'

'What was The Hole, Aaron?'

'It's the coal pits. M'paw and Samuel worked thair.
All the men worked thair.'

'Samuel's your brother?'

'Was. Samuel was killed in a car accident.'

'Tell me about The Hole.'

'Ever since I can remember *any*thing, I was afeared of
The Hole. I don't remember ever a time when just the
thought of goin' down thair din't strike me cold. From
when I first knew what The Hole was, I dreamt 'bout it
and dreaded of't.'

'What kind of dreams?'

'Like goin' down to hell, critters crawlin all over me,
demons hidin' in the darkness, no air t'breathe. I read
this verse once – "What torments of grief you endured,
from evils that ne'er arrived". Emerson wrote that.'

'You've got a very good memory.'

'I remember things I like, that un in particular 'cause
it reminded me what I felt like, tormented by that fear.
That's the way t'was, 'tween me and The Hole. 'Cept the
evil did arrive.'

'So you did go into The Hole?'

He nodded.

'And you thought that was wrong?'

'When I were nine yairs old, on my birthday, when I
woke up? On the chair next t'my bed, there was a hat
with a lamp on it. M'paw got it made especially for me.
I sat thair on the bed and I cried 'cause I knew it was
gonna be that day, that was the day he was gonna take
me down. At breakfast it was like a celebration.
M'brother, Samuel, took off from school to go with us.
And me? I was so scared I near threw up on the way to
th'pits. Twelve of us were on the elevator. I remember
Mister John Canaan and Bobby Aronski were thair, I
remember because both of them was killed later in the
cave-in at number Seven. And all the men were bent over,
like they were eighty yairs old. It was worse th'n all
m'nightmares. I remember I begun to shake when that

elevator started down. That light at the top of the shaft, it shrank smaller n'smaller until you couldn't see it 'tall and nobody turned their lights on. We just kept goin' down and down and it was darker than I ever thought it could be, the air smellin' like bad eggs, and my mouth so dry m'tongue was stuck t'my teeth, down 'n down . . . didn't know a hole could be that deep. Then suddenly we come on the shaft and the elevator stopped real hard and everybody piled out into that black tunnel, so black the hat lights . . . the lights din't go anywhere, t'was that black . . . like the darkness just swallered up the light. The tunnel was only 'bout four feet high, they had t'stoop over t'work. Every once in a while somebody'd yell, "Fire in th' hole", and there'd be this terrible blasting and great clouds of black dust'd come swirlin' through the tunnel at us. No nightmare I ever had was that bad. Seven hours. I truly thought I was gonna die that day. I could imagine that shaft fallin', the earth fallin' in on us, smashin' us all down to nothin'. When we finally came up, I looked up, waitin' for that hole at the top of the shaft to appear, and finally it did and it grew bigger and bigger and it were like . . . were like resurrection. Once't we were up, the men all set to pattin' me on the back, all those bent-over men, thair faces coal black 'cept for thair eyes and mouths, like a pack a demons. My paw took the strap t'me many a time after that, but I nair went back down. Ever.'

'Did he beat you a lot?'

'Oh, once in a month, maybe.'

'Once a month!'

'Sometimes he'd come home from Bailey's drunk and I'd know 'cause of th'meanness in his eyes. "Take em down!", he'd beller at me and I would take down m'drawers and lean 'crost the chair and he'd pull off that fat belt a his and lay into me. Sometimes three licks. Maybe four or five. But it was worth 't. Any beatin'd be better than The Hole.'

'Do you still resent it?'

'I suppose. Not so much that m'paw whack'd me, as that he ever took me down thair 'tall.'

'Do you hate your father for that?'

'For that one thing? I guess I do. Not for th' lickin's, that were the penance I paid for refusin' m'paw.'

'Penance?'

'Well, that's what Bishop Richard called't. Y'know, payin' for when y'do somethin' wrong.'

'Do you believe in that? Paying penance, I mean?'

'Well . . . I guess I ha'nt fully made up m'mind yet. Sometimes I do, sometimes I don't.'

'What bothers you about it?'

'Maybe . . .'

'Yes?'

'Maybe it started with Reverend Shackles.'

'Tell me about him.'

'Well, when I was – like maybe seven r'eight? – we had this preacher – Josiah Shackles. Big, tall man, skinny as a pole with this long, black beard down t'his chest and angry eyes – like the picture y'see in history books, y'know, of John Brown? When they had him cornered at Harper's Ferry? Have you seen that picture, his eyes just piercin' through you? Reverend Shackles were like that. Fire in his eyes. He din't believe in redemption. You did one thing wrong, *one thing*! You told one simple lie, and you were hellbound. He'ud stare down at me, "Look at me, boy," he'd say, and his voice were like thunder, and I'd look up at him, was like lookin' up at a mountain, and he'ud slam his finger down hard toward th'ground and say, "Yer goin t'hell, boy!" '

'Did you believe that? That you were going to hell?'

'I believed it at the time, I sure did. Reverend Shackles put that fear in me. Thair was no redemption'r forgiveness in Reverend Shackles' Bible.'

'So there was no reason to pay penance, right?'

'Yes, m'am, that's right. It were like penance without redemption, so why bother.'

'Do you still believe you're going to hell?'

'I don't know. Bishop Richard once told me hell is in your own mind.'

'What do you think he meant by that?'

'Not sure yet.'

'So you feared The Hole and Reverend Shackles. Were you afraid of your father?'

'Just that he'ud somehow force me down thair ag'in.'

'But you never went back?'

'N'um, and nair will.'

'Tell me more about your mother.'

'Well, like I said, she nair had much t'say. Didn't care 'bout education. I think she felt . . . she felt like it were a waste a'time.'

'Did she ever read to you, tell you stories?'

'No, m'am, m'maw couldn't read. The only stories she ever told were Bible stories and she'd start but never finish, like she'ud forgot how they ended.'

'Did you read the Bible?'

'T'was the first book I e'er read. T'was the only book in our house.'

'How old were you then?'

'Dunno. Six, maybe. Seven.'

'And you read the whole Bible at that age?'

'Yes'm.'

'And what did it mean to you?'

'Y'know how it is with the Bible. Ev'ry time you read it, it takes on a different message.'

'And how about Miss Rebecca?'

'She were my teacher, from when I was nine 'til I finished up in high school. Well, in high school I had lots a'teachers, but until I went to Lordsville, Miss Rebecca were my *only* teacher.'

'So all the children went to the same schoolroom?'

'Yes'm. One room. T'were divided up – some sat over

thair, some sat over thair, some sat here. Rebecca . . .
Miss Rebecca . . . she ud move around the room, teachin'
first one bunch a us, then t'other.'

'And she was a good teacher?'

'Smartest person I ever met.'

'Smarter than the Bishop?'

'Smarter than anybody.'

'How about your friends?'

'Didn't have a lot of friends. Y'see, most of the boys
I grew up with, they knew they would go to th'mines
when the time come. They didn't truck much with me.'

'Did they shun you?'

'I guess it were more like I shunned them.'

'The girls, too?'

'Until high school. They were all of a same mind. You
grow up, go t'school 'cause you have to. The boys quit,
go to The Hole, and the girls quit and marry 'em.'

'And that was unacceptable to you?'

'Kind of hopeless, w'nt y'say?'

'Yes, I'd have to agree with that. So you were alone a
lot growing up?'

Molly watched him as he considered the question. His
face clouded over. She saw consternation in his look, as
if he did not know the answer, or perhaps more accu-
rately, had never even considered the question before.

Finally he said, 'I didn't feel bad about it, if that's what
you mean.'

'Did you feel that you were different from the others?'

'I was. They all thought alike. They din't have dreams,
they din't ask questions, they just took everything th'way
'twas put to 'em. Yes m'am, I was diff'rent than all of
'em and thankfully so.'

'Can we talk about sex for a minute?' she asked,
watching his expression.

'Yes m'am.'

'Are you a virgin, Aaron?'

He smiled. 'No m'am. Lost that when I were sixteen. First yair in high school.'

'Was it a pleasant experience?'

'Well, yes m'am.'

'How old was the girl?'

'Same age s'me. T'were a girl I knew since we were kids. From Morgan's Crik.'

'Did you feel it was wrong?'

'I s'pose if I was talking to say, Reverend Shackles, it might've made me think badly on't. But I din't grieve over't, if that's what you mean.'

'Did the girl have any problems with't?'

'She never said, if she did.'

'Have you ever had a homosexual experience?'

He hesitated for a moment, then shook his head. 'No. Never really thought much about that.'

When he appeared to tire, Molly ended the interview. It was an interesting first meeting but she had only flirted with the peripheries of Aaron's life, the fringes of its structure. What she had solicited was elementary; that he feared the dark, hated authority, distrusted his elders, dismissed his peers, and that The Hole might well be the symbol for all in life that he dreaded. Phobia, disassociation, alienation, religious disorientation, all were present, yet these were not necessarily the symptoms of disorder. Who but a fool would not fear The Hole, with its connate disasters, foul air, and foreboding darkness? Or the evangelical madness of a Reverend Shackles? Rather they were testimony to that dark, forbidden locale in his mind where lurked the real 'crawling critters and demons' of his disobedient dreams. So they had walked the rim of the escarpment together, but they had yet to look into the chasm.

Sixteen

Goodman went across the street to Early Simpson's liquor store and found, covered with dust on a back shelf, a fairly decent bottle of red wine that probably had been there since KC&M was a one-shaft operation. He bought it and drove up the road, following Rebecca's instructions. Her cabin was on the other side of the roaring stream, embraced by a thicket of pine trees. Darkness approached early in the deep valley, particularly here, where the trees blotted out the last of the sunlight. The house was incompatible with the rest of the village, a small A-frame structure with a large window overlooking Morgan's Creek, its porch protruding to the edge of the rivulet. A one-lane wooden bridge carried him over the torrent. He parked beside her three-year-old Chevrolet and climbed the stairs to the porch. Her boots were beside the mat. He was removing his wet shoes when she opened the door for him.

'You don't have t'do that,' she said. 'I just like to wear plain old wool socks around the house.'

He was stunned by her appearance. She had taken off the denim jacket and skirt and replaced them with a grey sweatshirt and trousers cuffed tightly at the ankles. She had on bright red wool socks and had unbound her flaming red hair which cascaded down around her shoulders like hot lava. She seemed smaller without the boots, more vulnerable, less in control, perhaps because here she felt safe and comfortable. The room was lit with candles which haloed her hair and softened her features.

She had started a fire and the cabin was a warm and personal relief from the austerity of the rest of the village. A sleeping loft covered the kitchen in the rear of the peaked great room. Books were jammed and stacked into shelves that lined one wall. There were stacks of magazines on both sides of the window and a table in the corner was covered with photographs. Some were framed. Others, snapshots, leaned helter skelter against the frames. There were several stacks of records, some of them old 78 rpm's, beside the cheap stereo against the other wall. The place was clean but not necessarily tidy, almost as if things had been left exactly where she had used them last. He did not see a telephone.

'Hope you don't mind candles,' she said. 'I only use the electric lights when I read or sew. Hate to waste things.'

'It's very pleasant,' Goodman said. 'I like the way they smell.'

'I make them myself,' she said. 'Aaron loved candles. His favourite poem was from Edna St. Vincent Millay. Perhaps you know it.' She recited it almost wistfully:

> ' "My candle burns at both ends;
> It will not last the night;
> But ah, my foes, and oh my friends—
> It gives a lovely light!" '

'I remember it from college,' he said. 'Sort of.'

'It's a cliché, I know,' she said. 'One of the charming things about Aaron was that he didn't recognise stereotypes. Everything was new to him.' She waved towards the corner. 'Put on a record – they're over there. I've got to tend to dinner. I hope you like stew.'

'I love stew.'

'Good. It should be good and tasty by now, been brewing since yesterday.'

He flipped through the stacks of records – Crosby, Stills and Nash, Buffalo Springfield, the Stones, Jefferson Airplane, it was like a musical trip through the sixties and seventies – and finally chose 'Cheap Thrills' by Janis Joplin and Big Brother. He strolled over to the bookshelf

192

and stared down the rows of books. There were strips of paper protruding up from the pages, like the tabs on file folders. He was surprised at how many pages had been marked. He slid one volume out, a slender tome called *Quotations for Living*, and flipped it open. A phrase had been underlined lightly in pencil. 'Evil comes to all us men of imagination wearing as its mask all the virtues. William Butler Yeats.' He flicked to another, a Chinese proverb: 'There are two perfect men – one dead, the other unborn.'

'Those are Aaron's bookmarks,' she said from across the room. 'He marked things he liked in pencil and then when he had them memorized, he'd erase them. He was still working on those when he left.'

'Must have quite a memory,' he said, snapping the book shut and replacing it on the shelf.

'Remarkable.' She ladled out a helping of stew, sucking it noisily off the spoon, then smacking her lips with satisfaction. He popped the cork on the wine as she brought the stew pot over and ladled generous helpings on both their plates. He held her chair for her when she came back and she smiled grandly as she sat down.

'*Déjà vu*,' she said, almost to herself.

'Beg pardon?' Goodman asked.

'Just reminiscing,' she said, reaching out and tilting the wine bottle so she could read the label. 'Did you find this here?' she asked with surprise.

'It was hidden behind the bottles of Thunderbird and Hurricane.'

She laughed. 'I haven't had wine for a while,' she said. 'The school marm in Crikside doesn't drop by the liquor store and pick up a jug when she gets thirsty.'

The stew was a thick, succulent mixture of potatoes, okra, tomatoes, cabbage, and a tough but tasty meat, which he learned later was rabbit. There was cornbread to sop up the stew juices with and they ate and drank wine and talked more about Stampler; about his father's obsession that his sons should follow him into the coal mines; about his mother, who was afraid to disagree with old man Stampler, who talked to the spirits, and who blamed Rebecca for her son's contrariness; and how Stampler meted out punishment with his belt – the number of lashes contingent on the seriousness of the offence.

'Sometimes when he came over, he'd be laced so bad . . . his backside would be strapped raw . . .'

He looked up at her quizzically. She looked away quickly and hurried on, switching the subject to Aaron's insatiable appetite for knowledge.

'Tell me more about his mother. Did she have mental problems?'

'Never went out that last year. She would have starved to death except for her neighbours. Maybe the loneliness finally got to her. As badly as she treated Aaron? – when he left she didn't know what to do. She depended on men all her life and when they were gone, she couldn't handle it.'

'I mean before that. Was she always, you know . . . the grocer and Koswalski both implied she was always kind of weird.'

'She was a very religious woman. She used to chat with God from time to time. A lot of them around here do that, however.'

'Maybe they don't have anyone else to talk to,' Goodman said.

She laughed. 'Very possibly.'

'And she didn't think much of education.'

'Noooo, but that's not rare, either.'

'Sounds like Aaron was pretty much a free soul.'

She nodded somewhat wistfully. 'Everything excited him,' she said. 'He read anatomy books when he worked for Doc Koswalski and law books when he worked for Agent Daggett. When he was a sophomore in high school he played Biff in *Death of a Salesman*. He was wonderful

– he really loved acting. Of course people around here hated the show but he didn't care because he *became* Biff every night. But like everything else, there was no outlet for it. Fact is, he never mentioned it again after that.'

'Where did he go when he left here?'

'Lexington, I think. I heard he worked in the hospital there for a while.'

'He never wrote you?'

She shook her head. 'I didn't expect him to.'

The room fell silent again. A question nibbled at Goodman's brain but he pushed it back into a dark chamber of his mind.

She leaned across the table, studying him.

'What did you do before you became a cop for the defence?' she asked.

'I was a prize-fighter.'

She looked shocked for a moment. 'Really?' she asked. 'You did it professionally?'

'Yeah. I was working my way through law school,' Goodman said. 'Smashed up my hand and Marty talked me into doing this.'

'Is Marty the lawyer?'

Goodman nodded.

'Is he good?'

'Best there is,' said Goodman. 'If Aaron has a chance, Marty's it.'

She stared into her wine glass, suddenly lost in thought, and they ate in silence for a while longer.

'Were you in Vietnam?' she asked suddenly.

He nodded. 'Sixty-nine and seventy.'

'Those were bad years.'

'Any year was a bad year over there. I didn't have it that tough. I'd go in-country for a couple of weeks, then they'd pull me back, send me to Saigon or over to the Bay to fight. I'd train a couple of weeks, do a fight, get a couple of weeks R&R, and they'd send me back on the line. It went like that the whole time.'

'Did you always win?'

He nodded. 'All but that last one.'

'And what happened?'

He held up his hand. The bones had healed badly and were twisted and deformed. It was a gnarled fist, like the knob on a tree. She moved closer to him, took his hand in hers, felt its imperfections, imagined the pain it must have caused.

'Did you like to fight?' she asked, still staring at his broken hand.

'The amateurs were fine. Young fighters with style. But not professionally. I did it for the money. It was kind of a relief when I ruined my right.'

'It's not ruined,' she said, watching her thumb trace its irregularities. 'It's different. It has character.'

'Thanks. Where are you from, anyway?'

'Santa Fe.'

'Santa Fe. I couldn't place the accent.'

'I ran away when I was sixteen. Spent six years in the Haight.' She stopped for a moment, her mind spinning back to a psychedelic dream that had lasted more than half a decade. 'God, we tripped day and night. For six years, I thought the sun was tie-dyed and clouds were whipped cream – LSD reality.'

'How did you end up here?'

She emptied the wine bottle, sharing it between both glasses.

'Answered an ad in the *Lexington Tribune*,' she said with a smile. She got up and walked a bit too precisely to the kitchen, got a pack of cigarettes from a drawer and walked just as cautiously back.

'Sometimes I like a cigarette,' she said. 'I smoke a couple every three, four months. It's a cheap high, although I really don't need a high right now.'

She lit a cigarette.

'What happened after Haight-Ashbury?' Goodman asked.

'Oh, I bummed around,' she shrugged. 'Spent some time in communes, like that. I was just out of a rehab house and I read this ad for a school teacher. No references, that's what got me. For about a year I lived in a commune outside Toledo, teaching the kids – you know – ABCs, start them reading, so, I thought, why not? No references. When you've been high for six years that's important. And I figured there'd be no place better to go dry.'

'You've been here ten years now?'

She nodded. 'Since I was twenty-four. I was a mass of neuroses. Used to dream my mind was being invaded by spacemen.'

'C'mon,' Goodman said. 'Next you'll be telling me there's h'ants up on Sackett's Ridge.'

'They were like silhouettes at the window over there,' she wiggled her fingers towards the picture window. 'They were space miners, I could tell because they had psychedelic lights on their caps, like kaleidoscopes? And I could feel them seeping into my brain.' She stopped and giggled to herself and added, 'I don't dream it anymore. Maybe they're in there for good.'

'Maybe you got over them,' Goodman suggested.

'Oh no – I just switched to other kinds. And by the way, there is a ghost up on the ridge. Some very prominent people have run into her.'

'It's a she?'

'I assume it's Mary Lafferty.'

'Ah . . . well, do you want to jump in the car and drive up there. Maybe we can shake her up.'

'No.' Candlelight flickered in her green eyes. 'No ghosts tonight.'

'Well, guess I better find someplace to spend the night,' he said. 'I hear there's a rooming house about eight miles down the road.'

'Yes, in Morgan Creek.'

'Right,' he said with a smile, 'they got the name first.'

'You been talking to Clyde Boise.'

'He own the grocery?'

'Um hmm. That's his best joke.'

'I see what you mean – about the sense of humour in this town. He's the one told me Sam and Mary were killed in a car wreck. Some wreck.'

She leaned her elbows on the table and rested her chin in cupped hands and studied Goodman in the flicker of the candles. He had a wonderful face. Scarred by the abuse of fighting and etched by turmoil, it fell short of being handsome, for which she was grateful. In the wine's giddy cosmos, she felt as if she could see through his soft eyes, deep inside him, and what she saw was an architect for the havens of lost souls, creatures laden with hapless causes; a man who could withstand a slash of the sword but not a cut to the heart. She moved closer to him and reached out and ran her fingertips over his face. The harsh cicatrice hidden in one eyebrow and the bony ridge of his crooked nose became part of the aphrodisiac and her breath came short and finally she stood up and took his hand and led him up the stairs to the sleeping loft.

The bed seemed the size of a continent and was covered with a handmade feather mattress and soft, yellow flannel sheets. She lit a single candle on the night table beside the bed and then she slowly unbuttoned his shirt, spreading it open and exploring his chest lightly with the palms of both hands, like a blind person studying an alien texture. He responded by stroking her hair, letting it run between his fingers and then caressing the back of her neck. Their breathing was spasmodic, out of rhythm. She pulled her sweatshirt off and her breasts tumbled from under the cotton sweater and she pressed them against his chest and rose up on her toes until their nipples met. He kissed her and her tongue flicked out, traced his mouth, found his tongue, then her mouth opened and she sucked gently on his lips drawing them between hers and tracing them with her tongue. His hands slid into her slacks, embraced the mounds of her buttocks, pressed her against him and she began to move ever so lightly against him, her breath setting an erratic cadence for a slow-motion ballet of discovery. She undid his trousers, the zipper tracing priapic geography, and let them fall away and he did the same, slipping her slacks down and then she stepped back and they studied each other before she drew him down on the bed.

She kissed his chin, his throat, traced his earlobes with her tongue while her hands swept over his stomach, touched him and stroked him and his hands searched her soft down, felt her grow hard and wet under his fingertips, trembling as she rose to his touch. They stroked each other, their moans and whimpers became a rhapsody, time and place dissolved in seizures of ecstasy, until she rolled over on top of him, straddled him, staring into his eyes and crying out as she guided him into her. He stared up at her and she leaned forward on stiffened arms, arched her back, pressed herself against him, her hair whisking his face, and they moved faster and faster, racing, holding back, racing, holding back, until finally they surrendered in frenzied rapture.

She collapsed on top of him, lay there for several minutes until her breathing was almost normal and finally lifted herself off him and lay beside him on her stomach, her head nestled against his shoulder, her breath still unsettled.

'Oh God,' she murmured in his ear, 'How glorious to want something that badly. I mean to be attracted to you that way. It hasn't happened in a very long time. It was so good . . . just to . . . to *want* something again.'

'Are you that lonely?'

'Crazed,' she giggled. 'I knew I wanted you the minute you came in the school today and said that — you know — about learning something? I thought, my God, a man with a sense of humour — a real sense of humour, one that doesn't involve some kind of body function.'

He stroked her back with one hand, soothing her, feeling her pulse — in sync with his — return to normal. She lifted herself on her elbows and kissed him softly and rolled over on her back.

'Wouldn't a cigarette be just grand now,' she said softly. He lit one and handed it to her.

She smoked for a while then reached over and laid her free hand on his arm, stroked it then leaned very close to him. 'Spend the night with me,' she said softly in his ear. 'I want to feel you beside me when I wake up in the morning. I want to smell you before I open my eyes. You can make breakfast and I'll be late for school. In twelve years, I've never been late for school.'

'They're liable to descend on us, tattoo an "A" on your forehead.'

'Then I'll change my name to Abigail,' she said.

He raised up on one elbow and stared down at her.

'What the hell are you doing here?' he asked.

'I told you. I was attracted to . . .'

'No, not with me,' he laughed. 'I mean, here? What are you doing in Crikside-damn-Kentucky?'

She did not answer for a minute or two.

'I guess I'm hiding,' she said plaintively.

'From what?'

'From what the world's become,' she answered. 'Maybe . . . I'm afraid to go back out there.'

'Don't you ever miss it?'

'I miss a laughing man. I miss caring . . . strong arms around me. It's funny but I always did like the smell of aftershave lotion. Oh, at first I missed the museums, hearing good music, things like that. But you get over it. I even learned to play the fiddle. I can play a very wicked reel. And I like my independence. I don't work for KC&M, I work for the county. KC&M doesn't own the land, I bought it from the county 'cause nobody wanted it. This house came in a kit. You know, like an airplane model? It was in an ad in the Sunday paper. I tutored for two years, trading out with carpenters and plumbers and electricians to help me put it up.'

'Aren't you ever going to leave?'

She stared at the ceiling for a while and then said, 'No, I guess not.'

'Can I ask you something very personal?'

'It's about Aaron, isn't it?'

'Yes. That's why I came to Crikside, remember?'

'All right, ask it,' she said with resignation.

'It occurred to me because of what you said – about his father lacing him. The marks on his backside?'

'Yes . . . ?'

'Did you see them?'

She didn't answer.

'Did you sleep with Aaron?'

He watched her expression taper from irritated to cold to inquisitive to curious. And then back to resignation – or acceptance.

'Why would I do that?' she asked.

'I don't know,' Goodman said. 'It was a question, okay? Just say no.'

'I can't,' she said.

He didn't say anything, just waited.

'Yes,' she said truculently, lying on her back with her eyes closed. 'From the time he was fourteen until he left.'

'Fourteen?' he said.

She nodded. 'It was like a ritual. We made love two, three times a week. Except for about four months when he went with Mary. Then again after she died.'

'Mary?'

'Mary Lafferty.'

'The girl who was with his brother . . .'

She nodded. 'She was Aaron's first crush, right after he started in high school over at Lordsville. She was from Morgan's Creek and they dated for about four months and – you know, it's really strange – even though they weren't making it, Aaron had this funny sense of – not loyalty, exactly — more like monogamy. He stopped sleeping with me during that time. Sam was a year ahead of Aaron. He was on the football team and I guess Mary found him more desirable. Aaron's first heartbreak. We all go through it.'

'Did it shake him up, the way it happened?'

'Not really. When he first found out about it, he just . . . erased them from his mind. He could do that. If somebody hurt him, he could just, you know, X them out.'

'A fourteen-year-old kid?'

'If you've never lived in a place like this, you wouldn't understand.'

'Give me a try.'

She drew deeply on her cigarette and blew the smoke out in a slow, steady stream, never looking at him.

'I was attracted by his passion,' she said. 'He was a very passionate young man, even before his teens. Passion is a rare quality here.'

'Just passion?'

She stared at him scornfully. 'Is this part of your investigation?'

'Yes,' he said, although somewhat uncertainly.

'Hmph.' She stared at the ceiling as she spoke, stopping between sentences, dragging on her cigarette.

'I told you, he was very bright. And smart . . . We could talk about things, things nobody else here would understand. I remember once, we lay in bed for two, three hours talking about the composition in Ansel Adams' photographs and how we . . . the feelings we got from each picture. Things like that . . .

She was sitting crosslegged on the floor and he was facing her, reading to her from Sherwood Anderson's Winesburg, Ohio, *which was one of his favourite books. He was at the end of the story called* Mother, *a bitter-sweet story about rites of passage, and the inability of mother and son to reveal joy or sorrow or elation to each other. When he read, it was without accent. The quaint contractions of the valley vanished, replaced by orderly vowels and concise consonants and by the beauty of words spun into masterful narration.*

' "He fumbled with the doorknob",' he read. ' "In the room, the silence became unbearable to the woman. She wanted to cry out with joy because of the words that had come from the lips of her son, but the expression of joy had become impossible to her . . ." '

He stopped reading half a paragraph from the end and looked up at Rebecca and there was a time, it seemed interminable, when he sat there with his breath coming in short gasps and looked at her with a question in his eyes she had seen there many times before. She knew it was inevitable for she had seen, through the years, the fabrication of his desire, look upon look, thought upon thought.

'Kin I touch you?' he said, fearfully.

'Don't say "kin", say "can".'

'Can. Can, can, can . . .' he repeated, closing his eyes for a second, his breath coming harder, as if he had been running.

She gazed back at him and saw the fever in his eyes. It was a moment she had dreaded, anticipated, fantasised about and ultimately longed for, but had never encouraged. It was past time for denial. Past time to consider conscience or custom. Her skin was electrified, humming with desire. She unbuttoned her blouse slowly but did not spread it open and she sat adrenalised, her heart throbbing in her temples and her mouth dry. He stared at her, short of breath, licked his dry lips, and reached out with trembling hands. His fingertips barely touched her skin in the small gap of the open shirt. He drew the hand down – lingering, uncertainly, not probing but sensing her, as if he could perceive every molecule. Then just as slowly he spread the shirt open and gazed in awe at her breasts. He moved his hands back up but stopped and pulled them away and held them out in front of him, an inch away from her nipples.

'It's all right,' she said in a whisper. She felt her bust swell and reaching out, she took his hands in hers and placed them on her and felt her nipples harden under his palms. And he continued his delicate exploration with fingers as soft as feathers.

'I'm not ashamed of it, y'know,' she said. 'I didn't seduce him. It happened over a long period of time. I guess starting when he was . . . I don't know . . . about twelve. It was a very gradual thing. When it happened it was because we both wanted it to.'

'Like you said, people get married here when they're fourteen. A little chancey though, wasn't it? I mean, seems to me that could be a lynching offence in Crikside.'

'Maybe that was part of it.'

'Did you love him?'

She thought about that for a long time, trying to blow smoke rings at the ceiling which fell apart very quickly.

'I felt sorry for him,' she said, finally. Then she closed her eyes and after a minute, added, 'No, I felt sorry for both of us.'

She suddenly turned away from Goodman, lay on her side for a moment then sat on the side of the bed, her fair skin hidden behind the cascade of fiery hair.

'It was just part of it,' she said with neither rancour nor embarrassment. 'Why not? I taught him everything else.'

Seventeen

When Naomi Chance arrived at the office at eight thirty
a.m., Vail was already at work. Unshaven, his shirt as
rumpled as a wad of paper, he was staring at the photographs and taking more notes, as he had been doing the
night before when she left the office. A half-eaten meal
was on the desk beside the legal pad. Steam rose from
his coffee cup. He was so deeply concentrated he did not
hear her come in. She was accustomed to that. Vail called
it 'diving' – for it was like going under water. It was a
different world, one without sound, one in which all the
data and faces of the case were jumbled together and he
sought to categorise them, to rearrange them into a logical chronology until they formed a picture that made
sense to him. Like a legal jigsaw puzzle, the picture
occasionally would become clear even though some of
the pieces were missing. She ignored him and went about
her daily routine. Twenty minutes later he was in her
doorway.

'What time is it?' Vail, who never wore a watch in the
office, asked.

'Almost nine.'

'Tommy's back. He and the Judge will be in before
noon.'

'Strategy meeting?'

Vail nodded. 'I'm anxious to hear Tommy's report.'

'I doubt that even Tommy could find out much in
a town called Crikside,' she laughed. 'How about the
doctor?'

'Coming in for the day,' he said. 'I want her to hear
what Tommy has to say, too.'

At about the same time, across town, Lieutenant Stenner had gathered his task force in his office, a large, barren room totally devoid of personality or warmth. His large desk contained two telephones, a Rolodex, and two stacks of field reports – incoming on the left, outgoing on the right. His chair, rigid, straight-backed, without padding, looked about as comfortable as a rack. There were no photographs in this stark chamber, no books, no awards or citations on its walls, only two large cork-boards, one containing the photographs of the Rushman murder and xeroxed copies of several reports, the other a catalogue of all active cases and their current status. It was obvious that Stenner was a man so totally devoted to his duty that anything remotely personal was barred from the premises.

The task force consisted of Bill Danielson, the medical examiner, Dr Harvey Woodside, the obese and asthmatic coroner, and a team of six detectives headed by his personal assistant, Sergeant Lou Turner. They were all hand-picked veterans, a force of efficient experts, each of whom had earned citations and departmental awards for their competence and expertise. Jane Venable observed from an uncomfortable chair near the door.

Stenner removed his jacket, draped it over his chair and stood in the front of the room, bright red braces – the only colour in the room except for the blood in the coroner's photographs – supporting his dark blue trousers. He carefully adjusted his wire-rim glasses over his ears and rubbed his hands together.

'We are a week into this investigation,' he began in his flat, formal, no-nonsense voice. 'Let's see what we've got. Mister Danielson, will you please lead off?'

'Yes, sir.'

Danielson, a man in his late forties, was a devout fisherman with leathery, sun-stained skin and hard biceps which strained the sleeves of a pale blue shirt. His collar was open and his tie was pulled down. Originally from the south, his deep voice was a resonant composite of flat mid-west and soft, Georgia accents. He took a pencil from his shirt pocket and walked to the board of photographs. Stenner sat to one side and everyone in the room was poised with pens and clipboards, ready to take notes. Before he started, Danielson took out a cigar and started to peel off the cellophane wrapper.

'I'd prefer you don't smoke,' Stenner said. 'Stinks up my office for days.'

Danielson stared at him for a moment. 'It's your office, Abel,' he said and began to speak, emphasising his remarks by pointing at appropriate photos with his unlit stag.

'The victim, Bishop Rushman, experienced a total of seventy-seven different wounds. At least nine, possibly as many as twelve, of these wounds were fatal. Death could also have been caused by extreme exsanguination – that's bleeding to death – traumatic shock or sudden cardiac collapse, all due to the extensive damage of the wounds. An antemortem incision or a stab wound of the body that severs a large artery or vein or a highly vascular organ will produce profuse haemorrhaging, shock, and death within a short period of time – certainly the circumstance here.

'Wounds due to pointed and edged weapons are divided into four categories: stab wounds, incised wounds and cuts, chops, and therapeutic/diagnostic wounds, which are the type usually made by a physician or surgeon. This victim suffered stabs, incised cuts, chops – and possibly one therapeutic wound. In stab wounds, the most common weapon is the knife, in this case a kitchen knife of the carving variety with a twelve-inch blade, four inches in width at maximum. We can attribute all of the wounds in Bishop Rushman's body to that single weapon.

'Now in stabs, the length of the wound in the body exceeds its width on the surface of the skin, and the edges of the wounds are sharp, without abrasions or contusions. The size and shape of the stab wound in the skin is dependent on the configuration of the weapon, the direction of the thrust, the movement of the blade in the wound, the movement of the individual stabbed, and the state of relaxation or tension of the skin.' He pointed to several punctures in the photographs. 'The victim experienced thirty-seven separate and distinct stab wounds. Fourteen to the chest and upper torso, seven of which pierced either the heart or lungs, four to the left forearm and three to the right, three in his left palm, one in his right, eight to the abdomen and three to the right leg. The arm and palm wounds most likely were caused when the victim attempted to protect himself . . .'

'Excuse me, Bill,' Stenner said. 'But I think we can save the technical description for the trial. Right now I think we're interested in the number of wounds and cause of death, okay?'

'Right,' Danielson said. 'Incised wounds are those in which the instrument is inserted into the skin, then drawn along the body. We had twelve incised wounds the most serious of which was to the throat. This wound almost severed the head. Incised wounds of the neck are frequently extremely deep and often extend completely to the vertebral column. Fact is, the spinal column is probably the only thing that prevented this victim from bein' beheaded. It's difficult to tell which of these wounds were administered first but my educated guess is that the throat wound was the first and was sufficient to cause almost instant death. It's interesting that normally a throat wound this deep and complete would be performed from the back of the victim. This wound was administered from the front. Death from incised wounds of the neck may be due not only to exsanguination but to massive air embolus. Our X-ray of the chest for detection of air in the heart and venous system indicates this was the case.'

'So he probably saw it coming,' said Turner.

'I should think so,' Danielson answered. 'Frequently in throat wounds this massive, there is also cadaveric spasm – that's instant rigor mortis – but I don't believe that was true here . . .'

'Why not?' Venable asked.

'Because of the wounds to his forearms and particularly the palms. Obviously he was trying to protect himself.'

'Okay. Sorry to interrupt,' she said.

'Other incised wounds were to the face, scalp, chest and abdomen and on each leg. None of these were sufficient in itself to cause death.

'Finally we had cuts. Seventeen in all, most of which were superficial compared to the traumatic wounds. And then we had the removal of the genitalia which were placed in the victim's mouth. Incidentally, this amputation was performed with some degree of surgical skill, particularly when you consider it was done with a carvin' knife. That's the cut I believe approached diagnostic skill.'

'You think the perpetrator had some medical background?' Stenner asked.

'Possibly. Certainly he had some acquaintance with these procedures.'

'Humph,' Stenner responded.

'The bleeding was profound,' Danielson, whose train of thought stayed remarkably on course despite the interruptions, went on. 'The cadaver contained less than a pint of blood when we did the p.m. That's rare. Usually bleeding slows down when the organs stop functioning, particularly when the heart stops pumping. After that you get seepage. I believe that despite the severity of this attack, the victim may have survived longer than might normally be expected.'

Stenner asked, 'Did he put up much of a fight?'

'Judging from the wounds in the forearms and palms,

I would say yes. But not for long. This man died very quickly.'

'How about pain?' Woodside asked.

'Intense while it lasted.'

'How long do you think that was?' asked Stenner.

'The length of time it takes to die following an incised wound of the neck depends on whether the venous or arterial systems are severed and whether there is aeroembolism. In this case there was both. But judging from the wounds in his arms and palms, he could have survived for as long as a minute, minute and a half. If the throat wound was the first cut, I don't see how he could have been conscious for any longer than that – but it's possible he managed to fight for a minute or so.'

'How about that picture on the right. The back of his head. What is that?' one of the detectives asked.

'I was coming to that,' Danielson said. 'I have no explanation for this. Notice this photograph here, which was shot during the p.m.' He pointed to a shot of the back of Rushman's head. Just below the hairline, 'B32.156' was written in blood. 'I can't explain the numbers,' he concluded. 'But they were definitely printed with the Bishop's blood, as are the numbers "666" on his stomach – an obvious reference to the Devil.'

'Any other conclusions?' Stenner asked.

'Just that there was a certain amount of surgical skill in this job,' Danielson answered. 'Several of these wounds were very accurate, as far as hitting vital organs, causing trauma, what have you. And others were just random butchery. I also believe the killer was left-handed.'

'Thank you,' Stenner said and Danielson returned to his chair.

'Ms Venable?' Stenner asked, looking at the prosecutor.

'Nothing at this point,' she answered.

'Lou, what've you got for us?'

Turner went to the board and pinned a diagram of the murder scene on the board.

'We have the three interviews which are not admissible but do establish his story. He claims he came in through the front door here, heard something upstairs in the Bishop's apartment and went upstairs. He says he went into the Bishop's bedroom and that's where it gets crazy. Stampler says there was someone else in the room, someone he is afraid of, that he – Stampler – blacked out, and the next thing he remembers is leaving the bedroom. Claims he heard someone downstairs, panicked, ran down the hall here, out the back door and down the stairs, then saw a police car here in the alley so he ducked back into the church, ran down this corridor, and hid in the confessional where he was found.'

'What do you think?' Stenner asked.

'Pure, unadulterated bullshit. Excuse me, ma'am.'

Venable smiled. 'I've heard the word before, Sergeant. And I tend to agree with you.'

'We searched his stander but it had been ransacked before we got there,' he went on.

'By whom?' Venable asked.

'Other . . . uh, residents . . . of The Hollows. I doubt there was very much to take. We are also trying to locate his girlfriend . . .' he checked his notes, '. . . Linda ??? So far no luck on her, apparently she left about three weeks ago. There's no record of last names at Saviour House but we did get a possible fix on her. We think she's from someplace in Ohio, possibly Akron or Dayton. I can't blame her much for leaving, nobody could stand The Hollows for long.

'Our interrogations of his friends at the House and the staff at the church haven't turned up much of anything. They all tend to back up his contention that he and the Bishop were very close. This Stampler's a very smart kid, probably has an I.Q. in the 130s, 140s. He's from Crikside . . .' there was laughter in the room, '. . . that's

211

right *Crikside*, Kentucky, population about 250,' he said with a chuckle. 'Not too many phones in Crikside but we talked to several people there who know him. No record of any kind of abnormal behaviour there, no arrests.

'Apparently he was an independent kid. Father died of black lung, brother was killed in a car wreck. The mother died last year – about a year after he left home. She apparently suffered some mental disorder before she died but her doctor never diagnosed it. According to him, she was – and I quote – "lonely crazed".'

'Lonely crazed?' Woodside echoed.

'Lonely crazed,' Turner repeated. 'Moving along, he was an excellent student in grammar and high school and we're still missing a few months between the time he left there and showed up here in the city so we've still got homework to do on background, Lieutenant.'

'Any police record here, any record of any trouble before this?' Venable asked.

'Nothing so far,' Turner answered. 'He worked as an orderly at the hospital for a few months. Gets good marks from the staff there, but he quit, and then got a job cleaning up at the library, also good references from his supervisor there. He was taking extension courses at City College but we haven't pulled his transcript yet. That's about it so far.'

'Like to take a stab at the numbers on the back of his head?' Danielson asked.

'Not a chance,' Turner said with a smile. 'Anybody else?'

The other detectives all shook their heads.

'Thanks, Lou,' Stenner said. 'Woodside, you're up.'

Woodside hefted his enormous bulk from his chair and waddled to the front of the room.

'Without boring you with a lot of technical ying-yang – I'll save those for the big show – here's what we can prove,' he gasped with a rather smug smile. 'The knife taken from the perpetrator at the time of arrest is definitely the murder weapon. Blood on the perp's clothes and body is that of the victim. There was also some bits of the victim's flesh on the weapon *and* on Mister Stampler's clothing. Fingerprints on the doorjambs, walls and on the murder weapon match those of the perp. We also have fibres in his clothing that match fibres from the carpeting and we can track him from the scene of the crime to the kitchen by the blood stains on the carpeting. We also can show he left through the kitchen door and went down the back stairs, then re-entered the church through the back door and made his way through the corridor to the church and the confessional where he was found hiding.'

'How about the knife drawer?' Venable asked. 'Any prints?'

'Oddly enough, no,' Woodside said. 'We lifted some fibres off the drawer but we haven't matched them to anything yet.'

'It would be nice if we could prove he came in the back door and carried the knife to the bedroom,' Venable said. 'It would help to establish premeditation.'

'I'll keep that in mind,' Woodside said.

'Very good,' Stenner said. He looked back at Venable with what passed for a smile. 'Anything so far?' he asked.

'It's looking good,' Venable said, walking to the front of the room. 'But we need two more things to lock this case.'

'Motive?' said Stenner.

'That's right,' she answered. 'I feel sure the shrinks will let him stand trial but that doesn't rule out a possible insanity plea by Vail, it just means Stampler's competent to stand. Let's just hope our shrinks don't decide he's a mental case. Which reminds me, Vail's also got himself a shrink.'

She flipped open her notebook.

'Molly Arrington. Thirty-four, graduated *magna cum*

laude from Indiana State, been working with deviant mental cases at the Justine Clinic in Indiana for six years or so. She's supposed to be damn good, so you can bet she'll come up with something to counter the state psychs. Hopefully we can overcome that obstacle. But, if we get Stampler for trial what we need is a motive, Abel, something that'll put the jury's teeth on edge, otherwise Vail may try to use the nature of the crime itself to prove his client's a fruitcake.'

'Well, then,' Stenner said stoically, 'I guess we'll just have to find you a motive, Madam Prosecutor. What's the other thing?'

'Prove to me nobody else was in that room when the Bishop was sliced and diced,' she said.

At a few minutes before noon, Vail collected the defence team in his office. Molly Arrington was the last to arrive, looking harried and almost out of breath.

'This is Dr Molly Arrington, our resident psychiatrist,' Vail introduced her with a smile. 'Sorry to pull you back from Daisyland so soon but I wanted everybody to get to know you and I want you to hear what Tommy learned in Kentucky.'

'It's a pleasure to meet all of you,' she said quietly.

'I've already explained the rules of the game. We all say what we think, no holding back. Naomi, you've read the autopsy report. Anything we *don't* know at this point?'

'You noticed the "666" on Rushman's stomach?'

'Yeah,' said Vail. 'We'll have to check to see if Aaron or any of these kids was into Devil worship.'

'There's something else. We don't have this picture but according to the report "B32.156" is printed in the Bishop's blood under his hair on the back of his head.'

'B32.156? What the hell could that mean?'

Naomi shrugged. 'Who knows?'

'Probably a symbol,' Molly suggested.

'What kind of symbol?' the Judge asked.

'I don't know,' said Molly. 'Symbols are universal language. To the ancient Egyptians, the dung beetle or scarab was the symbol for resurrection. The cross is the symbol for Christianity. The triple six on the Bishop's stomach is a symbol for the devil. It's a conundrum. It's a symbol to whoever put it there.'

'There's something else we need to talk about,' Goodman said.

'Okay, shoot,' said Vail.

'It's these pictures,' said Goodman. 'I thought a lot about them on the trip. Seems to me they set up a pretty good case for premeditation.'

'Oh?' Vail said with a vague smile. 'Prove it to me.'

'First, the knife. The perp must've carried it from the kitchen. I mean, what would a carving knife be doing in the Bishop's bedroom?'

'I don't know,' Vail said. 'But it *could've* been in there. They have to prove the knife *wasn't* in the bedroom, we don't have to prove it was.'

'Pretty skimpy,' Goodman said.

'Tommy, at this point it's all skimpy but we have to start somewhere. Remember, we're working on the assumption he's innocent so everything we do must lead to that conclusion. It's their problem to prove he's guilty.'

'There's something else,' Tom said. He went to the photo board and perused the pictures, stopping at the photos of the bloody footprint and the medium shot of the kitchen with bloody smudges on the floor. Naomi walked over beside him.

'What do you see?' Vail asked.

'Well, he definitely went out the back door.' Naomi said.

'That's a given,' said Vail.

'Look at this close-up,' said Tom. 'That's not a footprint, it's a smudge. Now look at the other shot. The smudges end here, at the corner of the counter. No smudges the last six feet to the door.'

'So?'

'So my guess is, the smudges are from his socks. I think he had his shoes off. He comes in the kitchen door, takes off his shoes so the Bishop won't hear him, takes a carving knife out of the sliding drawer, walks eighteen feet down the hall, enters the bedroom and gives the Bishop forty whacks.'

'Seventy-seven, according to the autopsy,' Naomi said. 'Which, incidentally, is almost as bad as the photos.'

'We'll bypass it in testimony,' said Vail. 'Admit to the number of wounds, location, cause of death, et cetera. That'll take the edge off. The report will be admitted as an exhibit but most likely the jurors won't read it, they'll have other things to occupy their time.'

'Anyway, the shoes seem to indicate premeditation,' Goodman said. 'Not sudden anger, not temporary insanity. Careful planning and execution.'

'If in fact it happened that way,' Vail said.

Naomi said, 'How else could it have happened? He lied about it to you and the cops. Says he came in the front door and was scared by somebody when he left so he ran out the back. Obviously he came in the back door to start with.'

'Maybe. But they can't use the interviews and we don't have to. What we *do* have to find out is if he lied and why.'

'Why did he – if he did?' Goodman asked.

'Could have been confused. Scared. Intimidated,' said the Judge. 'Could be innocent but afraid to tell the truth because he looks guilty.'

Vail shrugged. 'Once again it depends on whether somebody else was really in that room with him. Look, suppose he came in the front way, took off his shoes and stuck them in his coat pocket or held on to them. When he left he got scared by somebody downstairs, went to the kitchen and then put his shoes back on before he went out in the cold.'

'C'mon,' Goodman said sceptically.

'Can you prove it didn't happen that way?' asked the Judge.

'No.'

'Then we're talking reasonable doubt and the shoes and bloody footprints become moot,' said Vail. 'Neither choice can be proven so either choice is possible.'

'And in most cases,' added the Judge, 'the jury will discount both rather than make an assumption on which way it really happened.'

'Same thing with the knife,' said Vail. 'We admit he left with it, we don't admit he brought it with him from the kitchen.'

'That's good,' the Judge said. 'Let them prove otherwise.'

'Fingerprints on the tray?' Goodman suggested.

'We'll know that when we see the forensics report.'

'Maybe he was wearing gloves,' Naomi suggested.

'Maybe he danced with the Bolshoi Ballet, too, so what?' the Judge offered.

'In other words, immaterial unless they can prove it,' explained Vail.

'Fibres from the gloves on the tray?'

'Once again, let's see what forensics says.'

'How do you think Shoat will rule on admitting the photographs?' Naomi asked.

Vail looked at the Judge and raised an eyebrow. Spalding scratched the bridge of his nose with a forefinger while he pondered the question.

'Tough call for him,' said Spalding. 'Personally, I think they're germane. But if he lets them in, it could become grounds for an appeal.' He thought a moment more. 'My guess is, he's going to permit them.'

'Jesus!' Naomi said.

'Hold on,' said Vail. 'It could work for us.'

'How?'

'Depends on motive,' the Judge suggested.

'Exactly,' Vail answered. 'You can bet the loyal opposition is working overtime on that one. If they don't come up with one, we can make a pretty good case for McNaghten by using the pictures.'

'Who's McNaghten? Molly asked.

The Judge offered the answer. 'McNaghten shot and killed a member of the British Parliament in 1843. The court found him not guilty by reason of insanity and the public went berserk so the Queen's Bench – that's the British appeals court – formulated the McNaghten Rule. It says that in order to acquit, it must be clearly proved that at the time the act occurred the accused was labouring under such a defect of reason, caused by a disease of the mind, that he did not know the nature and quality of the act he was committing.'

'Or even if he knew it,' Vail added, 'he didn't know it was wrong.'

'Translation: only a nut case would do something like that without a reason,' said Goodman. Molly winced at his use of the term 'nut case'.

Vail stood up and began pacing. 'Then we have the concept of "irresistible impulse",' he said. 'People who know the difference between right and wrong but can't control their actions because of some mental disorder. There are a lot of ways we can go with this – we've got to determine which is the most convincing – *and* the one that we can logically whip the D.A. with.' He smiled at Molly Arrington. 'Which brings us to the good doctor. I realise you've only talked to Aaron once but . . .'

'I'd like to defer until after I hear Mister Goodman's report,' she said.

'It's Tom,' Goodman corrected with a smile.

'Fair enough,' said Vail. 'How about it Tommy?'

'Look, I'm not a shrink, okay? It's just what I learned

and what I think. In fact, I'm not real sure what I think.'

'What the hell did you find out down there?' Vail asked.

'It's not that, exactly, it's just, uh . . .'

'Yeah . . . ?'

'I don't know, Marty. This kid really got fucked over when he was growing up. I've got mixed feelings about him.'

'We all do, Tommy.'

Goodman stared at the photographs as he talked, as if the horror of the pictures somehow grounded him in reality. He described Stampler as a misplaced child who had grown into a gifted but frustrated young intellectual, his accomplishments scorned by a stern and relentless father determined that the boy follow him into the hell of the coal mines and a mother who considered Aaron's education akin to devil's play; a boy whom the strap and the insults of his parents had done little to discourage from a bold and persistent quest for knowledge, abetted by Miss Rebecca, who saw in the lad a glimmering hope that occasionally there might be resurrection from a bitter life sentence in the emotionally barren and aesthetically vitiated Kentucky hamlet; a loner, attracted to both the professions and the arts, who had wanted – as do most young people at one time or another – to be lawyer, doctor, actor, and poet – and whose dreams were constantly thwarted except by his mentor, Rebecca.

And he talked about Rebecca, who appeared to be Crikside's only beacon, a lighthouse of lore and wisdom in an otherwise bleak and tortured place mired by its own stifling traditions; a woman whom some of the townsfolk regarded as a necessary evil; a woman who threatened the bigotry of their narrow and obdurate heritage, a notion possibly vindicated by Rebecca's 'education' of Aaron Stampler. And finally he talked about the sexual liberation of Aaron Stampler.

Goodman checked his little black notebook, the one in which he always kept copious notes.

'There're a couple of other things,' he said. 'On the table in the living room there were half a dozen pictures of Aaron at various ages – reading a book, sitting beside the creek, fishing, a class picture showing eleven children of various ages with Rebecca in the centre, all standing kind of stiffly in front of the schoolhouse, you know how those pictures go, they all looked so serious. But there were no pictures of Rebecca and Aaron except that group shot.

'He also marked a lot of quotations in books. He stuck slips of paper in them and wrote down the references. I wrote down two of them. "Evil comes to all us men of imagination wearing as its mask all the virtues." And there was a Chinese proverb: "There are two perfect men – one dead, the other unborn." '

Goodman had written some questions to himself. *Was Stampler physically or sexually abused in the legal sense? Was his sexual orientation as perverse as it might seem? Did these two factors alone contribute to an inner rage that led Aaron to Bishop Rushman's bedroom and the mutilation killing of the prelate?*

Perhaps, he suggested, Molly Arrington could answer these questions.

'You know what I'm beginning to wonder?' Tommy concluded.

'What?' asked Vail, who had listened without emotion, his eyes narrowed, as Tom Goodman detailed the short, unhappy life of Aaron Stampler.

'If maybe he didn't escape from one set of frustrations in Crikside and end up with a different kind of frustration here. Maybe . . . maybe it all just fell in on him.'

'You think he did it?'

'Christ, I don't know, Marty. That kind of background? Shit, that's enough to screw up anybody's head.'

Vail didn't answer. He turned instead to Molly.

'Okay, Doc, you're up,' he said.

'Let's watch the tape first,' she said. Her voice suddenly became sterner, authoritative, commanding.

And Vail thought, my God, she's taking over the meeting.

'Okay,' he said and wheeled over to the tape machine and slipped Molly's video interview into the slot.

'Before it starts,' Goodman said, 'how can you tell somebody's got a mental disorder?'

'It's a very structured procedure just like medicine,' Molly said. 'You look for symptoms, manifestations, influences – the same way a physician identifies physical diseases.'

'Is there some kind of standard for all this?' Vail asked.

'Yes. It's called the *Diagnostic and Statistical Manual of Mental Disorder*. DSM 3 for short. The American Psychiatric Association publishes it and it's our bible. It's to psychiatry what *Gray's Anatomy* is to physiology.'

'I know this is a dumb question,' said Naomi, 'but why do they always lie on a couch with you sitting behind them?'

'Simply to put the subject at ease. Not being able to see the analyst minimises distraction. It's like they're talking to themselves rather than conversing with someone. Removes the personal barrier.'

'What's the ultimate objective?' Vail asked.

'Free association. Encourage the subject to concentrate on inner experiences . . . thoughts, fantasies, feelings . . . hopefully create an atmosphere in which the patient will say absolutely everything that comes to mind without fear of being censored or judged.'

'How does that help you?' Naomi asked.

'Eventually it brings on a state of regression. They remember things from the deep past – traumatic events, painful encounters – very clearly. The re-experience and the fears and feelings that go with it are all clues to the

221

diagnosis. This first session was pretty much surface stuff, but it was an excellent beginning.'

They all watched and listened in silence until the tape ended. Nobody said anything for a few moments.

'Well, Molly, what do you think so far?' Martin asked.

She sat with her hands folded in her lap and said nothing for perhaps three minutes. *What did they want to know? Did he do it and if he did, why? Is he a cold-blooded killer or is his reality an illusion? Is he puppet or puppeteer?*

'I'm not sure yet,' she said finally. 'As I see it, we're all faced with the same challenge, how to save Aaron Stampler from the electric chair. The difference is, your approach involves legal strategy and tactics, mine involves scientific logic which can sometimes take years, if it ever gets solved at all.'

'And we have fifty-one days left,' Goodman said.

'*Any* conclusions yet?' Vail asked.

She shook her head.

'Nothing at all?' said Vail.

'I'm not ready yet.'

'Look, we're getting mixed signals on this kid,' said Martin. 'He says he got laid when he was sixteen. The teacher says she seduced him two years earlier. He says his brother was killed in an accident, we hear differently.'

'It didn't sound like a seduction,' said Tommy. 'It sounded more like . . .'

'More like what, Tommy? Bottom line – a woman in her thirties balled a fourteen-year-old kid.'

'I know, I know, but she made it sound, I don't know, very natural.'

'Yeah, well I'm sure our prosecutor won't look on it as natural. She'll paint this woman as a pervert and worse. We can't even subpoena her. If she *volunteered* to testify, Venable would have her in chains for raping a juvenile before she got off the witness stand. Hell, even if her testimony could help save him, I'd advise her to take the fifth. We couldn't let her incriminate herself.'

'Excuse me,' Molly said stiffly. 'That's tactics and that's your problem not mine. It's also meaningless at this point. Perhaps he seduced her. Or maybe the event is so painful he doesn't want to admit it. The brother and his girlfriend? It's a local myth, why is it so odd that he should choose to perpetuate it? As far as the quotes go,' she shrugged, 'they probably appealed to him. My guess is, his I.Q. will go off the charts. For God's sakes, he read the Bible when he was six years old. He probably should have been in Harvard med school instead of cleaning up the library.'

The Judge smiled. Well, he thought, it appears we have a live one. He said, 'I take that to mean you want to get back to Daisyland?'

'Tomorrow,' she answered. 'I have a lot of work to do.' She turned to Tommy. 'I do want to congratulate you, Tom. You learned a great deal in two days.'

'None of which seems to matter.' There was irritation in his voice.

'In time,' she said with a smile and then added, 'I think you should try to find the girl.'

'Stampler's girl, Linda?'

'Yes.'

'She probably split,' said Goodman. 'A lot of kids clean up at Saviour House and then go back where they came from.'

'To what?' Molly said. 'Whatever ran them off in the first place? Do you think Aaron would have gone back to Crikside?'

'So maybe she didn't go home,' Vail said. 'Maybe she's still around someplace. Maybe she's hiding out.'

'Maybe she knows what really happened,' Tom said.

'Stampler says she left three weeks ago,' said Naomi.

'Maybe he's covering for her,' Tom suggested.

'You think *she* killed Rushman?' said Naomi.

'Not necessarily,' said Vail. 'Maybe they did it together. Or maybe she was there. Maybe he's really afraid for her, not himself.'

'You're reaching, Marty.'

'Did we ever have a case when we weren't reaching?'

Tom laughed. 'Well, now that you mention it . . .'

'The Doc says find her, Tommy,' said Vail. 'Go find her.'

Eighteen

The street was deserted. He could hear the rumble of traffic a few blocks away on the highway. A freezing breeze rattled the dead limbs in the trees that lined Banner Street. Otherwise it was quiet. Even the kids had deserted the brown Chevy near the corner.

When he entered Saviour House, he heard the hesitating notes of a saxophone as someone upstairs picked away at 'Misty'. He found Maggie in the TV room. She was pleasant but an hour of interrogation brought him no closer to solving the riddle of Aaron Stampler than when he arrived.

'I'm sorry,' Maggie said. 'You got to understand, there's a lotta trust among us here. Nobody wants to talk about anybody else. It would kind of, I don't know, break the spell. It's the one thing that the Bishop was real good about, protecting people. That's why we don't give away last names or hometowns.'

'I respect their privacy, Maggie. Thanks for your help.'

'But if something comes up that might help, I'll call you,' she said.

'What are you, the den mother?'

'I was going to be the next mascot of the altar boys,' she said with a melancholy smile.

As he approached the VW, he saw a slip of paper flapping under his windshield wiper. It was a folded paper napkin, with a message written on it in a small, delicate hand:

'Alex. B Street. Batman and Robin.'

Goodman looked up and down the street but there was no one in sight. He got in his car, cranked it up, and sat for a minute, waiting for the ancient heater to warm up. As he looked back at Saviour House he saw the curtains moving in a second-storey window.

'Shit,' he said. And headed for B Street.

In years gone by, B Street had been one of the more fashionable shopping districts of the city. Dowagers and debutantes arrived in chauffeur-driven limousines to be fawned over by eager merchants who caressed mink and ermine pelts, wafting the soft fur with their garlic breath, or flattering throats and fingers with dazzling creations described by colour, point, and carat. The shops had retreated to skyscrapers with breathtaking views, indoor parking lots and uniformed guards at the elevators, leaving behind four blocks of dismal storefronts, most of them boarded up except for bars, where burned-out strippers waddled dispassionately on littered runways, and pawnshops whose barred windows flaunted Saturday night specials, retirement wrist-watches and guitars.

The strip was convenient to a ramp leading to the main suburban four-lane and had become a popular quick stop for bisexual and homosexual businessmen on their way home from the office, a minute market of young hustlers with something for every taste and desire.

Goodman swung into the line of two-door Caddys and bottom-of-the-line Mercedes cruising the wretched street while their jittery drivers checked the meat market; nail-studded leather boys, college types in blazers and polo shirts, acned pre-teens, transvestites, all displaying their wares in a strolling carnival that reached its peak between the hours of six and eight. In a kind of perverse reversal of custom, some even had pimps who flashed obscene pictures of their clients and made front-end deals with the trade.

'Batman and Robin.' Pimp and hustler. Robin would have to be Alex. But who was Alex?

The procurers walked down the line of cars, flashing their pictures, making their pitches . . . 'Hey cutie, how 'bout this? Twelve inches all for you . . . Catch him while he's hot, leaving for La La land next week . . . Lookit the tongue on my boy, huh? Lookit at that red banana . . .' to which Goodman answered, over and over, 'Lookin' for Batman and Robin . . .' and finally, after a half-hour of degrading interrogation, pay dirt.

He was a hulking cretin; bald and bullet-headed, diamond stud in one ear; thick, black moustache waxed on the ends; heavy rings flashing from thick fingers; a black leather cape over neanderthal shoulders; and, of course, a mask, one of those thin, black papier mâché Hallowe'en masks.

'Batman?'

'Who else, lover-boy?'

'Lookin' for Robin.'

'Yer new, aincha?'

Goodman sighed. 'What do you want, a recommendation?'

'Sensa humour, huh?' He looked over the battered VW. 'I ain't sure this peanut's big enough fer two.'

'Why don't we give it a try? Dinner's waiting.'

Batman's eyes narrowed behind the slits in the mask. He didn't like banter.

'It's fi'ty, sevenee-five you do him. I ain't sure you can bear the freight.'

Goodman held up a hundred dollar bill in his right hand, holding it over the shotgun seat, away from the window.

'Wanna bet?'

Batman's eyes twinkled. Money talked on B Street.

'Follow me. Next alley down. You got a heater in this thing?'

'Who needs a heater.'

Batman laughed and led the way. Goodman turned down a dark, narrow alleyway between two brick buildings, eased around an overflowing dumpster and past garbage cans bulging with trash, empty bottles and cans and refuse that reeked of maggots.

Marty, you son of a bitch, you're gonna pay for this trip.

Batman waved him deeper into the alley, then held up a hand. Goodman stopped. The big man knocked on a sagging door and a moment later, Robin stepped out, squinting into the harsh glare of the headlights.

'Kill the lights,' said Batman.

Alex was tall and reed-thin. Dirt-matted blond hair curled down from under a dark pea hat and over the shoulders of a scarred, tan suede jacket. His shoulders were hunched against the cold and his hands were buried in the side pockets of the jacket. The beginnings of a young beard pocked his jaw like tufts of grass. Dull eyes appraised the darkness.

'We gonna do it in that?' he asked, nodding towards the VW.

Goodman got out of the car, his hands hanging loose at his sides.

'We're not gonna do it at all,' he said. 'You're Alex, aren't you?'

'Motherfucker,' Batman growled. The kid turned and bolted towards the door. Batman lunged towards Goodman, a fist the size of a grapefruit cocked by his ear. Goodman blocked the roundhouse punch with his right forearm and stepped in close, smacking him under the chin with the flat of his left hand. The big man was jarred, reeled back against the brick wall. Alex tried to get around Goodman but the ex-fighter lashed out with a leg and swept the skinny kid's feet from under him. He sprawled face down on the alley floor.

Batman grabbed a piece of pipe from a garbage can and swung it back with both hands. Before he could complete his swing, Goodman charged him and hit him under the nose with a vicious left jab, then another and another. The big man's head snapped with each blow as he reeled backwards, trying to block the punches. Then Goodman feinted with his right, stepped in and sent him sprawling backwards with a vicious left uppercut. Batman flew backwards knocking over a garbage can and fell flat on his back among the debris. Blood spurted from his shattered nose. Whimpering, he rolled over on his side holding his face with both hands to stem the blood.

'M'nose,' he cried. 'Yuh broke m'nose.'

'You stand up again and I'll break both your Goddamn kneecaps,' Goodman growled.

He heard a crash behind him and saw Alex duck into the building. Goodman followed, darting through the door and crouching just inside. It was dark as a dungeon except here and there where light filtered through broken windows and fissures in the walls. The first floor was a *mélange* of disrepair. Goodman was suddenly back in Vietnam, hunched in a dark jungle of broken-out walls, fallen joists, and collapsed ceilings. He reverted back to his old training, squatting still as a statue, his ears keened for the slightest sound, his eyes scrutinising the grim interior for signs of movement. He waited patiently. Two or three minutes passed and he heard a board creak to his left. His muscles tensed. Then he saw vague movement in a streak of light. Alex was moving stealthily through the ruined interior. He followed quietly, keeping to the shadows and closing the distance between him and his quarry. The boy suddenly saw him and bolted. Goodman charged behind him, snatched up a shattered two by four, and skimmed it back-hand towards the dodging figure. The board hit Alex behind the knees and he staggered and plunged forward through a plaster and plywood wall section and fell face down in a billowing nimbus of dust. Goodman leaped through the hole, grabbed Alex by the collar, dragged him to his feet and slammed him against the brick exterior wall. The kid's breath shushed out of him like wind rushing out of a punctured balloon. The kid stared wide-eyed at him, his eyes darting around the dismal space. Goodman grabbed the one remaining ear-ring.

'Chill out, you little bastard, or I'll rip your other ear off,' he snarled. He reached in his pocket, took out the ear-ring he had torn from the boy's ear at Aaron's stander and held it in his palm in a sliver of light.

'No!' the kid squealed.

'We're going to have a talk,' Goodman said. 'Or we're going to dance. *Capish*, Boy Wonder?'

'Please don't hurt me,' the boy whined.

Goodman jabbed a forefinger in his chest. 'What were you after in Aaron's stander?' he demanded.

'Uh, uh . . . I thought, y'know . . . maybe he had a . . . a radio or sompin' hid out . . .'

Goodman tugged on the ear-ring and the boy's face squinched up in pain.

'How'd you know I was there?'

'I live there. The first stander on the right. I heard you talking to the old crock when you come in. I figured maybe you knew sompin' so I followed you down there.'

'What? What did you figure I knew?'

'You know . . . maybe Aaron told you he had sompin' stashed.'

'Bullshit.' He pulled harder on the ear-ring.

'Owww . . . hey, I . . .'

'Try again?'

'You don't know jack shit, man,' Robin whined. 'You ain't even a cop.'

'I'll tell you what I do know. I know your name's Alex and I know I got one of your ear-rings and I'm about to take the other one.'

He pulled on the ear-ring and Robin's earlobe stretched a half inch. The kid screamed.

'Don't hurt me. Please don't hurt me,' he begged.

'Then get level with me.'

'He had some books . . .'

Goodman pulled harder.

'Ow! God, please, man . . .'

'One more lie and I take off the ear.'

'It was a television tape!' he cried.

'Of what?'

'You don't know?'

'Just answer my question, what was on the tape?'

'It was a show!'

'What kind of show?'

'Altar boy shit.'

'What do you mean, altar boy shit?'

'You really *don't* know, do you?'

Goodman leaned very close to him, pulled hard on the ear-ring and held it. The boy writhed with pain. 'You got one more answer, Alex.'

'Porn,' he yelled.

Goodman snapped back with surprise. He eased off the ear slightly. 'Porn?' he said.

'Yeah. A fuck tape.'

Goodman let go of the ear-ring and leaned back, staring at Alex.

The boy was breathing heavily. 'An altar boy special.'

Goodman could hardly suppress his shock. 'Keep talking,' he said.

'We'd go to this place on Prairie, it was this old building the church owned and he had it set up with the bed and all and we'd do it and he'd direct. Like Hollywood, y'know? Do this, do that. He'd say who'd go first. Sometimes we'd all do it, sometimes just one. Then, whenever he got steamed up, he'd turn off the machine and go at it himself.'

'Who's he?' Goodman asked.

The boy's smile was twisted. 'Who else?' he said. 'The Bishop.'

'Bishop *Rushman*?'

'Yeah. The Saint himself. Called it gettin' rid of the Devil. Ain't that a crock?'

231

Goodman was incredulous. 'And you were one of the altar boys?'

'Yeah. Me, Aaron, Billy and Peter.'

'Just four of you?'

'You don't think we were the first ones, do you? You can bet there were others before us — but ain't nobody gonna admit it. You think anybody's gonna admit that? Shit, who'd believe us anyway?'

'Why would Aaron want the tape?'

'Because his girl was on it, man.'

'Linda?'

'Sure. She was the bird.'

'Let me get this straight.' Goodman's head was spinning. 'There were four of you, the Bishop, and one girl?'

'That's the way it went.'

'And you were all at the Bishop's the night he was killed?'

Fear crept into Alex's eyes. 'We didn't have no meeting that night, man. We broke up like a month ago.'

'It's in the Bishop's date book.'

'I don't now nothin' about that. Maybe he was gettin' together a new group. Look, first Aaron and Linda took a hike. Then I quit, okay? Then Peter and Billy Jordan split town about two weeks ago. Right after that, Linda bagged Aaron and took off. Maybe it was a new bunch, y'know. Shit, maybe Aaron was recruitin' for the old bastard.'

And Maggie was going to be the next 'mascot'. My God!

'So you didn't know for sure whether Aaron had the tape?'

'All I know, the last time I seen Aaron, which was a week or so ago, he said he was goin' up to the Bishop's pad and snatch the tape because he was worried about Linda bein' on it.'

'There was only one tape?'

'Yeah. We'd do it and then the next meeting, he'd

show the tape and we'd all get off on it.' He sneered. 'The Bishop was big on gettin' rid of the Devil. Then he'd erase the tape.'

'So you never had a meeting after that last time? Never actually saw that tape?'

'That's right. Aaron moved in with Linda right after that and I figured fuck it, long's I was into that shit I might as well get paid for it.'

'You're going to have to testify to all this at Aaron's trial, you know.'

'*Bullshit*, man. You think I'm gonna tell anybody that? I'll say I don't know shit. Nobody's gonna admit that. You think Linda or Billy or Peter's gonna own up? Think a-fuckin'-gain.'

'It could save Aaron's life.'

'I don't owe Aaron shit. Smart little asshole, always thought he was better'n the rest of us.'

'We'll find somebody who will and you'll get pegged anyway.'

'Yeah? What're you gonna do, put a fuckin' ad in the paper? You got no last names, no hometowns. You can't prove shit without the tape and anyways, the Bishop ain't in the show. It was Billy Jordan, Peter and Linda that last time and they're long gone.'

'Why would Aaron do that to the Bishop? I mean chop him up like that?'

'How should I know?'

'Did he have a bad temper?'

'Not exactly. He had a razor strap and if we couldn't get it up, he'd whack us one, tell us the devil had his hand on us.'

'I was talking about Aaron.'

'Oh, I thought you meant His Excellency,' he said and shrugged. 'Wasn't any worse'n anybody else. Shit, he was teacher's pet. Him and the Bishop was tight as a fist. Maybe the old man got himself a new boy, pissed Aaron off.'

'Enough to stab him seventy-seven times?'

'*Holy shit*!'

'And cut off his dick and stuff it in his mouth?'

'Holy *shit*! I didn't think he was that weird.'

'Well, how the hell weird was he?'

'Y'know, quotin' shit all the time, actin' like some kind of genius. He always knew everything.'

'Did it disturb him? That Linda was making it with the other guys?'

'I don't think so. I always figured he kind of got off on it. Hey, we all did once we got used to it.'

'Jesus!' said Goodman, half aloud. 'When did this all start?' he asked.

'Almost two years ago.'

'The girl couldn't have been more than . . .'

'She just turned fourteen,' Alex said, finishing the sentence for him.

'And the rest of you?'

'Aaron was seventeen. Me and Peter was fifteen. I think Billy Jordan was the oldest. Eighteen maybe. He's a big guy, has a huge wacker – a nine incher – I guess that's why the old man kept him around, even when he was twenty.'

'What makes you think you weren't the first ones?'

'Hey, the old Bishop knew what he was doing, man . . .' He lowered his eyes suddenly. 'Uh . . . that first time with us, that wasn't the first time for him.'

So intent was Goodman on his conversation with Alex he did not hear Batman until he was twelve feet away. He spun around to see the hulking figure advancing towards him grasping a four-foot slab of wood like a baseball bat over one brutal shoulder. Instead of backing off, Goodman charged into him. The big man made the same mistake he had made the first time. He swung the weapon too late. Goodman moved inside the arc, knocked his arm askew, and shifting sideways, slammed his foot into Batman's kneecap. The big man roared like a wounded lion. The slab spun away into the darkness and without thinking, Goodman threw a hard right straight to his jaw. Pain streaked all the way to Goodman's shoulder. The big man grunted, fell straight backwards, hit the floor and lay spread-eagled.

'You never learn, do you?' he said to the fallen pimp.

He heard sounds behind him and whirled in time to see Alex – a fleeting figure – dashing through shards of light as he ran to the rear of the building and crashed through a door. Goodman did not follow him. He had other things on his mind.

Half an hour later, an angry but excited Goodman was in a phone booth, checking the yellow pages. He found an electronics store on Plains Avenue, drove by it and bought a fresh video tape. When he got back in the car, he tore the cellophane wrapper off, reached behind him and slipped the tape under his belt in the back, pulling his sweater down over it. Then he went back to Lakeview and headed towards the cathedral.

The cop at the door to the Bishop's apartment had moved an overstuffed chair from the living room and was slouched in it with one leg over the arm rest, reading a paperback book.

'Hey,' Goodman said. 'I came to check the premises. Here's my ticket.' He held up the subpoena. The cop stared at it.

'A little late, ain't it?'

'Yeah. Guess we both got bad hours, huh? The D.A. finished in here?'

'How the hell would I know? And who are you?'

Goodman took out his wallet and flipped it open to his licence.

'Goodman,' he said. 'P.I. I'm with the defence.'

The cop looked at him with disdain. 'You must have a bad time sleepin' nights,' he said. 'They shoulda blew the little bastard away when they found him, save every-body a lotta trouble.'

'In the church?' Goodman answered innocently.

'You know what I mean, wise guy. Figger of speech,' he said as he reluctantly cut the paper seal with a pocket knife and unlocked the door.

'Sure. What the hell, I'm just a workin' stiff like you, right? Everybody's gotta make a living.'

'Why don't you become a dog catcher?' the cop said nastily.

Goodman bristled but his voice remained cheery. 'Same reason you're not out there freezin' your stonies on the bricks, 'stead of sitting in an easy chair, reading and mooching off the church.'

'Okay, wise guy, raise 'em, I gotta pat you down.'

Goodman raised his hands. The cop started under his armpits and did a cursory frisk. He didn't even touch Goodman's back. When the cop was finished, Goodman entered the room. It smelt of old incense, Pine Sol and stale air. The cop started in behind him and Goodman stopped.

'I won't need any help,' he said. The procedure permit-ted him to conduct his search alone.

'You don't take nothin', you don't move nothin', you don't leave nothin',' the cop snapped.

'Right.'

'We'll just leave the door open,' the cop said.

'Whatever makes you happy.'

Goodman walked into the room and stood with his hands in his pockets, surveying the damaged premises. Several swatches had been cut from the carpet. The walls were still streaked with splattered blood which had turned an ugly shade of brown. Goodman took out his notebook, make a quick sketch of the room, walked past the bed and stared down at the outline chalked into the enormous, hardened blot where blood had soaked into the carpet. The table and lamp still lay where they had fallen in the corner. A sudden chill passed through Goodman and he shook it off. This was a room still oppressed by pain and fear, by hate, anger and retribution.

To Goodman, there was always something incomplete, yet eerily personal, about the scene of a homicide, a sense that somehow the victim would not really be dead until the place was cleaned and painted and restored to its old order and until all evidence of violence had been eradicated. The chalk figure on the floor seemed to be part of the victim's persona. Such a radical termination was like the pause in a conversation with the rest of the sentence still trapped somewhere in the room, waiting to be said.

Subconsciously, his imagination played out the Cardinal's final brutal moments, terror ash-like in his mouth as life was carved from his body. And while Goodman now held the victim in utter disdain, he wondered whether Cardinal Rushman realised, in those last fleeting moments of life, that his life had been a lie and that he was stepping across the threshold of hell.

Goodman shook off his thoughts and turned to the closet. He entered it, saw the tape machine and recorder in the corner. He fingered through robes hanging neatly from padded hangers, looked behind them, checked the stainless steel shoe rack, the drawers of shirts and sweaters. In the rear of the closet, he found the tapes, two stacks piled neatly on a shelf near the recorder. There were maybe thirty of them. His eyes raced down the labels, checking the handwritten titles, most of them labelled 'Sermon' and the date. Then near the bottom of the stack, his eyes froze on one label.

'Altar boys. 9/2/83.'

There it was! He stared at it for several seconds, moved back along the rows of clothes and looked out the door. The cop was still reading. He slipped on a pair of nylon gloves, returned to the stack of tapes, knelt down and carefully peeled the label off the altar boy tape and placed it on the new tape, smoothing it out with his thumb. Then he edged the altar boy tape out a few inches and pulled it sharply free of the stack. The stack dropped down with a thunk. He heard the guard's chair creak and reaching up, flipped a couple of tapes off the top of the stack on to the floor, and dropped the new tape among them.

He slipped the altar boys tape under his belt and pulled the sweater down over it as he knelt down to pick them up. The guard appeared in the doorway to the closet.

'What the fuck?' he said with irritation.

'It's okay,' Goodman said, replacing the tapes back on top of the stack. 'Just a little clumsy.'

'Yeah, well watch it, huh. Break sumpin', I gotta take the heat.'

'I'll be more careful,' Goodman said.

Goodman returned to the bedroom with the guard, who went back to his chair and resumed his reading. Goodman went into the bathroom, opened cabinets and slammed them, rattled around, making noise and whistling. He quietly unlocked the bathroom window and swung it out, leaned over and looked down. The garbage can was directly under him. He quickly pulled out the tape, aimed it and let it go. He pulled the window shut before it hit and went back into the hall, notebook in hand, jotting down aimless notes.

'Get everything you need?' the cop asked.

'I think so. This the kitchen down here?'

'Yeah.'

'I'll just check it out,' Goodman said. 'Maybe go down and look over the grounds. Want to let me out.'

'Okay. Need a flashlight? It's black as a nightmare down there.'

'Got one,' he said, taking it out of his pocket.

He did a cursory check of the kitchen, then went out the back door and stared down the stairs.

'Wonder why he ran back inside the church?' Goodman said, half to himself.

'The way I heard it, the beat cop happened to be walkin' past in the alley back there. Stroke a luck, otherwise the little shit woulda been on the street and gone.'

'I'll just go down and look around. You can lock up behind me. Thanks.'

'Yeah. Colder'n a witch's tit out there.'

'You can say that again.'

He went down the wooden stairs to ground level, strolled aimlessly a while, then walked around the corner to the can and reached in, rustling around the loose papers. He felt the tape, quickly removed it from the can and slipped it back under his belt.

Ten minutes later he was on his way to Vail's house.

Nineteen

Molly's bedroom door was open and she was sitting at the small desk in her room, writing notes and leafing through a half-dozen thick, official-looking books, when she heard the tapping and the indistinct sound of singing. She stuck a pencil between the pages to mark her place and went cautiously down the hall. The sound was coming from the second-floor den. A door led to a large closet adjacent to it. It had been converted into a mini greenhouse with a six-foot long zinc-lined table with a small sink at one end. A row of grow lights plugged to an automatic timer created the illusion of daylight twelve hours a day. Beneath the lights was a row of small, delicate blue flowers surrounded by fern-like leaves. On the other side of the narrow room was a plastic-covered cubicle, its sides misty with man-made dew. Four puny orchids were suspended from the ceiling inside the tiny hothouse. Vail was pruning the flowers and doing a sub-dued tap dance and singing along. 'Me and my shadow, strolling down the avenue . . .' He looked up, embarrassed to see Molly standing in the doorway.

'I'm sorry,' she said. 'I didn't hear you come up.'

'You had your nose in the books.'

'Just trying to make some sense out of all this. Is this your hobby?'

He seemed embarrassed and even a bit annoyed, as if she had invaded his private space, but he recovered quickly and nodded.

'I started out growing orchids,' he said. 'Not too successfully so far. They're pretty skimpy.'

'What are these?' she asked, nodding towards the blue flowers.

'They're called blue belles,' he said. 'Not the kind of bells that ring, belles like beautiful young ladies. They're winter flowers, grow wild. This is my fourth shot trying to cultivate them. I may just have beat the odds this time.'

'Odds?'

'They don't like a false habitat,' he said. 'Probably yearn for real sunshine.'

She looked around the small alcove. 'So you're a closet horticulturist,' she said with a chuckle.

'Don't tell anybody.' He smiled and winked at her. 'My mother loved blue belles. They grew along the bank of the river. I used to pick them and take them home to her and she'd put them on the piano and sometimes I'd hear her talking to them. "This is Mozart," she'd say, and tell them a little bit about him while she played.'

'Is that why you grow this particular variety?'

'I suppose.'

'What was she like?'

'Actually she gave up a spot in the city symphony to marry my dad. Moved to a little town and taught piano. Every day she taught piano. I don't think she liked teaching as much as she just loved the piano. Kids came with the territory.'

'What did your dad do?'

'School teacher. He was also the band master in the high school. They both were musicians but my mother was the one with the talent. My dad, he was kind of a Henry Hill. He liked the flash more than the music.'

'Sounds like a happy family.'

He looked at her for a long time before he answered, 'Not particularly. She was an alcoholic. Died when I was in the eighth grade.'

'I'm sorry.'

'Why? It wasn't your fault.'

'That's a funny answer,' she said.

'Impertinent, probably. It's just that . . . it's always

241

struck me as strange. I say my mother's dead and some-body says "I'm sorry" yet they didn't know her.'

'I was sorry for *you*,' she said. 'She was obviously important to you. I'm sorry for your pain.'

The answer seemed to surprise him and it was a moment or two before he answered, 'That's a lovely thought. Thank you.' He wafted his hand gently across the tops of the blue flowers and watched the tiny petals fidget, his mind drifting with the tiny blossoms.

The past fall, Vail had returned to his home for the first time in ten years, a trip he had avoided since he had started his legal practice in the city. He chose to make the three-hour drive at night and he set off on the journey with enormous apprehension. The first two and a half hours were pleasant enough, it was the last thirty minutes, after he entered what was ironically known as Rainbow Flats, that the bad memories began, rushing at him from the dark. Old names and faces he thought he had purged forever nibbled at his brain. Worst of all was Rainbow Flats itself.

A century and a half before, some half-lost exploring party had stumbled across the vast ridge that sprawled for almost fifty miles, defining the banks of the white-water river. Elm, oak and pine trees abounded. Wild flowers etched the shores of the river. Deer and bear scurried from their watering places as the party invaded their land. What was truly ironic was that it would take so little time for the name to be defiled.

He was forewarned, his headlights leading him on the grim and baleful drive over a weary, potted two-laner. Then he saw the glow on the horizon. The stench came next, before he burst from the state park into the open place. Forms began to materialise through smoke and steam. Then the sounds began. He seemed to grow a little smaller, to shrink into himself as he wound past great chemical plants, paper mills, steel furnaces and oil refineries. Nothing had changed, the place had simply spread like a scourge on the land. The vast and violent landscape was a shadowy, disfigured inferno beyond Dante's wildest imagination. It assaulted and numbed all his senses.

Tall stacks spewed clouds of acid smoke into the vulnerable sky. Steel mills belched up blinding balls of flame that seemed to feed on the chemicals swirling through the air. Gases bubbled up through murky rivers and streams. Hissing sounds and clanging sounds and roaring sounds and whistles screaming and horns howling and heavy iron wheels screeching on steel rails all created man-made thunderclaps. And from it all, from this holocaust of America at work, foul odours burned his nose and eyes. The earth around him seemed to have been reduced to a great, rotting cadaver.

It went on mile after mile: the blazing lights, the belching furnaces, the cacophony of progress, the disgusting stink of success. Mile after mile without a tree or blade of grass to hide the copper-stained earth. Mile after mile without seeing a soul. It was as if he had stumbled on some burned-out, robot-driven planet frantically manufacturing its own destruction.

The 'industrial park', as it was called by the Chamber of Commerce, ended when the river curved under the highway bridge, forming a natural barrier between the Flats and Oakdale, the town of his birth. On impulse he suddenly pulled off the road and stopped in a turnaround just before the bridge. He got out of the car, leaned on a fender, and lit a cigarette, as he stared across the river.

From this vantage point, nothing seemed to have changed. The tannery, a long, low warehouse of a building, still dominated the river-front on the south side of Bridge Road and the drab brick building housing the shoe mill, commanded the north side.

This was the place that had spawned Martin Vail and nurtured him to manhood – and which he had finally fled, abandoning family and friends and disdaining its tarnished heritage. The past was a kaleidoscope, its fragments tumbling through his mind; the jaunty brass of the high school band practising on the afternoon of a football game; appraising the cheerleaders and particularly Elaine Golanka's long, lovely legs from the sanctity of a football huddle; the smell of boiled coffee in his grandmother's kitchen; the fearful anticipation of his first kiss in the back seat of Paul Swain's Chevy; the excitement of testing the ice on the river after the first freeze of the year and the muffled hiss of the first snow fall; the stark finality of his mother's funeral; the joyful cheers as Dr Nolan handed out the last diploma on commencement day; the wondrous gaze of Pal, his first puppy and the dreadful hurt in his chest when he realised it was Pal who lay crushed under the wheels of a semi up on River Street; the smell of sour milk at the end of the night when he worked in Jesse Kraft's ice cream shop; the smell of Emily Grantham's hair and how hard her nipples were and how warm her thigh was up under her skirt; that awful heart-stabbing moment when she told him she thought she was pregnant and the rush of relief when her period finally started.

Now he had been drawn back here to say goodbye to the woman who had put him through college and urged, almost demanded, that he leave Oakdale and never come back. Catlain Vail. Ma Cat, his grandmother.

A police car pulled up beside him and he shielded his eyes against the harsh beam of a flashlight.

'Need some help?' a youthful voice asked pleasantly.

'No thanks, just taking in the view,' he answered.

'Better put your flasher on,' the cop suggested. 'Those big trucks really come barrelling through here.'

'Thanks, I'll do that,' Vail answered.

The cop car pulled away and went on across the bridge. But when Vail got back in the car to switch on his warning lights, he realised the spell was broken. He cranked up and followed the blue police car across the narrow span.

The main street had changed very little in ten years. The stores all looked the same except several had been bought out by the big chains and the Ritz, the movie theatre which had shown old classics on Sunday night and introduced him to Cagney, O'Brien, Robinson, Bogart, Tracy and Busby Berkley, had been converted into a flea market. He passed Shick Madson's barber shop and a tinge of hurt stung his chest. He stopped for a minute and stared at the sidewalk in front of the shop.

He was in the dairy foods with the gang that day when Dick Hurst had rushed in. 'Hey Marty, you better come quick. Somethin' happened to your dad.'

He was lying on his back, one leg bent under the other, his hands at his sides, staring through half open eyes at the sky.

'What happened?' somebody said, and somebody else answered, 'It's Larry Vail, the band master from the school. Must have had a heart attack. Just got a haircut, walked out the door and fell over dead. Just like that.'

Staring at the spot, what he remembered most was sitting in the funeral home later thinking, *why does death always come at me so suddenly, without any warning at all. His mother, his first puppy, his best friend, now his father.*

The old hospital, once a rambling collection of wooden buildings, was gone. In its place was a five-storey glass and brick medical centre. He drove past, not quite ready yet to face Ma Cat, and went up Pine Road to his grandmother's house, a stately old anachronism sheltered by trees that protected it from the low, rambling ranch houses that encroached on it. All the other old houses were gone except that one proud two-storey Victorian, still clinging tenaciously to the past. He pulled up the curved driveway. It was obvious Ma Cat was no longer there. The lawn was overgrown, the bushes needed pruning and the night-light was either burned out or someone had turned it off. There was about the place a vestige of capitulation. At least grammar school scoundrels had not started breaking the windows yet. To Martin, broken windows tolled the death knell for any structure.

Memories flooded over him and choked his throat. It was on that front porch that he had learned his mother was dead and it had been Catlain Vail, not his father, who had passed on the dreadful news. He had dropped the clutch of blue belles he was bringing to her and run off, seeking the solace of the elm grove to deal with his sudden grief and with his sense of betrayal, for they had not prepared him, not warned him that his mother was dying. He had stayed there until old man Watkins had come with the hearse and then had run back, first fighting and kicking them, then pleading with them to leave her there a little longer, as if there was still some small breath of life left in her and taking her away to the funeral home would snuff that out. The others had treated his grief as an annoyance, an interference with the commerce of death, but Ma Cat understood his agony and his instant sense of loneliness and had consoled him and had nursed and healed his broken heart.

Ma Cat and this house were Martin Vail's last ties to family and past. He was about to shut the door on over half his life. He shook off his melancholy as he drove back down to the hospital.

He thought he was prepared to deal with it but he was not. Cancer had whittled Ma Cat down to a mere twig of a woman; her hands so bony it shocked him when he squeezed one of them; her arms mere bone and skin, all muscle and fat long since devoured by the scavengers that raided her body. Grey skin, like wax paper, stretched tightly around her skull. And her eyes, those once glittering mirrors of a wise and mischievous soul, were lifeless marbles, staring dolefully from pits deep within her ravaged face. Plundered, what remained of her hardly caused a ripple in the covers. There was about her, too, the musty smell of death and the same heartless and inhuman sounds of progress that characterised Rainbow Flats: the heart machine beeping her life away, an oxygen feeder cachunking in the corner, a monitor somewhere in the darkness of the room, humming ominously. She stared up at him from the brink of eternity through half-open eyes, each breath a desperate, rattling plea to turn off the machines and let her go.

Could she see him? Could she hear him? Was she even aware that he was there beside her?

'Ma, it's Marty,' he said, leaning close to her ear. 'Can you hear me, Ma?'

There was no sign of recognition but he kept whispering in her ear, telling her that he was there and how much he had missed her. The nurse came in and did all the things nurses do. He could see her peripherally, puttering around, adjusting the cocks on tubes, checking EEG readouts, looking at the chart before she drifted out of sight.

'Marty?'

He turned. The nurse was standing at the foot of the bed, a tall, chunky woman in her mid-thirties, her dark hair cut short and tucked under her cap. She was smiling down at him.

'It's Emily.'

'Jesus, Emily, I'm sorry. I'm so distracted, I . . .'

'It's all right. Gosh, it's good to see you again. You look terrific, Marty.'

'Thanks. You look great, too, Em. When did you become a nurse?'

'After working a year in the tannery. If you don't have any ambition, that'll give it to you in a hurry.' He smiled and his eye caught the wedding ring on her finger. She saw the glance. 'I'm married. Have two girls.'

'Who was lucky enough to get you, Em?'

'Joe Stewart. Do you remember him? He graduated two years ahead of you.'

'Tall guy. On the wrestling team, wasn't he?'

'Bowling.'

'Oh, right.'

'How about you?'

'Never got around to it. I wouldn't want to wish me on anybody.'

She cocked her head slightly to one side and her face softened into a memory smile.

'Don't say that,' she said. 'It broke my heart when you left. I still think about you. You know how it is, somebody will bring something up, it shakes up my memories.'

'I think about you, too.'

She stopped for a moment, embarrassed by how suddenly the conversation had become personal. 'I'm sorry about Ma Cat,' she said. 'She really fought hard, Marty. You would have been proud of her.'

'I am proud of her.'

'Good. It won't be much longer. I'll be right outside at the nurse's station.'

'Thanks.'

An hour passed. He kept talking, hoping he would stir a moment of recognition from her. And then there was an almost imperceptible pressure as she tried to squeeze his hand.

'Can you hear me, Ma Cat?' he asked softly. 'I love you, Ma.' He kissed the back of her fragile hand, rubbed it softly against his cheek. 'Hear me, Ma? I love you.'

The pressure loosened and her hand relaxed.

'I'm sorry I didn't come sooner.'

When it was over and they had taken her away he sat in the room for a long while, watching them strip the bed and move the equipment out. Emily appeared in the doorway.

'I'm off duty,' she said. 'Want to go over to Sandy's and get some breakfast?'

'Sounds like a great idea.'

They walked to the city park behind the hospital and strolled along the river bank towards Main Street.

'Bet I know what you're thinking,' Emily said.

'You too?' Vail answered.

She nodded. 'Every time I come to the park.'

'I still think about that day all the time,' Martin said. 'I'll be doing something, you know, see an old movie or some kids playing sand lot ball and it'll remind me of him. I guess it never goes away, losing your first friend that way. First time we realised we aren't immortal.'

'It was like we made fun of him. I mean, it wasn't really that way, but it seemed so for a long time after.'

'You remember it that well?' Martin asked.

'Don't you?'

Vail nodded. 'Oh yeah. I can still see him out there in the river, flailing his arms, bobbing up and down. We all thought he was kidding around.'

'I just stood there laughing,' said Emily.

'We all did.'

'Then you and Art Hodges both went in after him at the same time.'

'And you ran for the cops . . .'

'And you and Artie were still out there when we got back, still diving for him . . .'

'Little Bobby Bradshaw . . .'

'God, when they brought him out . . .'

'I know, I dreamed about that, I saw that little kid all blue like that for a couple of years after.'

'His mother still works at the shoe factory. I see her now and again. She never has got over it, you know? After all these years – how long has it been?'

'Twenty-two years. I was ten, Bobby was eleven.'

'After twenty-two years she still looks down when we pass. Never speaks. Know what I think, Marty? I think

I remind her. I mean, I'm sure she never forgets but I make it . . .'

'Valid,' Vail said. 'She sees his old friends, it all comes back like a bad show. I'm sure in her own way she blames us for it.'

'Or maybe because it was Bobby instead of one of us.'

'That too.'

She reached out almost reflectively and took his hand and they stood on the bank. The river was brownish-green with ash-grey foam broiling along the banks. Further up, steam rose from its murky banks. It seemed somehow to demean Bobby Bradshaw in death, as if the river when it was healthy and pure had been a living memorial to him. Now, bubbling with poison like the witch's cauldron in Macbeth, it abused his memory.

'Bobby was always the defendant,' she said. 'Used to make him so mad, that he was always the bad guy.'

He looked over at her, confused by the remark, but she was staring at the polluted stream, lost in her day-dream.

'And you were always so . . .' she lifted her chin impudently, 'well-spoken. Strutting up and down, preaching all that made-up law to us.'

Vail had known he wanted to be a lawyer all his life but he could not evoke the moment or time at which he first became obsessed with the goal. Her description of him playing first defender, then prosecutor, then judge, with his friends forced into the roles of defendant or juror, sitting patiently while he paced back and forth acting out his fantasy, all that seemed as if she were talking about somebody else, a boy he did not remember – an artefact from his youth. It wasn't that he was embarrassed by the reminder, or that he didn't want to remember, it was a void in his memory; even her reminiscence did not jar loose any visual recollection of his perform-ances. But he didn't tell her. He smiled and went along with it.

'Do you ever wish,' she said and hesitated for a moment, 'do you ever wish time stopped then, that we never grew up? That the river still smelt kind of earthy and fresh and the sky was still the colour of bluebirds? Do you ever wish that Marty?'

He smiled sadly and said, 'Yeah. Ain't progress a bitch.'

'You know Artie's president of the Chamber of Commerce now.' She snickered. 'Got a real bad attitude problem about it – thinks he's important. People laugh behind his back.'

Artie, president of the Chamber of Commerce? That self-serving league of losers, a club of flawed little failures who deluded themselves into thinking greed was accomplishment and blight was achievement.

'Maybe we can get some of the old bunch together,' she said brightly. 'Go out to Barney's for dinner.'

His memories were suddenly tainted by the children of his youth, now grown to pitiful, small-minded syco-phants, begging greedy scavengers to bring the plague they called 'progress' to the land of his adolescence. He did not want to see any of them, did not want to be ashamed for them, did not want to be reminded that they had all sprung from the same roots, roots they had corrupted by their betrayal of their homeplace.

'I'd rather not,' he said.

'Everybody's forgotten the case by now,' she said.

'I haven't.'

'You did a great job. Everybody says you did a great job. I mean, you were just starting out and you were up against all those big-shot lawyers from the east.'

'It wasn't lawyers, it was money, Em. It's always money. All those people, fighting to keep the industrial park from spreading into Pine Hill, trying to hang on to a way of life – all they had was me. No, it wasn't the lawyers, it was the big corporations. They bought out the country politicians, the Chamber, hell, they even bought the Goddamn judge. I lost the case, those people lost homes that had been in their families for a hundred years, and the predators gobbled up a little more of the town's tradition.'

'But the town's grown some, hasn't it?' she said.

'It's grown all right,' Vail said. He looked across the river at the corporate slum they called an industrial park. 'Trouble is, the growth is malignant.'

She was surprised at his vehemence.

'Even animals know better than to foul their own nest,' he said.

And Emily had looked up at him sadly and the memories of good times gone faded with her smile.

'If I didn't know better I'd swear you just had a small fugue experience,' Molly said with a smile. 'You were a long way from here for about three minutes.'

'Day-dreaming. Or night-dreaming as the case may be,' he said. 'Is that a fugue state?'

'In a way, yes. You were temporarily out of touch with reality.'

'Tell you what,' he said. 'There's a window box outside one of your windows. What say we give these guys a chance at living outside in the real sunlight.'

She watched as he poured rich, dark soil into the box, filling it about half-way up, then spreading it out evenly with the palms of his hands. He spread a second layer of top-soil into which he carefully planted six of the plants, pressing gently around the stems until they were well supported. Then he covered the earth with a thin layer of moss and dribbled water slowly across the entire surface.

'These are river flowers,' he said. 'They love water. I always re-plant at night. Flowers die a little at night, then they spring back to life with the sunlight. We'll see how they do. They may make it.'

'Thank you,' Molly said. 'Do I water them every day?'

'In the morning,' he said with a nod. 'Just that way. Kind of sprinkle the water gently over the moss. It holds the water, gives them a little drink at a time.'

He had performed each step precisely and with almost loving care and Molly had watched entranced as this man, who was so protective of his past, revealed what she was certain was a vulnerability few people had ever been permitted to see. He broke the spell.

'Let me ask you,' he said, wiping his hands with a towel. 'Knowing what we do about Aaron, do you think if he actually saw somebody killing Rushman it would have been shock enough to put him into this fugue state? I mean, he's had a lot of shocks to his system. Wouldn't he be pretty insulated against that kind of thing?'

She answered immediately. 'No. The mind might cope with many different types of shock, then one particular act, one visual experience can short circuit it. There's no telling what his mind will absorb and what it will reject. Hopefully we can find out.'

'So the science isn't that exact.'

'Let's just say we know what we know. There are some grey areas. We're dealing with the human mind, remember.'

'What I mean is, it isn't exact the way two and two equals four is exact?'

'That's right. All *homo sapiens* react differently to different stimuli. That's what thought is all about. If it was as absolute as mathematics, we'd all be robots.'

'That's very interesting,' Vail said.

'It's basic.'

'That's what I mean. It isn't as precise as, say, a fingerprint. A fingerprint is unequivocal. You can't really argue about it. If it's there, it's there. But a mental disorder? There you have variables.'

'We're learning,' she said. 'We know the symptoms, we usually can peg the disorder itself, even tell what caused it. And a lot of times, we can cure the patient.'

'Let's just say Aaron did kill the Bishop, that he was acting from some dark disorder. Do you really think he can be cured after doing something that . . . insane?'

'If I didn't, I'd quit.'

'What got you into this business?'

'My brother's been catatonic for almost ten years.'

'My God! What happened?'

'Vietnam happened. He came back and just gradually slipped into another country, someplace he created. I suppose subconsciously I blame myself for not getting him help but we didn't know. We knew he was suffering but I guess we thought he'd get over it. They've just recently begun to deal with the problem. In World War I, it was called shell-shock. World War II, it was battle fatigue. Now it's been identified as a form of mental trauma called Post Traumatic Stress Syndrome.'

'How do you deal with it?'

'It depends on the individual. But I have a theory that affection, love, touching . . . and forgiveness . . . might have a lot to do with it.'

'Forgiveness?'

'There's tremendous guilt involved. I think part of that is because they were really badly treated when they came back. They were kind of sneaked in, like unwanted children. There was a lot of alienation.'

'I defended a Vietnam vet who shot a clerk in a hold-up. Didn't kill him but it was just luck he didn't.'

'What happened to him?'

'Three years for armed robbery and aggravated assault, he did eighteen months. The court was lenient because of the Vietnam experience. He claimed he always carried a gun – it was like a fetish with him . . .'

'A conditioned obsession,' she said. 'Probably because it was such a critical part of his survival for so long.'

'That's what he said. Anyway, the store owner was a Korean. They got into an argument about something stupid and Jerry lost control, started flashing back to

Vietnam. The guy was Oriental and bang – shot him in the shoulder. Then – and here's the part that the court couldn't swallow – he says he didn't want to admit he went berserk, so he grabbed twenty bucks from the register to make it look like robbery. Fact is, I didn't use that. The jury would never have bought it.'

'It was probably true.'

'I know it was true, I believed him from the start, but in court the truth sometimes can be detrimental to the health of your client. Some jurors won't accept the fact that truth can be stranger than fiction.'

'Yours is a strange business, Mister Vail.'

'Look who's talking.' The front doorbell ended the discussion.

'What time is it?' Vail asked.

'About eight.'

'Wonder who the hell that can be?'

He went downstairs and opened the front door. A disheveled Goodman was standing in the doorway.

'Want to see a movie?' he said.

Twenty

'What happened to your hand?' Molly said.

Goodman looked down at his swollen fist and half-smiled. 'Well, for one thing I found out it still has a little TNT left in it,' he said.

She took the damaged hand gently and ran her fingers across the back of it.

'Is anything broken?'

'I don't know,' he said. 'It's been numb for five years.'

'Come in the kitchen, we have to put some ice on this and get you to a doctor.'

'No doctor. Ice is okay but I have an allergy to doctors – medical doctors that is.'

She smiled and led him to the kitchen with Vail tagging along.

'What about the tape?' Vail said.

'Let's fix his hand first,' Molly said.

'Forget his hand. It always looks like that.'

'Well, thanks,' Goodman said and then looked at Molly rather pitifully. 'It's very painful,' he said.

Vail rolled his eyes as Molly got out an ice tray and rolled up several cubes in a dish towel. She laid it on the back of the battered fist.

'Wow,' he groaned, closing his eyes.

'He's faking,' Vail growled. 'I know when he's faking and that is definitely a fake.'

'How do you know?' Goodman demanded.

'I know fake when I see it. It's one of my talents. Can we hear this saga of yours now?'

As Molly wrapped a towel around the ice pack she had jerry-rigged for Goodman's swollen hand, Goodman slowly detailed his confrontation with Alex and Batman and the conversation afterwards. His remarks were greeted with a combination of stark amazement and shock by both Vail and Molly.

'The Bishop took part in it and directed it?'

'That's what the kid said, but let's check out the tape first.'

They went back in the office where Martin put the tape in the machine. He sat across the room from the monitor and pushed the 'play' button on a remote unit connected by a long cord to the video machine. The first ten minutes was a recording of a mass. There were two altar boys serving the Bishop, neither of whom Goodman recognised. They were in their early teens and Goodman assumed they were not members of the 'Altar boys'. Perhaps the tape was a genuine study tape, Goodman thought to himself, feeling a little foolish. Then the screen went blank and a few moments later a new scene came on. It was a bedroom.

Here we go, Goodman thought.

The girl entered the scene first. She was tiny, her blonde hair pulled back in a pony-tail, her breasts mere buds, her face, despite garish black make-up around pale blue eyes, a veil of innocence. She was dressed in a shin-length summer cotton pinafore and looked about twelve years old. She did not look scared, rather apprehensive, even a bit insolent. Somewhere off-camera a stereo was playing the Bee Gees' 'Stayin' Alive'. She walked into the frame and began to dance to the music, at first with lacklustre indifference. There was a ripple of applause from two or three people off-screen. Spurred by the small unseen audience, her dancing became more spirited. She spun around and the skirt billowed out to reveal a glimpse of black stocking. As her dancing became more spirited, the skirt swelled more and they could see she was wearing a trashy garter belt and black panties under the innocent dress.

At that point, a voice off screen said, 'All right, Billy,

your turn,' and a tall, skinny boy wearing tight pants and a silk shirt entered the screen and began dancing with her. The performance became more spirited and sexy. The off-screen voice started giving directions, ordering what was a slow strip tease until they both were naked. Then his directions became more specific, more sexually oriented. Eventually he ordered Peter into the scene.

Molly, Tom and Martin watched speechlessly as the off-screen director orchestrated what was ultimately a *ménage à trois*. Then the tape abruptly ended. The three of them sat without speaking while Vail rewound the tape. Vail turned to Molly. 'Will you excuse us for a just a minute, Molly,' he said.

She didn't seem perturbed by the request.

'How about a drink?' she asked. 'We could probably all use one after that.'

'Good idea,' Goodman said.

She went into the kitchen.

'Okay, where'd you get the tape, Tom?' Vail asked when she was out of the room.

'Look, what you don't know . . .'

'Where'd you get the fucking tape?'

'The Bishop's bedroom. It was in the closet with the rest of his taped sermons.'

'You lifted evidence from the scene of the crime?'

'I just borrowed it.'

'Christ, they have an inventory list of those tapes.'

'I took a blank tape and switched them.'

Annoyed but impressed, Vail didn't know whether to laugh or be angry.

'For all we know, they've already seen it,' he said.

'Not a chance. It would be in the evidence room. They wouldn't leave something like that lying around.'

'If Venable finds out about this your career will end before it starts. We'll probably both be doing paralegal work in Bolivia.'

'So . . . I'll go over and switch it back.'

'I didn't say to do that either,' Vail said. 'It's a hell of a hit. Now we've got to figure out what to do with it.'

Molly returned to the room carrying the drinks on a small serving tray. As she put them on the table, Vail said, 'Molly, I don't want you to discuss what you just saw with anybody, not even the Judge or Naomi unless I say so.'

'Not even Aaron?'

Vail thought for a minute, then said, 'Don't tell him you saw the tape, just tell him what Tom reported. Aaron's not in it anyway. Do we know who the others are?'

'The tall boy is Billy Jordan,' Goodman said. 'The short one is a kid named Peter. And the girl is Linda.'

'Aaron's Linda?'

Goodman nodded.

'Jesus!' Vail said. He looked at Molly. 'Bishop Richard Rushman, the Frank Capra of child porn. No wonder the kid's screwed up!'

'So how do we handle it?' Goodman asked.

Vail did not answer. Instead, he stood up and started pacing the room. 'He's thinking,' Goodman told Molly.

'Martin, the implications here are enormous,' said Molly. 'Religious and sexual disorientation are leading causes of mental disorders. So first Reverend Shackles damns Aaron to hell. Then his father takes him into a living hell, The Hole. He's seduced by his teacher. The Bishop not only perverts his sexual experience, but tells him he's ridding himself of the devil doing it. And his girlfriend is a sexual victim! It seems to me . . .'

Vail held up his hand and stopped her. He turned to Goodman. 'How are we going to prove it?' he asked.

'Prove what?'

'That the ominous voice in the background belongs to Bishop Rushman? We never see the Bishop. Without iron-clad corroboration, the prosecution can claim that voice could belong to anybody. You said yourself Alex won't testify.'

'My guess is that Alex is probably on his way to Alaska by now,' Goodman said, dejectedly.

'How about Peter or Linda?' Vail asked.

'We'll have to find them first – and convince them to go on the stand.'

'So it's Aaron's word against the unseen – and dead – director.'

'That's right.'

'Was anyone else in the church involved?' Molly asked.

'I don't think so,' Goodman said. 'From what I can piece together from Alex, Rushman recruited these kids under the guise of proselytising them. The altar boy thing was just a front for his private porn club. I believe Aaron met Linda when she was brought in as the "mascot". She was fourteen at the time and they all lived at Saviour House.'

'Which is another reason they were afraid to blow the whistle on the Bishop.'

'Possibly,' said Molly. 'But I should think the real reason is humiliation and embarrassment. They'd fear censure from the public more than from their peers.'

'And there's the power of the Bishop in the community,' said Vail. 'A bunch of teenage runaways and ex-junkies attacking the Bishop? Forget it.'

'Unless we can prove that's Rushman's voice in the tape,' said Goodman.

'Would you swear to a jury that the man speaking is Bishop Rushman?'

'Hell, I didn't even know him. But we can get the voice analysed. We can't cover this up!'

'We're not covering anything up, Tommy,' said Vail, still pacing. 'We're considering what's best for our client. We're in the same boat those kids are in. If we introduce that tape, use it in any way to discredit Rushman, we'll be accused of trying to destroy the so-called Saint of

Lakeview Drive to save Aaron Stampler. And if the whole story comes out – that these kids were in a sex club for two years and never said anything about it – it could provide Venable with a perfect motive for the murder – jealousy – and make everyone look bad *but* Rushman.'

'You can't ignore it.'

'I can if it's going to help burn my client,' Vail said, whirling on Goodman and stabbing his finger towards him. 'Forget your anger towards the Bishop, Tommy, he's dead and his problem died with him. Our job is to keep Aaron Stampler alive.'

'And what if Aaron brings it up?' Molly asked.

'I'll worry about that if it happens.'

'A very hot potato,' the Judge was saying over breakfast at Butterfly's the next morning. 'If either side introduces this evidence into the trial, they are risking serious back-lash from the public and the jury.'

Vail did not show the tape to either Naomi or the Judge. But he had filled them both in and Goodman had given them a complete report of his conversation with Alex. Molly had left before dawn, anxious to get back to Daisyland and further sessions with Aaron.

'What if the prosecutor finds out about it?' said Goodman.

'She doesn't have to use it,' the Judge answered.

'Why not?' Naomi asked.

'If I were the prosecutor, I'd pass on it,' the Judge answered. 'The only reason to use it would be to establish a motive for the murder. Even if Venable suspects the voice belongs to His Excellency, the tape itself isn't proof of anything. It's three kids screwing. She would claim the evidence is inconclusive and she chose to ignore it.'

'But we could get it in discovery, right?'

'If we asked for it, yes. They would have to turn it over to us. You know, I find it difficult to believe that

261

somebody doesn't know about this except those five kids and us.'

'None of the altar boys or the girl would talk about it, they'd be afraid to and probably ashamed. Look at it from their point of view: Rushman's one of the most powerful men in the city. Are five kids going to squeal on him? I don't think so.'

He laid the torn slip of paper on the table and Vail stared down at it.

'This is how I got the lead. It was stuck under my windshield at Saviour House.'

'So,' Vail said, 'is the whistle blower one of the group or somebody on the outside who knew about it?'

'I don't know,' Goodman answered. 'I talked to several of the kids at Saviour House. The way I put it to them, I was looking for character witnesses for Aaron, kids that would stand up for him. I didn't know about the altar boys at the time, I was just fishing. Maybe some of them do know about it. I could go back . . .'

'Not yet,' said Vail. 'Let's not tip our hand until we know how we're going to use the information.'

'You mean we're really going to protect Rushman after what he did?' Goodman said.

'That's not the point, Thomas,' the Judge said.

'Well what the fuck *is* the point? You once said that facts don't cease to exist just because they're ignored,' Goodman said, an edge in his voice.

'Right, m'boy,' the Judge answered. 'I've also said that sometimes people don't want to hear the truth because they don't want their illusions destroyed. This isn't a philosophy debate, a boy's life is at stake here. If Rushman is a paederast, the man on the street – or the jury – may not want to hear about it.'

'I always thought truth and justice went hand in hand,' said Goodman.

'Very noble,' said the Judge. 'But naive. Unfortunately truth has nothing to do with justice.'

'It's perception,' Vail said. 'In photography it's called selective focus. You show the viewers only part of the picture, but the image is so strong they perceive it to be the whole truth.'

The Judge smiled rather sadly, and said, 'Truth is what the jury thinks.'

That afternoon, Vail had a copy made of the tape and gave the original to Goodman who returned to the Bishop's apartment and switched it for the blank. If Stenner and Venable discovered the tape, it would be their problem. If they didn't use it, Vail would have the option.

Vail wrapped the copy in a plain brown envelope and mailed it to himself from the down-town post office. Two days later when it arrived, he put it in his safe deposit box.

Twenty-one

It was Friday the eleventh, well into the middle of March, and Martin Vail was on his way to have lunch with Roy Shaughnessey.

The day Guido Signatelli became an American citizen he celebrated by opening a restaurant three blocks from City Hall called *Avanti!* The name included the exclamation mark. It precisely expressed Guido's exuberant perspective on life. Handsome, debonair, the perfect host, and master of the best Italian kitchen in the state, Signatelli had but one flaw: hopelessly tacky taste. Plastic grapes and dusty Chianti bottles dangled from phoney grape arbors that criss-crossed the ceiling and the booths that lined the walls were shaped like giant wine barrels. But Guido and *Avanti!* had survived on the strength of personality, discretion, and dazzling cuisine. Through the years, Guido's (the regulars never referred to the place by its name) had become the lunch-time county seat. And on Fridays, the legal profession dominated the fake landscape. The pecking order was obvious and predictable. On the bottom rung of Guido's ecological chart were the lobbyists, their mouths dry and their palms damp as they paid homage to everybody. They were followed by young lawyers eager to be seen as they cruised the room, hoping for a handshake. Next came the assistant prosecutors, huddled over out-of-the-way tables and whispering strategy. Then came the king-makers, the politicos who greased the wheels of the city from behind closed doors in what was jokingly called 'executive session' – to avoid the state's sunshine laws. Many a shady executive decision had been made in the quiet of one of Guido's booths. Finally there were the judges, the emperors of justice, each at his own pre-ordained table, each patronised by his or her own table of mewing sycophants, and each pandered by the rest of the room. And lording over it all from his booth near the bar was Roy Shaughnessey, his power impervious to change or political climate. Even the judges stopped by to kiss his ring.

When Vail came in, Guido greeted him with a bear hug. 'Where you been, Marty? You gettin' a be a big shot, win all those cases?'

'You been reading the newspapers, Guido? Watching television?'

'So, they hand you a hot potato, you still gotta eat,' he said, leading him to Shaughnessey's booth. Heads followed their journey across the room like waves in the wake of a boat.

Vail, Roy Shaughnessey's guest? Could a deal on the Bishop Rushman case be simmering?

'We'll probably make the columns, Roy,' Vail said as he sat down. 'The executioner and his victim, breaking breadsticks at Guido's Friday lunch.'

'Come on,' Roy said with a wave of his hand. 'That was Harry's choice. He wanted the best so he got you.'

Vail laughed. 'Roy, Hangin' Harry calls you every night to get permission to go to bed.'

'Watch your step, he's in the room.'

'Of course he's in the room,' Vail answered as the waiter approached. 'He needs his weekly fix of bondage from the peons, he doesn't get enough in court.' He looked at the waiter. 'I'll have a draft beer, a glass of tomato juice, and an empty frosted mug.'

'*Si,*' the waiter said and hurried away. Guido's waiters, all of whom were related to him in some way, many of them recent arrivals from Sicily, always hurried. In eighteen years, nobody had ever complained of waiting too long for their food or drink at *Avanti!*

265

'So? How's it going?' Shaughnessey asked, buttering a breadstick.

'How do you think? I go to trial in a month.'

'A month and fifteen days to be exact,' Shaughnessey said. 'Everybody's going to breathe a sigh of relief when this one's over and we can get back to business.' He chewed off half the stick in one bite and washed it down with a glass of red wine, then dabbed his lips with his napkin.

Vail leaned across the table and said softly, 'What is this, Roy, my last meal? Some kind of public humiliation?'

'No, no!' Shaughnessey said seriously. 'Nothing like that. I thought it was time we broke bread together. Got to know each other. Drinking brandy in the back seat of a limo's no way to get to know a man. By the way, you like oysters? The oysters are superb, today. Guido sent a sample by.'

'Where are they from?'

'What difference does it make? I told you they're superb.'

'I want to know if they come from polluted waters. You don't want your defence attorney to get hepatitis, do you?'

'You never did get over that case, did you?'

'You do a lot of homework. Roy.'

'So do you, son.'

'That's what lawyers are for.'

'Speaking of which, how's your case coming?'

Vail smiled and handed him one of the business cards with the embossed 'No comment' printed across the centre.

'Cute,' Shaughnessey said. 'I heard about these business cards of yours.' He filled his wine glass and added, 'I hear Venable's looking under beds for a motive.'

'It always helps to have one in a murder case.'

'She's got Abel Stenner doing handsprings trying to establish something.'

'Smart police work, smart lawyer work,' Vail said. 'What else do you hear?'

'This and that. What're you eating?'

'Guido's fettucini on the appetiser. Veal and lemon. Why don't we start with "this"?'

'Okay. The state shrinks are gonna give the boy a clean bill,' Shaughnessey said, waving over the waiter to give him the order. Shaughnessey was a man who savoured food. He prised the meat from an oyster and laid it on his tongue like a pearl, then closed his lips around it, drew out the fork, and sucked the juice from it before swallowing.

'The grand jury will indict. Murder one and they're going to max him out.'

'Surprise, surprise.'

Shaughnessey smiled. 'Everybody expects you to put on a super show. I think Venable's a little nervous.'

'Venable thinks it's an open and shut case. Why should she be nervous?'

'So much for "this", you wanna know about "that"?' Shaughnessey said.

'I'll take anything you're willing to give.'

'They hear maybe *you* got a motive under wraps.'

An alarm bell went off inside Vail's head.

Was this just a rumour or did somebody break security?

Perhaps Venable and Stenner had copped the altar boys tape and figured he had it, too.

Was that what it was all about – who's going to burn the Bishop first?

Vail laughed. 'Hell, *I* haven't even heard that one yet.'

'You've got no idea why he did it?'

'Who?'

'Stampler, for Christ sake,' Shaughnessey growled.

'I got an idea he *didn't* do it.'

'You still grabbin' that straw, Martin?'

'Roy, I could probably make the *Guinness Book of World Records* for all the straws I've grabbed.'

'You understand you're not only dealing with one of the most well-liked men in town, he was one of the most powerful.'

'Really? I didn't know saints were into power trips.'

'Hell, you know what I mean. He's got . . . had . . . his own agenda. His charity works, abortion, censorship, the school situation, capital punishment.'

'You know, I've always wondered about that. Since when is capital punishment a Catholic thing?'

'It was a personal thing with Richard, deterring crime and what have you.'

'Personal or Catholic, that is bullshit, is what it is. People who premeditate murder *plan* to get away with it – the consequences never occur to them. In fact, I've never met anyone who broke the law who didn't think he'd get away with it.'

'Talking about some of your clients? You know what they say about you up in the governor's office?'

'No, what do they say?'

'That you put more felons on the street than the parole board.'

'You know what else they say? Everybody's guilty of something.'

'You talking about anybody in particular?' Shaughnessey asked with a scowl.

The waiter arrived before Vail could answer and put a mug of beer, a glass of tomato juice, and the frosted mug in front of him. Vail poured half the beer into the mug, topped it with tomato juice and salted it.

'What the hell do you call that?' Shaughnessey asked, turning up his lip.

'I call it a Bloody Joe. Some people call it a San Francisco Bloody Mary. Excellent for the digestion.'

'It looks disgusting.'

Vail smiled and held the mug up in a toast. '*Skol*,' he said, smacking his lips after his first sip.

'What do you mean, everybody's guilty of something?'

'Just that we all have skeletons in our closets. Even the Bishop's life isn't an open book, I'm sure there were things in his life that're better left unsaid.'

'Like what?'

'It's just conversation.'

'You know something?'

'About what?'

'Jesus!'

'Are you always this paranoid?' Vail asked innocently.

'Paranoid? Who's paranoid?' Shaughnessey answered and changed the subject. 'So you figure your client's just a whacko, that it?'

'No, sir — I figure he's innocent.'

'You're really going with that defence?'

'I said "no comment". What I think is one thing, how I defend my clients is another.'

'Think Stenner'll find a motive?'

'You don't give up, do you?'

'Do you?'

Vail didn't answer. He took another sip of his Bloody Joe.

'Know what I read?' Shaughnessey said. 'I read that most people give up a fight just as they're about to win it.'

'That's probably true,' said Vail. 'They either burn out, get scared, or fuck up. Can't go that last ten per cent. Kind of like the Cubs.'

'Incidentally, I was talking to Jane Venable the other day.'

'You don't keep very good company.'

Shaughnessey smiled. 'She says one of your tricks in a murder case it to low-rent the victim.'

'Did she really say that?'

'Actually she used the term assassinate.'

'Ah. That sounds more like her.'

'You're not gonna bash the Bishop, for Chrissake, are you Martin?'

'Let me try one of those breadsticks, please.'

Shaughnessey passed the basket. 'The man's dead, Counsellor. Don't walk on his grave.'

'My man's alive, Roy. I'll dance on the Bishop's grave if I think it will do any good.' Vail crunched down on a breadstick. 'I hear he had a drinking problem.' He said it as a joke, although Shaughnessey took it seriously.

'That's a lot of crap,' he complained. 'He was a two-scotch drinker. I ought to know, I spent more time with him the last few years than I did with my wife.'

Vail laughed. 'Is that what this is all about? You think I'd try to taint the memory of the Saint of Lakeview Drive? Why worry?'

'He's got a lot of important charity projects in place. You create the illusion of scandal, it could hurt. It could hurt the whole city. Hell, it could backfire, hurt *you* in the long run.'

'Wasn't that the idea when Shoat dumped this case on me?'

'I told you, it's a little wrist slapping. Be done with it and move on. You've got big things ahead of you.'

'Why is everybody so worried about Rushman's charitable works?'

'He was a brilliant administrator. Everybody on his list is worried things'll fall apart with him gone.'

'What kind of things?'

'Afraid the trustees'll cut them out. Or the Charity Fund'll dry up without him. The usual panic.'

'What are *you* worried about, Roy?'

'Me? Nothing. The Rushman Fund will live on. We'll make it work.'

'Are you one of the trustees?'

'Now why would you ask that?'

'Just curious.'

'I've been a trustee of the Rushman Fund since he started it. Fact is, there're at least half a dozen trustees in this room right now.'

'What's a trustee do for the Bishop's Fund?'

'Oversee the operation. Approve the gifts. Of course, the Archbishop made most of the decisions.'

'Rubber-stamp board, huh?'

'Not exactly. We all had input. I think we all know how Richard felt about things. Which means I'm confident we'll keep the faith.' He paused a moment and said, 'You thought any more about what we talked about?'

'What was that?'

Shaughnessey's manner turned slightly brittle. 'Don't play games with me, son. It's bad for my digestion.'

'Did we ever get around to what's in it for me?' Vail asked.

'You know damn well. Want me to say it again? You get on the right side of the fence, you can write your own ticket. Where do you want to go? The Mayor's mansion? Up to the capital? You want to change the world, son, change it from the inside. You get to be D. A., you can make changes.'

'Judges make changes, not lawyers. You know, a couple years ago I sneaked into your lecture to the Judges' Association, when you were talking about *malum en se* and *malum prohibita*. Pissed me off for a month.'

'How come?'

'Your philosophy that *malum prohibita* is the way society defines the limits of acceptable behaviour. As a lawyer I disagree with that theory – it's absolutely prejudicial.'

'I didn't say I agreed with it, I said it's the way the system works,' said Shaughnessey, casually.

'What you're saying is that justice is doled out by social status. That's what it boils down to, right?'

'White-collar crime has always been dealt with as a kind of popular law. Look, eight, nine years ago, the

Supreme Court legalised abortion. The law changed. But mark my words, in a few years it'll swing the other way. God knows what the country'll be like after Reagan. A lot of laws can change once that bunch gets in office.'

'What's your point?'

'My point is that judges interpret the law. They also swing with the mood of the country. *Malum prohibita* laws are the way society defines behaviour. So if everybody in the country wants to drink booze and booze is against the law, the law gets changed. But *malum en se* never changes. If everybody in the country suddenly went kill crazy, they wouldn't legalise murder.'

'So a banker or a stock broker screws a lot of people out of their savings, the judge slaps his wrist because he wears the right colour tie and gives him six months in some country club prison. That's *malum prohibita*. On the way out of the court-room, some poor slob goes ballistic because his life savings have been wiped out, blows away the banker, and ends up doing hard time life because his offence is *malum en se*.'

'That's about the sum of it. Look, you get to be D. A., you can put the banker away for ten to twenty and go lenient with the little man who got wiped, how's that?'

'That's a damn perverse argument in favour of public service.'

'It's a perverse world, son, and money makes the rules. You found that out ten years ago when you took on Tidy Chemicals and Good Earth Petroleum and the rest of that bunch down state. You want to change it, change it from the inside. What the hell, you could even be a judge.'

'That's fat bait, Mister Shaughnessey,' Vail said. 'I'm after a big fish.'

'You know, I had a feeling you were on a fishing trip but I figured you were snooping for Venable. Or Shoat.'

'I know better'n that. Nobody bluffs you. You don't

284

talk about your cases to anybody — half the time you don't confide in your own staff.'

'Maybe I don't want them to know how dumb I am.'

'Bullshit.'

'I appreciate your confidence.'

'Just don't kick the Bishop around, okay? We got a lot of people waiting for their annual contribution.'

'I play 'em the way they fall. If Archbishop Rushman has some nasty little *malum prohibita* secret in his closet and I think it will help save my client's life, I'll pump it up like a hot air balloon and float it all over the state.'

'Don't go off half-cocked, I'm not even implying there *is* anything, Martin. I'm just asking you not to go on a bashing expedition. If there's a little smoke somewhere don't fan it into a Goddamn forest fire, that's all I'm saying.'

'I'm not going to screw up your charity works, Roy,' Vail leaned back, smiled, and took his gamble. 'Not unless he chased little boys and girls or something weird like that.'

Shaughnessey looked horrified, then rolled his eyes. 'Jesus, don't even make jokes like that,' he said with a hollow chuckle. 'I got all the problems I need.'

Vail continued smiling. 'Why is it when we get together, I always come away feeling like the affairs of state are in such sturdy hands? I always feel reassured, Roy.'

'No kidding?' Shaughnessey answered sourly. 'Why is it when we get together, I always feel nervous?' And he wasn't smiling.

The day before, Naomi Chance had found a slip of paper Vail had given her just after the case began. She had stuck the slip of paper in a file and forgotten it. It was a notation Vail had jotted down from Bishop Rushman's date book: 'Linda: 568–4527' and the date, March 8, which had been the previous Sunday. She was embarrassed. Goodman had been trying to track down Linda for weeks and this was possibly the lead they had been looking for. She had dialed the number and a receptionist answered: 'Good afternoon, the Berenstein Clinic, can I help you?' Naomi had cradled the phone.

The Berenstein Clinic? Was it possible Linda was in the snobbish Berenstein Clinic? Was that why she couldn't be located? Doctor Simon Berenstein was *the* Gold Coast gynaecologist, his patients limited to the Rolls Royce trade. No one got to his door without a triple-A Dun & Bradstreet rating. A gossip columnist on the *Trib* had once remarked to Naomi that Berenstein had felt-up every debutante in the city – *and* all their mothers.

What was the elusive Linda doing there?

Actually Berenstein was more than a gynaecologist. Mister Banker's little girl gets knocked up at the Lake City Club dinner dance? Never fear. His little boy gets some unacceptable waitress in Boston in a family way? No problem. Had a bad day at the club, need a valium? Old Si will fix you up. Need a little tuck here or a transplant there, call your friendly surgical cosmetologist. All very legal, of course, and Si Berenstein didn't keep any embarrassing records and he didn't talk out of school.

So, while Vail was being entertained at lunch by Roy Shaughnessey, Naomi took a cab through a cold, early spring drizzle to the Gold Coast – a half-mile of the most valuable property in the state. Jacked-up taxes and development predators had squeezed out the individuals who had once dominated this area, tearing down monumental old mansions and city landmarks and replacing them with sterile condominiums and office buildings. Having destroyed beauty and heritage in the name of progress and growth, the scavengers, like a pack of hyenas, had moved on seeking other areas of charm and grace to destroy.

Waterview Towers was a masterpiece of cold sophistication, an impotent twelve-storey glass and brass office building with a mini shopping mall in the lobby. Mauve and brass with a grey marble floor lined with oblong brass flower boxes thick with living, white mums, it vaunted a flower shop, an upscale toy store, a gift shop, a book store, and a sprawling pharmacy. The resident list beside the bank of elevators in the rear of the lobby included several prestigious law firms and half a dozen doctors. The Berenstein Clinic occupied floors nine through twelve – enough space for a small hospital.

Naomi took the elevator to twelve and stepped out into a waiting room roughly the size of Rhode Island. White leather furniture and smoked glass tables covered with current issues of *Town and Country*, *Vogue*, *Vanity Fair* and *Smithsonian*, dominated the big room. An array of expensive perfumes had scented it and a solitary Degas painting commanded one wall. Far below the floor to ceiling windows, a solitary sailboat struggled against the wind and rain on the lake while a thick bank of lead-grey clouds hovered claustrophobically just above the windows.

The receptionist would have been more appropriate in an interior decorating salon. She was in her late forties, her hair fashionably frosted with grey, and was dressed in a black Chanel dress adorned with a single strand of pearls. She looked at Naomi through hooded eyes, appraising her from top to bottom.

'Yes?' she said, icily.

Naomi laid her card in front of her.

'I'd like to speak to Doctor Berenstein, please,' she said brightly.

The receptionist frowned at the card. 'You don't have an appointment.' Her tone implied that Naomi's mere presence in the room was some kind of affront.

'This won't take long.'

'That's impossible. The doctor has consultations, examinations. What is this about?'

'It's confidential.'

'Just what is a paralegal?' The receptionist continued her third degree.

'I'm a trained lawyer but I haven't passed the bar yet,' Naomi explained.

'Oh. Kind of like a legal chiropractor?'

'Just a minute,' Naomi said, cutting off the insults. She took back her card and wrote on the back, 'Re: Linda and the Bishop' and returned it to the receptionist. 'Just show him the card – both sides. I'll wait.'

'It won't do any good. If you were the President you couldn't get in today without an appointment,' the receptionist snapped contemptuously.

'Well, lucky me,' Naomi said.

'What do you mean?'

'I'm not the President,' Naomi said, smiling sweetly.

The receptionist left and came back a few minutes later. 'Follow me,' she said curtly, and led Naomi across the waiting room to an office in the corner. 'Wait in here, please,' she said and pulled the door shut behind her.

The office, like the waiting room, was bordered on two sides by floor-to-ceiling glass windows. Naomi checked the doctor's framed credentials. Choate, Harvard, Princeton Med. The perfect pedigree. Berenstein came in a minute or two later, an impressive man in his mid-fifties and well over six feet tall, trim as an athlete, with wavy, pure white hair, hawk-like features, and a tennis tan. He had the patronising attitude of a man who expected respect and thrived on control.

'Miss Chance?' he said in a deep, explicit voice. 'I'm Doctor Berenstein.' He regarded Naomi down the length of his equine nose. 'You're a very impatient woman. What's so damned important?' He looked at Naomi's card, motioned for her to sit down and sat opposite her behind his desk.

'I work for an attorney, Doctor. I need to ask you a few questions. It shouldn't take long at all.'

'Today's impossible. Absolutely impossible.'

'I can wait until the end of the day. We can chat on the way to your car.'

'Absolutely not. I'll have Miss Thomas set up an appointment for next . . .'

'Sorry, Doctor, that's unacceptable.'

'Your attitude's offensive. I don't like that,' Berenstein snapped.

'You don't have to, it's not a requirement,' Naomi said nonchalantly.

'I think you'd better leave right now.'

'You can answer my questions angrily,' Naomi said. 'You can be surly. You can even write the answers down if you don't want to say them out loud. But you *are* going to answer my questions, Doctor.'

Berenstein chewed on the corner of his lip and snapped the business card back and forth across his fingertips several times.

'Perhaps next week,' he said finally.

'That won't do.'

'Who the hell do you think you're talking to!' Berenstein demanded. His lips began to tremble with anger. He stood up suddenly, his eyes reflecting his barely-controlled rage. 'I think you better leave before I call the police,' he said.

Naomi looked up at him for a few moments and said quietly. 'Okay. The man you'll want to talk to is Lieutenant Abel Stenner. Want to know what he'll tell you? He'll tell you I'm fully licensed and doing my job. Then he'll probably show up to find out why I was here. He'll also tell you that you can either talk to me now or I'll be back with a subpoena and you can talk to my boss. His name's Martin Vail.'

Berenstein seemed to deflate a trifle when he heard the name. The fire went out of his eyes and his mouth went slack. He unconsciously smoothed the back of his hair down and snapped back his shoulders. He looked down at Naomi's card again.

'Am I supposed to know what this means?' he asked. 'My people make dozens of appointments for me. Who are Linda and the Bishop? Linda who? And who's this person, Bishop?'

Naomi shook loose a cigarette and lit it. She leaned back and said, 'Why don't I make this real easy and go straight to the main course. We're investigating the Bishop Rushman murder case.'

'That has nothing to do with me.'

'It has to do with Linda.'

'Linda who? I don't know who you're talking about.'

'Linda is a possible material witness. She was living at Saviour House until a few weeks ago so we don't know her last name. You know the policy I'm sure.'

'I repeat, I don't know any Linda.'

'The Bishop made an appointment for her here last Sunday. It's in his book, Doctor.'

'As I told you before . . .'

'Doctor Berenstein, if the Bishop called here on behalf of Linda whatever-her-name-is, he didn't talk to that sphinx at the desk or some other receptionist. Bishop Rushman talked to you.'

'I don't recall . . .'

Naomi held up her hand and silenced him. 'Here's what I'd like you to tell me. What Linda's last name is – I'm sure it's on your records – where she's from, when you saw her last, where she is now, and why the Bishop sent her to you. That's all. Five answers and I'm out of here.'

'You're crazy, Miss Chance. Even if she were a patient her file is confidential . . .'

'Or I *will* get a subpoena and you can talk to Mister Vail – probably in court. Which way's easiest for you, sir?'

Berenstein, a man who knew when to cut his losses, pondered the options for a minute or so, then unlocked a deep file drawer in his desk. He fingered through the folders, finally drew one out and laid it on the desk.

'I have to check on a patient,' he said. 'I'll be back shortly. I trust you'll be gone by then.' He left the room. Naomi opened the folder, took out the file, and started reading. Then she started taking notes.

She beat Vail back to the office by ten minutes, excited with her news.

'How was the lunch?' she asked as he entered the office.

'At first I thought it was a fishing expedition. But I think it was more than that.'

'Why?'

'Shaughnessey told me to lay off the Bishop. No, actually he *asked* me to lay off the Bishop.'

'You think he knows about the altar boys?'

'Oh no. He's jumpy but not that jumpy. If Roy Shaughnessey knew about the altar boys, he'd be in cardiac arrest. He'd be in intensive care with about eighty-six different machines plugged into him. But he's worried about *something*. What the hell do we know about the Bishop, Naomi?'

'A lot more than we should.'

'I mean besides the altar boys?'

'What do you want to know?'

'Well, Shaughnessey's very jittery about the charity fund. How much money do you suppose the good Archbishop raises every year? You don't suppose there's a problem there, do you?'

'Nah,' Naomi said, but her eyes twinkled mischievously. 'But I think I've got a list of the Board of Trustees and the recipients of the fund. Be a good place to start.'

'Why don't we do that, just for the hell of it.'

'Yeah. Why don't I just pull the whole file?'

'Bring it all in. What are these books doing on my desk?'

279

'Martin, you've been moving those books from one place to another since Tommy brought them in two weeks ago. Those are the books he found in Aaron's place down in The Hollows.'

'Oh. What am I supposed to do with them?'

'I don't know, why don't you ask him?'

Vail shuffled through the battered paperbacks and one hardcover. He opened it. A stamp on the title page said, 'Property of the City Library, Down-town Branch.'

'What do you know,' Vail said dropping it back on the desk. 'One of these books is overdue at the library.'

'I'll bet Aaron's worried to death about it,' Naomi said from the other room.

She decided to wait until Tom Goodman and the Judge came for their usual afternoon meeting to spring her news. They arrived together. Goodman got himself a cup of coffee and flopped on the couch. The Judge waited until Naomi brought him his coffee, a deference to age and position.

'I've run my string dry,' Goodman said dejectedly. 'Not a sign of Linda, Billy Jordan or Peter.'

Naomi said, 'I know where Linda was supposed to be last Sunday.'

They all looked at her with surprise.

'Do you know who Dr Simon Berenstein is?' she asked.

'Sure,' Vail answered. 'He administers to the landed aristocracy. Spends more time on the society pages than he does in his office.'

'That's whose phone number was in the Bishop's book, the one you gave me a couple of weeks ago. The Berenstein Clinic over in Waterview Towers.'

'Linda had an appointment with Berenstein?' Goodman said.

'Made by the Bishop himself. I went over and had a chat with Doctor Si today. In fact, she had two appointments. One a week before Rushman was murdered, which you missed in his book, Marty, and the one last week. Her real name is Linda Gellerman. She listed Akron, Ohio, as her home town. And she's a year younger than we thought.'

'You mean she started with the altar boys when she was thirteen?' said Goodman.

'That's right. Also, as of February nineteenth, which was when she had her first appointment with Berenstein, she was seven weeks pregnant.'

'You're kidding,' Vail said. The Judge just shook his head.

'She was supposed to have an abortion last week, but she didn't show,' said Naomi. 'Berenstein claims he hasn't seen or heard from her since that first meeting.'

'I thought the Bishop was radical on abortion,' said Goodman.

'According to Linda's file, Rushman claimed the girl was raped at Saviour House. It says they dealt with the problem "in-house" and want to keep the whole thing hush "for Linda's sake".'

'Sure. I wonder who the father really is?' Vail said.

'She probably doesn't know,' said Naomi. 'It could be any of the altar boys.'

'Or the Bishop,' Vail said. 'Okay, Tommy, you know the drill.'

'Yeah. I hope there aren't too many Gellermans in the Akron phone book,' he moaned.

Twenty-two

'Hey Zwick, catch nine. It's long distance.'

Detective Eric Zwicki was about to check out for the day. He had to go to a Little League meeting on the way home and after that it was his night to cook, his wife having been liberated from that chore two nights a week, among other emancipations, as a result of the woman's movement and a subscription to *Ms* magazine. He was late already and he hadn't even left the office yet.

'Shit,' he said and snatched up the phone.

'Missing persons, Zwicki,' he said.

Tom Goodman, who was calling from Naomi's desk, introduced himself, explaining he was an investigator for the lawyer involved in the Rushman homicide.

'I read all about it,' said the detective. 'Some kid whacked a Catholic Cardinal.'

'Bishop.'

'You been gettin' a lotta press on that.'

'Yeah. Big case. The reason I'm calling, we're looking for a girl who might be a material witness in this case. She's only fifteen years old. My information is that she's from Akron, probably left there a little over two years ago. I'm just playing a hunch – thought maybe missing persons might have her listed.'

'Is her name Linda Gellerman?'

'You're a mind reader, Detective.'

'Nah. Two years ago? Thirteen years old? Girl never turned up? Been bugging me for two years, wondering whether she was dead and who killed her. Shit, her folks drove us crazy for at least a year. You're not telling me she's still alive, are you?'

'She was two weeks ago.'

'Jesus Christ! Man, I gave that one up a long time ago. She walked out of her house on her thirteenth birthday and it was like the earth swallowed her up. Not a fucking clue.'

'Well, she's been living here, in a place called Saviour House, for almost that whole time.'

'Never called home. No card. Nothin' for two years.'

'So you haven't heard from her in the last month or so?'

'Hell no. And I'm sure if her parents heard anything they would've called.'

'Can I have their number?' Goodman asked.

'Why not?'

Ten minutes later, Goodman was back in Vail's office.

'I think Linda was bullshitting Aaron,' he said. 'She never planned to go home. I talked to her parents and to a missing persons detective in Akron. They all thought she was dead. Not a peep in two years.'

'I wonder if Aaron knows she's pregnant?'

'There's only one person who can find out.'

'I'll call Molly in the morning,' Vail said. 'So where do we go from here? She didn't show up at the clinic. Where the hell is she?'

'Marty?'

'Yeah?'

'You don't suppose she's the one who put that napkin under my windshield, do you?'

'Hiding out at Saviour House, maybe?'

Goodman shrugged. 'That's where I got the message. But why didn't she show up at Berenstein's clinic?'

'Because the Bishop's dead, Tommy. Assuming nobody else at the church knows about this, who's going to pay the freight at Berenstein's? Maybe she's scared Berenstein'll turn her up to the cops. She's fifteen years old, where's she going to run? She's probably scared to death.'

'Or maybe she was there when it happened.'

Vail nodded. 'Yeah, that's the big one.'

He got up and began his custom of pacing the room, thinking out loud.

'We get her, we can bring in the altar boys tape and the Bishop because she can corroborate the voice on the tape. She can testify that he also screwed her, which takes the onus off the other boys. That she got pregnant and he arranged with Berenstein for an abortion and lied about the reason. Hell, she was never raped. He probably told her to leave Aaron and come stay at Saviour House – out of sight until after she was aborted.'

'What does that do for our case?' Naomi asked.

'It takes the heat off Aaron and puts it on the Bishop,' said the Judge. 'A pillar of the Catholic church sexually abusing kids who trusted him? We bring in Aaron's background. Sexual abuse, physical abuse, humiliation, mixed religious signals. It sets up a motive for outrage and sudden anger.'

'So maybe he went into a fugue state, killed the Bishop, and doesn't remember it,' said Vail.

'Or maybe Linda did,' Tom said. 'Aaron is there with her, sees it happen, decides to take the rap.'

'So he grabs the knife and makes a run for it only a cop car happens to be in the alley and he gets trapped in the church.'

'And she goes underground to cover her own ass,' Tom concluded.

'Might be enough for reasonable doubt,' the Judge thought aloud. 'Or not guilty by reason of. We can certainly keep him out of the chair with that kind of case.'

'Of course you're going to need Rebecca and Linda to testify. Unless we can find Peter or the Jordan kid,' Naomi offered.

'I told you the teacher's out,' Vail said. 'Self-incrimination. Besides, she'd have to testify she slept with Tom.'

'How the hell do you know?' a surprised Goodman said.

'Tommy, you're good but not that good. You don't

284

get that kind of information over a cup of coffee at Rosie's cafe.'

The Judge and Naomi nodded accord. Obviously they had all made the same assumption. Embarrassed, Goodman said, 'It didn't happen the way you all think.'

'Oh? How did it happen, were you swinging from the chandelier?' Vail said and laughed.

'That's not what I mean.'

'Tommy, I don't care how it happened, okay? I don't care if it was love at first sight, or full moon madness, I don't care. It's your business. The point is, we can't afford to bring her in and she can't afford to come. But Linda's a different case. Unless she's directly implicated in the homicide, she could save Aaron's ass. Judge?'

'It's certainly looking better than it did yesterday,' the Judge said. 'But without the girl or the other two altar boys, it would be suicidal to bring in Rushman.'

'You still going for not guilty?'

'Yes,' Vail answered.

'And amend later to guilty but insane?' Naomi asked.

'There are three ways we can go. Not guilty and try to beat them on reasonable doubt, not guilty by reason of insanity *or* guilty but insane.'

'What's the difference between the two insanity pleas?' Naomi asked.

'If they return not guilty by reason of insanity then what they're really saying is that he was temporarily insane at the time of the crime – in which case he could walk,' the Judge said.

'Guilty but insane means he's whacko,' said Vail. 'He goes to the rubber room and if they cure him, he has to serve the rest of his sentence, which in this case could be life. I'd like to go for the first but it's the toughest to prove and the riskiest.'

'Yes, we lose, he's dead,' said the Judge.

'So we go for the rubber room?' said Goodman.

'That really depends on whether we find Linda Geller-

man – and what our good doctor tells us about Aaron,'
answered Vail.

It was late in the day and the drizzle had turned into a
cold, intermittent rain when Goodman returned to Saviour House for the third time. The halls were virtually
deserted. He walked to the end of the hall and took the
steel and concrete stairs to the second floor, checking
the old classrooms which had been turned into sleeping
rooms. The beds were made and the rooms were neat,
clean, and empty. Friday afternoon. The refugees of Saviour House were obviously off frolicking for the weekend.
He went back to the stairs and went to the third floor.
A sign by the door at the top of the stairs said, 'Infirmary.
Visiting hours 1–4 p.m.' He entered a long, dismal hallway that ran the length of the building. Two ceiling lights
illuminated the bleak corridor. There was not a sound.
He walked down the hall past empty rooms and stopped
in front of one. In one room, the bedclothes had been
stacked neatly at the foot of the cot. He flicked on the
light and went inside but it was obviously deserted.
'She's gone,' a voice said behind him. Startled, he
turned to face the shrouded figure of a nun, silhouetted
against the hall lights. She stepped closer to him, the light
from the bedroom falling across her young face. The
mischief Vail had seen in her eyes was gone, replaced
with sadness and suspicion. 'I'm Sister Mary Alice,' she
said. 'What are you doing here?'
'Gone where?' Goodman said, ignoring her question.
'I have no idea,' she said.
'Sister, I really don't want to dispute your word . . .'
'I said I don't know where she is,' she said coldly.
'Now who are you and what do you want?'
'My name's Tom Goodman. I'm Martin Vail's investi-
gator.'
'Who are you looking for?'
'Who's gone?'

She sighed and her shoulders slumped. 'She's a scared little girl, Mister Goodman. Why don't you leave her alone?'

'She's a material witness in a murder case, Sister. She could save Aaron Stampler's life.'

'She doesn't know anything about that.'

'How do you know?'

'We talked about Aaron a lot.'

'How long was she here in the infirmary?'

'I don't remember exactly. About three weeks.'

'So she was here the night the Bishop was killed?'

'Yes. She couldn't stay down in that awful place with Aaron. The poor child was sick.'

'She's pregnant, Sister.'

The nun looked shocked. 'Where did you hear that?' she said. 'Aaron doesn't even know.'

'Do you know she hasn't called home in two years? Her parents thought she was dead.'

'I don't even know her last name, sir.'

'Please call me Tom,' Goodman said. 'Did you know she was scheduled for an abortion last week at the Berenstein Clinic?'

She looked down at the floor. 'Yes,' she said in a barely audible voice.

'And you approved?'

'It wasn't my decision.'

'Whose decision was it?'

'The Bishop's. She was raped here at the House . . .'

'That doesn't float, Sister,' Tom interrupted. 'He may have told you that, but it doesn't work. She was sleeping with Aaron before they moved out of here. Even if she had been raped, which I doubt, the odds are that it's Aaron's baby.'

'As I said, it was the Bishop's decision.'

'Why didn't she show up at the clinic?'

'I think she was scared to death. And she had some moral objections.'

'Was she a Catholic?'

'Yes. A convert.'

'When did you see her last?'

'She left sometime Friday.'

'And you haven't talked to her since?'

'No. Mister Goodman, she can't tell you anything. I told you, we talked about it. Please leave her alone. Isn't her life miserable enough? Do you have to add more tragedy to all our sadness?'

'We're trying to save Aaron Stampler's life, Sister.'

'At what cost?'

'What is a life worth?' She did not respond so he followed with, 'Did she tell you about the altar boys?'

'What about them?'

It was obvious from her casual reaction that she knew nothing about the Bishop's private club and its implications.

'That perhaps they were all at the Bishop's earlier that night?' he answered, diverting the subject.

'So?'

'So maybe one of them did it. Maybe she could enlighten us on that.'

'That's silly. Even she thinks Aaron killed Bishop Rushman. But she says she has no idea why.'

'Can you get a message to her to call me?'

She shook her head. 'I told you, Mister Goodman, I have no idea where she is and I don't expect she'll be calling or coming back here.'

Molly Arrington leaned forward as she guided the rain-slashed rental car along the antiquated two-laner. Cars coming from the opposite direction showered her windshield as they raced through puddles; the truck in front of her skewed water at her from its rear tires. The wipers struggled vainly against the steady assault. She squinted her eyes as she passed a sign which read, 'Easton, 3 miles.' She looked at her watch. It was a little after eight.

Only thirty-three miles to go. With any luck she would be at Martin's before ten.

Her heart was pulsating so hard she could feel it in her throat, a combination of excitement from her discovery that afternoon and the stress of driving under what, to her, were absolutely terrifying conditions. But she had to get back. This news was too important to wait or to talk about over the phone.

A mile outside the little town of Easton, the truck's rear lights began to weave. She slowed down cautiously, her nose almost touching the windshield, eyes squinted. Was he turning? Stopping?

Suddenly a barrage of red lights flashed in her face. It seemed the whole rear end of the truck had become a giant stop light. Then the truck swerved and she was driving straight at its side. She yanked the steering wheel, felt the tyres hit the soft gravel of the shoulder. The back end began to fishtail. She whipped the wheel into the turn as dirt and gravel spewed from under the truck wheels and riddled the front of her car. Her car lurched back on to the highway, for a moment she thought she'd make it but as the tyres hit the rainswept pavement, the car started to spin. Car lights, trees, the out-of-control truck – all whirled past her as if she were on an errant merry-go-round. The car just as quickly straightened out and vaulted straight towards the ominous pillar of a culvert.

Advice from her father years ago flashed suddenly through her mind. She fell sideways across the passenger seat and stiff-armed the dashboard to brace herself against the coming crash.

The truck slammed into the opposite side of the culvert, climbed up on the railing and screeched almost the entire length of the concrete abutment before it stopped. Molly was not as lucky. Her car hit the end of the culvert dead-on. The front of the car was thrown up. Inside, Molly's arm gave way and she saw the dashboard rushing towards her. She lowered her head a moment before it slammed into the instrument panel.

Outside, the rain continued to shower down. The truck was poised crazily on the bridge railing. Molly's car lay half on its side, the hood folded back over the windshield. There wasn't a sound except for the spattering of the rain and the hiss of steam from Molly's ruined radiator.

Vail's table was a wasteland of legal pads, law and medical books, newspaper articles and reports. Once arranged neatly into subject piles by Naomi, they were now strewn out in a chaotic mess. He was making notes to himself; listing reference cases, items from the forensic and autopsy reports, witnesses, evidence, questions to himself, the Judge, Goodman, Naomi and Molly. It was a nightly ritual, this updating and collaboration of information as he challenged himself to take the best course possible in defence of Aaron Stampler. His ashtray was full and his coffee had grown cold in the cup. So consumed was he that he did not hear the doorbell until it rang the second time. He went to the door, grumbling to himself and snapping his elbows back to ease the cramps in his shoulders.

She was tiny, a waif-life figure in a yellow rain slicker, her head pulled down into its flared collar, saucer-eyes fearfully peering up at him. Vail recognised her immediately.

'Mister Vail?' she said in a faltering voice.

'Linda! Come in, please,' he said, swinging the door open wide and leading her inside by the elbow. 'What a great surprise. I'm glad you came. Here, get that wet coat off.'

'I can't stay long,' she said in a minuscule voice as he helped her off with the slicker and hung it on the hat tree.

'Can I get you something to drink?' he said. 'A coke? A cup of coffee?'

'Coke'd be nice.'

'You like it in the old-fashioned six-ounce bottle or in a glass with ice?'

Her smile was cautious. 'I always drink it out of a can. Bottle might be fun.'

She followed him into the kitchen, her eyes appraising the surroundings, then watched as he popped the cap off. She took a deep drink and sighed.

'Haven't had a coke for a while,' she said, then hurriedly, 'I can't stay long.'

'So you said. You have a place to live?'

She nodded but did not offer an address, then she blurted, 'Mister Vail, I didn't see Aaron for three weeks before he killed Bishop Rushman.'

'You think he killed the Bishop?' Vail asked, freshening his coffee.

'Doesn't everybody?'

'Were you there, Linda?'

'Where?'

'At the Bishop's the night he was killed?'

She looked shocked at the suggestion. 'Of course not!'

'Then how do you know Aaron did it?'

'Well,' she shrugged, 'because he was hiding in the church with the knife and all . . .'

'How do you know it wasn't Peter or Billy Jordan?'

'You know about that?'

'About what?'

'Nothing,' she said, defensively. 'Why would they want to kill the Bishop, anyway?'

'Why would Aaron?'

'I don't . . . no reason I know of.'

'He never showed any anger towards Bishop Rushman?'

'No . . .'

'Was he jealous of you?'

'Aaron isn't the jealous type. Anyway, why should he be jealous of me?'

'I don't know, that's why I asked.'

'Look, I called Sister Mary Alice and she said I should talk to you. I told you, I don't know why Aaron would want to do a thing like that. I don't know anything about what happened.'

'Did he blow up often?'

'Aaron? He never blew up. He takes things as they come.'

'You think he killed Rushman but you don't know why, is that it?'

'Yes.' She hesitated a moment and added, 'You talked to my mom and stepfather, didn't you.'

'I didn't. A man who works for me did.'

'They don't care.'

'On the contrary. They looked for you for a year. They gave up because they thought you were dead.'

'I want them to think that. I'll never, ever go back there.'

'Want to tell me why?'

'My stepfather used to beat hell out of me.'

'Why?'

'I got in trouble in school.'

'What did you do?'

'Smoking pot.'

'When you were thirteen?'

She nodded. 'I started when I was eleven. I even tripped a couple times but it wasn't fun, too scary, y'know. I got caught and Everett, my stepfather, he hit me with his hands. Hard. Once he blacked my eye and another time he knocked one of my back teeth loose. It was like Aaron's father with the belt. You know what Everett did? Every morning before I went to school he'd smack me around. Then he'd say, "You do any drugs, I'll finish the job". And my mom was just like Aaron's, she didn't do doodly shit, just went out of the room. Maybe that's why it felt good to be with Aaron, he understood things.'

Her lips began to tremble.

'Every day Everett . . . did that. Then the morning of my thirteenth birthday . . .'

She stopped for a moment. Tears seeped down her cheeks.

'. . . he said for my birthday he . . . wouldn't hit me anymore . . . and I was crying I was so happy and then, just as I was going out the door, he grabbed me and he swung me around, and . . .'

The tears were coming hard now. Vail put his arms around her and held her. Her arms were limp at her sides and she sobbed as she spoke.

'. . . and said, "Well, just . . . one . . . more time" and he smacked me so hard . . . from way back over his shoulder . . . and knocked me across the room and then he just went upstairs laughing and my lip was bleeding . . . it hurt so bad . . . I can still remember how bad it hurt . . .'

She stopped and let the sobs come, wracking her body like chills.

'It's okay,' Vail said. 'Let it loose, you've got a right. Listen, you've dried out now, Linda. That's something to be proud of. There's no reason for him to hit you anymore.'

She moved back away from him, her arms still hanging loose at her sides, the coke forgotten in one hand.

'No, it's worse. I'm pregnant, Mister Vail. Sister told me you know. You know what he'd do? It isn't much of a guess.'

'Do you think Aaron's the father?'

'Most likely he is.' She finished the coke and put the bottle on the counter. 'Thank you,' she said.

'How about another?'

'I have to go.'

'Linda, why did you come here?'

''Cause I can't help Aaron and I want you to stop looking for me.'

'Maybe you can help him.'

'How?'

'I need you to testify.'

'About what?'

'The altar boys.'

She panicked. She backed away from him, terrified, her eyes like the eyes of a cornered animal. She whirled and darted for the door. Vail caught her arm as she reached for the doorknob and turned her away from it.

'Listen to me . . .' he began.

'I won't do that!' She spat the words out. 'I'll never admit that!' Then her eyes narrowed. 'I'll lie. I'll tell them it isn't true.'

'Linda, it may help for the jury to know what really went on. What the Bishop made you do.'

'You want me to do that? People will hate me . . . hate us all. How can that help Aaron?'

'It explains why Aaron did it. The awful things the Bishop did to you all . . .'

'Don't you understand?' she yelled, cutting him off. 'He didn't make us do anything! After a while it was fun. We *liked* it!'

She turned and ran out the door and vanished into the rainswept night. Back in the office the phone started ringing.

'Ah, shut up,' Vail snapped at it and decided to let the machine answer. He went back to his desk and lit a cigarette. The machine clicked in and a tough, no-nonsense voice said, 'Mister Vail, this is trooper John Leland of the State Patrol. If you know Doctor Molly Arrington will you please call . . .'

Vail snatched up the phone.

'Yes!' he almost yelled into the phone. 'This is Martin Vail.'

It had taken Vail thirty minutes to round up Naomi Chance and get on the road to Easton and less than an hour to get to the small hospital, which was a block off the main street. The emergency room consisted of a single operating room and an adjoining recovery room. As they entered, a doctor in a white gown and paper shoes left the OR carrying a clipboard.

'Excuse me, Doctor,' Vail said. 'My name's Vail.'

'Oh yeah, Doctor Arrington, right?'

'Right.'

'I'm not the doctor,' he said casually, leading them down the hall. 'I'm a nurse.'

'Sorry,' said Vail.

'That's okay, common mistake. Actually my wife is the doctor. She's in Emergency working on the truck driver. He wasn't as lucky as Ms Arrington.'

'How bad is she hurt?'

'Well, she's got a knot the size of a tomato on her head and a nose full of Demerol. She'll be groggy for about twelve hours, but she'll be okay.'

'Can we take her back to the city tonight?' Vail asked. 'We can put some blankets on the back seat. She should be comfortable.'

'I'll have to check with the doctor but I don't think it'll be a problem. She'll probably have a bad headache for the next day or two. Her coat and briefcase are at the receiving desk, you can pick them up on your way out.'

'Thanks for everything.'

'Well, she was very lucky. I hear the car's a wipe-out.'

'That's Midwest Rental's problem,' Vail said, shaking his hand.

The nurse ushered them into a small recovery room. 'There she is. Good luck,' he said. 'Come back sometime when you can stay longer.' He smiled and left the room.

She was lying on a bed in the corner, staring at the ceiling.

'Hey,' Vail said. 'Where'd you learn to drive, Doc?'

She looked at him crazy-eyed. 'Not 'round here, tha's

295

f'sure,' she said groggily her eyes trying to focus on Naomi and Martin.

'Marty?' she said groggily.

'Right here.'

'Don't call m'Doc, 'kay?'

He laughed with relief.

'Never again, Molly.'

'Truck forced m'off the road. M'I hurt?'

'You're fine. Just a bump on the head. You've got a snootful of Demerol, that's why you're so dizzy. Naomi's here, we're taking you home.'

'Than'you. Marty?'

'Yeah?'

'There's tape in m'briefcase. You . . . must look at't. Tha's why . . . was comin' back.'

'Sure.'

'Be sure . . . look't the tape.' She paused, her eyes roving crazily from the Demerol. Then she said, 'Marty, I met the Bishop's real murderer today.'

Twenty-Three

Covered with a wool blanket, Molly was curled up on the back seat of Naomi's sedan, wavering between sleep and Demerol-induced hallucinations. But the revelations of the past twenty-four hours so dominated her mind that the event intruded on her painless daze. She was neither asleep nor awake but instead was suspended in that alpha state between dreams and reality, drifting aimlessly from past to present. It was a bright day and she was standing at the edge of the cornfield where her mother's ashes had been spread. The golden stalks wafted gently in a spring breeze. Dogs zig-zagged through the field, barking at butterflies. Her brother, young and mischievous with the horror of Vietnam still ahead, lured her into the field, hiding among the tall stems and laughing at her as she thrashed deeper into the bountiful meadow. There was no sound or scent in her fantasy, just bright colours and a feeling of great joy. Was it ever thus, she wondered. Were these facsimiles of the past or were they real? Had their lives ever been that free and gay or was this remembrance a narcotic revision of the past? It did not matter, for a fragment of time she was sublimely at peace with the world. Then the present intruded. Her brother led her out of the cornfield and in the background was a structure she knew but did not immediately recognise. His spirit of gaiety changed and he seemed suddenly melancholy, a mime whose smile had become cheerless, whose joy had become a lament. He led her into the building. She was back at Daisyland. In that claustrophobic room. And when her brother turned to face her, it was Aaron. He lay on the cot. She sat behind him. The video camera was focused on them both. So compelling were the events of that day that fantasy became fact; her dreams became veritable.

For six weeks, Molly had interviewed Aaron twice a day, six days a week. Almost fifty hours of talk as she probed deeper and deeper into the young man's mind, looking for clues, looking for discrepancies in his story about blacking out, jumping back and forth in time, at times focusing for days on specific events. This was intense therapy and there were days when they both burned out. The physiological tests had shown no brain damage and her interviews had turned up nothing new except that Aaron had suffered from fugue attacks for years, although he was sure that sometimes he was not aware he had 'lost time' because the interval had been too short to notice.

During the weeks of therapy she dutifully avoided two subjects: Rebecca and the altar boys. She sensed the tension when she approached these areas and veered away rather than lose the ground she had gained. She sensed he was getting closer to transference, to accepting her as confidante and friend. But moving too quickly into danger areas could cost her the progress she had made.

On a Tuesday morning of the seventh week, she decided to test the dangerous waters. Now, with only six weeks left before the trial, she had decided to lead him gently into what could be a mental minefield.

'I want to go back to Crikside for a little while,' she said that morning.

'Okay.'

She checked her notebook. 'You said the first sexual experience you ever had was with Mary Lafferty when you were in high school.'

'Yes m'am,' he said. He began to get nervous, shifting on the cot. He looked back at her and smiled.

'It's okay,' she said. 'You trust me, don't you?'

298

He turned back around and got comfortable. 'A 'course,' he said.

'Did you and Rebecca ever talk about sex?'

'We talked 'bout ev'ryth'ng,' he said, distrust creeping into his tone.

'So she discussed sex with you.'

'Y'know, birds 'n th'bees, like thait.' He chuckled, uncomfortably.

'Did she talk specifically about making love?'

'You main how t'do it and thet?' he said, suspiciously.

'Yes.'

'Well, I s'pose so.'

'Did she touch you, Aaron?'

'Why d'you want t'know thet?' he said and there was an edge in his voice.

'Because I want to make sure you're being perfectly honest with me. And I have some questions that must be asked. Did Rebecca make love to you?'

'Daym. *Daym!* Why'd you have t'say thet? Why'd you aisk her thet?'

'I didn't, Aaron. She volunteered the information to Tom Goodman. It's all right, I'm not accusing you or judging you, I just want to make sure we have everything straight before we go into court.'

'I won't talk 'bout thet. Ain't got nothin' t'do with all this.' He was getting angry for the first time. He sat up suddenly, swung his feet to the floor and sat stiff-armed, clutching the side of the cot. He looked away from her and his body seemed to sag. His eyes narrowed. He looked down at the floor.

'It might,' Molly said. 'Back here you said — let me find it.' She looked down at her notebook, leafing through the pages.

Suddenly it seemed as if all the air had been sucked out of the room. She gasped for breath in the void. She felt chilled. The back of her neck tingled. A hand reached out and covered hers and a voice she had never heard before, a sibilant whisper, a hiss with an edge to it, an inch or two from her ear, said, 'He'll lie to you.'

She jumped and looked up. He had moved closer to her, sliding to the end of the cot so quietly she had not heard him. He was leaning forward, only a few inches from her face. But this was not Aaron. He had changed. He looked five years older. His features had become obdurate, arrogant, rigid; his eyes intense, almost feral, lighter in colour, and glistening with desire; his lips seemed thicker and were curled back in a licentious smile. Even his body seemed straighter and harder. She felt an instant of terror, feeling his hand on hers, watching him lick his lips very slowly.

'Surprise,' he said, his voice a soft rasp. There was not a trace of Appalachia in his accent. It came straight from the city's west side. She drew her hand very slowly out from under his. He looked down as she did, then held his hand up quickly as if taking an oath.

'Sorry, no touchee, right? Talk but no touch? Typical.'

He swept the hand down suddenly and grabbed her by the throat and squeezed, his fingers digging deeply into her flesh. 'You can't scream so don't even try.' He smiled. 'See this hand? I could twist this hand and break your neck. *Pop!* Just like that.'

She was terrified. She prayed the guard would look through the peep-hole but she had been explicit in forbidding anyone from observing her sessions with Aaron. Then just as suddenly he let her go. She backed away from him, her mouth dry, her pulse rampant, rubbing her neck.

'I didn't hurt you, Doc,' he whispered with a sneer. 'I coulda hurt you. Know why I didn't? 'Cause, Doc, we're gonna be friends.'

He sat in her chair. Even his body language had changed. He was contentious, insolent, aggressive, intimidating. She sensed that he was close to the edge, a man about to explode, just barely in control, except for the venomous, grating whisper.

To her, he was suddenly disconnected from the room, a body sitting in a chair suspended in light and surrounded by darkness as she subconsciously isolated him from reality.

She could see the spasms of her pulse in her wrist and she was breathing fast and trying to modulate it. She knew what was happening, had seen it before, but it was always exciting when it happened, when she lost control of the interview and then subtly tried to get it back without disrupting the delicate balance of the moment.

'Who are you?' she asked pleasantly.

'Oh, you're very cool, Doc,' he said in his flat, edgy tone. 'You're one cool lady. But I knew that already. I'm Roy.'

'Roy?'

'Yeah.'

'Roy who?'

'Just Roy. Make believe I live at Saviour House.' He laughed contemptuously. 'What a crock that is, huh?'

'Do you come out often, Roy?'

He looked at her suspiciously. 'That depends. How often is often?' he asked.

'Once a day, once a month.'

'I come out whenever I feel like it,' he said with a sneer.

'So you make the choice?'

'That's right.' He stood up and strolled to the end of the room and back. He walked with a strut, an arrogant kind of hitch in his stride that she had seen in street toughs.

'Why haven't you come out before?' she asked. She was still standing against the wall. He turned her chair around and sat backwards on it, his arms wrapped around it, one wrist clasped with his other hand.

'It wasn't time to meet you until a couple of weeks ago. You two were becoming such fuckin' buddies . . .'

'And that upset you?'

'Sometimes I come out for a minute or two, say something just to get him in trouble. He ends up catchin' shit and he doesn't even know why.' He chuckled.

'Can you give me an example?'

'How about the first time? Shackles – you know about Shackles, I heard him tellin' you about that freak – Shackles is tellin' him how he's goin' to hell and Sonny's standin' there, shakin' in his boots, scared to death, and I sneak out and I say, "If you had a dick between your legs instead of a worm, you'd go right down there with me." And I pop back in and Shackles goes totally apeshit and Sonny takes off like a rabbit with a fox on his ass. I used to think one of these times he's gonna act like a fuckin' man. *Yeah, suuure.*'

'You call him Sonny?'

'Yeah. I knew this kid in the second grade – a real sissy – name was Sonny Baxter. That's who Aaron reminds me of: sissy . . . Sonny . . . Baxter.' He paused between each of the words for emphasis.

'How long have you lived with Aaron?'

'Why?'

'I'm just curious.'

Is he faking, she wondered? Was he a psychopath who had invented this other personality to cover up a homicidal psychosis? She had seen a couple of patients try to fake multiple personality but they were never very convincing. Roy was *convincing*. If he was faking, she felt sure it would come out in therapy sessions. It would be, she believed, impossible to fake the condition for long. She had to play along, let him make the moves and study everything he was doing: his body language, his tone of voice, his attitude.

One thing she was now sure of – either Aaron had a

multiple personality or he was psychotic as hell. Time would tell which.

'You tryin' to catch me up?' Roy snapped. 'I know all about you, lady. You can fool him but you can't fool me. You're really needling your way in there.'

'No. I'm trying to get to know him. And you, Roy.'

'No shit. Why? Why do you want to get to know me?'

'Because you want to know me. Isn't that why you came out?'

'Well, you got me there.' He smiled again, a cold, insolent smile that was neither humorous nor sincere. 'You know the answer anyway. I've known him all his life.'

He never took his eyes off her and he slowly flexed the fingers of his free hand as he spoke.

'But he doesn't know you, right?'

The smile passed, replaced with apprehension and distrust. 'No,' he said insolently. 'That's our little secret. You and me.'

'You've been together nineteen years?'

He nodded. 'But I'm twenty-eight.'

'Oh? What did you do before you met Aaron?'

He grinned and leaned slightly forward against the back of the chair, his voice even lower than usual. 'I was warming up,' he said. 'I didn't come out until when he was about eight.'

'Why?'

He shrugged. 'He didn't need me until then. Then for a long time, he wouldn't let me back out.'

'I thought you were in control.'

He rolled his eyes and shook his head. 'Jesus. Not in the beginning, Doc. Took time.'

'Why do you dislike Aaron so?'

'Never has the guts to *do* anything. Oh, he *wants* to do it all right, but I'm always the one that ends up doing the dirty work while he runs and hides.'

'Hides?'

'Stands in the corner facin' the wall. He doesn't wanna watch. Holier-than-fuckin'-thou,' he said nastily. His eyes narrowed. 'But he's the one gets off. He's the one has all the fun. So he takes all the heat, too. You blame me for that?'

'No, I don't blame you.'

'Go ahead, butter me up,' he smirked. 'I love it.'

'Where's Aaron now?'

'Ah, he's hiding,' he said with a disgusted wave of his hand.

'What if he wants to come back?'

'He has to fight for it,' he hissed, his lips curling back with scorn. 'That night with the Bishop and all? I waited until we were in the kitchen before I let him come back . . .'

Laughter.

'. . . I'll tell you, he didn't know *what* the fuck t'do. There he is, covered with blood . . . on his hands . . .'

He wiggled his fingers in front of his eyes.

'. . . face . . .'

He stopped, held his hand up in front of his face and stared at it, as though, like Macbeth, he actually could see that brutal blade, its handle towards his hand.

'. . . knife in his hand . . . shoes sittin' by the door.'

He leaned forward and whispered softly. 'I whisper in his ear, "Come out, come out, wherever you are . . ." '

Laughter.

'*Shiiit*, he pops out and goes totally bananas, sticks on the shoes and runs for it. Next thing y'know, the cops pop open the confessional and he's tellin' them he didn't do it! For Christ sake, he didn't have a clue what he was talkin' about.'

He jumped up and began pacing from one side of the room to the other. But he never took his eyes off Molly. 'He's yellin', "I didn't do it!" and he didn't even know what it was he didn't do. See what I mean, Doc? All wimp and a mile long, that's our fuckin' little Aaron.'

'Then *you* planned to kill the Bishop?'

'Who says I killed the Bishop?'

'Then who did?'

'Nobody.'

'Nobody?'

'Nobody *killed* him. He was *executed*.'

'Executed?'

'Don't you understand? He let the mask down.'

'Mask?'

'Work it out.' His lip curled up in a half laugh, half sneer, his eyes narrowed, his voice became more threatening. 'Let me tell you something, sister, I know everything he knows. Ever knew. I got a better memory than he has. Sonny couldn't remember shit without me.'

'Who let the mask down?'

'His fuckin' Excellency, who else?' he snarled. 'You wouldn't believe it if I told you.' He sighed and stared at the ceiling. 'I'm talkin' too much.'

'No you're not. Tell me about the Bishop.'

'C'mon, that's Sonny's story. Sonny says . . .' he raised his voice in a falsetto, ' "Oh he's the devil, he's evil. He must be eradicated." That's the way he talks. *Eradi-fuckin'-cated*. Shit, he was a dirty old man. The world needed to know he was a dirty old man.'

'Did you put the numbers back there, on the back of his head?'

He smiled. 'B32.156. Right?'

'That's right.'

'You'll figure it out, Doc. You got a clue.'

'A clue?'

Throwing his head back, he laughed very hard. 'It's on the tape,' he said with his head still back. He peered down across his cheek at her, wiggled his eyebrows and laughed again.

She decided to take a chance although she was not sure what his reaction might be. 'You mean the altar boys tape?' she said, trying to sound casual.

He shook his head sharply as if he had been slapped. He was obviously stunned and he glared at her. His eyes sparked with incredulity and anger, jumped around the small room almost frantically before they settled back on her.

'You know about that?' he said, squinting.

'Yes.'

'Who told you that?'

'We found the tape.'

'Jesus!' He railed in his vicious whisper. 'I told him, get that goddam tape! But the door to the closet was locked so we had to run for it. Jesus! He can't do *any*-thing right.'

'Tell me about that night, Roy.'

'He never does. He never did.'

'Roy? Tell me about the night the Bishop was executed.'

'But as usual Sonny let *me* plan it and do it, right? He stands in the corner and gets off on it and then he screws up and now we're both in deep shit.'

'Did you really think you'd get away with it?'

He started pacing between the side walls of the room again, shaking his head. 'We would have gotten away with it, wasn't for that damn cop car in the alley. Would you believe that, a minute earlier, a minute later . . .' The veins stood out on his forehead and he began to sweat. 'Can't do anything right,' he said, angrily. 'Nothing! Never, never!' He slammed his hand into the wall.

'Roy!'

He whirled on her. 'Leave me alone.'

She was losing him and she was desperate to establish some method to communicate with him again — if, in fact, Roy was real.

'Roy, suppose I want to talk to you and Aaron's out. How do I do that? How do I speak to you?'

'You figure that our, Doctor bitch. How do you know

I want to talk to you? You're *his* friend, not mine. I know you, lady, you're gonna tell him about me.'

'I'm your friend, too, Roy . . .'

'Gonna ruin it all, aren't you!' He stood with his back to the wall, slapping his open palms against it. 'God damn, I shoulda known better than this.'

'Ruin what, Roy?'

'*Everything!*' His head nodded and he seemed out of breath. He splayed both hands against the wall as if holding it up. He stood that way for a full minute before he looked back up.

'I lost time,' Aaron said fearfully. His features had softened and his eyes were scared, rather than wrathful. He seemed to collapse within himself, to diminish physically.

'You had a little fugue attack,' Molly said calmly. 'It didn't last long.'

'How long?'

'Five or six minutes.'

'I were layin' on that cot. Next thing I was over hair. Wha'd I do.' He looked up sharply. 'I din't try to harm you, did I Miss Molly?'

'No. It was kind of like a nap.'

'Why'd thet happen, you s'pose?'

'I don't know yet,' Molly said. 'Hopefully we'll find out.' She realised she was breathing hard. 'Aaron, do you know someone named Roy?'

'Roy who?'

'Just Roy?'

'Did he live at Saviour House? Thet why he don't have a last naim?'

'I'm not sure. It's just a name that came up.'

'Well, if I think a someb'dy, I'll tell yuh, Miss Molly.'

'Let's call it quits for the morning, John,' she said. 'Maybe we can talk again after lunch.'

'John?'

'What?'

'You called me John,' he laughed.

'My mind's out to lunch,' she said. 'Steady the tripod while I take this camera off.'

The first person she had ever seen with a dissociative personality disorder was John Neckerson. It was when she was a senior in college, studying abnormal psychology at the state institution. Neckerson. Bank manager. Age forty-five. Manic depressive. Two suicide attempts. Institutionalised after he took thirty-two hundred dollars out of the teller's drawers one morning, in full view of the three employees, walked out of the bank and up the street and made a thirty-two hundred dollar down-payment on a new Cadillac.

One afternoon John Neckerson had suddenly changed before the eyes of the entire class. Everything changed: his demeanour, his appearance, his voice. Suddenly John Neckerson was a five-year-old *girl!* She was pleading with them to keep her father away from her. Sexually abused by his own father, Neckerson had invented a girl to assume his guilt and the abuse, and to rid himself of what he felt was the taint of homosexuality. She had seen many cases of multiple personality disorder since then.

She was detaching the video camera when the voice spoke again. She jumped. He was inches from her, staring intently into her eyes. 'You want to hear about it, doncha?' Roy whispered.

He reached out and stroked her cheek. She did not move. She stared back at him. 'Bet I know what you'd like. You'd like me to drop you right there on the floor and fuck your brains out, wouldn't you? Shit, I know you women – you want it but all you do is talk, talk, talk.'

He moved closer again and flashed his Cheshire cat smile. When he spoke it was in a breathy whisper she had to strain to hear.

'You'd like me to talk, talk, talk, wouldn't you? Maybe

next time, Doc, huh? Maybe next time I'll tell you what you wanna hear. About His Excellency?'

'You're a real tease, aren't you, Roy?'

'You oughta know.'

'I think you're making it all up.'

His hand shot out before she could move and the fingers wrapped around her throat again. His lips pulled back from his teeth.

'I could kill you right now and stop you,' he said, his voice trembling. 'You live lucky, Doc.'

He let go of her again and jabbed his forefinger at her.

'Don't pull that shit on me, tryin' to trick me into somethin'. Listen, lady, if I want to tell you somethin', I'll decide when.'

'I'm sorry,' she gasped.

'Hurt a little that time, din't it? Huh?'

'Yes.'

'You remember that. You want to get along with me, you watch your ass.'

'We should stop for now. Why don't you come back out . . .'

'Tryin' to get rid of me?'

'You hurt me,' she said firmly. 'I don't trust you.'

'You trust him but not me?'

'He's never hurt me. Never wanted to hurt me. Roy, this is all your doing.'

'Okay . . . *okay*.' He smiled up at the camera. 'Next time I'll be a good boy . . . Doctor Camera.'

Twenty-four

Three a.m.

Vail's house was dark except for a single light that burned in his first-floor office. Anyone who might have passed the place at that ungodly hour could have seen him through the half-open blinds, pacing the room, stopping occasionally to jab a finger at an imaginary jury, like the childhood Vail addressing a command performance of his pals. Yellow legal pads covered with hand-scrawled notes, open legal books, medical journals, newspaper clippings, all littered his desk. Occasionally he would stop, move to the desk and root through the piles of information looking for some obscure reference and scribbling it on a fresh page of a fresh yellow pad.

Strategy.

Instinct told Vail that more than law, more than facts, more than truth, strategy and colloquy would win this case.

The tape changed everything. For weeks he had been developing his case, scrutinising every report, every photograph, every detail he could find, searching for discrepancies no matter how minute, digging into the backgrounds and credentials of the expert witnesses the prosecution would call. Now, in the space of a one hour tape, everything might change. Three weeks from the trial and he might have to start over.

The postscript on the end of Molly's interview with Aaron and Roy had sent his mind tripping. She had returned to the chair and facing the camera, was slightly out of focus and almost out of the frame. But her voice was clear and concise.

'Martin, I realise this tape will shock you just as the

appearance of Roy shocked me,' she began. 'So I want to pass some quick thoughts on to you while they're fresh in my mind. I'll try not to be too technical.

'This could be – and I say could be because I can't make a reasonable analysis on the basis of one interview – but this could be a classic case of multiple personality disorder. What lay people call split or dual personality. Very often, the initial reaction to this kind of exposure is disbelief and rejection so it's important for you to understand that this is a specific and recognised mental disease.

'It's easy to understand how this could have happened, considering what we know about Aaron's childhood and his teen years here. There are strong possibilities that he has been abused, sexually, physically and mentally, and that he could be sexually and religiously disoriented – which are the two main causes of mental illness.

'A simplified assumption is that Aaron created Roy to assume the guilt and responsibility for acts which he, Aaron, could not perform himself. In other words, Aaron transferred his guilt to Roy. As I said, this is an over-simplification of a very complex problem, but it is not psychiatric hocus-pocus or black magic or voodoo. One thing we can be sure of – if he's faking or for real, this boy is very sick. And if Roy does exist, he's very dangerous.'

She stopped for a moment and looked away from the camera, then added, 'Either way, he is obviously suffering a serious mental disorder. It raises the question of whether he should stand trial.'

The tape went blank.

Nice.

Was he faking?

Was this other personality for real?

One thing he agreed with Molly about, Aaron was definitely one sick boy. And if Aaron did have a duplicate personality, who the hell was he defending, Aaron or Roy?

Roy was easy to pin it all on. He appeared bereft of compassion, sensitivity, response – everything but passion. Hate seemed to be his passion, his fire and fuel, the brain that focused the energy, the muscle that propelled the knife.

The question was, whose hate was it?

Did Roy draw his passion from Aaron? Or did Roy invent his own enmity? How detached were Aaron and Roy? Were they umbilically bonded like brothers, or were they enemies at heart? Did they share the same id, the same headaches, the same desires? Did Roy want to rule their singular universe, ascend to host? Or was he simply an errant clone?

Who really killed Archbishop Rushman? Aaron? Roy? Both of them?

Strategy, not truth, would keep them alive because it didn't matter who killed the Bishop. If one of them died, they both died.

He sat on the edge of his table, hands poised pyramid-fashion in front of his lips, staring into the fireplace. Then finally he stood up and started pacing around the room.

'When I was a child my best friend was Beanie McGlaughlin,' he said aloud, addressing the fireplace as if it were a jury box. 'He had three brothers and two sisters and they were always in trouble. And when one of them did something wrong, his mother would swat them all. "That way I'm sure to get the right one," she used to say. It was effective, but it wasn't equitable.

'Justice is equitable. Justice is fair, impartial, and unbiased. Justice is truth. That's why we're here today, ladies and gentlemen. To seek the truth.'

He stopped and shook his head. 'Shit,' he muttered.

'Sounded pretty good to me,' Molly said from the office doorway. She had been standing in the shadows watching him, listening to him developing a case through

312

oration. Vail was startled. Shaken from his reverie, he seemed at first annoyed but that quickly changed to empathy.

'Hey,' he said, smiling, 'how's the head?'

'Worst hangover I've ever had.' She sat on the over-stuffed sofa. 'And my knees are made of rubber. But I think I'll survive.'

She was huddled in a long, satin bathrobe. Her hair was loose and flowed down over her shoulders. He was stunned at how vulnerable, how young, how naturally beautiful, she was. Stripped of her professional veneer, she sat like an injured bird and there was about her a softness she had not revealed before. He felt suddenly protective of her. She seemed a different person than the tough professional who had faced down this shadow killer in a small room – a killer who had threatened her verbally and physically – and beaten him at his own game. He went over, draped a blanket over her knees and inspected the knot on her head.

'You got a tomato growing out of your head,' he said.

'Don't make me laugh,' she groaned.

'How about a cup of coffee?'

'Actually, I'm starving to death.'

'And well you should be,' he said. 'You've been out of it for almost twenty-four hours. How about eggs and bacon? I make a mean poached egg.'

'You cook?'

'I suppose you can call it cooking,' he said, heading for the kitchen.

'What do you think of the tape?' she asked.

He stopped at the kitchen door and looked back at her. 'I've never seen anything like it,' he said.

'I don't think many people have, unless they're in the business.'

'I've heard of it, of course, seen some movies, but I never really thought much about it. That's the way it happens, huh? He just changes, pop, like that, almost in the middle of a sentence?'

She nodded. 'I've actually seen cases where personalities switched in the middle of a sentence.'

'Do you believe him?'

'That's a tough question on the basis of a one-hour interview. Let's just say I can't discount it.'

'He could be faking it, right?'

She nodded. 'I've dealt with at least thirty cases of dissociative behaviour in the last six years. If this is a real case of dissociative multiple personality disorder, I'll find out.'

He dropped the eggs in small containers in a frying pan half-filled with boiling water and turned the bacon over with a spatula.

'How long will that take?'

'I can't tell you that. It could take a few weeks or a few months. It will depend on how often he comes out, whether I can trip him up in analysis. We'll do tests . . .'

'*You'll* do the tests,' Vail said quietly. 'I don't want the State's people to know anything about this yet.'

'All right . . .'

'This is a specific disease, right?' he asked as he prepared breakfast.

'Yes. It's described quite explicitly in DSM 3. It's no different in my business than measles and heart disease are to a medical doctor.'

'To you, maybe. And other doctors, but it might not fly with a jury of people whose average I.Q. is probably 110, 115.' He buttered toast and put the eggs and bacon on plates. He lit two candles and put them on the dining room table.

'Breakfast is served, madam,' he said and offered his arm as she wobbled to the table.

'If this Roy character is for real, can he switch in and out whenever he wants?'

'Possibly.'

'Can you bring him out when you want to?'

She shook her head. 'Not at this point. If he is for real, I don't know what brings him out yet. It's going to take time.'

'Which we're running out of . . .'

'I know,' she said. 'But I have to deal with the situation very carefully. Aaron is either a very sensitive young man with an alternate personality or a psychopathic faker. If he is a split, the shock of finding out could have disastrous results. We could lose Aaron and Roy could become the dominant personality, and apparently an extremely volatile, amoral, psychopath.'

'What are the chances he's faking it?'

'I've seen a couple of feeble stabs at faking split personality but they're usually amateurish. We discount them very quickly,' Molly said. 'I'm sure it's been done, everything in the world's been done, but it would take someone with an explicit understanding of the disease and tremendous powers of concentration.'

'Why?'

'Because the faker can't just *act* like somebody else, he or she literally would have to adopt the psyche of the host *and* the alternate. Sustaining the charade would be the toughest part of it – and the body changes that frequently accompany it are hard to fake. Actually, it's more of an attitude change than a physical one. I don't think that's really the problem.'

'Then what is?'

'He is definitely suffering from some form of psychosis or none of this would've happened.'

'So now we're into an insanity plea for sure?'

'That's your call, Counsellor. But he definitely has a mental problem of some kind.'

'Give me a quick profile of a psychopath,' Vail said.

'I hate to stereotype it with quick brush strokes,' she said.

'It'll never leave the room,' he assured her with a smile.

315

'Well, psychopaths are totally amoral, usually paranoid, harbour great rage – which they successfully hide.
Remember the boy in the Texas Tower? Nobody knew
how angry he was. They also tend to consider others
inferior, have contempt for their peers. They're anti-
social, pathological liars, often homicidal. Laws don't
count to them.'

'Real charmers,' Vail said.

'Well, they can also be charming, intelligent, witty,
socially desirable.'

'I really don't know anything about this,' Vail said.
'How about legal cases? Are you familiar with any?'

She nodded. 'Very recently. A mentally disturbed man
over in Ohio named Billy Milligan. The last time I heard
he had over thirty different alternates.'

'Thirty!'

'And counting. Men, women, children. One's a very
talented artist.'

'You saying Aaron could have several personalities?'

'Yes. But it could be months before all of them come
out.'

'Let's just stick with two for the time being, that's all
the clients I need for now. What happened in the Milligan
case?'

'He was tried for rape and used multiple personality
disorder as his defence. He's in a mental institution
instead of prison.'

'You know, according to Roy, Aaron had an orgasm
when Roy killed the Bishop. Where does one stop and
the other begin?'

'We don't know at this point how disjunctive they are.
The complexities are enormous. I'm sure they both lie to
me at times, which doesn't help.'

'Is there any way to figure it out?'

She thought about the question as she ate. 'I don't
know. Certainly we have to study the tapes. Maybe
there's a clue there. Once I establish a strong rapport

with him, I might be able to bring him out by simply mentioning his name. That's usually what happens in cases like this. But right now, it's up to Roy to come out on his own.'

'If there is a Roy.'

'Yes. If . . .'

They finished breakfast and moved back into the office. He poured them each a fresh cup of coffee.

'I have to admit, these cases are absolutely fascinating,' she said. 'There's no telling what we can learn from this relationship.'

'Maybe we can have him classified as a valuable scientific experiment.'

'Very funny.'

'As I understand this, Aaron doesn't know about Roy, right?'

'Right.'

'He still thinks he blacks out from time to time when he's under stress.'

'Yes.'

'Then who does he think killed the Bishop.'

'I don't think he knows. He thinks somebody else was in the room and he fears whoever it was.'

'But he understands what a fugue state is?'

'Yes. He calls it losing time. It's a common term in the business, particularly among those who suffer from it. I had a case once, a woman who was obese. She was in therapy, Weight Watchers, everything but she kept gaining weight. Then one day her husband found dozens of Big Mac wrappers stuffed in the back of a cupboard. That's when I got her. She swore she didn't put them there. Turns out she would leave work and on the way home, she would get an eating attack and lose time, stop at the hamburger place, get a dozen burgers and fries, eat them all, and then hide the wrappers.'

'All this while she was in this fugue state?'

She nodded. 'Usually a fugue event is quite short. One

or two minutes. Even the victim doesn't realise it happened unless it's obvious. You're watching a football game on television and suddenly in the snap of a finger, *60 Minutes* is on. You *know* you lost time.'

'What would happen if you showed him the tape? If he saw Roy in the flesh?'

'It's hard to say,' she answered. 'It would certainly be traumatic. There's a chance Roy could come out and become the host personality and Aaron would withdraw into his own world. There's no way to predict what might happen.'

'So you don't want to take a chance?'

'No, not yet. Although he has to face the truth sooner or later.'

'We're running out of time, Molly.'

'I know,' she said.

'Tell me about your brother again' Vail asked.

'He's catatonic schizophrenic,' she said. 'He has a fixed stare, hasn't said a word for years, no recognition of where he is. He's in another world.'

'And you don't have a passport,' Vail said.

'Well put. One of the reasons I went to Justine is that they agreed to take him as a patient.'

'Doesn't it get to you, seeing him like that every day?'

'I got used to it. There are others far worse. It's a totally different situation than Aaron and Roy. They live in our world, they are dysfunctional in a different way.'

'Is that what you meant when you said we may lose Aaron?'

She nodded. 'He could retreat into that dark world.'

'So if it is a multiple personality problem, we could lose Aaron and be stuck with Roy.'

'Yes.'

He rolled his eyes. 'Wonderful. Their ids must really be a mess.'

'Actually, if Roy does exist, he doesn't have an id. He represses nothing. In a way, he's Aaron's id. I hope what drew Roy out is that I've achieved transference with Aaron.'

'Transference?'

'It's one objective in treatment. Hopefully, the patient comes to regard the analyst as a figure from the past – a parent or mentor – somebody they relate to and trust.'

'Like Rebecca?'

'Not really. I'm sure she became a surrogate mother to Aaron, but she's also part of the past.'

'You?'

She nodded slowly. 'I think it's possible he's beginning to transfer to me.'

'Then Aaron would have sexual desires for you?'

'Possibly. Which he suppresses.'

'And so Roy lusts after you?'

'That's one possibility. There's also a downside to transference. It creates a subconscious fear that all the old injuries and insults will be repeated – by children, friends, husbands, wives . . . just about anybody.'

'All the hurts are transferred from past to present?'

'That's right. And those fears can result in uncontrollable anger . . . frustration . . . unreasonable expectations. It's a double-edged sword. It causes great anxiety in the patient, what we call re-experiencing – living past injuries – but also it permits the analyst to make connections between the past and present. That's eventually how we diagnose the problem.'

'Can he be cured?'

'Possibly. Or, we could literally fuse Aaron and Roy into a single personality with an id strong enough to control Roy. And then there's the possibility we could end up with a totally new personality. The mind is a remarkable invention, Martin.'

'I'll tell you the truth, Molly, it all scares hell out of me. I can just see the jury sitting there, thinking I ought to be locked up with both of them.' He paused, sipped his coffee, and said pensively, 'If Aaron has a split personality, we have to bring Roy out. If we can't, we can forget the multiple personality defence.'

He lit a new cigarette off his old one and dropped the spent butt in his coffee cup. 'And what a defence,' he said sarcastically. 'Aaron Stampler's not guilty – Roy did it.'

He shook his head and laughed dourly. 'Hell, they'll fry 'em both – and me with them,' he said.

'Don't you ever explode?' Molly asked. 'Don't you ever get mad and kick things? Haven't you ever just lost it?'

'Anger wastes energy.'

'Oh hell, Martin, waste a little energy. Rail out at those bastards that stuck you with this impossible case. Nobody can be as cool as you are. It's scary.'

'I'm not cool inside. Inside, I'm a bundle of balled-up nerves and they all have frayed ends. I do a lot of silent screaming. If that's obsessive or compulsive or repressive, then so be it. People put their lives right here.' He held his hand out with the palm up. 'They have to come first.'

'That's very admirable.'

'It's not admirable, it's work. You open up minds and try to let a little light in. I defend felons. I think we both pay a price for our choices.'

'Yes,' she said. 'I guess both our ids runneth over.'

'Just what the hell is an id, anyway?'

'It's where all our repressed desires are stored,' she said.

Vail laughed. 'Well, mine all seem to be under lock and key,' he said. 'My last love affair lasted seven months. It ended during a trial. That appears to be the acid test, trials.'

'I lived with a guy once for eighteen months before I found out he was a manic depressive,' Molly said. 'I don't know which was worse, breaking up or realising it took me eighteen months to figure out there was something wrong with him.'

'Blinded by love?'

'I suppose. That doesn't seem to be one of your problems.'

'No, I seem to be blinded by *juris prudence*.'

They fell into an awkward silence, staring intently across the room at each other.

'I think I need another twelve hours sleep before I go back to Daisyland,' she said finally and stood up. 'Thanks for the breakfast. It took the wobble out of my legs.'

'So, what are we going to do about our over-crowded ids?' Vail asked.

'Well, for starters, I suppose we could stop repressing our libidos,' she said as she went up the stairs.

Twenty-Five

Molly had increased her daily sessions with Aaron to three a day, seven days a week. When Roy appeared for the second time, it was only for a few minutes – to deride her for asking Aaron about Rebecca. The next day he was back, this time to argue with her. After that it became a daily occurrence, sometimes twice a day, and always adversarial.

She tried to trap him to see if he was faking, checking the tapes for slip-ups, looking for him to go out of character for just a moment. But after almost fifty hours of interviews she was ready to accept Roy as Aaron's real-life alter ego. She was still not sure if any particular subject triggered Roy's appearance.

Then she had her most significant, and frightening, interview with Aaron and Roy. That morning, Aaron was quiet, almost sullen. Then ten minutes into their session he suddenly sat up on the cot and laughed. Molly felt her usual surge of excitement when Roy appeared.

'Good morning, Roy,' she said.

He looked over at her and the smile disappeared.

'The food here sucks,' he said.

'Have you complained?'

'Hey, I don't complain about anything and he hasn't got the balls to do it.'

'Any other complaints?'

He lay back down and stared at the ceiling. 'I'll tell you if there is.'

'What would you like to talk about today?'

'Well, aren't we being friendly,' he said.

'Why not. Do we always have to argue?'

'Not argue, Doc. We have discussions.'

'Where are you from, Roy?' she asked.

'Not from Shit Hollow, Kentucky, I promise you that.'

'But you've been with Aaron for a long time.'

'Cute. See, that's when we have trouble, when you get cute on me. Start prying, trippin' me up, or trying to.'

'I'm not trying to trip you up, just curious. I can't place your accent.'

'South Philly. Right off the street.'

'Aaron's never been to Philadelphia, has he?'

'Shit no. I come and go, Doc, come and go. You think I spend twenty-four hours a day at his beck and call? It was a couple years after that first one.'

'You mean with Reverend Shackles?'

'That's right.'

'When you insulted him.'

'Well . . .'

'You didn't lie to me, did you?'

'I don't lie to you,' he said, nastily. 'It was just longer than that.'

'Longer than what?'

'What I told you.'

'What do you mean by longer?'

'I was out longer than I said.'

'Oh? Did you say anything else?'

'Nope.'

'Did anything else of importance happen?'

'You could say that.'

'Do you want to tell me about it?'

He laughed. 'I might, just to see the look on your face.'

'What do you mean?'

'Maybe I wasn't being completely honest with you before,' Roy said. 'Maybe I did more than tell Shackles off, y'know.'

She tried a ploy. 'Come on, Roy,' she said with a snicker.

He hoisted himself up on one elbow and turned back

towards her. 'You don't really think I tell you everything, do you?'

'Do you even remember that far back?'

'Let me tell you something, I remember them all.'

Them all? Was he talking about all the times he had come out or something else?

She didn't want to push her luck. She looked down at him. He lay back down, hands clasped over his chest, feet crossed at the ankles. His eyes were closed and he was perfectly relaxed.

'We were up at a place called East Gorge See,' he said, in almost a monotone. 'Highest place around there. It's this rock that sticks out over the ridge and it's straight down, maybe four hundred, five hundred feet, into East Gorge. You can see forever up there. Shackles used to go up there and he'd stand on the edge of the See, and he'd deliver sermons. Top of his fucking lungs, screaming about hell-fire and damnation and it would echo out and back, out and back, over and over.'

'Did you go up there often? With Shackles, I mean?'

'He'd take Sonny up there all the time. That was my first time. That day he dragged Sonny along, points down over the edge and he tells him that's what it's gonna be like when he goes to hell, like fallin' off that cliff. Sonny's petrified. Then he grabbed Sonny and shoved him down on his knees and starts going at him.'

'Going at him? What do you mean by going at him?'

'It was like, he was warming up. Before he started sermonising. And when he started it was all that hate and hell-fire and damnation, and all of it was aimed right at Sonny. That's when I came out and said that, about his dick, and then ran off into the woods.'

'So you and Sonny were hiding in the woods together?'

'Yeah. We hid there watching him strutting around, talking to himself. Then he turns and walks back out to the cliff and he starts it again, yelling about how Sonny is hellbound, and how rotten he is. I sneaked down on him. Hell it was easy. He was yelling so loud he didn't even hear me. I picked up this piece of busted tree limb and I walked up behind him, jammed it in the middle of his back and shoved. He went right over. *Wheee.*'

Molly stared at him, trying to control her shock and surprise, trying to look casual as the hair on her arms rippled in cadence with his narrative.

'I couldn't tell when he stopped sermonising and started screaming,' Roy went on, 'but I watched him hit on the incline at the bottom. I didn't want to miss that. He rolled down to the bottom and all this shale poured down on top of him – what was left of him. It was wild. All that shale buried him on the spot.

'I went back down to Misses Neeley's place. Shackles had a room in the back. He didn't have much stuff. Travelled with it in a duffel bag. I stuffed it all in the bag and took it back up the Johansons' farm and threw it down their well. Nobody ever missed Shackles. They just figured he got a wild hare up his ass and split.'

'Sounds like you planned it very well.'

Roy's eyes turned ice cold. 'What're you gonna do, set me up, Doc? Thinking about premeditation? You can't testify against me. You're *my* shrink, man. What's said between us is privileged in the eyes of the law.'

'You keep forgetting, Roy, I'm on your side. So is Martin Vail.'

'Shit, you're on *Sonny's* side, not mine. Anyway, it wasn't planned, I just had enough. Sonny wouldn't do a damn thing so I did. Then I cleaned up afterwards. It was so great, I hated to go back in. I wanted to stay out forever. Sonny finally came back out when we got home. Drove him crazy, wonderin' what happened to all that time he lost.'

'How did you feel about that?'

'Feel? I told you, it felt great. But the best part of it was not getting caught. And old Shackles – he sure as hell knows what it's like to fall into hell.'

Molly said nothing. She stared down at the top of his head for a long time. A chill went through her. He had just described committing a murder when he was nine years old. She had dealt with a lot of dissociative behaviour in six years but had never experienced anything quite like this.

'Can we talk about Bishop Rushman?' she asked cautiously.

'Shit, another Christ freak. They always have to bring the devil, hell, and Christ into their thing. When he didn't have the answers, it was always the same old song, "Accept it on faith. Christ loves those who trust him most." Who could believe His Excellency about anything?'

'Was he mean to Sonny?'

'Ah, you know, he made fun of him because Sonny was smart, asked questions. The rest of them didn't give a damn. They'd go along with anything.'

'Tell me about the night the Bishop was killed. Why did you come out that night?'

'Because Sonny was scared shitless of him. So I had to do something.'

'Did you have a plan?'

'I didn't have time for a plan,' he said, turning slightly and winking at her. 'I improvised.'

He lay silent for a little while and she did not press him. 'Driving out the devil, that's what he called it,' Roy said. 'Driving out the devil! If you couldn't get a hard-on, it was the devil's fault. If you had a cold when there was a meeting, the devil had his hand on you.'

'Did you believe that?'

'Come *ooon*. None of us believed it, but what the hell, we were having fun, right? Let the old bastard make up any excuse he wanted. Sonny was the only one upset.'

'Because Rushman was a Bishop?'

Roy got up on one elbow again, leaned towards her and whispered, 'Because they were fucking his girl. I

326

mean, the first couple of times he maybe was confused – but after that he was pissed off because everybody was fucking his little Linda. Peter, Billy, Alex, and His royal fucking Excellency.'

'You really hated the Bishop, didn't you?'

'I told you, he was a pervert and a liar. One minute we were one big, happy, fornicating family, the next, he was giving us all this shit because we were "no good". No good? We were no good because he made us no good, that's why.'

'So you decided to execute the Bishop?'

'We . . . *we* decided to execute the Bishop.'

'Who's we? You and Sonny?'

He nodded. 'It was starting to drive Sonny crazy. He wanted him dead just as much as I did but I had to do it all, he wimped out as usual. Just like with Peter and Billy.'

There it was again. Peter and Billy? What did he mean, just like with Peter and Billy?

Roy was angry. And he was bragging.

'How about Linda and Alex?' she said. 'Why just pick on Billy and Peter?'

'They took off. Alex and Linda split.'

'Why?'

Roy shrugged. 'I dunno. Maybe they were getting nervous. After that last time, she went home to Ohio. I don't know what happened to that little fink, Alex.'

'What about Peter and Billy,' she asked cautiously.

'The usual. He always wimped out. He'd get steamed up and then . . . y'know, I'd have to come in and take care of things. It was no different than takin' down His Excellency.'

My God, is he hinting that he killed Peter and Billy, too?

'How did it happen?' she asked, keeping the question vague, hoping he would continue to talk about the two missing altar boys.

'What do you want, the gory details?'

'Yes. How you did it. How you felt when you did it. Everything.'

'Jesus, you're just as sick as everybody else,' he said.

Suddenly he jumped up and started pacing back and forth, rubbing the palms of his hands together as he spoke. He went on, describing the events of that night as if he were having an out-of-body experience, as if he were high in the corner of the room, watching what was happening . . .

'The Bishop had invited Aaron up for a "private screening" of their latest epic. Peter and Billy were gone, Alex and Linda had split, so nobody had seen the tape yet.'

Another reference to Peter and Billy, she thought. *What did he mean, Peter and Billy were gone? Gone where?*

'Aaron hated it but the Bishop really got off on it, as always. He started breathing heavily, rubbing himself. Aaron could see on the tape that Linda had really gotten into it with Billy and he started feeling jealous. The Bishop told them what to do and they were really goin' at it. Then of course, the Bishop's off-screen voice started telling them all what to do. Sonny hated the film and he hated the Bishop. The Bishop's voice told Peter, who was already primed, to come into the picture and Aaron went berserk inside.

'The Bishop, staring at the screen, said to Aaron, "You getting hard yet?" and he rubbed Aaron's leg.

' "No," Aaron answered and moved away from him.

' "The Devil's got you tonight," said the Bishop.

' "Ah'm not in the mood," Aaron mumbled nastily, and stood up. At first, the Bishop got a little testy but he shrugged it off. Aaron left and the Bishop went into the shower.

'Aaron went down to the Bishop's library to borrow a book. But he couldn't get rid of the anger. Linda had left him, she was gone — but the tape was very much alive. He started back up the stairs. He could hear the shower running and the Bishop singing. He stood by the door to the bedroom and then *whoosh*, it was as if the hand of God had reached down inside him and given a giant tug and he suddenly was turned inside out . . .

'I had to take over at that point, he would have really screwed it up. I was thinking to myself, maybe this time he'll go through with it, but forget that. Not a chance.

'I hustled down the hall to the kitchen and checked the kitchen door. It was unlocked. I went outside on the landing and checked around and the place was deserted. I went back inside, took off my sneakers and then got a Yoohoo out of the refrigerator and drank it. My heart was beatin' so hard I thought it was going to break one of my ribs and the drink calmed me down. I opened the knife drawer and checked them out. The thick carving knife was perfect. Be like carving a turkey on Thanksgiving. I checked it and it was like a razor. I nicked my finger and sucked on it until the bleeding stopped. Then I went down the hall to the bedroom.

'He had the music way up. "Ode to Joy". I could picture him standing in the bedroom directing that air orchestra of his. Shoulda been a Goddam orchestra conductor, maybe we never would've met him.

'That's just what he was doing. He had candles burning — cleaning the air he called it — some kind of incense. His ring was lying on the table beside the bed. He always took his ring off before he took a shower. He left his watch on, I guess it was waterproof, but he took his ring off. Make sense out of that. So there he stood, the fucking saint of the city. His naked holiness, conducting that imaginary band of angels.

'The music was building. I thought, now it's your turn. So I went over and got the ring and put it on. His Excellency was out of it. Arms flailing around, eyes closed, unaware. I just walked up behind him and tapped him on the shoulder with the knife and he turns around and I thought his eyes were going to pop out of his head when he saw the knife. He got the message real fast. I held out the hand with the ring on it and pointed the knife at it and he begins to smile. So I jabbed the knife towards the carpet and that wiped the smile off his face.

'He got down on his knees and I wiggled that ring finger under his nose. The Bishop slowly leaned forward to kiss the ring and I pulled away my hand and I swung that knife back with both hands and when he looked up, whack, I swung at his throat. I yelled "Forgive me, Father!" but I was laughing in his face when I said it. He moved and I didn't catch him in the throat, the knife caught his shoulder and damn near chopped the whole thing off.

He screamed and held out his hands. I don't know how he even raised up that one but he did. I started chopping on him but I kept hitting his hands and arms. Then I cut his throat and switched and swung the knife up underhand right into his chest. It was a perfect hit. Didn't hit any ribs, just went right in to the hilt and he went, "Oh", like that, and he fell straight back and the knife pulled out of my hand. I had to put my foot on his chest to get it out. Then I took that big swipe at his neck.

'I couldn't stop. It was like free games on a pinball machine. Blood was flying everywhere. I know every cut I made, they were all perfect. Thirty-six stab wounds, twelve incised, seventeen cuts and one beautiful amputation. I counted every one.

When he fell he knocked over a table and lamp. There was blood splashed on his blinds and he let out this one terrific scream. So I knew we had to get out of there. Sonny tries the door to the closet and it's locked. So we head back to the kitchen.'

She had to swallow hard several times during his description, his details reminding her of the photographs in

Vail's office. Her revulsion turned back to fear when he finished. He stood a few feet from her, staring through half-closed, insane eyes.

'I tell him, ditch the knife,' Roy said, his eyes memory-mad. 'Does he hear me? Shit no, he never hears me. I hear him, all right, but not Sonny, oh no. It's like I don't exist.'

'How did it feel, Roy? While you were doing that?'

'Usually it feels good . . . I like killing, if that's what you mean. But not this time.'

'Why not? Why didn't that feel good this time?'

His lip curled back again. 'Because we got caught. The stupid shit runs out the door with the knife in his hand, doesn't get the video tape. I do my part and he fucks up royally, as usual. See, you think he's this sweet kid but that's bullshit, Doc. Y'know the only difference between him and me?'

Molly shook her head.

'He wants it . . . I do it.'

Then in an instant, his expression changed, his shoulders slumped, and Roy was gone.

Questions swirled through her mind, but one clouded all others: *What happened to Peter and Billy?*

It was time to get Vail up to Daisyland.

Twenty-Six

It was Tom Goodman who solved the secret of 'B32.156'.

It was right there, in front of Vail's face, all the time. It had only been three weeks since Molly's wreck. Vail had received a call from Molly the night before and had cancelled all appointments and was preparing to leave for Daisyland. Vail had shown the Roy tape, as it was now known to the team, to Naomi, the Judge and Tom Goodman.

'What you're going to see stays in this room,' Vail said before he started. 'And I don't want a lot of discussion. I just want you to think about it until Molly decides whether it's for real.'

Their reactions had been expected. Naomi was awed, Goodman was perplexed, the Judge was sceptical.

'It would be interesting to see how many defendants have ever successfully appeared before the bench claiming their alter ego committed the crime,' was his response.

'Have you ever tried one?' Vail asked.

'Nope.'

'Naomi,' Vail said, 'work some magic – see what you can find out for us.'

On this morning, Vail had called them together before leaving for Daisyland and was running over notes. Goodman had been staring at the library book he had found in Aaron's stander and suddenly he bolted for the door.

'I'll be back in thirty minutes,' he yelled back at Vail. 'Don't leave until I get back.'

'What the hell . . .' Vail said, but Goodman was gone.

Naomi, meanwhile, had busied herself at the phone. It took her fifteen minutes to come up with some bad news.

'I just had a nice chat with the ABA research department,' she said. 'There were fifty-three felony cases last year involving mental disorders as grounds for defence. Seven of them involved dual or multiple personalities.'

'And . . . ? asked Vail.

'Six convictions, one hung jury, no acquittals.'

Vail whistled softly through his teeth.

'Odds are for shit,' she sighed.

'They aren't even odds,' said Vail. He paced the room, snapping his fingers. Then he stopped abruptly and turned to her.

'Okay,' he said. 'I want case citations on every MPD defence for the last five years. Judge, as soon as she gets the list, start reading.'

As he was leaving, Goodman wheeled up in his Bug. He jumped out and ran up to the door as Vail was walking out.

'Wait a minute! Listen to this,' Goodman said. He took out his little black book and read: 'No man, for any considerable period, can wear one face to himself, and another to the multitude, without finally getting bewildered as to which may be true.'

'That's very good, Tommy,' Vail said. 'I have to get back up to Daisyland. Can we discuss these creative attacks of yours when I get back?'

'I didn't write it, Nathaniel Hawthorne did,' Tommy said as Vail sidestepped around him. 'In *The Scarlet Letter*. I copied it out of one of the Bishop's books.'

'Good for him.'

Goodman grabbed Vail by the arm. 'Come here,' he ordered, walking back into Vail's office. He picked up the library book he had taken from Aaron's stander and held it up with the spine facing Vail.

'What do you see?'

'*East of Eden* by John Steinbeck,' he said.

'What else?'

'302.16,' the Judge said.

'That's right. It's called the Dewey decimal system. It's

333

the way they index books at the library. I remembered something – the books in Rushman's library also had index numbers on the spine, so I went over and checked. He devised his own index system, much simpler than the library's. Book B32 is *The Scarlet Letter*. The passage is on page 156 and it's marked the same way those two quotes were marked in the books at Rebecca's house.'

Vail took the book and stared at it a moment.

'B32.156,' he said. 'I'll be damned.'

'Molly said he was sending messages,' Goodman said. 'The numbers are symbols. Remember what he said? The clue is on the tape?' He leafed back through the notes he had taken while watching the tape. 'He said the Bishop dropped his mask.'

'So the face he wore to the multitude was a mask, and the face he wore to the altar boys was his true face,' Naomi suggested.

'There's only one way to find out,' Vail said, heading towards the door. 'I'll go ask him.'

What had brought Roy out? That was the crucial question now. Molly had taken copious notes on her taped interviews with Roy and she and Martin discussed them at length when he arrived at Daisyland.

'You don't think he's faking?' Vail asked.

'So far, I've heard nothing, seen nothing on the tapes, and found nothing in my notes to indicate he's faking. I think we have to assume Roy is for real.'

It was Molly's contention that the only way to draw Roy back out was to trick him, to find some clue in her previous interview that would enable them to lure Roy back out into the open. They watched excerpts from several of the tapes and pinpointed the precise moment when Roy had replaced Aaron.

'Notice he has a slight malaise, rolls his eyes and then seems to get drowsy for a few seconds,' Molly said, pointing out what she felt were significant moments from the hours of interviews. 'He looks away from me, his body seems to sag, his eyes kind of go out of focus. His whole body changes. When he looks back up, he's Roy. That whole procedure doesn't take more than a few seconds.'

'Have you ever seen it happen like that before?' Vail asked.

'It's not uncommon,' she nodded. 'We sometimes see it in epilepsy, just before a seizure.'

'You were looking away from him the first two times he came out,' said Vail. 'Could that have had something to do with it?'

'Maybe. Who knows?'

'Is there any common subject matter when it happens?'

'It frequently involves some sexual reference. This last time we were talking about Rebecca, about sex. I asked him if she ever touched him and he started getting angry. "Why do you want to know that?" he asked and I said something about being honest and that's when I said, "Did Rebecca make love to you?" and he got very upset, it was the first time I ever saw him approach anger. I looked down at my notes and that's when Roy came out.'

'So it had something to do with Rebecca?'

'Or sex. Or fear we were getting too close to him. Or maybe it reminded him of something else, something we don't know about yet.'

'Like what?'

'I don't know, Martin. We're dealing with anxiety, phobia, paedophilia, voyeurism, neurosis, dissociative behaviour, multiple personality, religious and, possibly, sexual disorientation . . .'

'Sounds like a list of every mental disorder in the book.'

'Yes,' she said. 'And I'm still not sure which problem – or combination of problems – tipped him.'

'What's the first thing Roy ever said to you?' Vail asked.

'He said, "He'll lie to you." '

'Sounds like he was already trying to come between you and Sonny. Or Aaron. Christ, I have a hard time keeping these people sorted out.'

'Yes, there's definitely jealousy there.'

'Maybe Aaron is harbouring unclean thoughts about you, Molly, and Roy's acting on them.'

'That's very possible.'

'It makes me nervous.'

'What?'

'You going in there alone.'

'He won't do anything to me,' she said.

'What makes you so sure?'

'Because Roy's very street smart. He knows we're all that stands between him and the electric chair. Besides, we're playing his game and that's very important to him.'

'Do you think Roy will talk to me, if he comes out?'

'That's up to him.'

Vail's biggest concern was to try to explain to the jury the immense complexities of this case, for he knew that without a basic understanding of the way the mind works, the jury would never accept the bizarre phenomenon known as multiple personality disorder or that it was a verifiable disease.

'Okay, you're on the witness stand,' he said. 'How would you explain all this to twelve laymen?'

'I would tell them that the mind is a marvellous instrument consisting of three parts, like three boxes. The first box is the ego which contains conscious, every day thoughts and learned responses, all the things that permit us to perform normally – everything from cooking eggs to arguing a case in court to sweeping the floor. Second, there's the superego. Also conscious. This is where our values are stored. Ideals, imagination, integrity. Consequently, it also controls our morals. It prohibits certain acts – and punishes us with guilt feelings if we commit them, like lying, for instance.'

'Your conscience?' Vail asked.

'Yes, that's a reasonable analogy,' she said. 'Finally there's the id, the subconscious. It contains our basic instincts, but it's also where all our repressions are stored. All our suppressed desires lurk in the id. Finally, there are two basic drives, aggression, which prompts most behaviour patterns, and the libido, which is the sexual drive.'

'Okay, let me try this. I work at the grocery store. I get up, go to the store, do my job. That's my ego at work. I know I shouldn't take money out of the cash register, that's my superego talking. But my libido is working overtime. I harbour sexual feelings towards the boss's teenage daughter and my superego tells me that's taboo. It makes me feel guilty for thinking about it and so I suppress those feelings and they go to my id.'

'That's very good,' she said.

'Then explain what happened to Aaron.'

'Well, on the simplest level, your mind is just like your body. A perfect machine except when it gets sick. There are strong boundaries in the mind between the ego and the id. When the mind gets sick, the boundaries, or walls, between the ego and the id break down and repressed thoughts seep into the ego from the id. They clash with the superego and the mind becomes confused. Suddenly it's getting mixed signals. Sometimes the id wins out and the repressed thoughts become normal. When that happens, the mind is disordered. And that's the disease. It can manifest in hundreds of ways. There are more than two hundred identifiable mental diseases. In many respects, it's worse than a physical disease because we can't take x-rays. We can't operate. We can't give him a prescription for antibiotics.'

'Can it be cured?'

'Sometimes. First we have to determine why the wall broke down. Then we decide the best way to fix it.'

'That's an evasive answer.'

'Okay. With proper therapy — maybe.'

Not bad, Vail thought. Calm, authoritative, concise, self-assured. She'll make a good witness.

For the next two days at Daisyland they got nowhere. Aaron had no objection to Vail being in the room during the interviews, but during the next four interviews she could not bring Roy out. Vail said nothing. He marvelled at how effortlessly she conducted the interviews, the economy of her questions, how subtly and instinctively she moved from one subject to the other. She continued to probe Aaron's childhood; his relationships with his family and Mary; they talked about Rebecca, although Aaron was steadfast in his refusal to discuss their sexual exploits; about his relationship with Rushman, which he described as benign; and about Shackles and the occasions when he had lost time in the past. It was obvious he was unaware that the mad evangelist was dead, if indeed he was. Perhaps Roy was lying about that, just as Aaron lied about his relationships with Rebecca and Rushman.

At night they went back to Vail's motel room and studied the tapes of the day's interviews, looking for leads. The only subjects Molly avoided were the altar boys and the existence of Roy, which she still felt were too dangerous to broach.

'I'll know when it's time,' she told Vail. 'Trust me on this.'

They studied the tapes and talked about the case, went to dinner and discussed the case, and dutifully avoided the subject of their respective libidos as if the subject had never been brought up.

On the third day, Vail was all smiles when he showed up for breakfast.

'I think I figured out how to get to Roy,' he said.

'How's that?' she asked, sceptically.

'B32.156,' he answered with a smile.

Vail despised the hospital. To get to the maximum security wing, they had to pass one of the wards. Patients wandered around the large room, talking to themselves, others sat in catatonic stupors, staring into space. Still others were curled up in the corners in foetal positions. There was a constant din as the patients babbled inanely or cried out as they were suddenly overcome by obscure pains or fears. He hated the odour of disinfectant that seemed to permeate the entire establishment, the sterility of the white walls, the cold, proficient, emotionless way in which the staff dealt with the patients. Each time he entered the institution, Martin was reminded that if he successfully defended Aaron Stampler, the young Appalachian could spend the rest of his life here.

In contrast, the max wing, as it was known, was almost pleasant, although monotonous. Muzak was piped softly into the rooms and the stark white walls and high windows gave them an airy ambience.

On this morning, Aaron seemed distracted and disinterested when he first entered the interrogation room. He flopped down on the cot with hardly a word of greeting.

'Something wrong?' Molly asked.

'It's them other doctors.' he said. 'They ain't really interested in me. They ask the saim questions over and over. Give me stupid tests, one after t'other. You wanta know the truth? It's boring. Sometimes I fail like makin' sompin' up just to see what they'd do.'

'Don't they ever ask you about your parents and Crikside?'

'T'aint like you, Molly. T'aint like they really care.'

'Have you ever lost time when you were talking to them?'

'No m'am. Leastways I don't think so.'

'But you're pretty sure you haven't?'

'Yes, m'am.'

'Do they ever ask you about your education, things you've read, what you remember?'

'They did at first.'

'What's your favourite quote, Aaron?'

'Gosh, I dunno. Got a lot of thaim. Told you that one from Emerson. Thomas Jefferson hardly wrote a word thet wasn't worth rememberin'.'

'How about Nathaniel Hawthorne?'

'Yes, m'am, a faivour't of mine.'

'Any favourite quotes of his?'

'Not thet I thaink of, offhaind.'

'Let me try one and see if you can finish it. Want to try that?'

'If you want.'

'No man, for any considerable period of time, can wear . . . can you finish that, Roy?'

A few seconds passed, then Aaron suddenly sat up and swung his feet to the floor. It was Roy who turned to face them, his eyes defiant, his lips drawn back in a sneer.

'Ain't you the clever one, Doc,' he hissed in his harsh whisper. 'Or maybe it was your boyfriend, here. Maybe he figured it out.'

'This is Martin Vail, Roy,' Molly said, ignoring the sarcasm.

'I know who the fuck he is. You think I been sleepin' for the last couple days?'

'He's going to defend you and Aaron.'

'*Shiit*. He's not gonna defend me,' he breathed softly. 'He's gonna lay it all off on me, that's what this is all about.'

'That's not true. You say Aaron and you planned everything together.'

'It was his *idea*,' he said in his threatening voice. 'He thinks, I'd like to kill that son of a bitch. Bing! Here comes old Roy to the rescue.'

'So that's the way it works?' Molly said.

'How the fuck you think it works?'

'I wasn't sure.'

His tone turned more venomous than usual. 'I told you

last time, he gets a beating, I get the pain. I get him laid, he comes. He gets pissed, I do the dirty work. It's called the shitty end of the stick.'

'What do you want out of this, Roy?' Vail asked.

'Well,' he leered. 'We don't want to get fried, do we, Mister Vail?'

'That's right,' Martin said. 'And maybe if you help, you won't get fried.'

'How'm I supposed t'do that?'

'I want you to come out and testify at the trial.'

'Ohhh,' he said softly. 'And you want me to confess, right?'

'I just want to prove to the jury there are two of you. And you both need help.'

'I don't need any fuckin' help,' Roy snapped. 'What you mean is, you're gonna put me through the ringer and get rid of me. I know that trick. We've read about all that.'

'All what?' Molly asked.

'Shock treatments, drugs, ice water baths,' he said, standing and walking into the shadowy corner of the room. 'Shit, I know about that. You're gonna get rid of me and he'll sashay out the fuckin' door free as a bird, as God-damn-usual. Well it ain't gonna happen.'

'Maybe you're right,' Molly said. 'Maybe we'll work it out so you share the pain and the joy.'

'That's bull.'

'Not if you help,' Vail said.

Roy started rubbing his hands together. 'You must really think I'm stupid.'

'Of course not,' Molly said.

He rolled his eyes and knelt down in an Indian squat, staying in the shadows. 'Bullshit. *Bull*shit! Look *I'm* the one knows the tricks, I'm the one with the smarts. You forgot that, Doc?'

'No, I didn't forget it. It's also you who's sending the message.'

341

His eyes narrowed again. He cocked his head to one side and stared at her, half-grinning.

'Message?' he whispered.

'From *The Scarlet Letter*. That's what brought you out, isn't it?'

He sneered at her. ' "No man, for any considerable period of time, can wear one face to himself, and another to the multitude, without finally getting bewildered as to which may be true." Which one of you figured it out?'

'Actually it was Tom Goodman,' Molly said.

'The one who gave Rebecca all that shit?'

'He didn't give anybody any shit, Roy,' said Vail. 'She told him. I think maybe she figured the information might help you and Aaron.'

He stood and walked slowly back to the cot where he stood for several seconds chewing on his lower lip, then suddenly he hissed like a snake and holding his two fists together, twisted them in opposite directions, is if throttling a chicken.

'Kill the chicken and leave the bones,' he said cryptically in his soft, sibilant voice.

'What does that mean?' Molly asked.

'You're so smart, figure it out,' he said.

'I think you want the world to know what a demon the Bishop was, that's why you picked that verse and that's why you emasculated him. You wanted to draw attention to the gravity of *his* crime and you knew Aaron wouldn't do it.'

'Aaron would never tell,' Roy said. 'You know why? Because he'd rather fry in hell than admit it. Same as those other two.'

'You mean Billy and Peter?' Molly asked cautiously.

'Who the fuck else would I be talkin' about, Mary and Sam? Shit, that was different anyway.' He suddenly pointed at them. 'You think he figured that one out? Never! Little bastard still doesn't know where he was that day. But he had me kill his own brother and his old girlfriend.'

Molly was trying to think a step ahead of Roy, trying to out-guess him. *Mary and Sam. Billy and Peter.* My God, she wondered, how many people has he killed?

'No, I'm sure it was your plan to make it look like an accident,' she said.

'Damn sure. I read about it in the newspaper.' He leaned back sideways on the cot, supporting himself on his elbows. 'It was an article about how if you get stuck in the snow, don't leave your windows closed or you can die from carbon monoxide. I knew when Sonny read it to me what he wanted. They used to go up to Sackett's Ridge and fuck their brains out. Then Sam'd brag to Sonny about it, knowing how Sonny felt about Mary. Shit, little wonder Sonny started thinking about it.'

'You mean Mary and Sam.'

'Of course.'

'Weren't you afraid they'd catch you?'

'C'mon.' He let his head loll back and closed his eyes. He began to breathe heavier. His smile turned lascivious. 'They'd go at it, you could throw water on 'em like a couple of stuck dogs, they wouldn't notice it. She was a real chunk, Mary was, and she loved her screwin'. We went up there once or twice and hid in the woods and watched. Couldn't see a hell of a lot, the windows were all frosted over, but Sam always left the window cracked and I could hear them in there, him grunting, her squealin' – like damn pigs.

'You would've been proud of me, Doc, I didn't miss a trick. I came out just after dinner. Sneaked down and got a bunch of towels from the Doc's operating room and the gas can Hiram Melvin kept on his tractor. I knew they were gonna do it that night. Took us almost an hour to walk up there. The ground was good n'hard so I wasn't worried about the sheriff finding any footprints around. After a while, here they came. He hadn't set the brakes good and they were in the back seat.'

He stopped and opened his eyes, as if he were trying to focus on something beyond the room. He spoke more slowly, savouring every word.

'Ten minutes. Ten minutes, the inside of the car looked like a fog settled in there. I sneaked down to the car, looked in the window. They were just getting started good. He had her sweater pulled up and I could see those big boobs of hers. His hand was up under her skirt and she was squirming around and moaning . . . a bomb coulda gone off, they wouldn't of heard it.'

He sat up and started acting out the story as he told it, his eyes transfixed. 'I stuffed the towels real tight in the crack in the window and waited. After a while, I could hear him, grunting like a hog. They were breathing real heavy.' He stopped and laughed. 'Using up that oxygen. She starts whimpering, then yelling.' He stopped for a moment.

'Quite a show. A half hour passed. They'd stopped talkin'. Finally I took a quick peek. She was on top of him and they were both sound asleep, naked as they was born.

'I opened the door real easy, the towels fell right in my hand.' He started acting out his narrative again. 'I roll up the window, I turn off the radio so it don't burn out the battery . . .' He revolved his hand and twisted the imaginary knob. He pushed an imaginary door closed with both hands. 'I close the door and we go over and sit on a stump and stare at the car, listening to the engine humming. Seventy-one Chevy, that bastard Sam spent half his life tinkerin' with it. Finally I got cold so I put two more gallons of gas in the tank from the can, just to make sure it wouldn't stall out and we went back down into the valley, ditched the towels and the can and went home. We were in bed when he came back out. Didn't know shit until the sheriff came by in the morning.' He stopped, still staring at some point in infinity. 'It was beautiful.'

He abruptly jerked out of his almost trance-like state, his whispered voice suddenly laced with anger. 'Except they made up that fucking story so nobody'd know what really happened.'

'Made you mad, didn't it?' Molly said, sympathetically.

'Everybody shoulda known.'

'So you made sure that never happened again, didn't you?' Molly said.

'That's right. Fuckin-A. *Fuckin-A*, Doc.'

'Were Billy and Peter going to tell what was going on with the Bishop?' she asked.

'Billy and Peter! Shit.' His tone became derisive. 'They woulda kept on doing it right up until he got him some new altar boys, which would've been soon because they were all too old anyways. He already had a new girl lined up. They would've clammed up. Or worse, like that freak, Alex. Robin the Boy Wonder, my ass, the little fag, he woulda been next if Sonny hadn't fucked up so bad.'

'Aaron doesn't want to talk about it either, isn't that why you really came out the first time?'

'He woulda jacked you around forever, Doc. Same as with Rebecca. He'll never admit that.'

'Why not?' Vail asked.

'Because he liked it. Because he knew it was wrong but he liked it. Right or wrong, he fuckin' *liked* it.'

'Did you come out when he was making love to Rebecca?'

'No such luck. I told you, he liked it. It screwed up his head but he handled it by himself. That's why he won't talk about it.' Then he unexpectedly changed the subject. 'Is old Clarence Darrow here always gonna be along for the ride.'

'Would you be more comfortable if Martin left?'

'More comfortable . . . shiit. On this cot? Hell, I don't mind if he's here. He's gonna watch the tape anyway, right Clarence?'

'Not unless you give me permission,' Vail said. 'The tape is privileged information between you and Doctor Arrington.'

'So, why'd you watch the last one?'

'She had to explain about you. Were you offended that I watched it?'

'Nah. What the hell's the dif? Don't you have any questions, Clarence?'

'Call me Martin. Or Marty.'

'No sense of humour, huh?'

'Sure. Tell me a joke and I'll laugh.'

Roy cackled at that. 'You're okay, Marty. No hard feelin's.'

'I do have a question.'

'Shoot.'

'What happened to Billy and Peter?'

He chuckled. 'Jesus, you jump right past the main event, doncha?'

'I figure you'll tell us about it when you feel like it.'

'I didn't do nothin' with them. I left them there. Nobody'll find them for another week or two.'

'How come?'

'Place is closed. Always closes until late April. Even the caretaker's off.' He turned on the cot and looked back at them. 'Know what? I don't think you think I did it. A mile past the diner, right on the lake,' he said. 'When you find them, come back, we'll talk some more.'

'How did you get there?' Vail quickly asked.

'The church pick-up. They let us use it all the time, never thought nothin' about it. That's all. Night, night.'

He closed his eyes and his body suddenly sagged. A moment later his eyes fluttered open. He lay there staring at the ceiling for a moment, then said. 'Yes, m'am, I know that one. It air one of my fayvrites. It's from *The Scarlet Letter*.'

'That's very good, Aaron.'

Twenty-seven

The town of Burgess was forty-five miles north-west of the city, a quaint lakeside resort town that bustled during the months between May and November, then settled into a quiet, lazy village during the winter months. Its four hotels and three lodges were shuttered from December through early April except for an occasional party. Although sequestered just inside the King's county line, Burgess paid little attention to county politics, set its own rules, and relied on the wisdom of three city council men and a curmudgeon of a mayor to maintain its autonomy. It was a clean, unstructured community whose eccentrically undefinable architecture contributed to its charm and whose 2,500 permanent residents were radically independent, politically conservative, gossipy by nature, and cozily upper middle class, thanks to the upscale tourists who provided enough seasonal income to keep the town prosperous and comfortable year round.

The political seat of Burgess was the Lakeside Diner (a misnomer since the lake was a half mile to the east) on the northern edge of town, which was owned by Hiram Brash, the mayor. In the off-season it was open from six a.m. until ten p.m., seven days a week. The city council met every Wednesday morning at ten a.m. in one of the back booths – anybody interested could crowd around.

It was at just such a meeting that the town had agreed to permit the Rushman Foundation to purchase the old Wingate Lodge and turn it into a camp for the residents of Saviour House. There was some grumbling about having 'juvenile delinquents and druggies wandering all over the county' but a letter from Archbishop Rushman had assured the locals that there would be no problems and indeed there had been none. Thus Wingate Lodge had become Wingate Shelter.

It had taken Naomi Chance three days of calls to the American Hotel Association, travel agents, and other sources, checking out lakeside hotels and inns in the state that were closed during the months of February and March before she had remembered the shelter. A call to the Burgess Chamber of Commerce had confirmed that there was, indeed, a diner in the town and that Wingate Shelter was 'down the road and off to the right, next to the lake.' It fit Roy's description: 'a mile past the diner, right on the lake.' If Billy and Peter were to be found, it seemed as good a place as any to start looking.

Vail and Goodman arrived in the town a little after dark and stopped at the diner. Brash, a short, chubby, red-faced man in his early sixties with wisps of white hair decorating his florid scalp, put cups of coffee in front of them both.

'Passing through?' he asked pleasantly.

'How did you guess?' Goodman asked.

'Been Mayor of this town for eighteen years. My son's Chief of Police. I know everybody in this end of the county, son. And since the hotels are all closed for the season and the motel's full, you're either visiting or passing through.'

'That's very astute,' Vail said with a smile.

'Where you headed?'

'Actually we're heading back to the city,' said Goodman. 'We've already been.'

'I see. Are you eating this evening?'

'Nope, just coffee to get us back to town.'

'How come you're not driving the interstate?'

'More trouble than it's worth this time of night,' said Goodman. 'I don't like driving bumper-to-bumper.'

'You got a point there.'

'Actually I used to come up here when I was a kid,'

Goodman lied. 'My family stayed at a lodge down by the lake. Uh, Winston Lodge, Winthrop Lodge . . .'

'That's the old Wingate place, right down the road here,' Brash said.

'That's it, Wingate. My dad used to hunt up around here. I was just a kid then.'

'Yeah, that'd be twenty years ago,' the mayor said. 'Hasn't been a deer or bear around here for fifteen years. Price of progress.'

'Where is that old lodge, anyway,' Goodman asked. 'I remember it was a big place down by the lake.'

'That's right. About a mile down the road here. There's stone posts on both sides of the road where you turn in. But it's closed up right now. And Benny Hofstader, the caretaker, he's down in Florida fishing. Won't be back till next week.'

'Is it really as big as I remember?' Goodman said, still fishing for information.

'Hell, it's bigger now. Place can sleep about thirty. Got a living room big as a stadium. After the Catholics took it over they fixed up the basement, too. Game room, TV room.' He leaned over and winked. 'Pretty fancy for a bunch of runaway teenage dope fiends, you ask me.'

'Well, maybe next time I come up I'll run out there and take a look.'

'Come back in the summer and spend a little time with us,' Brash said with a smile. 'We love your money.'

'Fair enough.'

The road was an unlighted two-lane blacktop bordered by thick pine trees, so dark it seemed to swallow up the headlights. They would have missed the entrance to Wingate except that a full moon, just rising through the trees, etched the stone post in grey. As Goodman turned up between them the headlights picked up a brass plaque that read:

Wingate Shelter
FOUNDED 1977
By The Rushman Foundation

The dirt road wound through a heavy forest for half a mile before they saw the dark, ominous, two-storey sprawling structure framed by the moon's reflection, rippling on the lake.

'Hell, they didn't even leave a night-light on the place,' Goodman said.

They parked near the front entrance and swept the place with their flashlights. A broad wooden deck surrounded the first floor of the big resort with a wide wooden staircase leading up to it. Beneath the deck, narrow windows opened into the basement. Large casement windows and french doors faced the lake and led from the deck into the first floor of the structure. They held their flashlights against window panes and peered inside. Fingers of light probed an enormous great room with a sweeping fireplace at one end.

'Christ, you could burn a whole pine tree in that fireplace,' Goodman said.

'And probably heat most of Burgess,' Vail agreed. 'I'll check all the windows and doors on this level. You check the basement windows.'

'We could break a window,' Goodman suggested. 'Wonder what you get in Burgess for B&E.'

'If Roy's been here, about twenty years,' Vail answered.

Goodman went around the side of the building. The beam of his flashlight picked up a basement window. It was half open. A tremor of apprehension swept through him, a moment of anxiety. The first clue that perhaps this was the place Roy was talking about and that Billy Jordan and Peter were inside.

'Marty,' he called out. 'You better come back here.'

Their flashlights explored the basement room, slender

shafts of light revealed a large room with old-fashioned desk tables and two large television sets on a shelf at one end of the room. A large see-through fireplace separated the TV room from the adjacent game room. Except for cold, grey ashes and firewood remnants in the fireplace, the room seemed spotless. They scrambled over the sill and dropped down into the room.

'It's colder in here than it is outside,' Goodman said, his breath condensing in little swirls as he spoke.

'It's that cold wind blowing in off the lake,' said Vail. 'Wind chill's probably below freezing. Comes straight in the window and settles down here.'

Goodman walked through the television room and entered the game room through an arched doorway. As he did something soft brushed against his leg and across his foot.

'Shit!' he yelped and fell back against the wall, his heart beating in his throat, his light searching the floor. A large raccoon ran past Vail and scampered up the stairs to the first floor. Goodman sighed.

'I'm glad I don't do this for a living,' he said. 'I still don't know why we didn't let the cops handle this.'

'What if it's a false alarm?' Vail said. 'How the hell would we explain it?'

Goodman went into the game room, his light reflecting off the light walls cast an eerie glow in the large room. The rats came next. Flushed by the light, they came squealing from behind a sofa and dashed about seeking the darker corners of the room.

'Jesus, it's like a zoo down here!' Goodman cried.

Vail did not answer immediately. He was immobilised. His eyes stared unblinking down the thin beam of his flashlight. It was focused on a hand which rose up from behind the sofa, its fingers bent as if clawing the air. The flesh was dark blue, almost black. He took a few steps closer to the couch and as he did he saw the rest of the arm, a petrified limb stretched straight up. Then the ray picked up the naked, bloated torso to which it was connected and then the face, or what was left of the face. Swollen beyond recognition, the eyes mere sockets; the cheeks, lips, and jaw were gnawed and torn by furry predators of the night; the gaping mouth was a dark tunnel in what was an obscene facsimile of a once human visage. The throat was sliced from side to side, a gaping wound further mutilated by the creatures that had feasted upon it. He moved the light down the torso, passed the stabs, cuts and incisions, passed the vast sea of petrified blood, now black as tar, in which it lay, to the butchered groin. The fossilised corpse beside it was a smaller version of the same. Coffee surged into this throat and he had to swallow several times to get it back down.

'Tommy,' Vail said hoarsely.

'Yeah?' Goodman answered from across the room.

'Naomi guessed right. This is the place.'

It was nine o'clock when Abel Stenner got to the diner. He came in followed by Lou Turner, who took a seat at the counter near the door. Stenner walked back to the booth where Tommy and Martin were finishing dinner.

'What's the matter with Lou, is he feeling anti-social?' Vail said.

'You said you wanted to have a private talk,' Stenner answered, staring at Goodman.

'Hell, I just didn't want you to show up with the National Guard,' Vail said, waving Turner back to the booth. The black sergeant joined them.

'I can recommend the coffee,' Goodman said. 'It was made sometime this year.'

'I don't have time for coffee.'

'You may need it,' Vail said.

'What am I doing here, Vail?' Stenner asked. 'This is way off my beat.'

'You're still in the county.'

'I work for the city,' Stenner said.

'Maybe the county'll forgive you,' Vail said, lighting a cigarette.

'Can we get to the point?' said Stenner. 'The sign in front says they close in an hour. And do you mind not smoking, gives me a headache.'

'I may have a bigger one for you,' said Vail, snuffing it out in a tin ashtray.

Stenner leaned back in the booth and appraised him. He took off his wire-rim glasses and cleaned them with a paper napkin.

'Okay, I'm listening,' he said.

'This is just a guess, but I think you may be looking for a couple of Rushman's altar boys – Billy Jordan and Peter, who doesn't have a last name as far as we know.'

'Why should I be interested in them?'

'According to the Bishop's datebook, they had a meeting the night he was killed. Aaron was one of them,' Vail shrugged. 'You don't miss stuff like that, Abel.'

'Peter's name is Holloway,' Turner said. 'He's from Kansas City.'

'Good homework,' said Goodman.

'We went through his things at Saviour House,' Stenner said. 'Found a high school year-book in the bottom of his foot-locker. His foster parents couldn't care less about him.'

'That's too bad,' said Vail.

'You wouldn't know about a kid named Alex, would you?' Turner asked.

'We might,' said Vail.

'We here to play twenty questions?' Stenner said stiffly.

'Alex flew the coop,' Vail said. 'Probably pearl diving someplace in Alaska about now.'

'How about the girl?'

'The girl's out of the circuit. She doesn't know anything about Rushman's killing anyway.'

'How do you know?'

'She came to see me. But I have no idea where she is now.'

'She could be a material witness,' Stenner said, sternly.

'What was I supposed to do, make a citizen's arrest?'

'You said something about Jordan and Holloway,' Turner said.

'We can take you to them,' Vail said. 'But I want to make it clear, we got an anonymous tip about them.'

'Have you seen them?'

Vail nodded.

'Talk to them?' Stenner asked.

'No.'

'Is there some kind of a deal in this somewhere?' Stenner asked, his cold eyes narrowing with suspicion.

'Nope. Just doing our civic duty.'

'Aw bullshit,' Turner said.

'Okay, Lou,' Stenner said, softly. Then to Vail, 'You want nothing out of this, is that the ticket?'

'I just want it understood that we got a tip and checked it out before we called you. I didn't want to be accused of sending anybody on a wild goose chase.'

'Okay, understood. Where are they?' Stenner asked.

'Follow us,' Vail said, picking up the check. 'It's not far from here.'

Chief Luther Brash turned out to be a pleasant and co-operative fellow. He was four inches taller than his father, a bear of man with a black beard, shaggy hair and kind eyes who wore a thick leather jacket and corduroy trousers. The only deference to his official position was his badge, which he wore on the crown of a brown felt hat, and the .45 strapped to his hip. He had no objection to Stenner taking over the investigation and calling in the county coroner and forensics experts.

'Hell, the only violence we get up here is when the teeny-boppers knock each other around after football games,' he said, volunteering his two night men to put up yellow crime ribbons around the place and then posting them at the entrance posts to keep people out. The Mayor had closed the diner fifteen minutes early and was hanging around as an observer although he did find the circuit box and turn on the electricity. Harvey Woodside and Bill Danielson got there about eleven. Woodside meticulously snooped around the place, his expert eyes checking every scrap of dirt and dust. Vail and Goodman stayed out of the way, watching Woodside from a corner of the room. By midnight, Danielson had completed a cursory examination of the victims and was ready to send the two bodies back to the county morgue.

'What a mess,' he said, hefting himself to his feet.

'How long you think they've been here?' Stenner asked.

Danielson shook his head slowly. 'Place is colder'n a deep freeze, that window being open. Retarded decomposition. Wild things have been feasting on them. Hell, could be two weeks or two months. Maybe when we get 'em down-town I can get a little closer to it but right now I'm not taking any bets on when this event occurred.'

'Think there was more than one perp?' Stenner asked Woodside.

'Well, I'm not sure, but I'd say no. See here . . .' he pointed to blood stains and dark marks on the floor. 'My guess is that the tall one was done in first, probably right where he fell. The shorter one was attacked here and dragged about ten feet and laid out beside him.'

'The tall one's Jordan, the little guy's Holloway,' Turner volunteered.

'Whatever. I'll tell you this, either it was done by the same culprit that did in the Bishop, or a damn good copy-cat. Same kind of wounds, privates cut off and stuffed in their mouths, numbers on the backs of their heads. Also I'm pretty damn sure they were both clothed when they were attacked. There's definitely fibres around the chest wounds on both of them.'

Danielson strolled back in the room and walked over

to the open window, checking it carefully before joining the group.

'They didn't come in through that window,' he said. 'There's a broken pane in the door around back on the first floor.'

'So why is that window open?' Stenner said.

'I'm not sure,' said Danielson. 'But if I were guessing, I'd say to keep this room as cold as possible.'

'So whoever did this *wanted* the room to stay cold,' Stenner said.

Danielson nodded. 'Pretty smart, I'd say. Going to make it that much tougher for Woody to pinpoint when it happened.'

Stenner turned to Vail. 'And you don't know who tipped you off about this?' he said.

Vail shrugged. 'You know how it is with tips,' he said. 'Besides, if you're thinking what I think you're thinking, I couldn't tell you anyway. It might be contrary to my client's best interest.'

'It might at that,' Stenner answered.

Twenty-eight

Naomi Chance had cleared off her desk except for the telephone and spread a large fourteen by seventeen inch sheet of graph paper out in front of her. For ten days she had been gathering information – and for the last two days her quest had been so intense she had not been in the office or called, which was uncharacteristic. She had returned with her briefcase bulging with copies of corporate files, tax records, bills, contract figures, political lists, and newspaper clippings. As always, she was excited when she was on to something. Usually it was Martin who put things into context but this time she had figured out exactly how to do it.

She was drawing boxes, entering information into each of them, then connecting them with lines. It had taken her two hours to fill in the matrix and now she sat back and studied her handiwork.

It was all so obvious when you put it into a graphic perspective. Simple. Clever. Almost foolproof. But not quite.

As she was putting the finishing touches on her display, Goodman and Vail came in from breakfast.

'Where the hell you been for the last two days?' Vail asked. 'I was ready to call Missing Persons.' He looked at the large link analysis which lay before her. 'And what's that?'

'I think I'm about to make you a happy man,' she said.

Goodman said, 'Before you start, listen to this. It's Roy's message to us, courtesy of the late Peter: "There never would have been an infidel, if there had not been a priest." '

'Thomas Jefferson,' Naomi said without losing her cadence.

'That's very good, Naomi,' Goodman said. 'How about this one that was on the back of Jordan's head: "There are few pains so grievous as to have seen, divined, or experienced how an exceptional man has missed his way and deteriorated."'

'Easy,' she said. 'It's from Nietzsche. *Beyond Good and Evil.*'

'You're red hot, lady. Batting a thousand.'

'He killed Billy and Peter before he killed Rushman,' Vail said. 'These quotations all refer to the Bishop, not the altar boys. Hell, he was leaving clues before he killed Rushman.'

'And that,' said Tom in a voice of doom, 'is called premeditation.'

'Or madness?' Vail answered.

'Maybe Stenner and Venable won't figure out they're quotes,' Naomi said.

'I wouldn't assume that,' Goodman answered.

'We assume they know everything we know,' said Vail. 'That way we don't make any mistakes.'

'Maybe they know more than we do. Maybe we've overlooked something.'

'Yeah,' said Vail. 'We sure overlooked Roy for a long time. It's all academic anyway. Venable can't use it unless she proves Aaron killed Jordan and Peter and that she won't do.'

'Why not?' Naomi asked.

'She's too smart,' Vail answered. 'It's a hell of a lot easier to prove one murder case than it is to prove three. She's not going to blow one open and shut case to take a chance on proving the other two.'

'Besides,' said Goodman, 'from what we hear, Danielson can't pinpoint when they were killed. The range is four weeks, starting a week before Rushman was murdered.'

'Yeah, she's too smart to bite on that,' said Vail. 'We'd wait until they establish the connection between the murder of Rushman and the killing of the two boys, then nail Danielson. According to his investigation, the chances are three to one that Jordan and Holloway were killed after Bishop Rushman, while Aaron Stampler was in custody.

'And farewell Madame Prosecutor,' said Vail. 'The jury would look cross-wise at all three cases. But it's moot, she won't walk into that trap.'

'Is that why you told Stenner about the murders?' Goodman asked.

Vail did not answer immediately then he shrugged his shoulders. 'It was worth a shot,' he said. 'Besides, did we have a choice? What've you got for us, Naomi?'

'The Gudheim Foundation,' she said.

'What the hell's the Gudheim Foundation?' Vail asked.

'It's one of twenty-two different charities, steering committees and holding companies in the Rushman Foundation,' she said. 'I've laid it all out so you can follow the paper trail.'

She traced the boxes on the matrix with her finger as she described them, Goodman and Vail following the trail avidly.

'It's like a pyramid. On the top is the Gudheim Foundation. It is the paymaster for all the charities. Whatever these charities spend, goes to Gudheim and it pays off. Three construction companies do all the maintenance work, from putting up new buildings to paint maintenance. Two automotive companies do all the maintenance on their vehicles. These two CPA firms handle bookkeeping for everybody. The Berenstein Clinic is their official "hospital" . . . twelve companies in all and they submit their bills directly to Gudheim, nobody in the charity even approves them. Why? Look here. The directors of the charities are all trustees of Gudheim. It gets a bill for twenty thousand dollars for repair work at

Saviour House, it sends them a cheque. Now look at this. Each of these companies has made the maximum contribution allowable under the law to certain political candidates.'

'Legal so far,' said Vail. 'The limit is twenty-five thousand dollars per candidate.'

'Except that by using these twelve companies,' Naomi said, 'they make twelve times the legal contribution to each of these eight candidates. That's almost ten per cent of their annual take – over five million bucks in illegal campaign contributions.'

'That's several felonies' worth,' said Tom.

'And in every case,' she went on, 'in the three or four months preceding the contribution, these companies have submitted large invoices to Gudheim. Look, Berenstein goes along for five months averaging three, four thousand a month. Then suddenly it jumps to twenty-two thousand, eighteen thousand, here's one for thirty thousand.'

'So they report the income and write the contribution off their income tax,' said Vail.

'There's more,' Naomi said. 'Four of the recipients are also the members of the Board of Trustees who specifically approve the payments ... including Mister D.A., Jack Yancey, and guess who?' She pointed to the name. 'Your friend and mine, Judge Harry Shoat.'

Vail whistled softly through his teeth. 'If this breaks, bye-bye Supreme Court for Harry.'

'Slick, too,' said Tom. 'A giant, illegal slush fund and nobody can talk because they're all guilty.'

'And most of the heavy hitters in town are trustees.'

'That's a lot of people to keep silent,' said Goodman.

'Probably only these four on the payola committee know about it,' said Vail. 'The politicians think the contributions are coming from corporations.'

'But the heads of the corporations have to know about the contributions,' said Naomi.

'What do they care,' Vail said. 'It's a break-even propo-

361

sition for them and they get on the Foundation payroll. If you asked them, they'd brush it off, tell you it's the way business is done these days.'

'Besides,' Naomi sneered, 'if the Bishop was behind it, how could it be wrong?'

'How do they pick their candidates?' Goodman asked.

'Check it out,' said Naomi. 'These are clippings from their campaigns. All of them are anti-abortion, pro-censorship, pro-capital punishment, anti-welfare . . . hard line right-wingers.'

'All the Bishop's favourite things,' said Goodman.

'They toe the mark, they get the money,' said Vail. 'The Bishop was a very busy bee.' He checked through the clippings. 'So this is what Shaughnessey is afraid of, what he was referring to at lunch the other day.'

Goodman laughed. 'Jesus, if he thinks *this* is a problem, what would he do if he knew about the altar boys?'

'Instant coronary,' Naomi said.

'But how can we use this in the trial?' Goodman asked.

'Oh,' said Vail, still checking the clippings, 'something'll come up. Naomi, darlin', you're an absolute jewel.'

She beamed. 'Praise from Caesar,' she said.

Jane Venable's split-level penthouse overlooking the lake had once been featured in *Architectural Digest*. An only child, she had sold the family mansion on Lakeshore Drive when her mother died, her father having passed away the year after she completed law school, and had her architect structure the sprawling apartment around the family antiques and paintings. It was unique, a late nineteenth-century home high in the clouds atop the most modern structure in the mid-west.

The only incongruity was her study, a bright, starkly modern room which was in harsh contrast to the dark hues of the rest of the suite. It was to that room that she had invited the key members of her team – Danielson,

Stenner, Charlie Shackelford, and Woodside — for a catered lunch. Sliced steak, roast beef, ham, hard rolls and strawberry cheesecake for the men; a salad for her. She wore a black double-breasted suit with a high-collared lace blouse, all business but feminine — to remind them that she was both a woman and the boss.

As the big day approached she became more paranoid about the people in the office. With only eleven days left before the trial, she had decided to narrow the inside circle, hold the meetings away from the office, and limit discussions to facts not strategy. She had moved the stacks of reports and books off a large, smoked-glass table and stacked them in a closet but she had left three stacks of thick, trial transcripts on one end of the table. The food was laid out on the other end. As usual, she cut to business after a minimum of small talk.

'What's the final word on Jordan and Holloway?' she asked Woodside.

'Same pattern as the Rushman kill,' the heavy man said. 'Same kinds of wounds, done with the same professional touch. Numbers on the backs of the skulls, emasculation, the whole bit. He killed Jordan first. My guess is, the perp took down Holloway when he saw Jordan's body. Slit his throat from behind, then dragged him over beside Jordan.

'We can establish that from the marks made by the heels of Holloway's shoes,' Danielson said in his quiet, southern accent. 'They were dragged through the blood. There was bark and wood splinters around the spot where he attacked Holloway. So I think what happened, they sent Holloway out to get firewood. When Holloway left, the perp hit Jordan — three or four fatal stab wounds. Then when Holloway came in with his arms full of firewood, the perp hit him from behind. He burned the logs in the fireplace while he undressed the two bodies and finished the work. Then he burned their clothes in the fireplace, too.'

'When, Bill?' she demanded.

Danielson shook his head. 'These two bodies were chewed up by predators and that basement was like a deep freeze. I really can't give you anything definite.'

'Can you say for certain they were killed before Rushman?'

'No. My guess is anywhere from a week before Rushman's murder to three weeks after it. I'm sorry. I know you'd like to add these two to the Rushman . . .'

'Absolutely not!' she said, cutting him off. 'We've got Stampler cold on the Bishop's murder. If we tie these to the indictment and we blow either one of them, we lose it all. But it would be nice to have it in our back pocket, just in case.'

'This is the most substantial physical evidence I have ever seen in a felony homicide,' Danielson said. 'We got everything but an eyewitness.'

'And a motive,' Shackelford said.

'Don't be too sure,' Venable answered. Stenner's eyes flicked over at her but she ignored him. 'We have three psychologists who will testify that Stampler is sane. The Bishop had forced him to move because he was shacked up with this girl, Linda. Our contention is that Stampler and Rushman had a falling out. He had to move to The Hollows. His girl left him. He probably was going to have to quit the college extension courses. We can make a very strong case that he felt betrayed by the good Bishop, and so he premeditated and committed his murder.' She turned to Shackelford. 'I know you have a problem with that, Charlie.'

'I think Vail will eat us up on the motive thing, mainly because it's all supposition and hearsay.'

'We have to provide a motive,' she said. 'If we don't he'll come down harder on us.'

'I'm just saying it's skimmed milk,' said Shackelford.

'Then come up with some cream.'

'That I can't do.'

'Remember,' she said, 'we have three shrinks – and one of ours is a woman which should balance off his female psychologist – and all three will testify that under that kind of stress he could have been motivated to this kind of response. Right now that's the best we can do.'

'How about this fugue thing?' Stenner asked.

'All three shrinks say he has never gone into fugue while they were talking to him – even under the worst kind of stress.'

'Which means?'

'Which means they don't believe him. Anything else, Bill?'

Danielson said, 'We can match fibres found on the knife tray to the gloves in his jacket pocket.'

'Beautiful,' she said, excitedly. 'So we can prove he came in through the kitchen.'

'Or went out there and got the knife,' Woodside said.

'Either way it blows his "mystery killer" theory,' said Stenner.

'Certainly puts a dent in it,' Venable agreed.

'As far as Jordan and Holloway go . . .' Woodside started to say.

'Forget them,' she said firmly, waving off the suggestion. 'Keep working on it but it doesn't relate to this case. Unless we can prove they were killed before Rushman and we can put Stampler on the scene when they died, I'm not touching it. Like I've told you, the best way to screw up a good murder case is to double up. Whoever succeeds me can worry about those two.'

'Have you seen Connerman's column?' Danielson asked.

'I saw it,' she said. 'So . . .'

'Well, he's picked up some bull from the Keystone Cops up in Burgess and he's speculating that Jordan and Holloway were killed by the Rushman killer and it could have been done after Rushman was killed, when Stampler was in custody.'

'Connerman isn't trying this case, I am,' she said slowly, with more than a touch of venom. 'And anybody that reads that garbage will not sit on this jury. It does not relate and it will not be mentioned in this trial, okay?'

They spent an hour talking testimony, the witness agenda, and physical evidence, but she would not get into strategy. When they left she asked Stenner to stay behind for a few minutes. The waiters cleared the table and Venable sat down behind it and gazed across the stacks of transcripts at Stenner who sat stiffly in a straight-backed dinner chair. She lit one of her long, slender cigarettes, then remembered Stenner's aversion to smoke and snuffed it out.

'These aren't just transcripts,' she said, leaning forward and patting the thick folios. 'These are transcripts of Vail's ten toughest cases. I've studied every one of them, Abel, looking for his Achilles Heel.'

'Did you find it?' he asked, his expression unchanged.

'I think so. See, Vail not only wants to win – he wants to win it all. He'll destroy witnesses, risk the wrath of judges, play to the press – do anything – to win big. To do that, he gambles. And when you gamble, there's no such thing as second place. Either you win, or you lose it all. Vail's *never* lost it all.'

'He's done some plea-bargaining in his day,' Stenner said with a shrug.

'Uh huh. The secret is, what does he want? Oh, he'll go for the whole package – but he's always got a compromise waiting in the wings and the compromise is what he really wants. If he settles for a plea, then the plea was always what he wanted.'

Stenner's eyes never strayed from hers. He did not comment, he sat quietly and listened. But he was thinking, *Why did she have to read ten transcripts to figure that out? They're exactly the same, she and Vail. They both have uncompromising sticking points. But the points are so far apart that the verdict will be a disaster for one of them.*

'What he'd like, his dream, is to walk that little psychopath out the door a free man. What he'll settle for is guilty but insane, which means Stampler goes to Daisyland until he's cured and then walks.'

'What will you settle for?'

'The chair.'

'That's not a compromise.'

'Who said anything about compromising? We've got him, Abel. The only weak link in our case is motive. We've got the strongest chain of physical evidence I've ever seen – more than enough to burn him. With all that, the jury will buy any motive, no matter how weak it is.'

'Then what are you worried about?'

'Who says I'm worried?'

'Any lawyer is worried before a big trial.'

'If I'm worried about anything . . .' she said and hesitated, staring at the transcripts. 'If I'm worried about anything, it's the myth.'

'Myth?'

'The Vail myth. Fear that the son of a bitch's got something up his sleeve. Well, this time we know he doesn't. Oh, he'll make a circus out of it. And I'll stay cool. Object every time he starts performing. That'll break his momentum. Vail's bullish on momentum. He likes to get on a ride, so I'll interrupt his rhythm. Distract him. Juries are intuitive about things like that. They sense when a lawyer's grandstanding. They can tell when they're on shaky ground.'

'Supposing he does spring something on you? You still won't compromise?'

'It's not going to happen. I mean, if I absolutely *had* to plea this case out, the least I'd settle for . . . the absolute *least* . . . '

She tossed her lighter angrily on the table and stood

up, going to the window, staring out at the city with her hands on her hips.

'. . . the absolute least, I guess, would be life without parole. In Rockford. Solitary confinement. Life in solitary confinement in the meanest sweat-box in the state. If I absolutely had to settle for less than max, I'd want him to be the leper of the state. I'd want him locked up so tight he couldn't find an ant to kill.'

She whirled around, her face clouded with anger at the thought of compromising the Rushman case.

'But it won't happen,' she snapped. 'Aaron Stampler's going to the chair, Lieutenant. Take it to the bank.'

Six days to go – five until Aaron was taken back to the city. Molly had to make her move, and a dangerous move it was. Revealing the existence of Roy could traumatise Aaron – or even worse, bring Roy out permanently. But it was essential to inform Aaron now to prepare him for the trial and the revelations that were sure to follow. How he would react was completely unpredictable.

She returned to the tall security building after dinner. It was unusual for her to see Aaron in the evenings but she felt the conversation should be done in a relaxed atmosphere. No heavy therapy, no delving. She would take him a piece of coconut cream pie, his favourite, and a coke. She would try to be as calm and casual as possible as she prepared him for the shock of discovering that within his skin, there was another entity – that his 'lost time' was being filled by an evil, psychopathic, killer.

He was surprised to see her.

'Sompin' wrong?' he asked, his startled eyes reflecting fearful anticipation.

'No,' she said. 'I just came by to say hello. Brought you a coke and a piece of coconut cream.'

'Awraight!' he said with a smile, taking the paper plate and plastic fork and sitting on the edge of the cot and putting the coke at his feet. 'Thaink yuh.'

'Sure.'

'Gonna move me to th'city Sunday,' he said.

'Yes. Getting nervous?' she asked.

'Ah reckon.' He took a bite of pie, and added, 'Wha'more kin they aisk me they ain't aisked awready?'

'It's how and when they ask – and why,' she said.

'Yes, m'am, ah understand all thet. I weren't mad at Bishop Richard and ah don't remember anythin' that happened. Saims t'me thet 'bout says t'all.'

'Maybe not,' she said, trying to sound blasé.

'What'a thet main?'

'You know. All these lawyers have tactics. Strategies. Never know what they might come up with.'

'What maiks a good lawyer is thet he figgers out what they're gonna do afore they do't.'

'I suppose that's true. I'm sure Marty will do that. But, you know, there's always those unexpected things that pop up.'

'Sech as?'

She smiled. 'Well, if I knew that, they wouldn't be unexpected, would they?'

He laughed as he finished his pie and washed the last bite down with his coke. 'No, m'am, not railly.'

'Do you always know when you lose time, Aaron?'

'Mostly, ah reckon. It's like, one eye-blink ah'm staindin' hair, next blink ah'm settin' down. Worst it gets, one blink ah'm hair – next, ah'm a mile away n'it's four hours later, like thet.'

'Ever wonder what happens when you lose time?'

''course ah do. But, y'know, tain't sompin' you feel easy askin' others 'bout. Cain't ask somebody, "How'd I get hair?" Know wh't ah main?'

'Sure. Do you remember I asked you once about someone named Roy?'

He nodded. 'Don't recall nary by thet name.'

She realised there was no easy way to do it.

'I do have something I want to talk to you about.'

He stared up at her with anticipation and grinned. 'Should I lay down?'

'No, no. This is just you and me talking.'

''kay.'

'Aaron, I know you've read a lot about mental disorders. Have you ever heard of a mental disease called Multiple Personality Disorder?'

He stared at her for several seconds. 'Thet's what th'call split personality?'

'That's the common term for it, yes.'

'Don't know much 'bout it.'

'But you do know what it means?'

He nodded slowly, still staring at her.

'I've worked with a lot of people who have multiple personalities,' she said. 'It isn't that rare.'

He continued to stare apprehensively. She could almost feel his anxiety.

'Supposing I told you that you have another personality, one that comes out when you lose time. How would you feel about that?'

He still did not respond.

'For instance, supposing you have another personality called Roy.'

'Roy? Roy who?' he said with alarm.

'He doesn't use a last name.'

'You sayin' thet this Roy is me?' he said, cautiously.

'In a manner of speaking. He is like your alter ego. You know what that means?'

'Laik the other side of me?'

'That's a very good description. You see, sometimes when we suffer great pain or humiliation, the mind invents another personality – another character – to suffer that pain and humiliation. Kind of like an escape valve.'

After a long pause, he said, 'The bad side?'

She hesitated before answering. It was moving too fast. She had hoped to approach Roy's divergent nature more

370

cautiously; to ease Aaron into the revelation that his soul harboured a secret killer.

'Not necessarily,' she said. 'You remember when Reverend Shackles scared you and threatened you?'

'Yes, m'am.'

'Did you lose time then?'

'Don't remember.'

'When is the first time you remember losing time?'

He thought about that for a long time. Finally he said, 'Reckon it was 'bout the time m'paw started strappin' me for refusin' t'go in The Hole.'

'Did you lose time when you went down in The Hole?'

'No m'am,' he said emphatically. 'I remember every second a'thet, every second . . .'

'Roy says the first time he came out was to cuss out Reverend Shackles.'

'You *talk* t'him?'

'Yes.'

'Kin ah talk t'him?'

'Maybe later. Not yet.'

His eyes narrowed. 'Y'got him on the taip, don't yuh?'

'Yes. But before we get into that, I want to make sure you understand exactly what has happened to you.'

'Is Roy me?' he demanded.

She started to explain the ego, the id and the superego in order to define Aaron's disorder but he was shaking his head.

'Roy killed Bishop Richard, din't he? Thet's what yer tryin' t'tell me. I really did it.'

'You didn't do it, Aaron, Roy did. And with help and time we can strengthen you and get rid of Roy.'

He sat up very straight and stared at the wall, then his shoulders sagged for a moment and he turned slowly towards her, eyes ablaze. He stood suddenly, smashed the cot against the wall and rushed her. She fell back into the corner as his right hand grabbed her by the throat, the strong fingers digging deeply into her neck.

'You whore bitch,' Roy bellowed, his eyes yellowing with rage. 'I knew it! You lied to me. You're trying to kill me . . .'

'No, no!' she begged, her voice barely audible as his fingers continued to cut off wind and voice. 'Please . . . listen . . .'

'I already listened. You're like all of 'em, say anything to get what the fuck you want.'

She grabbed his hand with one of hers but he laughed at her, applying more pressure as she tried in vain to break his stranglehold. He backed up, holding her at arm's length with one hand to prove his strength.

'Roy . . .' Her voice was a squeezed-off whimper. 'Don't you . . . understand . . . we're going to make . . . both of you well . . .'

'You're gonna get rid of me. Think I'm a fuckin' dork? You forget, baby, I get both sides of the conversation.'

She was getting faint. His hand was like a steel vice, crushing the life out of her. He began to diminish in size, his laughter hollow and far away, the muscles, veins and pipes in her throat numbing.

'Aaron?' she squealed. 'Help . . . me . . . Aaron . . .'

'Bitch,' Roy roared and the vice tightened. She could feel herself going, the room rushing away from her, all sense and feeling abandoning her.

'Aaron . . .'

Consciousness whooshed away from her as she plunged into darkness.

Molly stirred. Her eyes fluttered and opened slowly. She was staring at the ceiling of the white room. Her neck throbbed with pain as she rolled over on her side. She coughed as she gasped for breath through her bruised throat. She lay still for a full minute, slowly regaining her breath as the room racked back into focus. Finally she sat up. The cot was back in place and Aaron was lying on it. She rose on unsteady legs, grasped the corner of the cot for support and slid on to it. Aaron was on his side, facing the wall.

'Aaron?' she said. There was no response. She touched his shoulder. He was tense and curled into a semi-foetal position. Only his breathing appeared normal.

'Aaron?' she demanded, a little louder. There was no response. She sat on the edge of the cot and shook him.

Nothing. Aaron Stampler appeared to be catatonic. He had escaped to another world.

Twenty-nine

'You think he's gone catatonic?' Vail asked.

'I'm not sure. He could have gone into a trance. He may have been bluffing. He may have been avoiding talking to me. I just don't know, but I gave him a shot.'

'Why?'

'Just to be on the safe side. He'll be out for twelve hours. If he comes around, we're back where we started. If he doesn't . . .' She made a helpless gesture with her hands. 'I told the guard he was nervous about the trial so I gave him a shot. Anyway, he'll be out until morning – which gives us time to figure out what to do next.'

Molly had taken a hundred dollar cab ride back to the city after giving Aaron sixty milligrams of Demerol to keep him out until morning. Now Vail had gathered the team to discuss the latest crisis. Except for the discussion of the Gudheim Foundation, he had been almost reclusive for the past three days, silent and brooding, striding his office, sometimes speaking aloud, sometimes arguing silently with himself. It was an experience all of them but Molly were accustomed to, watching him prepare for battle; feeling the tension he was creating, the energy sizzling about the room. Now he was edgy, verging on anger.

'Hell,' Goodman said, 'we're home free, Marty. It's obvious he's sick. We go for commitment and it's over.'

'And what if he comes out of it?' Vail said. 'What if he sits up tomorrow morning and says, "Haiy, mayem, was I jest out to lunch?"'

'That's cruel,' Molly snapped.

'Let me tell you what's really cruel,' said Vail. 'Doctor Bascott and his two dinosaurs have given Aaron a clean bill of mental health but . . . *but* . . . they also say, that, uh . . . how did they put it, Naomi?'

' " . . . given the sress of the situation," ' she read from the report, ' "Aaron Stampler could have committed this homicide." '

'That's ridiculous,' Molly said. 'Under the stress of what situation?'

'They're manufacturing a motive,' Vail said. 'Rushman forced Aaron to leave the House, he was reduced to The Hollows, his girlfriend left him . . . blah, blah, blah.'

'What's the point?' Molly said angrily.

'The point is, you know he's sick and I know he's sick but the State's genius head shrinkers are dancing to the tune because they don't know shit,' Vail answered angrily. 'A three-headed fucking rubber stamp.'

'Haven't we got enough to get a postponement?' Tom said. 'Or get him committed without a trial?'

'I don't want a postponement, Tommy,' said Vail. 'We won't be any readier than we are now and the longer we postpone, the stronger their case can get.'

'You think you can win this trial, Marty?' the Judge asked.

'Immaterial. Now's the time to defend Aaron, not after he's been lying around Daisyland in a foetal position for ten years.'

'But he may anyway!' said Molly.

'We're going to proceed on the assumption that when he wakes up tomorrow we'll be back in the ball game. Am I right, Judge.'

The Judge shrugged. He gave the premise a lot of thought and finally nodded. 'I agree with Martin. The only chance Aaron's got is to go to trial. If Martin wins, the boy goes to Daisyland until he's cured and he's a free man. Otherwise it will play out just as he says.'

Vail started pacing, grinding his fist in the palm of his hand. His jaw was set.

'Okay,' he said, 'here's what we're going to do. First,

we're going to do a run-through of your testimony, Molly. We're going to do this because if he does come around, we have to be ready, okay? Then we're going back up to Daisyland so we can be there when the jolt wears off. And if it doesn't wear off, he stays in Daisyland and everything goes on hold. Molly, we're going to do this as if you're on the witness stand. I'll be asking the questions. Naomi and Goodman can cut in with adversarial questions by raising their hand. They can object, just like in a regular trial. The Judge will maintain order and rule on objections, if there are any. Up for it?'

'Sure,' she said.

'If there's a legal objection or discussion, I'll put the video machine on pause.'

'How come?' asked the Judge.

'Because I feel like it,' was the curt answer.

Molly was sitting in the centre of the room and Vail paced as he asked the questions, sometimes stopping to lean against the table or check his notes. He was warm but formal and his eyes never left hers as he interrogated her. The video camera rolled silently, focused on her.

VAIL:	Please state your name.
MOLLY:	Doctor Molly Arrington.
VAIL:	Where do you reside, Doctor Arrington?
MOLLY:	Winthrop, Indiana. I'm on the staff of the Justine Clinic.
VAIL:	And what is your profession?
MOLLY:	I'm a licensed clinic psychologist and psychiatrist.
VAIL:	Where did you attend college?
MOLLY:	Indiana State. I took my medical training at Emory University in Atlanta, Georgia.
VAIL:	What is the Justine Clinic?

MOLLY:	A privately endowed mental hospital and research institute.
VAIL:	And you are on the staff there?
MOLLY:	Yes, I'm associate director of the Aberrational Studies Department.
VAIL:	What does that mean exactly?
MOLLY:	I'm a specialist in the field of mental health specialising in antisocial and eccentric or bizarre behaviour as it relates to psychopathic conduct.
VAIL:	And as such, do you deal with violent behaviour?
MOLLY:	Yes I do.
VAIL:	How long have you been at the Justine Clinic?
MOLLY:	Six years.
VAIL:	And before that?
MOLLY:	I was an associate in private practice for a year and before that I spent two years interning at City Hospital in Indianapolis.
VAIL:	And in this position, have you been called upon to diagnose and examine patients suffering from mental disorders?
MOLLY:	Yes, many times.
VAIL:	And did you so diagnose Aaron Stampler?
MOLLY:	Yes I did.
VAIL:	Doctor Arrington, are you familiar with the collaborative diagnosis of Aaron Stampler submitted to the court by Doctors Bascott, Ciaffo and Solomon on behalf of the State?
MOLLY:	Yes, I've studied the report.
VAIL:	Do you know these three doctors?
MOLLY:	I have met Doctor Bascott. I'm familiar

	with Solomon and Carole Ciaffo by reputation.
VAIL:	Do you respect their work?
MOLLY:	Yes I do.
VAIL:	And do you agree with their diagnosis of Aaron Stampler?
MOLLY:	No, I do not.
VAIL:	Why not?
MOLLY:	I believe it's incomplete and inconclusive.
VAIL:	On what basis did you arrive at this conclusion?
MOLLY:	The three doctors were responsible for determining only whether Aaron is capable of understanding the charges brought against him and is capable of assisting in his own defence and is intelligent enough to comprehend the proceedings.
VAIL:	And you think they made a mistake?
MOLLY:	No. I believe their diagnosis of Aaron Stampler in these areas was accurate.
VAIL:	Then in what way do you disagree with them?
MOLLY:	I don't believe their examinations were comprehensive enough. Their conclusion is superficial. Their job was to make an evaluation and that's all they did.
VAIL:	Isn't that what they were supposed to do?
MOLLY:	May I give an example of what I mean?
VAIL:	Whatever is comfortable for you, Doctor.
MOLLY:	Let's say a man is injured in an automobile wreck. He has obvious head injuries. If the examining team confines

378

its examination only to head injuries and the man also has a ruptured spleen, that would be classified as either a misdiagnosis or an incomplete diagnosis. I believe that's essentially what happened in the State's examination of Aaron Stampler. By confining their tests and examinations to simply whether Stampler is competent to stand trial, I believe they overlooked a major – or combination – of major mental disorders. It wasn't done to deceive the court, they just didn't carry their examination far enough.

VAIL: How much time did you spend with him, Doctor?

MOLLY: Two hours a day for a total of forty-four days.

VAIL: About eighty-eight hours?

MOLLY: Approximately, yes.

VAIL: And have you formed a medical opinion as to what happened in Aaron Stampler's case – have you categorised his disease?

MOLLY: Yes. I think he suffers from a combination of Dissociative Multiple Personality Disorder combined with psychopathic schizophrenia.

VAIL: And how did you determine that Aaron Stampler suffers from a form of schizophrenia?

MOLLY: Well, schizophrenia tends to be genetic – that is, it runs in families. It is also caused by environmental or sociological factors. Usually a combination of all three. So these are the factors you look for in his background. They all exist in Aaron's past.

VAIL: Let's talk about genetics, Doctor. Do you have information pertaining to the mental health of Aaron Stampler's mother.

MOLLY: Yes, I do.

VAIL: Would you describe these conditions.

MOLLY: Based on the symptoms and the socio-economic conditions, I would say that Misses Stampler probably suffered from forms of schizophrenia.

GOODMAN: Your Honour, we strenuously object to the introduction of this testimony. Doctor Arrington may be the greatest thing since Freud but I think it's preposterous to ask the court to accept an analysis made over the phone with a country doctor who uses terms like 'lonely-crazed'.

VAIL: Please the court, Dr Arrington based her assumption on the symptoms described by the family doctor and half a dozen people in Misses Stampler's hometown, all of whom have said that she exhibited many of the symptoms of schizophrenia.

GOODMAN: She could be senile, she could have Alzheimer's ... the point is, there is absolutely no proof that the mother had schizophrenia. We move that it be stricken.

THE JUDGE: Sustained.

VAIL: Come on! This woman hid in her house, talked to imaginary objects, yelled at people passing by. Most of the time she didn't know where she was, didn't know the time of day. She would have starved to death if her neighbours hadn't fed her. She was dissociative . . .

THE JUDGE: The objection is sustained, Marty. Maybe she was just 'lonely-crazed'.

VAIL: Very funny.

THE JUDGE: (Laughing) Marty, knowing Shoat, you'll be lucky to get this far with that assumption. Get on with it.

VAIL: Okay. Now what do you mean by psychopathic schizophrenia?

MOLLY: Psychotics – psychopaths – suffer breakdowns in behaviour, thought, and emotion so profound they can't function in everyday life.

VAIL: Can you give us an example?

MOLLY: Well, let's say a man is afraid he's going to be fired, so he lies in bed rather than go to work and face his fear. He is dysfunctional. He feigns a cold or the flu when actually he is sick – the illness is mental. On the other end of the scale, perhaps he becomes so dysfunctional that he goes to the office and shoots his boss. In both cases, the subject is totally unaware that these perceptions and fears are abnormal, so he doesn't accept the fact that he's mentally ill.

VAIL: What are the symptoms of psychotics?

MOLLY: A personal history of chronic and continuous antisocial behaviour. It manifests in persistent criminality, sexual promiscuity, aggressive sexual behaviour . . .

VAIL: What are these subjects like?

MOLLY: Impulsive, irresponsible, callous. They feel no guilt over their antisocial acts

381

	because they are basically amoral, they don't recognise law or moral restraint . . . they fail to learn from their mistakes.
VAIL:	Now you also mentioned the term dissociative. Can you explain that to the jury?
MOLLY:	Psychopathic schizophrenia is a dissociative disorder. It's an unconscious mental attempt to protect or excuse the individual who acts out repressed impulses or emotions. This is done by disassociating that individual from the superego.
VAIL:	In other words, a defence mechanism caused by some kind of stress or emotional conflict?
MOLLY:	Yes. Dissociative disorders involve a sudden alteration in behaviour. It can affect a person's consciousness, his motor skills, even his sense of identity.
VAIL:	You mean he could assume a different personality?
MOLLY:	Yes. A whole new identity.
VAIL:	What else?
MOLLY:	It can be accompanied by amnesia, a loss of memory of an important personal event or activity.
VAIL:	So in effect the mind blots this out?
MOLLY:	Yes. What we call hysterical amnesia. A sudden loss of memory associated with a traumatic event. It can also be selective.
VAIL:	In what way?
MOLLY:	The subject might recall part of an incident and not recall another part.
VAIL:	What triggers it?

MOLLY: Usually severe stress. But even a simple event, like a phone ringing, can precipitate a sudden terrifying recollection and an exaggerated response.

VAIL: And is this also known as psychogenic fugue?

MOLLY: Yes. Patients call it 'losing time' because they do just that, they lose the time they are in the fugue state.

VAIL: But they are aware of it?

MOLLY: Only in the sense that they realise time has passed. They don't know what happened during that period.

VAIL: And what is a multiple personality disorder?

MOLLY: It is an extreme form of dissociative behaviour. When an individual is faced with divergent signals from the id and the superego the result can be extremely traumatic. In multiple personality disorders the individual's personality fragments into two or more independent personalities.

VAIL: And how do these fragmented personalities differ?

MOLLY: The way individuals differ. Each one has a distinct way of perceiving events, relating to them, and regarding him- or herself and the environment. One might have a very low self image while another is very comfortable with his ego.

VAIL: How many different personalities are we talking about?

MOLLY: There's no pattern. Sometimes the individual creates a second personality or a third . . . sometimes a dozen other personalities . . . to deal with the pain of these dilemmas. Sometimes one personality will receive the pain, another will deal with trying to decipher the mixed signals, another may be a sexual performer.

VAIL: And this is a subconscious... an uncontrolled response to the disorder?

MOLLY: Yes. These new personalities free the host to perform normally in society.

VAIL: This is not unique, then?

MOLLY: Well, every case is unique but the disease is not uncommon. Since 1974 at least eleven investigation teams throughout the world have reported clinical or research experience with ten or more multiple personality disordered patients each. That's one hundred and ten documented cases that we know about in the past six years.

VAIL: Do these other personalities differ only in attitude? By that I mean, are they all just like the host?

MOLLY: On the contrary. Sometimes an alternate personality can be a different sex, even a child or an old man. I have seen cases in which the alternate speaks a different language than the host, has a talent — painting for instance — which cannot be attributed to the host. In fact, the multiple personalities are usually very unalike.

VAIL: Are there any specific causes of these disorders?

MOLLY: About sixty per cent of all mental disorders are caused by either sexual or religious disorientation.

VAIL: By disorientation you mean . . . ?

MOLLY:	Mixed signals, mixed information, usually from parents or mentors.
VAIL:	Are Aaron Stampler's problems sexually or religiously oriented?
MOLLY:	Both. The libido – the sex drive – is as relentless as the drive for food or water. But you die without food and water and without sex all you do is become dysfunctional. Sex has become the moral battleground for Christian ethics and at the same time it has become a major cause of mental disorders.
VAIL:	So it is accepted psychiatric theory that sex and religion are frequently responsible for mental disorder?
MOLLY:	Yes. The libido responds naturally to sexual stimuli but religious or moral restrictions suppress them and the mind becomes confused. So you have a conflict between the superego and the id.
VAIL:	And it's your contention that Aaron Stampler was troubled by both?
MOLLY:	Yes.
VAIL:	Now Doctor I would like to go back to the examination by Doctors Bascott, Ciaffo and Solomon for a moment or two. You say you've read their report, which included background information on the defendant when he was a child in Kentucky.
MOLLY:	Yes.
VAIL:	Is that report compatible with your findings?
MOLLY:	No it is not.
VAIL:	In what way do they differ?
MOLLY:	There are several facts which are not included in the biographical notes on

	Aaron. For one thing, they state that Aaron had his first sexual experience when he was sixteen with a girl named Mary Lafferty. We know for a fact that his sexual activity began two years earlier. When he was fourteen he was seduced by an adult ...
GOODMAN:	Objection, Your Honour. Hearsay.
VAIL:	Your Honour, obviously we cannot put her on the stand. Her testimony would be self-incriminating.
GOODMAN:	Does Counsellor suggest that we take his word for it?
VAIL:	I am suggesting that we are looking for the truth and this thing, this event in Stampler's life could, and probably did, have a significant effect on his mental health.
JUDGE:	Objection sustained, Mister Vail. Produce the witness or a sworn and signed affidavit or drop it.
VAIL:	Exception, Goddamn it!
JUDGE:	Exception noted. You don't have a chance on that one, Marty, not without at least a sworn affidavit. Or if Molly testifies that Aaron described the events, in which case I would allow it.
VAIL:	Okay. Where was I?
NAOMI:	Uh ... when he was fourteen he was seduced by an adult.
VAIL:	Doctor, we are talking about sexual disorientation. Was there anything in his early years that might contribute to such a condition?
MOLLY:	Yes. He had a preacher named Shackles when he was in his preteens who told him that even thinking about sex would

damn him to hell *and* there was no redemption. So for several years, Aaron not only repressed his libido, he avoided thinking about it. Later, when he became sexually active, he had to repress all the guilt he felt. At the same time, he began to question the religious information he got from Shackles. The conflict between sex and religion began then. And the boundary – the wall – between his id and his ego began to erode at that point. Then later he got the opposite message from Bishop Rushman, who not only promised him redemption, but a place in heaven when he dies.

VAIL: Were there other disturbing facts in his early years?

MOLLY: He was beaten regularly by his father. According to Aaron, at least once a month. He was also ridiculed by his parents because he placed so much emphasis on learning. His father wanted him to be a miner, which terrified Aaron. He called it going in The Hole and that fear itself became a mild form of mental disorder and this went on for many years. Any kind of psychic trauma like this may lead to the ego becoming a battleground in the war between the id and the superego. It was during this period that his subconscious splintered and created Roy. Roy took the pain of the beatings and the humiliation. Roy also had to deal with fear of the mines, had to actually instigate sexual encounters for him because of Aaron's guilt.

VAIL:	Roy is the alternate personality?
MOLLY:	Yes.
VAIL:	And, in effect, Roy assumed all the punishment and guilt associated with these events?
MOLLY:	Yes. It's a classic case.
VAIL:	Would it be fair to say that Aaron suffers from Dissociative Multiple Personality Syndrome and Roy is the psychotic schizophrenic?
MOLLY:	Yes, that is my analysis. Roy has all of the classic symptoms of the psychopath. He feels no guilt or remorse, recognises no laws.
VAIL:	So Roy could kill?
MOLLY:	Yes, he's quite capable of murder. He is sexually aggressive, homicidal, and is completely dissociative.
VAIL:	Is Aaron capable of murder?
MOLLY:	No. He would repress any such urges. The problem is, when he represses them, Roy carries them out.
VAIL:	Now we talked briefly about a fugue or fugue state which you described as a temporary amnesia. Is that what happens when Aaron changes?
MOLLY:	Yes, he goes into a fugue state – it's amnesia. Aaron loses time while Roy is out.
VAIL:	Is it possible that Roy actually killed Bishop Rushman and Aaron was in a fugue state and did not know it?
MOLLY:	Yes. Aaron was not aware of it until I told him.
VAIL:	So now he is aware of Roy's existence?
MOLLY:	Yes.
GOODMAN:	Your Honour, we seriously object to

this entire procedure. We have been more than generous in letting Mister Vail ramble on about mental disease, but now we have a diagnosis that is totally in disagreement with three prominent psychologists. We have references to this homicidal playmate of Stampler's. Allegations that an adult seduced him when he was fourteen that cannot be substantiated. Some vague diagnosis of Stampler's mother that cannot be substantiated. If this Roy exists, let's see him. Let's talk to him. Otherwise, we move that this entire line of questioning be stricken.

VAIL: Your Honour, we can't produce Roy on order. He comes and goes. However, we do have several tapes of interviews . . .

GOODMAN: Objection, objection! We requested copies of the tapes and were advised by counsel for defence that they would not be used in the trial and were therefore exempt from discovery. Now we ask for the witness. Let him produce the witness so we can cross-examine or this whole conjecture of split personality is inadmissible.

VAIL: Your Honour, we cannot produce this witness at will. Even if you subpoenaed him, we could not produce him at will. The tape, therefore *is* the best evidence.

THE JUDGE: All right, all right. I overrule the prosecution's objection to the introduction of psychological data. It is important for the court and the jury to understand the nature of the disorder, if in fact there

389

	is a disorder. The key question here is, are the tapes admissible? And I agree with the prosecutor in this instance. The witness is the best evidence. If you can't produce him, that's your problem.
VAIL:	Bullshit!
THE JUDGE:	That's contempt. A thousand dollars and ten days in jail. (Laughs)
VAIL:	Thanks a lot.

He punched the 'stop' button on the tape recorder and threw down the remote unit.

The Judge leaned back and perused him for several seconds.

'Tommy's right on this,' he said. 'If you excused the tapes from discovery, you cannot introduce them without giving the opposition a chance to let their experts study them. And if you can't put Roy on the witness stand, it's Molly's word against the State's three experts – the weight favours the State. Anyway, a videotape is not a substitute for the real thing.'

They all looked back and forth at each other. Vail sat down behind the table, lit a cigarette, and glowered into space.

'Marty,' said the Judge, 'you can't use the altar boys tape without corroborating that the voice belongs to Rushman; you can't use the mother's schizophrenia as a genetic link to Aaron on the basis of a telephone diagnosis; and you can't use the multiple personality defence without direct cross-examination of Roy or permitting the D.A. to have Molly's tapes for study.'

He paused for a moment, then added, 'In fact, at this moment, Counsellor, I'd say you're up shit creek.'

Thirty

Vail hated motels. He hated the smell of disinfectant, the soggy feeling underfoot of the napless carpeting, the twenty-dollar Degas prints on the wall, the threadbare towels, the strip of paper over the commode assuring guests that the seat has been thoroughly doused with Lysol, the knobby mattresses and foam-filled pillows. He hated motels because the ice machine would be down the hall somewhere and the switchboard would go down about ten-thirty. They were all clones. If this were an episode of the 'Twilight Zone', Vail would enter the room in Daisyland and walk out the next morning in Dubuque. He took the ice bucket and wandered about until he found the machine. When he got back, he tapped on the connecting door to Molly's room. She opened it and smiled.

'How about a little bourbon to help you sleep?' he said.

'What will the desk clerk think?' She followed him into the room, flopped on to her side on the bed.

'He already said it with that look when I asked for connecting rooms.'

'You know what they say in the old shrink business — he's the one who's drawing the dirty pictures.'

He dropped two ice cubes in each of the plastic glasses and poured Jack Daniels over them and handed her her drink. 'Motels,' he said quietly. 'They're your hell away from home.'

They tapped glasses. 'Here's to an open-minded jury,' he added.

'You really want this to go to trial, don't you?' Molly said.

'Of course,' Vail answered. 'I want to know Aaron will get out – if he's cured – and the only way I can be sure of that is with a jury. Shoat'll fight it. The hanging judge wants to max him out as badly as Venable does. So if he can't burn him, he'll do the next best thing, he'll put him away forever.'

'Is that the only reason?'

'Only reason for what?'

'To go to trial. How much is personal pride involved? All the time we've invested in Aaron, the build-up, the strategies. You remind me of a long-distance runner. You're trained to perfection. You *want* to go to trial.'

'Molly, we're down to the wire, now. From here on it's up to me. You have to trust me to know the best way to save Aaron's life.'

'I've always trusted you, Martin, although it isn't easy. You're a very armoured man. You're surrounded by shadows.'

'What're you gonna do, Doctor?' He laughed. 'Give me a free hour on the couch?'

She laughed. 'I wouldn't dare.'

'I'll make a deal with you,' Vail said. 'No more talk about Aaron or the trial until tomorrow.'

'You're on,' she agreed. There was a momentary lapse in the conversation, an awkward silence, broken when they both laughed at how ludicrous the situation was. 'The Judge says you were a lawyer in the army,' she said, finally, changing the subject.

'Yeah, Judge Advocate's staff in Germany for two years. I was a defence counsel in court martial cases. You think this is rough? Hell, it's a picnic compared to the army's peculiar notion of justice.'

He sat down on a nondescript Naugahyde chair, slipped off his shoes and propped his feet on the coffee table.

'Was it during Vietnam?'

He nodded. 'I was lucky. I went east instead of west. It was a thankless job – but great experience. For all practical purposes, in a court martial, the defendant is guilty until proven innocent. There'll be palm trees growing in Milwaukee the day anybody beats that system.' He stopped and sipped his drink, then added, 'Not unlike the situation we're up against.'

'Were you an officer?'

'I was a captain.'

'Did you volunteer?'

'Drafted, just after I finished law school. I was your standard long-haired protester right up until they came and dragged me away.'

She laughed. 'I can picture you as a captain a lot quicker than I can as a sixties hippie.'

'Well, I was both. Got beat up in Chicago during the convention in sixty-eight. Hell, I even went to Woodstock.'

'You were at Woodstock!' she said.

'That surprises you?'

'Yes, but I guess it shouldn't.'

'I was seventeen that summer, had a summer job in New York. There were six of us, four girls and two guys. On the spur of the moment we piled into an old Corvair and headed up the Interstate. It was unbelievable. We had to walk the last six miles. All those kids, trekking to Valhalla. It was like nothing before or since.'

'Somehow I don't see you at Woodstock,' she said. 'There's something . . . I guess I don't see you putting up with all the inconvenience.'

'Hell, it wasn't inconvenient, it was magical. For three days there wasn't a single act of violence, not even a fist fight. Three hundred and fifty thousand people, dancing naked, making love in front of each other, flopping in the mud, bathing together in the pond, scrounging for food. And nobody complained.'

'That's because everybody was stoned out of their minds,' she said with a laugh.

'I had a great conversation with a grasshopper. He had

a deep tenor voice, almost operatic. He was sitting right here, on my sleeve, and we were discussing Richie Havens, who was at that moment singing "Freedom". I was lying in the grass and there were people everywhere. There were half a dozen people around me, caressing me, fondling me, kissing me, humming in my ear, guiding me through my trip. There was this one girl, she just kind of – hovered over me – didn't have a stitch on. Had long, red hair, it kept blowing across my face. When I came down, she drifted away. But I remember how that girl felt. How soft her skin was. That we laughed a lot when we were making love. It was . . . an infinite moment . . . that beautiful red hair . . . tickling my face.' He stopped for a moment, staring into his drink, then looked back at Molly. 'How about you? Were you a protester?'

'In Iowa? My God, no,' she said. 'I lived in Patriot City, U.S.A. I'm sure protesting was a hanging offence. Every house had a flag in front of it, everybody was gung ho the war. When one of the boys went away the American Legion always had a parade for him.'

'How about when they came back?'

She tapped an ice cube with her forefinger, watching it bob in the amber liquid. 'My brother Bobby didn't *come* back, he sneaked back. As if he was embarrassed.' She tapped the ice cube a few more times, then added, 'And I guess he was, we just didn't know how to deal with it. My dad would say, "Leave him alone, he'll work it out for himself." ' She paused and then said, 'And he finally did.'

Her eyes began to mist over and Vail got up and went over to the bed. 'I'm sorry,' he said, squeezing her hand. 'Maybe we better talk about the trial again.'

'No, I'll be all right. I was just remembering the day he left. How grand he looked in his uniform, marching all by himself in front of the band, and everybody was cheering him and when he went by he winked at me.' She stopped and after a moment, said, 'I lost my virginity that night before a parade just like that – when I was nineteen.'

'Deflowered by a uniform,' Vail said with a chuckle.

'No, deflowered by Walter Jenkins who now has a pot belly and very little hair and owns the Ford dealership. God, I hope he's forgotten that night.'

'Not a chance,' Vail said. 'Nobody could possibly forget you.'

She looked up at him and he slid his hand around to the back of her neck and eased her up to him. 'I think I better warn you,' she said. 'I haven't been with a man for over a year.'

She moved a little closer.

'Your libido must be a wreck,' Vail said, closing the gap a little more.

'My libido is in a museum somewhere,' she whispered.

'I'm sure it's by choice.' They were inches apart. 'You're a beautiful, intelligent woman. I would think men would line up at your door.'

'I haven't seen you forming any lines,' she said, and brushed his lips with hers. Her lips were soft and wet and he drew her to him and kissed her and she fell back on the bed, pulling him down beside her.

'How's *your* libido?' she whispered.

'Rampant.'

He was a surprisingly considerate lover. And he was funny. He made her laugh and put her at ease. He teased her, his hands gently exploring her clothed body, then undressing her a bit at a time as his mouth continued the journey. He talked softly to her, made her laugh more. Undressed, they lay facing each other and she could feel him hard against her. Finally she moved a leg over his leg, opening up to him, inviting him into her.

'Be gentle,' he whispered in her ear. 'This is my first time.' And she laughed out loud as she rolled over on top of him and enveloped him.

He moved around the room very quietly, dressing in the bathroom so as not to awaken her. She was sleeping soundly when he slipped out the door at six thirty. As he headed towards the institute he passed a small flower garden. A single, purple wild flower had pushed its way through the softening earth. Vail picked it and went back to the room. He put it in a Coke bottle and left it on the table beside the bed.

A wet, cold early-morning fog shrouded the grounds and the old brick buildings of the hospital looked particularly grim and ominous stretching away through the cottony mist. As he hurried towards the ultra-modern max wing, he remembered something he had read by Jung. Jung had written that symbols were the primitive expressions of the unconscious, a universal language, and the unconscious could best be reached through the use of them.

As he neared the place, he stopped for a moment and stood, shoulders hunched against the cold, thinking. Then suddenly he reached down and swept up a handful of coarse dirt from beside the concrete walk.

A young male nurse was seated at a table beside the door to the security section when he entered the maximum wing. His name was Linc, a beefy youth in his mid-twenties with thick blond hair and a surfer's complexion.

'Mornin', Mister Vail. Little early, aren't you?' he said pleasantly. 'How about a cup of coffee? I just made it.'

'Thanks, I can use it.'

'Doctor Arrington gave him a shot, you know. He was nervous about the trial and all. He's still in the therapy cell.'

'I know. I thought it'd be nice if I was there when he comes around – to reassure him.'

'Hey, that's real thoughtful,' Linc said, filling a plastic cup and handing it to Vail before admitting him to the section. 'Nobody really cares about them, you know, all the lost souls back there. Nobody ever visits them or thinks about them. Ain't their fault, right? That Aaron, he's a real nice boy. He shouldn't even be in this place.'

Vail entered the antiseptic therapy room and waited until the door clicked shut behind him. He stood by the door until his eyes adjusted to the fog-filtered dawn light that streaked through the high window.

As he stood there, Vail, for the first time since the case began, felt he was in the presence of pure evil. The room was cold and almost airless and his steamy breathing became laboured. Hate seemed to permeate the cubicle, like a human presence. In the deep shadows in one side of the room, he could hear Aaron breathing; a shallow, harsh sound like a large snake hissing at its foe. He shivered uncontrollably and shook it off. It was the weather outside, he assured himself. The cold, damp fog had invaded the room. Evil was not that tangible. Evil was a thing of the soul, self-contained, not pervasive.

He did not turn on the lights. Instead he walked slowly over to the cot and stared down at the still form, curled up on the makeshift bed. He sipped his coffee as he watched Aaron's deep, steady breathing. Then the rhythm changed slightly. The breathing became more normal and Vail knew that the drug was wearing off.

He leaned over close to the boy's ear and whispered, 'Peter. C14.136. "There never would have been an infidel, if there had not been a priest." Right, Roy?'

No response.

'How about Billy Jordan, Roy? P21.365. "There are few pains so grievous as to have seen, divined, or experienced how an exceptional man has missed his way and deteriorated." Sound familiar?'

The youth turned over very slowly but did not open his eyes.

'I thought that would get your attention,' Vail said. He reached out, hooked the chair leg with his foot, slid it over beside the cot and sat down. He took a sip of coffee and lit a cigarette.

The youth blinked and stared up at him through squinted, yellow eyes, aflame with loathing.

'Hi, Roy,' Vail said, pleasantly.

Roy swung his feet off the cot, sat rigidly on the edge of it and glared at Vail with contempt. Then, without warning, he jumped up, swinging behind Vail and using both hands, snapped Vail's head sharply to one side. His thumb was pressed hard into Vail's voice box. Pain rippled from the base of the lawyer's brain down his neck.

Roy hissed in his ear. 'This's the way I did Floyd. Snap, crackle, pop! He never knew what happened.'

'Wwwho's Floyd?' Vail managed to squeal.

Roy twisted Vail's head a little further and more pain rippled down Vail's spine. 'Worked in the morgue at the hospital in Lexington, right after I left Crikside. I worked for the funeral home.'

'Wwwhy did . . .'

'Because I felt like it. Because he used to rag me about working in the funeral home. He was stupid and he was loud and he liked to insult people. I was in the crematorium by myself setting up for a service. Man named Metzenbauer. And Floyd came in and started his shit. I was standing behind him and I just walked up and pow! Then I put him under Metzenbauer's body and they went into the furnace together. Bet they're still looking for that moron.'

My God, Vail wondered. *How many others has he killed?*

'Just a little pressure,' Roy went on. 'You'd be lying on the floor with your tongue waggin' outa your mouth just like he did.'

'You're too smart for that,' Vail squeaked, his voice sounding like air being let out of a balloon.

'You're out to destroy me. You and that fucking doctor.'

'We've been over this. Nobody's out to do you any harm.'

'Bull*shit*!'

'Okay. If this is the way you want it . . .' Vail squealed. 'You're so anxious to fry, go ahead. Finish the fucking job.'

Roy applied a little more pressure and Vail moaned as the pain streaked into his brain.

'It's power,' Roy hissed softly in his ear. 'Power isn't about money. Power is control. I got control. At this moment, your life is in my hands. Think about it. Death is just a twist away.'

Then suddenly, Roy let go, swinging his hands out to his sides, and Vail dropped in a sitting position on the cot. He gasped for breath and rubbed his throat. Then he stood up and started for the door.

'Where the fuck you going?' Roy demanded.

Vail whirled on him. 'First you hurt Molly,' he said, his voice still a half-whisper. 'Now you hurt me. Christ, we're trying to help you, you stupid bastard. You want to talk or do you want to stay stupid?'

Roy started rubbing his hands rapidly together. He backed up a few steps, then paced back and forth a few times, still rubbing his hands.

'Okay, I'm scared,' he snarled through bared teeth. 'I'm fuckin' scared to death, that what you want to hear?'

'That's okay, you got a right to be. It's understandable. But relax,' said Vail. 'Just listen closely to me. And when we're through, I have to talk to Aaron . . .'

A bright morning sun was dissipating the fog as Molly rushed up the walk towards max wing. She was angry because Martin had let her sleep. Would Vail know how to deal with Aaron? The wrong words, the wrong actions, could send Aaron back into never-never land.

She refused Linc's offer of coffee, impatient to get into the therapy room. The young man fumbled with the keys, finally opened the main door and then he unlocked the door to the therapy cell. She entered cautiously and with apprehension. Vail, who was sitting in the chair facing the patient, smiled as she came in.

'Hi,' he said. 'Sleep well?'

The young man turned to face her and smiled. 'Hi, Miss Molly,' he said. 'Sure is good t'see yuh.'

She smiled with relief. 'It's good to see you, too, Aaron,' she said.

Thirty-one

As was always the case with any notorious trial, there was a carnival atmosphere about the court-house the day the trial started. But Vail had never seen quite the spectacle that greeted the car as they turned into Court-house Square. It was a bright, unseasonably warm day and the crowds had gathered early to get seats in Court-room Eight on the second floor of the King's County Superior Court. Half a dozen TV remote trucks were angled haphazardly against the kerb in front of the historic old building. The sidewalk and wide marble stairs were choked with radio reporters, TV personalities, photographers and writers.

'This is the big time, Aaron,' Vail said as the car pulled slowly through the throng of media jackals. 'The hearing was a barren wasteland compared to what you're about to witness.'

Stampler, who wore a tweed sports jacket and grey flannels, an outfit Naomi had picked out, waved out the window as the press converged on the car and surrounded it.

'You only say two things,' Vail said.

'Yes suh. Ah am happy th'trial is finally going to start so I can prove my innocence. And I feel good.'

'Terrific. Let's do it.'

They jumped out of the car and battled their way up the steps with microphones and cameras in their faces and reporters' questions assaulting them. Vail led the way. Behind him, he could hear Aaron, repeating over and over, 'I fail rail good. A'm happy the trial is finally startin'.'

In the lobby, Bobby, whose news-stand had been in

the corner of the towering foyer since before any of the sitting judges were elected, had doubled his regular order of apples and oranges, as well as cigarettes, chewing gum, candy bars and cheese cracker sandwiches. Bobby was praying for a long trial.

Room eight at the court-house was the hottest ticket in town. Hotter than fifth row centre at *Chorus Line* or a front row seat at the 'Donahue Show'. The room held two hundred and it was full an hour before showtime, with at least another fifty people sitting in the hall waiting for a vacancy. The crowd was eclectic: little old ladies with their knitting, housewives brown-bagging it, stock market types with their briefcases on their laps, grabbing an hour or two of the circus before they report to their glass caverns, at least two dowager types who arrive in limos, and the usual court-room hangers-on who normally wander from one room to the next looking for the action.

The bailiff at the door, like the *maître d'* at an exclusive restaurant, kept a running list. When someone left, someone else got in.

Margaret Booth, the dean of the court-house stenos, who had a voice like Casey Stengel and was affectionately known among pressroom *habitués* as Lady Macbeth, peered out of her office and growled, 'It's Armageddon. The last time we had crowds like this was when Jerry Geisler defended the mayor on a morals charge. And that was in fifty-two.'

The spectators in the court-room were loud and aggressive, like Romans waiting for the Christians to be thrown to the lions. Molly, who was in the first row with Tom and the Judge, decided about two-thirds of them were housewives taking the day off. Seated in the back of the room, there were four priests and two nuns. The press box, already almost full although many of the reporters were still outside following Stampler into the court-room, consumed a third of the seating capacity, prompting continuous verbal abuse from the spectators. Three artists were already at work sketching the crowd in the elegant mahogany room, while Jack Connerman was in the front row, his hand tape recorder lying on the railing, his notebook on his knee. He jotted down a note to himself: 'comment on the times and the legal carnival – when killers become celebrities' and another 'is it possible to find twelve people in this city who do not have an opinion already?'

At five minutes to nine, Stampler and Vail entered the court-room through a side door. The room almost fell silent, but the rumble of conversation started up again almost immediately. They joined Naomi at the defendant's table and a moment later Venable and Charlie Shackelford entered the room. She nodded rather curtly to Vail who smiled and blew her an air kiss.

Molly had hardly seen Vail since the night in Daisyland although he had sent her flowers the night before she and Aaron came back to the city. She had not expected anything more. She knew that for three days before a trial, Vail sequestered himself behind the doors of his office, roaming the room, making arguments, throwing them out, honing his defence up to the last minute. And she would be heading back to Justine as soon as the trial was over. He had stoked both her libido and her ego in the best possible way and she expected nothing more than that.

At exactly nine o'clock Shoat, master of the domain, entered with his black robes swirling about him.

'All rise,' the bailiff said.

And let the games begin, Vail said to himself.

'You may be seated,' Shoat said as he settled behind the bench. 'Before we begin I would like to make it clear that this court will not tolerate outbursts of any kind from the spectators. No applauding, nothing like that. Please conduct yourselves accordingly. Bailiff?'

'Case Number 80–4597, the State of Illinois versus

Aaron Stampler on the charge of murder in the first degree.'

'Motions?' Shoat asked, his eyebrows directing the question to Vail and Venable.

'Yes, Your Honour,' Vail said. 'Defendant wishes to change his plea at this time.'

Venable was surprised. A change in strategy at the last minute, she said to herself. Oh well, it would not affect her presentation. Her case was on ice. All Vail had going for him was grandstanding.

'Mister Vail, to the charge of murder in the first degree, you have previously entered a plea of not guilty. Do you now wish to change that plea?'

'Yes sir.'

'And how does the defendant now plead?'

'Guilty but insane.'

Venable's eyes narrowed. My God, he was going to go with that fugue defence, she thought. He must not have anything.

'Mister Vail, I'm sure you're aware that three professional psychiatrists have concluded that your client is sane.'

'I'm aware of that, Your Honour. We believe they screwed up.'

Shoat showed visible pain at Vail's analysis of the diagnosis.

'I would also respectfully point out to the court that their decision and the indictment does not mean my client is either sane *or* guilty,' he added.

'Well, of course,' said Shoat with annoyance. 'I also assume you understand, Counsellor, that you must prove the defendant was insane at the time of Bishop Rushman's murder. The state psychiatric board has deduced that Mister Stampler is sane. It is not up to the prosecutor to prove he was sane, it is your responsibility to prove he wasn't at the time the act was committed.'

'I understand that, Your Honour. But we are not

inclined to accept the diagnosis of the three State experts. It will be our contention that Doctors Bascott, Ciaffo, and Solomon mis-diagnosed the defendant.'

'You intend to challenge the testimony of all *three* expert witnesses?'

'If necessary,' Vail answered. 'Three psychiatrists examined the defendant but according to the witness list, the prosecutor has produced only one of them to substantiate this diagnosis,' said Vail.

Venable fired back, 'Your Honour, a single diagnostic report was prepared and submitted *and* signed by all three of these doctors. Doctor Bascott was head of that team. He is fully capable of testifying in support of it.'

'Then I can assume that whatever Doctor Bascott says is substantiated without exception by all three doctors, is that correct?' Vail asked.

She hesitated a moment and tossed a quick glance back at Bascott who was seated behind her. He squirmed very slightly in his seat.

'Well, Madame Prosecutor?' Shoat asked.

'Doctor Bascott?' Venable asked, looking at the psychiatrist.

Bascott stared at her for several moments. It was obvious to Vail that she had not prepared Bascott for the possibility of a challenge to all three of the State's experts. Now he had to assume responsibility for the report and for what the other two doctors concluded. *Had there been a disagreement?* Vail wondered. But Bascott nodded.

'Yes,' he said finally. 'We all examined him at the same time. We all arrived at the same conclusions.'

'Satisfied, Counsellor?' Shoat asked.

'Yes, Your Honour,' Vail said. 'Thank you.'

Great, thought Vail, *all I have to do is nail Bascott and I shoot down all three of them.*

The surprises began early. The jury selection, which most

of the old timers had concluded could take days or even weeks, was over in one day. Vail, normally manic when it came to selecting jurors, did not probe the prospects. He asked one or two questions and waved assent. Both Venable and Shoat were surprised at his almost cavalier attitude towards the selection.

Seven women, five men. All Christians, two of them Catholic. Four black, eight white. A mix of upscale businessmen, homemakers and bureaucrats.

By day two they were ready to do battle.

Venable's opening statement was relentless. She painted Stampler as a jealous teenager, involved in a sexual affair with a younger girl who struck back at Rushman after he kicked them out of Saviour House.

'You will see the pictures and they will shock you. You will see the overwhelming physical evidence. You will hear expert witnesses testify that Aaron Stampler — and only Aaron Stampler — could have committed this vicious and senselessly brutal murder of a revered community leader. Aaron Stampler is guilty of coldly, premeditatedly killing Archbishop Richard Rushman. In the end, I am sure you will agree with the State that anything less than the death penalty would be as great a miscarriage of justice as the murder itself.'

Not bad, thought Vail. A little underplayed but that was smart. Let the shockers come later.

'Mister Vail?' Shoat said.

Vail walked to the jury box and unbuttoned his jacket. He walked slowly down the length of the box, staring each juror in the eye.

'Ladies and gentlemen of the jury, my name is Martin Vail. I have been charged by the court to represent the defendant, Aaron Stampler. Now, we are here to determine whether the defendant who sits before you is guilty of the loathsome and premeditated murder of one of this city's most admired and respected citizens, Archbishop Richard Rushman.

'In criminal law there are two types of crime. The worst is known as *malum en se*, which means wrong by the very nature of the crime. Murder, rape, grievous bodily harm, crippling injuries – purposeful, planned, premeditated crimes against the person's body, if you will. The murder of Bishop Rushman is obviously a case of *malum en se*. The accused does not deny that.

'You will see photographs of this crime that will sicken you.

'And you will be asked to render judgement on what is known as *mens rea*, which means did the accused intend to cause bodily harm – in other words, did Aaron Stampler intentionally commit the murder of Bishop Rushman.

'Aaron Stampler does deny that he is guilty of *mens rea* in this murder case.

'Finally, you also will be faced with extenuating circumstances because there are extenuating circumstances in this case, as there are in almost all crimes.

'Let me offer an example. A man is accused of hitting another man with his car and killing him – a man whom he hates and has threatened on a previous occasion. The prosecution accuses the defendant of purposely hitting the victim. But during the trial you learn that the accused was driving in a heavy rainstorm. That he was blinded by headlights reflecting off his wet windshield. That when he slowed down, his car skidded. And the victim, who was walking beside the road, was struck and killed during this series of events.

'*Mens rea*. Did the accused intend to run the victim down and kill him? Or was it an unavoidable, and tragic, accident? Is there a reasonable doubt – were the extenuating circumstances enough to cast doubt on this event?

'The extenuating circumstances in the case of the State versus Aaron Stampler are of an unusual nature because they involve mental disorders. And so you will be made privy to a great deal of psychological information during the course of this trial. We ask only that you listen carefully so that you can make a fair judgement on *mens rea*, for in order to make that judgement you will be asked to judge his conduct. Did Aaron Stampler suffer a defect of reason? Did he act on an irresistible impulse? Was he capable of understanding the charges brought against him and assisting in his own defence?

'These and many more questions will hinge on the state of Aaron Stampler's mental health at the time the crime was committed. And as you make these judgements, I would ask also that you keep one important fact in the back of your mind at all times: if Aaron Stampler was in full command of his faculties at the time of this crime, why did he do it? What was his motivation for committing such a desperate and horrifying act? And if he did, was he mentally responsible at the time. In the final analysis, that may be the most important question of all.

'And so, ladies and gentlemen, your responsibility will be to rule on the believability of the evidence the prosecutor and I present to you. Who do you believe? What do you believe? And most important of all, do you accept the evidence as truth "beyond a reasonable doubt".

'We claim that Aaron Stampler is not guilty of this crime but is insane. Ms Venable, the prosecutor, must prove that he planned and committed the crime "beyond a reasonable doubt". That is her responsibility. I must prove to you that Aaron Stampler was insane or so mentally impaired that he could not resist the impulse to kill the Bishop. That will be my responsibility.

'In the end, when you have heard all the evidence, I sincerely believe that you will find on behalf of my client, Aaron Stampler.'

Vail smiled and bowed slightly. 'Thank you very much,' he said and returned to his desk.

'All right, Ms Venable,' said Shoat, 'you may call the State's first witness.'

'The people call Doctor Harcourt Bascott.'

Thirty-Two

Venable seemed uncomfortably confident. Vail had already figured her first witness would be Doctor Harcourt Bascott, head of the state mental health institute. She would establish his credentials, limit her examination to establishing Aaron's sanity, and that would be that. Short and sweet, straight to the point. She'd make it seem cut and dried. Aaron was as normal as the boy next door – just a little psychopathic, that's all. Likes to carve up Bishops when there's nothing good on at the movies.

Dressed conservatively in a dark blue suit, Bascott was an imposing man, six-two or six-three, in his early fifties with long, flowing white hair and soft, brown eyes, who balanced his potentially intimidating size with an uncommonly soft voice and a gentle nature. Crowd pleaser, thought Vail. Instant father figure, this bear of a man. The jury loves him. It would be dangerous to destroy him. Vail would have to tread carefully in discrediting him.

'You are Doctor Harcourt D. Bascott?' Venable began.

'That's correct,' he answered with a comforting smile.

'Are you a physician licensed to practise medicine in this state?'

'Yes I am, and in six other states.'

'Where do you live, Doctor?'

'At the state mental health facility in Daisyland.'

'And what is your speciality?'

'I am a licensed psychiatrist.'

'And where are you employed?'

'I am Director of the Stevenson Mental Health Institute and Chief of the state's mental health department. I am also a professor of psychiatry at the state university.'

'And how long have you been a specialist in this field?'

'Since nineteen sixty-four.'

'Please tell the court where you attended college, Doctor.'

'I have a bachelor's degree from Reed College in Portland, Oregon, my M.D. degree from the University of Oregon Medical School, and I took my psychiatric training at the University of Cincinnati.'

'And do you have an opportunity to treat patients?'

'Oh yes.'

'How many mentally ill patients do you treat or see annually, Doctor Bascott?'

'I supervise and oversee the treatment of probably five hundred to eight hundred patients confined in various state institutions and my consultative arrangement with the state permits me to treat another seven to eight hundred patients a year.'

'All right, sir, how many ... have you written any books or papers in this field?'

'I'm the author of nine books in the field of psychiatry and over two hundred scientific articles in the field.'

'And in your practice, sir, do you treat people who would generally be considered criminally insane?'

'Yes, frequently.'

'And in this capacity were you called upon to diagnose Aaron Stampler?'

'I was head of a team of three psychiatrists assigned to examine Mister Stampler.'

'And can you identify Mister Stampler?'

'Yes. He's sitting over there. The young man in the tweed jacket.'

'Now Doctor, you say you were head of a team who examined Mister Stampler. Can you briefly describe the procedure you followed?'

'Of course. Doctors Ciaffo, Solomon and myself each conducted individual and extensive evaluations of the patient. Then we had three joint meetings with him.'

411

'And would you consider this a normal procedure?'

'Yes, the three of us frequently are called upon to make psychological evaluations of patients.'

'And did you also examine hospital and medical records pertaining to Mister Stampler?'

'No. There were none available.'

'Now Doctor, just to help the jury, I would like to explore some basic psychiatric principles. Is it true that mental disorders are classified as a disease?'

'Yes.'

'The study and treatment of medical disorders is a recognised and accepted branch of medicine, is it not?'

'Yes, it is.'

'And you diagnose mental disease just as you would a physical ailment?'

'More or less. The techniques are different but the methods are similar.'

'Doctor, will you please explain to the jury how you diagnose a mental disease?'

'We look for the most significant symptoms and assign these to a category, much the same as a medical doctor.'

'And these categories are described in a manual known as DSM 3, are they not?'

'Yes.'

'What is DSM 3, Doctor?'

'The *Diagnostic and Statistical Manual of Mental Disorders*, or DSM 3 for short. The American Psychiatric Association publishes it.'

'And this is the so-called Bible of psychiatry, is it not?'

'Yes.'

'And did you so diagnose Aaron Stampler?'

'Yes. The team conducted all the usual tests.'

'Were any other tests administered?'

'Yes, he was given physical and neurological tests as well as an I.Q. test.'

'Why did you order physical and neurological exams?'

'Because mental disturbance can result from brain damage or physical defects to the brain.'

'And was there brain damage?'

'There is no evident physical brain disease.'

'And the I.Q. test?'

'To determine the intelligence level of the patient.'

'What is Aaron Stampler's I.Q.?'

'Between 138 and 140. Genius level.'

'Did you perform any other tests?'

'Most of our testing was in the realm of interrogation of the subject, Stampler. What you would call therapy.'

'And all three of you worked together and separately in this analysis?'

'That is correct. Myself, and Doctors Ciaffo and Solomon on behalf of the State. We jointly prepared our report.'

'And what is your conclusion?'

'That Aaron Stampler is not suffering from any serious mental disorder.'

'Did you find any evidence of what is known as fugue or temporary amnesia?'

'No, ma'am. Nor was he observed to suffer any evidence of fugue by the orderlies.'

'Capable of standing trial?'

'Absolutely. In fact, we found him quite normal.'

'And he understands the charges that have been brought against him, does he not?'

'Excuse me, Your Honour, if she wants to lead the witness she should get a leash,' Vail said.

Shoat glared down at him. 'Is that in the nature of an objection, Counsellor?'

'It's an objection, yes.'

'I'll rephrase, Your Honour,' Venable said, and smiled at the jury. 'Does Mister Stampler understand the charges that have been brought against him by the people?'

'Yes he does.'

'Thank you Doctor. No further questions at this time.'

Bang, just like that. Short and sweet. Almost too casual. Okay, Doc, time for a little damage control. Vail walked to the witness box and laid his arm on the railing. Friendly, unthreatening. Just Vail and the bear having a friendly chat.

'Doctor Bascott,' Vail began. 'Would you please explain schizophrenia to the jury.'

'Well, schizophrenia is the most common of the psychoses. About . . . two per cent of all the people in Western countries are treated for schizophrenia at some time in their lives. And, of course, many schizophrenics never receive clinical attention at all.'

'What are we talking about in actual numbers here?'

'Hmm. Maybe . . . half of the in-patients in mental hospitals in the United States.'

'That prevalent?'

'Yes.'

'And what exactly is schizophrenia?'

'It's the collapse or erosion of the boundaries between the ego, which controls your everyday thoughts and actions, and the id, which is the repository for all suppressed thoughts and actions. When that happens, the subject's repressions are released and the result is a kind of mental chaos.'

'How exactly does that manifest?'

'He or she can become dysfunctional. The symptoms include hallucinations, spatial disorientation, delusions, thought and personality disorders.'

'Delusions?'

'Delusions are false beliefs that are usually absurd and bizarre.'

'In lay terms, what exactly does that mean?'

'In the extreme, a patient might believe he or she is being persecuted by others. They may believe they are important historical personalities, even someone who is dead. Or they can even believe that a machine controls their thinking. I had a case in which a woman thought that her mind was controlled by her toaster. She would sit for hours, talking to a toaster, taking orders from it.'

A ripple of laughter swept across the room. Shoat smacked his gavel and it ended abruptly.

'So this kind of bizarre behaviour is not uncommon, is that correct?'

'It's relative.'

'Within the context of a mental institution?'

'Not uncommon at all.'

'And there are different kinds . . . different categories of schizophrenia?'

'Oh yes, many of them.'

'Tell me about genetics, Doctor. Does genetics figure into this? Does schizophrenia tend to run in families?'

'Well, yes to varying degrees.'

'In fact, Doctor, isn't it true that about twelve per cent of all schizoids are the children of one schizophrenic parent and about forty-five per cent have two schizophrenic parents?'

'I am not sure of percentages, but that sounds generally correct. It is a significant sample.'

'So schizophrenia can be either genetic or caused by environmental or sociological factors, is that correct?'

'Yes. Usually a combination of all three.'

'Are you familiar with Aaron Stampler's hometown, Crikside, Kentucky?'

'It has been described to me, sir.'

'You haven't been there?'

'No, I have not.'

'From what you understand, Doctor, is it possible that environmental factors in Crikside might contribute to schizophrenia?'

Venable stood up. 'Objection, Your Honour. Hearsay. And what is the relevance of this testimony?'

'Your Honour, we're dealing with a homicide which we contend is the result of a specific mental disorder. I'm simply laying groundwork here.'

'Are we going to get a course in psychiatry, too?' Venable snarled.

'Is that an objection?' Vail asked.

'If you like,' she answered.

'Excuse me,' Shoat said, his voice tinged with annoyance. 'Would you like a recess so you can carry on this private discussion or would you two like to address the court?'

'Sorry, Judge,' Vail answered. 'We contend that the study and determination of mental disorders is somewhat ambiguous in certain areas, particularly where it concerns differing theories. Freud and Jung, for instance, are not entirely compatible. What we are trying to do is determine where the good Doctor and the defence are in concert so we can proceed along those lines. If there are areas in which we disagree, they should be resolved before we go any further. What I am saying is, we do not challenge Doctor Bascott's expertise but we do question whether his theories are compatible with ours.'

'Your Honour,' Venable said with acid in her tone. 'Mister Vail is creating a forum for the discussion of various psychiatric theories here and I object to that.'

'I just want to find a common ground for the whole Q and A on psychiatric theory. Doctor Bascott may believe one theory, Doctor Arrington may believe another. If that happens, we must bring in other experts to resolve the differences. Unless, of course, we can put aside those problems now.'

'Only as it pertains to this case,' countered Venable. 'I object on the grounds that this line of questioning is too broad. We should cross those bridges when we come to them. It isn't a debate.'

'I tend to agree with the prosecutor on this,' Shoat said. 'If there is a specific area of disagreement, then I will permit introduction of witnesses supporting one theory or the other. But I will not open the court to a debate. Objection sustained.'

'Okay,' Vail said. 'Doctor, are you familiar with Jung's theory that the unconscious can be reached only through the use of symbols? That symbols are the universal language, the primitive expressions of the unconscious?'

'Yes, I am.'

'Do you agree with that theory?'

'In part.'

'So you disagree?'

'Objection,' Venable jumped in. 'Doctor Bascott answered the question.'

'No, Your Honour,' Vail disagreed. 'He said, "In part".'

'Perhaps I can explain,' Bascott offered. 'I also believe that dreams are a window to the subconscious. I do not think these two theories are incompatible. We would not rule out *any* accepted theory in making a diagnosis.'

'Didn't Paul Tillich say, "Symbolic language *alone* can express the ultimate"?'

'Yes, but that still does not preclude the use of dream analysis in determining mental dysfunction,' Bascott said.

'Did you use dream analysis?'

'Mister Stampler claims he does not dream.'

'He claims he never dreams?'

'To be more precise, he does not remember them.'

'Is that uncommon?'

'Not particularly.'

'How about hypnosis?'

'We tried. Stampler was a poor subject.'

'Is that uncommon?'

'No . . . some people just subconsciously resist hypnosis.'

'You do not consider that odd or out of the ordinary?'

'Not really. No.'

'So your analysis of the defendant is based solely on interviews with him, is that correct?'

'No, we talked to some people in his hometown. People he lived with at Saviour House and at work.'

'How much credence did you put on the interviews with the people in Crikside, Kentucky. That is Aaron's hometown, is it not?'

'Yes, it is. These were telephone interviews. Largely informational.'

'Did you conduct them?'

'Some of them. I talked with his former teacher, uh . . .'

'Rebecca Kramer?'

'Yes. Kramer.'

'And what did she tell you?'

'That he was an excellent student. Somewhat of a loner. That he aspired to much more than that area had to offer.'

'Bad tempered? Angry? Violent?'

'No, none of those.'

'Did you discuss his sexual orientation?'

'Objection, Your Honour. Relevance?'

'If I may have a little latitude, here, Judge, I think it will be apparent.'

'All right, Counsellor, I'll give you a little room here but don't get lost on us.'

'Yes sir. Doctor, did you discuss his sexual orientation?'

'We didn't question her about that.'

'Why not?'

'It hardly seemed appropriate. She was just his teacher, after all.'

'I see. I want to talk about Aaron's religious orientation for a moment. Are you familiar with the defendant's relationship with a Reverend Shackles?'

'Yes. Josiah Shackles.'

'Did you interview Shackles?'

'No, sir. We were informed that nobody has seen or heard from him in years.'

'What do you know about him?'

'Apparently he was a fundamentalist, basically, but he had very severe attitudes about sin.'

'Did the defendant discuss this with you?'

'Yes, he did. We also had had your interview with him in the jail.'

'What was your analysis of that relationship?'

'Unfortunate.'

'Why?'

'As I said, Reverend Shackles was a fundamentalist. From what I understand, he believed once you are tainted with sin, there is no redemption.'

'In other words, he believed in abstinence from all sin?'

'Yes.'

'How about prayer?'

'As I recall, Aaron quoted Virgil on that. He said that Shackles believed what Virgil wrote.'

'Which was?'

'May I refer to my notes?'

'Of course.'

Bascott leafed through several pages of a black notebook before stopping. 'Here it is,' Bascott said. 'Quote: "Cease to think that the decrees of the Gods can be changed by prayers." Unquote.'

'Shackles believed that, right?'

'According to Aaron.'

'Did Aaron accept that thesis?'

'Well, he was a child at the time. Eight, nine years old. Naturally it impressed him.'

'Did he *believe* it?'

'Objection, Your Honour,' said Venable. 'The defendant would be the best source for that information.'

'Except the defendant does not have to testify,' said Vail. 'In which case I believe the State's witness would certainly be the best source. After all, he and his team are responsible for determining that Stampler is sane. And this information will be corroborated in defence interviews conducted by Doctor Arrington.'

'Overruled,' Shoat said. 'Continue, Counsellor.'

'Did Aaron believe Shackles when he said there is no absolution on earth for sin?'

'I think it had an effect on his religious outlook.'

'Do you believe it? That there is no absolution on this earth?'

'Objection. Immaterial.'

'On the contrary, Your Honour. The Doctor's viewpoint is quite material in analysing this information.'

'Overruled,' Shoat said, looking at Venable and raising his eyebrows.

'Well, it would seem to nullify the basic premise of Christianity,' Bascott said.

'I asked if you believed it,' Vail pressed.

'No.'

'So you believe in absolution?'

'Well, I . . . Not really. I, uh . . . I'm an atheist.'

His answer caught Venable completely off-guard. Suddenly it became obvious that Vail was trying to taint Bascott in the eyes of a jury that was comprised of devout Christians.

'Objection,' she roared. 'The Doctor's religious beliefs are immaterial!'

'He said it, I didn't,' Vail said with a shrug. 'Okay with me if you strike it.' He smiled at the jury as he returned to the desk and picked up a legal pad. 'The point is, Doctor, that Aaron Stampler was definitely affected by his exposure to Shackles, was he not?'

'Yes.'

'So his original religious orientation was somewhat distorted.'

'Unless you agree with Shackles.'

'Did Aaron change his mind about that?'

'Yes. Years later he was studying to be a Catholic with Bishop Rushman. The Catholic viewpoint, of course, is exactly the opposite.'

'So his religious message was mixed, correct?'

'Absolutely.'

'Is religion important to Aaron?'

'Well, he talks about it a lot. Yes, I think so. But I think the Bishop helped him to resolve the conflict.'

'So the Bishop convinced him that there is absolution on this earth?'

'I believe Aaron when he says that, yes.'

Vail flipped through his legal pad. 'Doctor, in your third interview with Aaron, page seven, there is this exchange:

' "Bascott: So you believe in absolution then?

' "Stampler: Well, the Bishop was very convincing about that. But Ambrose Bierce wrote, 'To ask that the laws of the universe be annulled on behalf of a single petitioner is unworthy.' And absolution comes through prayer.

' "Bascott: So you still have doubts?

' "Stampler: Well, I do think about it, sir." '

Vail dropped the tablet on the desk.

'Now, Doctor, don't you see a conflict present there?'

'Because he thinks about it doesn't necessarily mean it's a conflict. We're talking about a very intelligent young man. He asks a lot of questions.'

'So is it your opinion that this conflict did not cause any stress in the defendant?'

'It did not appear significant to the team.'

'Is it not true, Doctor, that a large percentage of mental diseases can be attributable to religious and sexual disorientation?'

'I suppose you could say that.'

'Is it not true, Doctor, that more than *fifty per cent* of cases involving schizophrenia are attributable to these two factors – sex and religion?'

'I believe that's fairly accurate, yes.'

'So if Aaron Stampler received, let's say, divergent religious and sexual signals from Shackles and Rushman, this very likely would create the environment in which schizophrenia thrives?'

'Well, I suppose you could say that. Thrives might be a bit strong . . .'

'Fifty per cent of all cases . . . ?'

'Well, hmm, yes, I guess I would have to agree with that.'

'But you didn't consider this radical difference in religious messages to him as significant?'

'We did not see any effect,' Bascott said. 'Therefore we didn't look for a cause.'

'I see.' Pretty good answer, Vail thought. 'Doctor Bascott, was there ever a time when you had reason to believe that Aaron Stampler's mother suffered from schizophrenia?'

Venable's antenna went up. *Where the hell's he heading now*, she wondered. *Well, all the phone interviews were borderline hearsay – if he gets too far out of line.* She focused on Vail's interrogation.

'Not . . . really,' Bascott answered.

'Did you talk to anyone else in Crikside. I mean, did you personally talk to anyone else?'

'Objection, Your Honour. This is all hearsay.'

'All his testimony pertaining to Crikside is hearsay, Judge,' Vail said, holding his hands out at his sides. 'If he considered this information in his analysis, then we feel it's pertinent and open to cross.'

'All right, I'll let you go on but tread carefully, Mister Vail. Restate the question, Ms Blanchard.'

'Did you talk to anyone else in Crikside? I mean, did you personally talk to anyone else?'

'Yes,' Bascott answered. 'Her doctor.'

'That would be Doctor . . . Charles Koswalski?'

'Yes.'

'And what did he tell you about Aaron's mother?'

Bascott chuckled. 'He said that she was lonely-crazed.'

The court-room erupted in laughter, prompting Shoat to again gavel them quiet.

'Lonely-crazed?' Vail asked. 'Is that a specific mental disorder, Doctor?'

'I'm afraid not, sir.'

'What did he mean?'

'Her husband and oldest son were both dead and when Aaron left, she became eccentric.'

'Eccentric?'

'Yes.'

'Is that how he described her? Eccentric?'

'Not in so many words.'

'I refer to my notes, Doctor. Did he describe her as "Crazy as a full moon dog"?'

More laughter from the gallery. Shoat glared out at the audience and this time they quieted down without the gavel.

'I believe that's the expression he used.'

'And what were her symptoms?'

'Uh . . . she was reclusive. Never cleaned the house or cooked for herself, her neighbours took care of her. She did not relate to her peers. Talked to herself. Yelled at people passing her house.'

'Dissociative?' Vail asked.

'Uh, yes.'

'Spatially disorientated?'

'. . . yes.'

'Doctor, aren't these the symptoms of schizophrenia?'

'Well, yes . . .'

'So would it be fair to say that it is possible that Mrs Stampler was schizophrenic?'

'Object!' Venable bellowed. 'There is no way Doctor Bascott could possibly make such an analysis, sir!'

'Your Honour, we are merely saying that Aaron Stampler's mother suffered some kind of mental disorder before she died and that should have been enough to raise serious questions about Aaron Stampler's mental health in the minds of the State's team. Perhaps enough to follow up by going to Crikside – as the defence did.'

'Your Honour, prosecution moves to have that entire testimony about Mrs Stampler stricken from the record as hearsay.'

'Your Honour,' Vail shot back, 'we submit that the facts concerning her condition are certainly admissible. And it is a medical fact that her symptoms are indicative of schizophrenia. What's to object to?'

'I repeat, Your Honour, this is off the cuff analysis and it is meaningless.'

'All right, all right. I'm inclined to agree with Miss Venable's position here, Counsellor. I understand your argument, but since the information is blatantly hearsay I must rule it out. The jury will disregard it. Move on will you, Mister Vail?'

'Exception,' Vail snapped.

'Noted. Get on with it.'

'I'd like to go back to symbols for a moment. Doctor, will you explain very simply for the jury, the significance of symbols. What they are, for instance?'

'Symbolic language is the use of drawings, symbols, uh, recognisable signs, to communicate,' Bascott said. 'For instance, the cross is a symbol of Christianity while the numbers 666 are a universal symbol for the Devil. Or to be more current, the symbol for something that is prohibited is a red circle with a slash through it. That symbol is recognised both here and in Europe. A stop sign along the road, for instance.'

'In other words, symbols transcend language?'

'Yes, but not always.'

'Could a symbol come in the form of words? A message, for instance?'

'Hmm. Possibly. Yes.'

'So symbols can come in many forms, not just drawings or pictures?'

'Yes, that is true.'

'Now Doctor, you have testified that you have seen the photographs of the victim in this case, Bishop Rushman?'

'Yes, I have.'

'Studied them closely?'

'Yes.'

'Were there any symbols on the body?'

'Uhh . . .'

'Let me put it more directly. Do you think the killer left a message in the form of a symbol on the victim's body?'

Venable was thinking a question ahead of Vail. *He's going to make something of the numbers on Rushman's head*, she thought. *Possibly use it later to discredit Bascott in some way. Or maybe he's fishing – trying to find out whether we know what the symbols mean. That was more likely.* Venable wrote out the word 'symbols' and 'B32.156' on her legal pad and turned it over so no one could read it. But she decided now was not the time to spring it. She would wait until Arrington was on the stand and trap her into admitting the message came from Aaron.

'I can't say for sure,' Bascott answered. 'It appeared that the killer was indicating *something* but we never figured that out and Stampler was no help.'

'Did he say he didn't know what the symbol meant?'

'Objection, Your Honour. We have not established that it *was* a symbol.'

'Sustained.'

'Doctor, we are talking about the letter and numbers on the back of the victim's head, correct?'

'I assumed that is what you meant. Yes.'

'Do you recall what the sequence was?'

'I believe it said, "B32.146".'

'Actually, "B32.156",' Vail corrected.

'I'm sorry. Correction, 156.'

'And do you believe that this was a symbol left by the killer?'

'Uh. Well, yes, I think we all made that assumption.'

'Did you try to analyse the symbol?'

'Well, we asked Stampler about it.'

'And he professes no knowledge of its meaning, correct?'

'Yes.'

'And that is as far as you took it, correct?'

'We did discuss it with Ms Venable.'

'When?'

'Early on. I think before we ever talked with Stampler.'

'And what was the conclusion?'

'That it was probably immaterial to our responsibility.'

'Which was?'

'To analyse the patient.'

'Wouldn't that be a significant piece of evidence in your analysis?'

'If we understood it. It takes years, sometimes, to break through, to decipher all these subtleties . . .'

'In other words, you really didn't have time to examine all the facets of Mister Stampler's problems, did you?'

'Objection, Your Honour,' Venable barked, jumping to her feet. 'Defence is trying to muddle the issue here. The Doctor has stated that it might take years to decipher this symbol, as the Counsellor calls it. We are here to determine this case on the best evidence available. This line of questioning is completely irrelevant. The numbers could mean anything – maybe even an insignificant phone number.'

'Then let the Doctor say so,' Vail countered.

'Rephrase, Counsellor,' Shoat said, rather harshly.

'Doctor, do you think this symbol is relevant?'

'Anything is possible.'

'Do you think it is irrelevant?'

'I can't really answer that.'

'But what do you *think*?'

'Objection! Can we stick to the facts, Your Honour?'

'Yes, Ms Venable. Objection is sustained. Let's keep conjecture out of this,' Shoat said.

'Doctor, are you saying that the numbers and letters

on the back of the victim's head probably have some significance, but that you just haven't figured out what it is?'

'Yes, possibly they are significant.'

'Thank you. Now I believe you testified earlier that the diagnosis of mental diseases is as precise as the diagnosis of physical diseases, correct?'

'Yes.'

'Doctor, during your interviews with Aaron Stampler, did he ever offer an explanation of what happened the night Bishop Rushman was killed?'

'Yes he did.'

'And what was his explanation?'

'That he blacked out before the killing started.'

'Did he claim someone else was in the room at the time?'

'Yes he did.'

'Who was that person?'

'He could not identify him – or her.'

'So the defendant admits being there but denies committing the crime, is that correct?'

'Yes.'

'Is that possible? What I mean is, could Stampler have blacked out in that fashion?'

'Well, yes . . .'

'Is there a medical term for that condition?'

'Yes. It's called fugue. A fugue event is another term for temporary amnesia.'

'And is it uncommon in the study of abnormal psychology?'

'Well, it isn't rare.'

'So you have treated people who suffered a fugue event?'

'Yes.'

'How long does it usually last?'

'Anywhere from a few minutes to, well, I know of one case where a patient went into fugue for several months.'

'And this person was able to function normally in this state?'

'Yes. She just didn't remember what happened during that period.'

'What would cause someone to go into this fugue state?'

'Undue stress, anxiety, recall . . .'

'Recall?'

'Remembering a traumatic event from the past. Also it can be triggered by something very simple. A doorbell ringing, a combination of words that is reminiscent of an event from the past.'

'So witnessing a brutal murder like this one could initiate a fugue event?'

'Yes, I would have to agree with that.'

'And when Aaron Stampler says he went into this fugue state, it is not a preposterous explanation, is it?'

'No, it could happen.'

'And if it did happen, it would be a form of mental disorder, would it not?'

'Yes.'

'But you say he never exhibited signs of fugue during your investigation?'

'No, sir, he did not.'

'Doctor Bascott, let's say a patient has emphysema, goes out in a cold rain improperly dressed, catches a cold, and does not seek medical help. These conditions could possibly lead to pneumonia in the patient. True or false? Understand what I'm saying?'

'Yes. Cause and effect.'

'Right. And knowing the conditions, if you diagnosed the patient, you might predict that pneumonia could develop and take the proper precautions to prevent it, is that a fair assumption?'

'Your Honour, I am not comfortable with this line of questioning at all,' Venable said. 'It's all supposition and word games. Where is counsel going with this?'

'Give me another question or two, Your Honour.'

'One more chance, Counsellor. Make your point or I'm going to rule this whole line out of order,' Shoat said.

'Doctor Bascott, here you have a young man and you are conducting tests to determine whether or not he is culpable in this case and you know that these conditions exist – first, that he has a confused and possibly disorienting religious background and, second, that his mother was possibly schizoid. Would it not be fair to expect you to take extra steps to determine whether, in fact, schizophrenia exists here?'

'Well, yes. That's what we did.'

'You specifically zeroed in on the possibility of schizophrenia?'

'We examined him for all types of mental disorders.'

'It is my impression, and correct me if I'm wrong, that you merely determined whether or not the defendant is capable of standing trial.'

'That was our responsibility. But that included diagnosing him for mental disorders.'

'So you can tell this court with assurance that he does not suffer from schizophrenia?'

'Well, I can say it does not impede his ability to recognise right from wrong and assist in his own defence.'

'In other words, it is immaterial whether he suffers from mental disorders or not.'

'Objection. Argumentative.'

'Sustained.'

'I'll put it another way. Is it possible, Doctor, that Aaron Stampler *could* be suffering from a serious mental disorder and you overlooked it in your examinations? Is that possible?'

'Well, sir, anything is *possible*.'

'Are you saying, then, that it is unlikely?'

'Sir, two other noted psychiatrists and psychologists examined Mister Stampler. I would say it is unlikely that all three of us could have overlooked anything of that importance.'

'So your answer is no?'

'Objection,' Venable said. 'The doctor explained his position.'

'Your Honour, I am trying to determine whether he is saying it's impossible or improbable, or if he's saying it's possible.'

Shoat sighed. 'Please read the question again,' he instructed the court stenographer.

' "I'll put it another way. Is it possible, Doctor, that Aaron Stampler could be suffering from a serious mental disorder and you overlooked it in your examinations? Is that possible?" '

'And what was the immediate answer?' Shoat asked the stenographer.

' "Well, sir, anything is *possible*." '

'It seems to me, Counsellor, that he answered the question,' Shoat said to Vail.

'Not exactly,' Vail answered. 'I would like the Doctor to go on record that the possibility of pre-emptive mental disorders was completely ruled out. This is key to the defence. It goes beyond the right-or-wrong test, Your Honour. Can Doctor Bascott swear that the defendant, Aaron Stampler, suffers no mental disorder which could result in either irresistible impulse or defect of reason?'

Venable stared over at Vail. *The son of a bitch, he's setting something up here*, she thought. *What the hell is he after?*

'Your Honour,' she said quickly, 'my objection stands. Doctor Bascott has explained his position.'

'Ambiguously,' Vail said.

The judge glared down at both of them.

'I agree with the prosecution,' he said brusquely.

'Okay, I want to be clear on this,' Vail said. 'The doctor is admitting that it is possible some things were overlooked in the defendant's examination.'

'Objection,' Venable yelled, standing and slamming her fist on the table. 'He's putting words in the mouth of the witness!'

'No, sir,' Vail countered, 'I am saying exactly what he said. It is possible they overlooked something.'

Doctor Bascott, realising his credibility was in jeopardy, suddenly spoke up. 'Sir,' he said, 'I will say that Aaron Stampler is fully capable of understanding why he is here. If he does suffer any kind of mental disorder, it is my opinion that it is not severe enough to legally excuse him from his own actions.'

Vail smiled.

Gotcha.

'Thank you, Doctor.'

Thirty-three

'Your Honour, the people call William Danielson.'

Vail doodled aimlessly on his legal pad as Venable ran through the routine questions establishing Danielson as the city's chief forensic specialist, where he went to school, and his expertise.

'As chief medical examiner on this case, what were your responsibilities?' Venable asked.

'To take all the information gathered pertaining to the crime and assimilate them into a single report.'

'So you, in effect, linked all the various elements of the crime together?'

'Yes.'

'That included medical reports, fibre samples, fingerprints, et cetera . . .'

'Everything, yes. I put it all together.'

Vail and Bill Danielson had gone a lot of rounds in the past and Vail liked him. He was good and had broken a few headline cases in his time. Vail listened as Venable led Danielson through the description of the scene and up to the introduction of the photographs, then he jumped up.

'Objection, Your Honour,' said Vail. 'The presentation of all thirty-or-so photographs is flagrantly prejudicial to my client. We submit that the prosecutor's point can easily be supported with a half-dozen of these pictures.'

'Yes, yes, Counsellor, I've heard this before. Overruled.'

'Excuse me, sir, I take exception to your ruling,' Vail said pleasantly.

Shoat's cheeks turned red. 'Exception noted, *sir*,' he snorted with a scowl. 'You may continue, Ms Venable.'

Venable introduced the photographs one at a time, giving Danielson the opportunity to describe each one in gory detail – the amount of blood from each wound, the type (Danielson seemed to take particular pleasure in describing the differences between cuts, stabs, slices, and incisions), how it was made, which ones were fatal, and which were merely painful. The object was to create anxiety among the more squeamish of the jurors, before the photographs were passed among them. The result would be even more shaking than simply exhibiting the pictures. The jury regarded each of the sanguine shots with abject horror, as she expected.

Under questioning, Danielson droned on, describing a litany of horror – the number of stab wounds and their location, the results of certain kinds of wounds, the differences between a stab, a puncture and an incision.

'So, Dr Danielson, did you conclude that death can be attributed to several different factors?'

'Yes. Body trauma, aeroembolism, cadaveric spasm, several of the stab wounds, exsanguination, that's loss of blood. All could have caused death.'

'Can you identify which you think was the primary cause?'

'I believe it was the throat wound.'

'Why?'

'Because it caused aeroembolism which is the sudden exit of air from the lungs. This kind of wound is always fatal, in fact, death is usually instantaneous. And this wound was profound. Exsanguination was also a factor.'

'Loss of blood?'

'Yes. The extent of the wounds caused excessive bleeding. Normally, when the organs cease functioning, bleeding slows down. You get seepage but not a flow of blood. But in this case, the wounds were so numerous and so devastating that he lost almost all of his blood. The human body contains six quarts of blood, there was less than a pint in his body at autopsy. As you can see in the photographs, it was splashed on the walls, lamp shades, windows, but to a large extent it collected around the body itself.'

'All right, Your Honour, enough is enough,' Vail yelled. 'We concede that there was a lot of blood on the scene. Is it necessary to continue subjecting the jury to these sickening details?'

'Mister Vail, let me worry about the jury.'

'Fine. I'll worry about my client,' Vail said. 'As I reminded the court earlier, the prosecutor's focus on the sick details of this case is highly prejudicial. What's the prosecutor going to do next, haul the Bishop's blood into the court-room in buckets so the jury can see it first hand?'

'All right, that's enough, Counsellor,' Shoat yelled back. 'Are you making some kind of motion here?'

'Yes, Your Honour. We concede that there were five and a half quarts of blood in the room. We concede it came from the victim, that it's red, viscous, and thicker than water . . .'

'All right, sir, that's enough!' Shoat bellowed.

'And we object, Your Honour,' Vail continued, jabbing a forefinger towards Venable. 'We object to any further discussion of the disposition of Bishop Rushman's bodily fluids.'

The exchange broke the tension in the room. Several of the jurors snickered. Vail had reduced the most damaging visual evidence to a joke and Venable knew it. To continue now would risk losing points.

'We'll move on,' Venable volunteered.

'Thank you, Madam Prosecutor,' Shoat said. He motioned Vail closer to the bench and said in a stage whisper, 'Curb your emotions, sir.'

'Is that like curbing your dog?' Vail mumbled half-aloud as he walked back to his desk.

'What was that?' Shoat demanded.

'Just clearing my throat, Your Honour.'

'Thank you. And are you one hundred per cent sure that the same person made *all* the various cuts, slices, incisions, punctures, and other graphically-described wounds in the victim's body?'

'Do you mean is there a possibility someone else might have made some of these cuts?'

'That's exactly what I mean.'

'The traumatic wounds – the throat wound, the wounds to the chest – I can say were definitely made by that knife and by a left-handed person. I can tell by the . . .'

'Yes, yes, Dr Danielson, we're not arguing that point. We will concede that those twelve wounds were administered by a left-handed person. How about the other . . . sixty-five wounds? Were all these wounds made by a left-handed person?'

'It's hard to say. You can't always tell whether the person wielding the weapon was left- or right-handed.'

'Depends on the wound, doesn't it?'

'Uh, yes.'

'A puncture, for instance, would be very hard to distinguish – I mean, between a right-handed and left-handed person, isn't that so?'

'Yes, that's true.'

'And weren't at least two of the twelve wounds you identified as fatal, or potentially fatal, in fact puncture wounds?'

'. . . yes.'

'Straight in, right?'

'Yes.'

'So, what you are saying is that someone else could have wielded the knife when at least two of the fatal wounds were administered, correct?'

'I suppose so.'

'There we go with that "suppose so" again, Dr Danielson. Could at least two of the fatal wounds have been struck by someone else, yes or no?'

'Yes.'

'Thank you, sir. Now let's talk a minute about the throat wound. In your opinion this was the first wound struck, is that correct?'

'In my best opinion.'

'You say aeroembolism occurred, correct? Here in your report, it says, "Evidence of aeroembolism in heart and lungs." '

'There was evidence, yes.'

'And you testified that aeroembolism is almost instantly fatal. In fact, your exact words were, "In *most* of the cases, cadaveric spasm occurs – which is instant rigor mortis." Correct?'

'Yes, that's right.'

'And yet you also testify that the Bishop put up a fight. That the stab wounds in his hands and arms were the result of his using his hands and arms to protect himself. Is that correct?'

'Yes.'

'So, while it is possible the throat wound was the first wound, it is more *likely* that it was not, isn't that true?'

'It is possible that he could have survived, even fought back reflexively, for a minute or so. Certainly long enough to administer the wounds in the hands and arms.'

'The knife entered here . . .' Vail pointed to a spot just under Danielson's right ear and drew his finger slowly across to the left side as he spoke, '. . . just under the right ear, slashed to just under the left ear, cut through to the spinal column, severed the jugular, all the arteries and veins in his neck, the windpipe, and all muscle and tissue. That's what your report stipulates, is that right?'

'Yes.'

'So there was some muscle and tissue trauma there, too, right?'

'Yes.'

'And aeroembolism, which is almost *always* instantly fatal, occurred, right?'

'Yes.'

'And you still contend that the Bishop fought on for another minute or minute and a half?'

Danielson stared Vail eye-to-eye and suppressed a smile. He was good, all right. This Vail was a shark.

'I judged . . . because of the amount of blood and tissue samples . . . that probably . . .'

'Probably? What is it, Dr Danielson? Probably, possibly, an outside chance, a fluke . . .?'

'It's certainly possible that it was the second or third strike,' Danielson agreed.

'So . . . if two of the fatal chest wounds could have been struck by one person and the rest of the wounds by another, it is also possible that one person actually struck the death wound and someone else then stabbed and cut the Bishop after he was dead, right?'

'I suppose . . . yes, that's true, but unlikely.'

'Why?'

'Why?' Danielson echoed.

'Yes, why is it unlikely?'

'Well, just think about it . . . I mean, it's just completely illogical.'

'So, Doctor, you can't prove that Aaron Stampler made all or even any of the actual stab wounds, and you can't prove whether one or two people stabbed the Bishop or even which wound was the fatal wound, isn't that so?'

Danielson thought about the question for several seconds and finally nodded slowly. 'That's all true,' he said.

'And the fact that Aaron is left-handed is really the only proof you have that he actually wielded the knife, true or false?'

'Yes, Mr Vail, that's true.'

'Thank you, Dr Danielson,' Vail said, walking away from him. 'You may come away.'

'Just a moment,' Venable said. 'Dr Danielson, in your twenty-six years as a forensics scientist, have you ever seen a case in which two people used the same knife to stab the same person to death?'

'No I have not.'

'Have you ever heard or read of such an occurrence?'

'No I have not.'

'Thank you.'

'Excuse me, Dr Danielson,' Vail said. 'How many cases are you familiar with in which the penis and gonads of the victim were cut off and stuffed in the victim's mouth?'

'Uh . . . none, actually.'

'So this event could have occurred exactly as I described it, true or false?'

Danielson sighed. 'True.'

'Thank you, sir.'

Harvey Woodside followed Danielson to the stand. It was his job to correlate the medical and forensics evidence into a single, hard conclusion: That Aaron Stampler committed a premeditated, cold-blooded murder.

He huffed his way to the witness stand, breathing heavily through his nose as he settled into the chair and took the oath. Vail listened quietly as Venable established his credentials. Woodside was also an expert at his job. Vail did not challenge him.

'So, in effect, Mr Woodside, you link all the various elements of the crime together, is that true?'

'Yes.'

'That includes medical reports, fibre samples, fingerprints, et cetera . . .'

'Everything, yes. I put it all together.'

In the ensuing cross-examination, Woodside used the combination of photographs, physical evidence, fibre samples, blood stains, and fingerprints to paint a mural of terror.

'Mr Woodside,' Venable continued, 'based on the physical evidence gathered at the scene of the crime, what is your assessment of this crime?'

'That Stampler entered through the kitchen, took off his shoes, removed the carving knife from the tray leaving fibres from his gloves when he did, went down the hallway to the bedroom and attacked the Bishop. Bishop Rushman fought for his life, as witness the wounds in his hands. He was stabbed, cut and sliced sixty-six times. He had less than a pint of blood in his body after the attack, which is one-eighth of the normal blood supply in the body. The final act was the removal of his sexual apparatus which Stampler stuffed in the Bishop's mouth. Stampler then returned to the kitchen, put his shoes on and ran out and the police car happened to be passing so he dodged back inside and hid in a confessional, where he was discovered by police and arrested.'

Vail buttoned his jacket and stood up. He walked around to the front of his desk and leaned against it with his arms crossed. Shoat looked down his nose at Vail, his mouth hanging half open.

'Was it something, Mr Vail?'

'That's a very interesting story, Your Honour,' Vail said with a smile. 'Of course we object to the entire presentation. It's pure conjecture.'

'Your Honour,' Venable shot back, 'Mr Woodside is one of the most honoured pathologists in the country. His job is to assess a crime based on the forensic evidence and that is exactly what he has done.'

'There's no proof that Stampler removed his – and I quote – sexual apparatus,' Vail said. 'The only basis for Mr Woodside's and Dr Danielson's assumption is that it had to happen that way or his whole theory is full of hot air.'

'Mr Vail,' Shoat said, leaning over the bench and glaring down at him, 'it is certainly within the realm of Mr Woodside's expertise to logically string these events together. That is what he does. He made it clear that it's an assumption and I am sure the jury will take that into consideration in weighing the evidence. Your objection is overruled.'

'I have no further questions at this time,' Venable said.

'Your witness, Mr Vail.'

Vail flipped through his legal pad and slowly approached the witness box, while reading from his notes.

'Mr Woodside,' he said, still reading from his pad, 'you checked the carpeting for fibres, correct?'

'That's correct. I worked with Dr Danielson in the analysis of all the evidence.'

'What else did you check the carpeting for?'

'Bloodstains, hairs, other foreign matter.'

'Indentations?'

'I don't understand the question.'

'Did you check for residual footprints, indentations in the carpeting to ascertain whether anyone else was in the room besides Bishop Rushman and Aaron Stampler?'

'That really isn't practical, Mr Vail. The maid cleaned the room earlier that day. Other people passed through the bedroom.'

'So what you're saying is, if there were other indentations in the carpet they could have been there since earlier in the day?'

'Yes . . .'

'And the same might be true for hair samples and fibres, isn't that correct?'

'Well, yes . . .'

'So the only physical evidence in the room that you can positively state was *not* there prior to the murder are the bloodstains?'

'Well, that's . . .'

'Yes or no, Mr Woodside.'

'I suppose you could say that. There's the bloody footprint, of course.'

'My client doesn't deny that it's his footprint,' Vail said, still checking his notes. 'Of course he was there.

440

But since he was in a 'fugue state and remembers nothing, we raise the question — was someone else there, too? And that's the question we'd like you to resolve, Mr Woodside, beyond a shadow of a doubt. Now, sir, based on these findings can you honestly say that Aaron Stampler and Bishop Rushman were the only people in the room at the time of the assault?'

'I am ninetey per cent . . .'

'Ninety per cent won't do, Mr Woodside. Will you tell the court that you are one hundred per cent sure that nobody else was in the room at the time of the murder?'

'I guess not.'

'Yes or no?'

'No.'

'Mr Woodside, I will remind you of the Wright case. Do you remember the Wright case?'

'Of course.'

'You were the forensics expert on that case, right?'

'Yes.'

'Tell the jury the details.'

'I object, Your Honour. Irrelevant. What is the point here?'

'The point is logic, Your Honour.'

'Logic?' Shoat echoed.

'Mr Woodside is basing a lot of his assumptions on logic. I would like to examine his perception of logic.'

'Oh, all right, Mr Vail. I told you I'd give you latitude in this case so you may proceed.'

'The Wright case, Mr Woodside.'

'Theodore Wright was a salesman. He was found shot to death in a hotel room. The murder weapon was later discovered behind a steam radiator in the corner.'

'So the logical conclusion was that he was murdered, right?'

'That's correct. Our original assessment was that Wright was murdered.'

'And was that, in fact, the case?'

'No, we later ascertained through tests that Wright shot himself. The kick of the gun threw his hand back and the weapon flew out of his hand and lodged behind the radiator.'

'So the logical conclusion – that he was killed – was wrong.'

'Yes.'

'Mr Woodside, judging from the evidence, would it have been logical to conclude that he committed suicide?'

'Not really.'

'You mean no.'

'No.'

'The point is, a great many criminal cases defy logic, don't they sir?'

'Well, you can say that, but in most of the cases . . .'

'Most of the cases. But not *all*, correct?'

Woodside sighed. 'Correct,' he said.

'Now Mr Woodside, you testified earlier that Mr Stampler's fingerprints were – as you put it – all over the knife and the body.'

'Yes.'

'And you also testified that fibres from Stampler's gloves were on the knife tray?'

'That's correct.'

'And so you assumed from that evidence that Stampler took the knife out of the tray, right?'

'It would certainly seem logical.'

'Is it also logical that he took off his gloves before committing the murder?'

'Uh . . . I don't understand the . . .'

'Sure you do, but I'll put it another way,' Vail said. 'You're very big on logic, Mr Woodside. Is it logical that Mr Stampler came in with his gloves on, took the knife, then took off his gloves so he could leave fingerprints all over the place – as you put it? Is that logical?'

'Uh . . . well, I would say . . .'

'Just say the answer, sir. Do you think it is logical that

a man premeditates a crime, plans it all out, then takes off his gloves before he goes to work?'

'Well, I don't know why he did that.'

'Is it logical? Does it make any sense at all?'

'Not really.'

'I think we can assume that's a "no",' Vail said. 'And as far as the other fibre samples you found, if Mr Stampler was there earlier in the evening, the fibre samples could have been left at that time, true or false?'

'True.'

'So the fibres in themselves really don't prove that the defendant was in the room at the time of the attack, is that a true statement?'

'Yes, that's true.'

'So, to sum up, Mr Woodside, you can't prove Aaron was alone in the room with the Bishop, can you?'

'Uh . . . well, I . . .'

'Yes or no?'

Woodside sighed. 'No,' he said.

'And you can't say beyond a reasonable doubt, that Aaron took the knife from the kitchen, right?'

'Not really.'

'We'll take that as another "no". Now let's talk about Aaron's escape, as you put it, through the kitchen door. It's your opinion that he came in through the kitchen door, left his shoes there, took the knife, and went to the Bishop's bedroom and stabbed him, then went back the same way, put his shoes back on, and exited through the kitchen door.'

'Yes.'

'And you base that opinion on what?'

'Logic. Logic says that he took off his shoes when he came in because the blood stains on his socks led straight back there. And since it is unlikely that the carving knife was in the bedroom we can also assume that he picked up the knife when he came in.'

Vail walked across the room.

'Supposing he did come in the front door, as he says he did. What's the first thing you do when you come in from the cold? You take your gloves off, right? Rub your hands together, breathe on them. So Aaron comes into the rectory, pulls off his gloves, then he hears something upstairs, and goes up. Someone else is in the room, so . . .' Vail leaned over, pulled off his loafers and stuffed one in each of his suit coat pockets, '. . . he takes off his shoes so nobody'll hear him, sticks them in his jacket pockets. He goes to the bedroom, looks in, and sees someone stabbing the Bishop – someone who *did* come in the back door, take the knife, and go to the Bishop's bedroom. The Bishop is trying to prevent the stabbing. He has his hands in front of him. But finally he drops his arms and the killer stabs him – according to your report, "wound number four, direct cardiovascular hit sufficient to kill almost instantaneously" – and the Bishop falls on the floor. The killer runs out of the room and Stampler, shocked into a fugue state, grabs the knife and goes berserk. Then he leaves the room, hears someone downstairs, runs to the kitchen, puts his shoes back on before going out in the cold, and exits via the kitchen door. Can you prove it didn't happen that way, Mr Woodside?'

'Nope,' Woodside said with resignation. 'I can't prove a duck didn't fly in the window and kill him, either.'

The arena broke up. Shoat smashed his gavel several times.

'If you people don't shut up, I'm going to clear this room,' he bellowed, then glared down at Woodside.

'Mr Woodside, that remark was totally uncalled for. You are no stranger to court-rooms or trials. You know better.'

Woodside lowered his head. 'Yes sir, I'm sorry,' he mumbled.

'I should think so. The jury will ignore that remark. It has absolutely no relevance to these proceedings.'

'I have no further questions of this witness,' Vail said.

The doorman delivered the first paper to hit the street that night to her door. She read it at her desk while she supped on chicken noodle soup and crackers.

Legal Eagles as Celebrities
Venable versus Vail is the
Best Show in Town
By
JACK CONNERMAN

'The toughest ticket in town these days is in Kings County Superior Court where yesterday the legal battle of the century began.

'It's a dream trial; a grisly murder case involving two legal superstars and one of the city's most prominent citizens as victim. At stake: the life a 19-year-old mountain boy named Aaron Stampler, who has a Himalayan I.Q., an accent like Sergeant York, and is accused of turning Archbishop Richard Rushman, "The Saint of Lakeview Drive", into an anatomy lab experiment one night last February. The details of the slaying were so brutal they were kept under wraps by the police until the trial started yesterday.

'It could be called Celebrity Court-room, this re-match between Assistant D.A. Jane Venable, a lady with more scalps on her belt than any other prosecutor in history, and the jugular wunderkind of the circuits, Martin Vail, who was saddled with what was considered an open and shut case as penance for taking the city, county and state for one mil, six just recently.

'The last time these two faced each across the banq was as main event gladiators in the infamous Rodriguez narcotics case a few years back. Vail waltzed away with the roses that time, thus there is vengeance in the air and it emanates from the D.A.'s office.

'The first day delivered all it promised; verbal clashes between Venable and Vail, several testy admonishments from Judge Hangin' Harry Shoat, photographs that would start a feeding frenzy at a vampire convention, and some hard in-fighting by Vail.

'Venable promises quick, Biblical-style justice. "Thank God the Supreme Court has given us back the electric chair in time for Aaron Stampler," is her best quote to date.

'Vail, as is his custom, has two words to say. "No comment." He saves it all for the court-room and Monday he was looking pretty good. Venable's open and shut case began to look a little more open than we were led to expect.

'Venable, decked out in a grey flannel double-breasted suit over a black turtleneck, her blazing red hair pulled back in a tight bun, her designer spectacles perched on the end of her nose, made it clear in her opening remarks that blood red was the colour of the day, characterising the defendant as a ruthless, jealous, vengeful boy-killer who literally butchered the man who had been his guardian angel and mentor for two years.

' "Seventy-seven times he struck while the Saint of Lakeview Drive tried to defend himself," she declared. "The Archbishop's hands were pierced and punctured as he tried to ward off that deadly carving knife. Twelve fatal wounds were struck. The Bishop was virtually decapitated. Aaron Stampler, who learned his skill with a knife working as an apprentice in a funeral home, showed no mercy as he destroyed and mutilated his benefactor . . ."

'Strong stuff. A straightforward, max-out pitch followed later by shocking colour photographs that backed up her verbal horror story.

'Vail, dressed haphazardly as usual, promised surprises. His contention: that Stampler went into a psychological blackout, clinically known as a "fugue state", and remembers nothing until police found him cowering in a confessional covered with blood and still holding the murder weapon. There have already been intimations that a third person was in the Bishop's bedroom when he was murdered.'

There were several paragraphs devoted to the testimonies of Bascott and Danielson and some snide lines about the overkill of the photographs. The last paragraphs of the story put her teeth on edge.

'Undaunted, Vail challenged the credibility of the State's psychiatric evaluation and raised a question: was the team's analysis incomplete or possibly misdirected? Stampler's blackout story, until now a media joke, became not only credible, but by Bascott's own admission, a fairly common occurrence. Is it possible that Stampler did, in fact, suffer a blackout? Vail has challenged and changed the perception that it was a feeble defence.

'Then too, there was Vail's testy cross-examination of Bill Danielson which has raised a lot of questions. The prosecution cannot prove Stampler was alone in the room, or that he actually made any or all of the stab wounds, or which wound was the actual fatal stab, or whether more than one person took part in the attack.

'There is no question that the physical and circumstantial evidence still weighs heavily in Venable's favour. But if Vail's first day in court is any indication, this trial is far from being over. Round two at nine a.m. Tuesday.'

Venable slammed down the paper after reading it twice. Connerman, the ultimate male chauvinist, rooting for Vail, as usual. She could read between the lines. She paced the room, listening to a tape recording of the testimony. She stopped at one point and replayed the tape.

It was at the series of questions regarding symbols. Vail went into it and then suddenly abandoned the line of questions. *Why?* Was he fishing to find out what the numbers meant? Did he get on shaky ground and change direction? Something had warned him off. Was it one of Bascott's answers?

Suddenly it had become obvious that Vail was avoiding the symbols on the back of the victim's head. He was trying to get information into the record without dealing with it head on. After having cracked the door with Bascott, he seemed to be dancing around the question. Did he know what the message meant? And if so, why was he avoiding dealing with it directly? It occurred to her that Vail might be trying, obliquely, to introduce testimony concerning the similar symbols on the heads of Billy Jordan and Peter Holloway.

That was it! The son of a bitch was trying to connect Rushman to the two altar boys without specifically bringing up what the messages meant. In so doing, he could then introduce the possibility that Rushman and the altar boys were killed by the same person and then show that there was a strong probability that the two boys were killed after Rushman's murder, when Stampler was already in custody. Also if he opened that door wide enough, he might force her into introducing the altar boy tape – which would definitely work to her disadvantage. At the same time, it would then allow him to introduce what the jury might consider a sympathetic motive for the killing.

Not a chance, she thought. No way.

On the other hand, if she could prove Stampler knew what the messages meant, it would be another proof of his guilt and possibly manoeuvre him into a court-room admission that he killed all three of the victims.

What a coup, she thought. She could turn the tables on Vail, nail the little bastard for Rushman's killing, and at the same time raise the issue of multiple murders in the mind of the jury. The jury would vote to burn him for sure and Shoat would love it.

But it was a dangerous manoeuvre. She would have to think more about that.

Otherwise, she had to admit Vail had done well today. He had set out to lower Bascott's credibility and he had. He had raised a question in the minds of the jury: could there be something Bascott and his team overlooked?

If there was, Vail would counter with Arrington's testimony. Venable would be ready for her.

Thirty-Four

For the next three days, Jane Venable led a parade of innocuous witnesses past the jury. Priests, nuns, kids from Saviour House, the most powerful businessmen in the city, and socialites who headed the major charities, all testified that Rushman was a prince among men and was indeed the Saint of Lakeview Drive. Vail responded with a few perfunctory questions and an occasional objection. The character witnesses for the victim were irrelevant – everyone on the jury knew who Rushman was – but Vail had no intention of attacking the credibility of either the Church or business communities. Besides, the jury appeared bored by the procession of 'important people', even Shoat began to relax as the tension in the court-room eased.

Then Venable called her final witness.

'The State calls Abel Stenner to the stand.'

Vail watched Lieutenant Abel Stenner walk to the witness chair and raise his hand as he took the oath. Stenner, dressed in a dark blue suit with a wine tie, looked more like a broker than a cop, except for those icy eyes behind wire-rim glasses and his aloof, almost patronising demeanour. He would make a good witness if he did not antagonise the jury with that remote manner. By this time, most of the testimony had been given and Stenner would be reduced to a corroborating witness – the clean-up man. He would put it all in perspective with that cold and wily air of his. A dangerous witness, perhaps the most dangerous of all. Vail leaned his chin in the palm of his hand and listened as Venable ran through the obligatory qualification questions, emphasising Stenner's four citations for meritorious service and twenty-three years on the force, ten as a homicide detective.

Stenner described his reaction on first entering the crime scene, his subsequent arrest of Aaron Stampler, and the care which was taken to, as he put it, 'preserve the integrity of the homicide area'. He was straightforward and blunt and sounded as formal as a police report. Having been sequestered, he was not aware of Vail's cross-examination of Danielson and Bascott. When he gave his 'appraisal' of what happened it was basically the same story Danielson had told.

'I object to the lieutenant's so-called appraisal, Your Honour,' Vail said, jumping up and feigning anger. 'For the same reason I objected to Mister Danielson's description of the events. It's pure conjecture.'

'And we've already gone through this, Mister Vail,' Shoat said curtly. 'These people are qualified as expert witnesses and as such their viewpoint is valid. The jury is intelligent enough to put the proper weight on their remarks. You are overruled.'

'I suppose it would be redundant to except,' Vail said, sitting back down.

'What is your conclusion regarding the defendant's claim that he saw someone else attack the Bishop, blacked out, and does not remember anything after that?' Venable asked.

'I believe the evidence points to a single assailant who premeditated the murder, carried it out, and got caught.'

'Would that be Mister Stampler?'

'Yes.'

'Thank you, Lieutenant,' Venable said. She turned to Vail. 'Your witness,' she said.

Vail stood up slowly, buttoned his jacket and approached the witness stand with his trusty yellow legal pad in hand. He leaned on the railing separating the witness box from the court-room and smiled.

'Lieutenant,' Vail said softly, 'would it be fair to say

that your main job is gathering evidence in homicide cases which is then turned over to the D.A. for prosecution?'

'That's part of it.'

'What else?'

'Well, there's that somewhat ambiguous area called deduction, or detection, if you will,' Stenner said. His voice, always with an edge to it, made him sound on the verge of anger.

'And that is taking all the evidence and putting it together, then making an educated guess about what it all means, right?'

'Objection to Counsellor's use of the word "guess", Your Honour,' Venable said.

'I qualified it with the word "educated",' Vail said. 'If there's a better way to describe it, I'm open to it.'

Shoat looked down at Stenner and smiled. 'Would you object, sir, if the Counsellor substituted the word "appraisal" for "guess"?'

Stenner shook his head.

'Excellent choice, Your Honour, thank you,' Venable said.

'Lieutenant, if you are provided with information which is detrimental to a case you're developing, how do you deal with it?'

'The same as any other piece of evidence.'

'In other words, you are not selective about the information you provide to the District Attorney?'

'Of course not.'

'So if you arrest someone and he has an alibi, do you check it out or do you expect him to provide the proof?'

'We would check it out.'

'That's part of the investigative process, right?'

'Yes it is.'

'Lieutenant, when did you first see Aaron Stampler?'

'He was cowering in a confessional at the Cathedral.'

'This was when he was arrested?'

'Yes.'

'And did he say anything?'

'He said, "Didn't do it, Mama. Mama, I didn't do it."'

'Did he appear frightened?'

'Yes, he was terrified.'

'And did you read him his rights at that time?'

'Yes I did.'

'Now Lieutenant, did you conduct three interrogations with the defendant . . .'

'Objection, Your Honour,' Venable interjected. 'That's inadmissible. Mister Vail had it excluded himself!'

'I'm not introducing testimony concerning the content of the interrogations, Judge, just that they occurred.'

'See that you don't,' Shoat snapped.

'Prior to your first interrogation, in the car on the way to the station, did you have a conversation with Mister Stampler?'

'We chatted,' Stenner answered. 'I asked him the usual. What his name was, where he lived, worked, that kind of thing.'

'In fact, didn't you ask Aaron, and I use your exact words, "Why did you kill the Archbishop, what did he ever do to you?"'

'I object, Your Honour. Counsellor's trying to get parts of the interrogation into the record without admitting the entire Q and A.'

'On the contrary, I am asking the Lieutenant about – what he himself characterised as – a chat which he had with the defendant on the way to the police station. I'm not referring to the three taped interviews which have been excluded from testimony.'

'Objection overruled.'

'How about it, Lieutenant, did you ask Stampler that question?'

'Something to that effect.'

'Isn't that kind of a "When did you stop beating your

wife" question? The fact is, you assumed he was guilty, did you not?'

'I suppose so.'

'How did he answer the question?'

'He said he didn't remember what happened.'

'In fact, didn't he say he blacked out?'

'Yes, he used those words.'

'And did he also say there was someone else in the room besides the Bishop?'

'Yes.'

'Did he tell you who it was?'

'No. He just said he was afraid of him.'

'Just like that?'

'I don't understand . . .'

'Let me suggest what was said. He refused to tell you who else was in the room. You said, "Are you afraid to?" and he answered, "Yes." Is that about the way it went?'

'I guess so. Like I said, it was two months ago.'

'My reason . . . why I bring this up, Lieutenant, is that I think you misinterpreted what the defendant meant. He did not say he was afraid of the other person, he said he was afraid to tell you. He was exercising his Miranda rights which you had just given him.'

'What's the point, Counsellor?' Shoat said.

'The point is, I believe Lieutenant Stenner misinterpreted the remark. And since the lieutenant interprets the comments of witnesses in preparing the appraisal to the D.A., which is the evidence for the prosecution, and if his appraisal is based on a misinterpretation of remarks made by witnesses, I suggest that this is a perfect example of the fallacy in the appraisal and therefore it is fair game for challenge.'

Shoat seemed confused by the explanation. 'Are you objecting to something here?' he asked.

'Your Honour,' Vail said, 'I just want to make sure that the line is clear here and that this so-called appraisal is not carved in stone and that we are not confusing fact with faulty guesswork.'

'Your Honour, please. Counsellor has already been admonished for using the term guesswork . . .'

'Yes, yes, Miss Venable, I'm ahead of you on this. Mister Vail, I think we all agreed that the word appraisal is better suited here.'

'I didn't agree with it.'

'Noted!' Shoat blurted. 'Now get on with it.'

'Okay, but if it please the court, I want to make sure the jury understands that when Lieutenant Stenner makes a statement such as saying Aaron said he was afraid of the other person in the room, that is not true. It is a supposition and an erroneous one and the record needs to show that.'

'Who says so?' Venable demanded.

'Your own witness. Page twelve of the interview submitted by Doctor Bascott that was taken March third by Doctor Ciaffo:

' "Ciaffo: And you say you were afraid of this other person in the room.

' "Stampler: No, ma'am.

' "Ciaffo: I'm sorry, what did you mean?

' "Stampler: I don't want to say anymore about it."

'Now I contend that Stampler never said he was afraid of the other person in the room. *He didn't want to talk anymore about it*. It supports my earlier contention that this is not a scientific evaluation, it includes human error and should be regarded lightly by the jury.'

'Mister Vail, I will instruct the jury, if you don't mind. You are out of order. Save your remarks for summation and get back on track.'

Vail walked back to his desk, picked up a file folder, leafed through it for a minute, then turned and interrogated Stenner from across the room.

'Lieutenant, did Aaron Stampler tell you he blacked

out and didn't remember anything until he was outside, running away?'

'Or words to that effect.'

'And what did you think when he told you that?'

'I thought it was a pretty feeble excuse for murder.'

'You didn't believe him?'

'No, I didn't.'

'Are you familiar with the medical term "fugue state" or hysterical amnesia?'

'Yes, I discussed it with Doctor Bascott.'

'As a matter of fact, you don't believe in the fugue theory, do you Lieutenant Stenner?'

'I have no firm opinion.'

'It is a scientific fact, Lieutenant.'

'As I said, I have no firm opinion.'

'Do you believe that two plus two equals four?'

'Of course.'

'Do you believe the earth revolves around the sun?'

'Yes.'

'Are you a Christian, Lieutenant?'

'Yes.'

'Go to church every Sunday?'

'Yes.'

'Do you believe in the Resurrection?'

'Yes I do.'

'Is the Resurrection a matter of fact or a theory?'

'Objection, Your Honour. Lieutenant Stenner's religious beliefs have nothing to do with this case.'

'On the contrary, Your Honour. If I may proceed, I think I can show the relevance.'

'Overruled. Read the last question, please Miss Blanchard.'

'Is the Resurrection a matter of fact or a theory?'

'Lieutenant?'

'It is a matter of faith, sir.'

'So you believe in scientific fact and you believe in religious faith, but you question the scientific reality of a psychiatric disorder which all psychologists agree exists and which is included in DSM 3, which is the standard by which all psychiatric disturbances are identified, isn't that a fact, sir?'

'It can be faked. You can't fake two plus two, but you could sure fake a fugue state.'

'I see. And how many people do you know for a certainty have faked a fugue state?'

Stenner paused for a moment, then said, 'None.'

'How many people do you know who have had experiences with faked fugue states?'

'None.'

'Read a lot of examples of faking a fugue state?'

'No.'

'So you're guessing, right?'

'It's logical. If there is such a thing, it could certainly be faked.'

'Have you asked a psychiatrist if it's possible?'

'No.'

'So you're guessing, Lieutenant, yes or no?'

'Yes.'

'Ah, so your reason for doubting Aaron Stampler's statement is that you guessed he was faking – or lying, right?'

'That is correct.'

'You didn't believe him?'

'No I did not.'

'So you assumed that Aaron was lying and that he killed Bishop Rushman, correct?'

'It was a very logical assumption . . .'

'I'm not questioning the logic of your assumption, just that it existed. You assumed Stampler was guilty, right?'

'Yes.'

'When did you ascertain that Aaron was alone in the room with the Bishop at the time of the murder?'

'I don't understand . . .'

'At what point, Lieutenant, were you positive from

reviewing the evidence, that Aaron Stampler acted alone?'

'From the very beginning.'

'And what evidence did you gather to prove he was alone in the room?'

'Forensics evidence. Uh . . .'

'Let me put it another way. Aaron Stampler tells you that he blacked out when he entered the Bishop's room, correct?'

'Yes.'

'What did you do to disprove his allegation? In other words, sir, what evidence or witnesses can you produce that will verify your contention that he was alone in the room and that he acted alone?'

'Forensics evidence, physical evidence, just plain logic . . .'

'You believe in the Resurrection yet it defies logic, does it not?'

'Not to a good Christian.'

'So you believe in an act of faith, but deny the existence of a fugue state, which is a scientifically proven fact. Isn't that true?'

'I said I don't trust Stampler.'

'Because you think it is logical that he was faking, right?'

'I suppose so.'

'Do you recall a case involving a man named John Robinson Jeffries?'

'Objection, Your Honour. Immaterial and irrelevant.'

'I intend to prove it's very material, Your Honour.'

'I'll keep an open mind and overrule, but don't stray, Mister Vail.'

'Thank you. Do you recall the case, Lieutenant?'

'I believe so.'

'Mister Jeffries was arrested for what?'

'Murder and armed robbery.'

458

'And you arrested him because it seemed logical at the time, isn't that correct?'

'Yes, there was . . . uh . . .'

Stenner hesitated in mid-sentence.

'. . . a great deal of physical evidence?' Vail said. 'That what you were going to say, Lieutenant Stenner?'

'Something like that.'

'Even had an eyewitness, did you not?'

'That's true.'

'A preponderance of evidence, right?'

'That's right.'

'Was Mister Jeffries convicted of this crime, Lieutenant?'

'Yes.'

'Was he tried?'

'Yes.'

'Found guilty?'

'Yes . . .'

'What was his sentence, Lieutenant?'

'He was sentenced to death.'

'And was that sentence carried out?'

'No.'

'Why not?'

'Jeffries was subsequently released.'

'Who arranged that?'

'I did.'

'Why? Why, after submitting the case to the prosecution and getting a guilty verdict, why did you then help get him released?'

'I discovered while working on another case that our eyewitness lied.'

'Why did he do that?'

'Because he was the guilty party.'

'You see, Lieutenant, I have a problem with some of these logical assumptions that have been made during this trial. Do you understand why?'

'Most of the time . . .'

'Lieutenant, my client's life is at stake here. Most of the time won't do. And so much for logic and a preponderance of evidence. Mr Danielson says he cannot say for sure that Aaron was alone in the room, cannot say for sure that only one person actually stabbed the Bishop, and cannot prove evidentially that Aaron even came in the back door or brought the knife to the murder scene. Yet you assumed Aaron Stampler lied to you because it wasn't logical, right?'

No answer.

'The fact is, Lieutenant, that you are willing to accept on faith that Christ was crucified and died, and that he arose from the dead, and went to Heaven. But you don't choose to believe the fact that a person, under extreme stress or shock, can black out and enter a scientifically described limbo called a fugue state. So you never actually tried to prove that Aaron Stampler was lying, did you?'

'The physical evidence . . .'

'Answer my question, Lieutenant. Did you seek any evidence that might substantiate Aaron Stampler's statement?'

'The evidence itself disputes it.'

'Really? At what point did you rule out the presence of a third person in the room?'

'He had the weapon, he was covered with blood, he left fingerprints . . .'

'My question, sir, is at what point did you specifically rule out the presence of a third person in the room?'

Stenner hesitated.

'Isn't it a fact, Lieutenant Stenner, that you never even considered the possibility?'

'Not seriously. No.'

'In other words, you never specifically ascertained that Stampler was lying, you simply assumed that his story was bogus and the jury would not believe it, right?'

'It's not my job to prove the defendant is innocent, it's yours,' Stenner snapped.

'On the contrary, Lieutenant, it's your job to prove he's guilty.'

Stenner glared at Vail, his eyes flashing with anger.

'It's your job to prove – beyond a shadow of a doubt – that this crime happened exactly as you claim it happened and to do that I would suggest you must also discredit the claims of the defendant which you have not done.'

'The physical evidence alone is overwhelming.'

'But not conclusive.'

'Of course it's conclusive.'

'How many witnesses did you interview about the altar boys' meeting in the room earlier that night?'

'Actually none . . .'

'Was there a meeting of the altar boys in that room earlier in the evening or not?'

'I can't say for sure.'

'Lieutenant, were there fibres recovered from the murder scene that have not yet been identified?'

'Yes.'

'So it's possible they were left by a third person in the room, is that correct?'

'I guess . . .'

'Or by one of the altar boys earlier in the evening?'

'There's no record of any meeting . . .'

'Ah, but there is a record, Lieutenant. The Bishop's date book which you introduced into evidence. On this page, the Bishop wrote altar boys critique, eight p.m.'

'The Bishop could have cancelled it.'

'Well, he could have danced in a topless bar, too, but he didn't.'

The gallery broke into subdued laughter, having been warned more than a few times about demonstrations by Shoat.

Venable said, 'Your Honour . . .'

'Yes, Miss Venable. Mister Vail, we can do without the metaphors and analogies. Stick to the facts.'

'Lieutenant, can you prove beyond a shadow of a doubt that only the defendant and the Bishop were in the room at the time of the murder?'

'I suppose not, but the preponderance of evidence indicates . . .'

'Indicates? *Indicates?* The evidence is *all* circumstantial,' Vail said. He turned back to his notes. 'I have only one more question, Lieutenant Stenner. You stated a few minutes ago that this crime was premeditated. You said it unequivocally, as a statement of fact. Isn't that just another one of your unsupported allegations, sir?'

'No, sir, it is not.'

'Well, will you please tell the court upon what evidence you base that supposition?'

'Several factors,' Stenner said confidently.

'Such as?'

'The symbols on the back of the Bishop's head.'

The answer was a shock to Vail. He had broken the first commandment in law – never ask a question unless you know the answer. So they had unravelled the mystery of the symbols. Vail realised he could not back away now. He was in it with Stenner. He had to pursue the line of questioning he had opened, and do it with great caution.

'And what about the symbols, Lieutenant?'

A flicker of a smile crossed Stenner's lips.

'They refer to a quote from a book in the Bishop's Library. The passage was marked in the book. We found similar markings in a book retrieved from Stampler's quarters in The Hollows. Same highlighter was used and we can identify the handwriting in both books as Stampler's.'

'Your Honour,' Venable said, 'I can offer both of these volumes in evidence at this time.' She carried both books to the bench.

'All right, mark them appropriately, clerk,' Shoat said.

Vail's mind was racing. Could he afford to continue? If he dropped the line of questioning at this point, Venable would finish it. If he went on, he would most likely shoot himself in the foot. What the hell, he thought, it's in the open. Better for him to pursue the point.

'Lieutenant,' Vail began, 'why do you believe these markings on the victim's head prove premeditation?'

'Because he planned it. He wrote in blood on the victim's head, the symbol B32.156. B32.156 is the way this book is identified, it's a method for cataloguing the books in the Bishop's library.'

'And what does it mean?'

Careful, Abel, Venable thought.

'It is a quote from the novel, *The Scarlet Letter* by Nathaniel Hawthorne,' Stenner said, opening the book. ' "No man, for any considerable period, can wear one face to himself, and another to the multitude, without finally getting bewildered as to which may be true." '

'What is the significance of that quote?'

'It is our belief that Stampler felt betrayed by Bishop Rushman, who made him leave Saviour House. His girl-friend left him, he was living in a hell hole. He felt the Bishop was two-faced. So he put this symbol in blood on the victim's head to add insult to injury.'

'Nothing more than that?'

'Just further proof that Stampler was planning to murder Bishop Rushman all along.'

'Why?'

'Because he memorized the index number of the quote, and put it on the back of the victim's head when he killed him,' Stenner said. 'I don't know what you call it, Mr Vail, but I call that premeditation.'

Vail had to make a fast decision. Should he bring in the whole sordid story of the altar boys or drop the questioning now? He decided to back off.

'I think you're reaching, Lieutenant,' he said. He

walked back to his desk. 'You can't prove the defendant was alone in the room with the victim, you can't prove he struck the fatal blow, you can't prove he came in the back door, or took the knife to the bedroom and you base premeditation on some highlighting in books and you can't even prove Mister Stampler made those markings.'

'We proved it to my satisfaction.'

'Well, I guess we should thank our lucky stars you're not on the jury, sir. I have no more questions, Your Honour. The witness may come away.'

The Judge stared at Vail as he sat down. Had Vail been ambushed, he wondered. It appeared to him, and probably to the jury, that Vail had backed away from the quote from the book. It seemed to have snapped his momentum and juries picked up on things like that.

'We have no more witnesses at this time, Your Honour,' Venable said. 'The State rests.'

Now it was Vail's turn. *What's he got up his sleeve?* the Judge wondered. He didn't wonder for long.

'Are you ready, Mister Vail?' Shoat asked.

'Yes sir, the defence is ready to proceed.'

'Please do.'

Vail said, 'The defence calls Aaron Stampler.'

And the court-room went berserk.

Thirty-Five

Although Aaron Stampler had been sitting in the front of the court-room for several days, the anticipation of the young killer on the witness stand created a minute or two of bedlam in the room. Shoat rapped the room into silence and an eerie quiet settled over the legal arena as Aaron stood up.

For five days, he sat quietly and attentively as the witnesses for the prosecution had painted him as an ungrateful psychopath who had turned on the Saint of Lakeview Drive in a brutal, senseless, and perverse combination of anger and vengeance. Throughout the trial, the well-dressed, handsome young man had listened with deep concern to the accusations made against him, seeming almost intimidated by the procedure. Now, as he approached the witness stand, the court-room became funereal, the spectators silently watching his every step, scrutinising his expression, as if his countenance might mirror the most perverse secrets of his soul. They were disappointed. All they saw was a baby-faced vulnerable youth, who appeared both confused and frightened.

When he answered the oath he said in a loud, clear voice, 'Yes suh, I will tell all the truth.'

Vail approached him with his hands in his pockets, the hint of a smile on his face, his attitude calm and reassuring.

'Please tell the court your name.'

'Aaron Stampler.'

'How old are you, Aaron?'

'I be nineteen years old.'

'And where were you born?'

'Town called Crikside in Kentucky.'

'That's C-r-i-k-s-i-d-e?' Vail asked, spelling the name to a ripple of laughter.

'Yes suh.'

'That's in the mountains in coal mining country, is it not?'

'Yes suh, 'bout an hour or so south of Lexington.'

'And where do you live now?'

'I had a stander down in Th'Hollows.'

'Was it pretty awful down there?'

'Yes suh. Dark dirty, smelt bad, n'air, n'water, n'toilets er showers. It were bad, yes suh.'

'And how long did you live there?'

'Three weeks.'

'Before you were arrested?'

'Yes suh.'

'Did you have a job at the time you were arrested?'

He nodded. 'Yes suh, clean-up man at the libury.'

'How much did you make?'

'Well, it were part tahm. Two-fifty an hour and I worked 'bout twenty-five hours a week.'

'About sixty-five dollars a week?'

'Yes suh.'

'Aaron, did you blame Bishop Rushman for that, for having to live in that awful place?'

'No suh, it were my choice.'

'Your choice?'

'Yes suh. M'girlfriend, Linda and I decided to live t'gether. We found this one room apartment and she had a job in th'supermarket s'we could afford it. Then she went back home to Ohio and I had t'move. But it weren't the Bishop's fault, I mean all thet what happened, t'weren't anybody's fault.'

'Was the Bishop upset that you were going to live with Linda?'

'He never said a thaing 'bout it, one way or t'other.'

'Aaron, did you ever have a serious fight with Archbishop Rushman?'

'No suh, I never had any kinda fight with th'Bishop. We talked a lot, mostly 'bout things I read in books, ideas n'such. But we were always friends.'

'So the Bishop did not order you out of Saviour House and you were still friends after you left?'

'Yes suh.'

Vail walked to the end of the jury box and leaned on the railing so Aaron was looking straight at the jury.

'You had access to the Bishop's library, did you not?'

'Yes, I did.'

'Could borrow books any time you wanted?'

'Yes, 'cept if somebody were in the office with him. His office and the libury were the same.'

'And this was after you left Saviour House?'

'Yes, suh.'

'So he trusted you?'

'Yes, suh.'

Not a mention of the books that Stampler marked with the highlighter, Venable thought to herself, *particularly the one book*. He was obviously tiptoeing around that one. She made a note to herself.

'How much schooling do you have, Aaron?'

'I finished high school and one yair a college in the extension.'

'You took night courses here in the city?'

'Yes suh.'

'How were your grades in grammar and high school?'

'I were always an A student.'

'Were you valedictorian of your high school graduating class?'

'Yes suh.'

'How about college?'

'Well, I taken fourteen hours altogether 'fore I had t'quit. It were five courses in all. Made all A's 'cept for a B in economics.'

'Why did you make a B in economics? Was it hard for you?'

'No, suh, it just didn't matter much t'me.'

'When did you leave Crikside, Aaron?'

'After I grad'ated high school. I were seventeen.'

'Why did you leave?'

'Was nothin' thair fer me.'

'No future?'

'Only coal mining, which I refused t'do.'

'Why?'

'I fear'd it. Killed m'paw. Killed lots of folks I knew growin' up. It were no way t'live.'

'Your mother was still alive when you left?'

'Yes suh.'

'Did she condone your leaving?'

'No suh, not partic'ly. She was fer me goin' into The Hole.'

'You mean go down in the mines?'

'Yes suh. I call it goin' in The Hole. M'paw whipped me 'cause I wouldn't go down and she stood with him on it, mostly 'cause it were all she knew t'do.'

'How did your father beat you?'

'I object, Your Honour,' Venable said. 'There's a significant difference between a whipping and a beating.'

'Never mind,' said Vail, 'I'll rephrase. How often did your father hit you?'

'Once er twice a month.'

'Did he hit you with his hand?'

'Sometahms. Mostly he took th'strap t'me.'

'The strap?'

'T'were his belt. Big, thick black belt, maybe two inches thick.' Aaron held up his hand and measured the thickness between two fingers. 'He would pull it off n'lick me with it.'

'How would he hit you?'

'Make m'bend over a chair and pull down m'britches, n'gimme licks.'

'How many licks?'

'Sometahms five, sometahms ten. Maybe more.'

'Did he break the skin with these licks on your bare behind?'

'Yes suh. Sometahms they took t'bleedin'.'

'And he did this once a month?'

'Sometahms more. Whenever he were drinkin'.'

Vail turned to the judge and said, 'Your Honour, I don't know how the State defines a beating but getting stropped once a month with a two-inch belt until you bleed qualifies in my book.'

'You made your point, Counsellor,' Shoat said with a nod.

'Aaron, could your father read?'

'No suh.'

'Your mother?'

'A mite. T'were she first read the Bible t'me – in a kinda falterin' way.'

'You had a brother?'

'Yes suh, m'brother Sam. He were killed in a car accident.'

'Aunts, uncles, other relatives?'

He shook his head. 'Nary.'

'Who was the most important influence in your life, Aaron?'

'T'was Miss Rebecca, m'school teacher.'

'She was your teacher until you went to high school, wasn't she?'

'Yes suh, it were a one-room schoolhouse and she was our teacher. She taught me ev'thin' I know. Taught me 'bout readin', history, the geography of the world. 'Bout science and psychology, adventure books and the like. She had lotsa books at her place and I were allowed to read one at a tahm. I read all of those books 'fore I went to high school, and all the books in th'Crikside libury – which weren't many. Like maybe half as many as were in the Bishop's libury.'

'Your parents didn't like you to bring books home to read, did they?'

'Uh, well, it were like an insult to m'paw, him not being able t'read n'all. I think he and maw considered it a waste a m'tahm.'

'Did Miss Rebecca encourage you to leave Crikside?'

'Ye suh. Told me t'were no future thair and thet sooner or later, I would end up in Th'Hole.'

'So you left when you were seventeen?'

'Yes suh.'

'Where did you go first?'

'Went to Lexington and I worked in a funeral home 'bout six months, then I came hair.'

'Why did you leave Lexington?'

'I always planned to come here to the city.'

Vail slowly walked down the length of the jury box, sliding his hand along the highly polished railing.

'What's the first book you ever read, Aaron?'

'The Bible. T'were the only book in our house.'

'How old were you then?'

'When I read it th'first tahm?'

'Yes.'

''Bout six.'

'You read the Bible when you were six years old?'

'Yes suh.'

'Is religion important to you?'

'Yes suh.'

'Why?'

'Well suh, I guess I'm tryin' t'figger it out.'

'Religion's in your thoughts a lot, is it?'

Aaron nodded. 'Yes suh.'

'Do you believe in God?'

'Yes suh.'

'Are you a Christian?'

'Yes suh.'

'Other than reading the Bible, when's the first time you became aware of Christ?'

'T'were from Reverend Shackles.'

'How old were you then?'

''Bout nine, I reckon.'

'Tell the jury about Reverend Shackles.'

'Well, he were a fearsome man, tall and lean like a pine tree, and he had terrifyin' eyes and a long beard, come down t'bout hair.' He pointed to his chest. 'N'he would put his hand on m'shoulder, and press down real hard till m'knees hurt, and he would sermonise over me. T'were like . . . he were pickin' me out to yell at.'

'And that embarrassed you?'

'No suh, scairt me outa m'wits. He preached hell-fire and damnation n'thair were no room fer sinners. T'were like, if you sinned, you were hellbound, an' nothin' to stop it. No absolution, no forgiveness, just hell awaitin' down thair. I mean, even if yuh jest had bad thoughts. Even when yer nine yairs old, y'cain't help havin' a bad thought now and agin.'

'So he was a frightening figure?'

'Yes.'

'And he said you were going to hell.'

'Yes, suh.'

'And that troubled you even at the age of nine.'

'Yes, suh, troubled me from then on.'

'So you tended to suppress your bad thoughts, as you put it?'

'Yes, suh.'

'Tried not to think bad thoughts?'

'Tried.'

'And when you did have a bad thought, what then?'

'I would be scairt . . . I would feel . . . uh . . .'

'Guilty?'

'Guilty, yes, suh, but also . . . y'know, like helpless.'

'Helpless in what way?'

'Thet I were going t'hell and nothin' I could do would stop it.'

'Aaron, are you familiar with the term fugue or fugue state?'

'Yes suh.'

'What does it mean?'

'Means forgettin' things for a while.'

'Do you have a term for it?'

'Yes suh. Call it "losin' time".'

'And did you ever "lose time"?'

'Yes suh.'

'Often?'

'Yes suh.'

'When?'

'Well, I'm not perfectly sure. At first you don't know it's happenin'. Then after a while you know when you lose time.'

'How do you know?'

'Well, one minute I'd be settin' here, a second later – jest a snap of a finger – I'd be settin' over thair, er walkin' outside. Once I was in the movies with a girl n'jest an instant later we were walkin' outside the movie. I don't know how the picture ended, I was jest outside on the street.'

'Did you tell anyone about this?'

'No suh.'

'Why not?'

'I didn't think they'd b'lieve me. Thought they'd make fun a me or maybe put me away.'

'So it was fear?'

'Yes suh.'

'Did it worry you?'

'Well, mainly I would wonder if I did somethin' wrong.'

'Like what?'

'Y'know, maybe I said somethin' wrong, made somebody mad, somethin' like thet.'

'Did you tell Miss Rebecca?'

'No suh. I din't tell anybody.'

'Did you know what caused it? By that I mean, were there subjects you avoided because you knew it might bring on this condition?'

'Reckon it were lotsa things. Sometahms when m'paw were lickin' me, I'd lose time. Next thing I know, I'd be in m'room and t'would be n'hour later. Sometimes when I were havin' sex, suddenly I'd be in the shower or on my way home. It was like that. First time I went in th'Catholic church it happened. Jest no way a tellin'.'

'How did you meet Bishop Rushman?' Vail asked.

'I was down on South Street, beggin' fer a meal, when this big black car pulled up and the door opened and the Bishop, he leaned out n'says, "C'mere son." So I went over n'he aisked where I were livin' and I told him sleepin' in unlocked cars n'he says, "Come along with me" and he took me to Saviour House and I moved in thet night. Reckon Billy Jordan had tole them 'bout me.'

'And you became friends after that?'

'Yes suh. From thet moment on.'

'And did you talk about religion with the Bishop?'

'Yes suh. He were tryin' to convince me t'become a Catholic.'

'And you resisted?'

'Not really. I were jest, you know, tryin' to get it all straight in m'mind. Reverend Shackles tellin' me one thaing, n'the Bishop tellin' me jest the opposite.'

'And you thought a lot about that?'

'Yes suh.'

'And sometimes when you were having sex with your girlfriend did you lose time?'

'Yes suh.'

'But you don't know why?'

'Not really.'

'And you have no recollection of what happens when you're in this state?'

'No suh. I jest lose time.'

'And this has been happening for ten years or more?'

'Yes suh.'

'And you never told anyone?'

'No suh.'

'Now I want to talk about the night Bishop Rushman was murdered. There was an altar boy meeting scheduled, wasn't there?'

'Yes suh.'

'Did any of the altar boys show up?'

'No.'

'Nobody else?' Vail was saying.

'No, suh.'

'Was the Bishop upset?'

'No. He said he were tired anyway and we could meet another time.'

'What did you do when you left?'

'I went over to Saviour House and found an empty bed. T'were real cold thet night and I din't wanna go back to The Hollows. Then I decided t'go over to the Bishop's office and borrow a book t'read. When I got there, I heard some noise – like people shoutin' – up in the Bishop's bedroom so I went up t'see if everything was all right. When I got to the top of the stairs I taken m'shoes off and stuck em in m'jacket pockets. The Bishop was in the bathroom and then I realised what I heard was him singin'. Then . . . I felt like there was somebody else thair, beside the Bishop, and that's when I lost time.'

'You didn't actually see anyone else?'

'No suh.'

'Did you see the Bishop?'

'No suh. But I could hear him. He was singin' in the bathroom.'

'You just sensed that somebody else was in the room?'

'Yes suh.'

'Then what happened?'

'Next thing I knew, I were outside, at the bottom of the wooden staircase up to the kitchen, and I saw a police car and the . . . there was a flashlight flickin' around, then I looked down . . . and uh, there was blood all over . . . m'hands . . . and the knife . . .'

Aaron stopped for a moment, staring at his hands.

'... and ... and then, I jest ran ... don't know why, I jest ran into the church and another police car was pullin' up front and I ducked into the confessional.'

'And what did you think, while you were hiding in there, before the police found you?'

'Don't remember except I was scairt, so scairt there was a lump in m'throat.'

'Aaron, did you have any reason to kill Bishop Rushman?'

'No, suh.'

'Did you plan his murder?'

'No, suh.'

'To your knowledge, did you kill Bishop Rushman?'

'No sir.'

'Thank you.' Vail turned to Venable and nodded. 'Your witness,' he said.

Connerman felt let down. When Vail had called Stampler to the stand, he had expected fireworks, it was such an audacious move. Where was the Vail flair? The surprises? The tail twisters? How was he going to prove insanity? Was he going to let her take her swipes and then come back with his heavy guns? Was his secret weapon the psychiatrist, Molly Arrington, who had been sequestered with Tom Goodman and the other witnesses since the trial began? So far, except for some nice dramatics and clever rhetoric, Vail hadn't unproven a damn thing Venable had thrown on the table. And now Vail had given her a shot at Stampler, who could not have been called to the stand unless he agreed.

Had Vail finally blown one?

Venable had a scattering of notes but the introduction of Stampler as a witness had thrown her. She was not sure exactly what strategy to follow in interrogating Stampler. She was faced with a critical decision; either she could excuse the witness, implying to the jury that Stampler's testimony in his own behalf was worthless and immaterial, or she could tread on dangerous ground, specifically, the marked books and the symbol on Rushman's head. Could she introduce this evidence and strengthen her contention of premeditation without getting into the volatile altar boy problem? It was her best shot and she decided to go straight for the jugular.

No prisoners.

'Mister Stampler,' she began, 'you say you did not plan the murder of Bishop Rushman.'

'No, m'am.'

'Or remember what happened?'

'No m'am.'

'You came up the stairs and heard the Bishop singing in the bathroom?'

'Yes, m'am.'

'Why did you take your shoes off?'

'Well, I thought I heard the Bishop arguin' with somebody and I wanted to make sure ever'thin' was all right but I didn't want him to think I was bein' nosey or anything. So I took off m'shoes so he wouldn't hear me.'

'And then what happened.'

'I heard him singin' back in the shower and that's when I lost time.'

'And you remember nothing after that?'

'No, m'am.'

'You have quite a memory for quotations and sayings that appeal to you, don't you Mister Stampler?'

'I have a good memory, yes, m'am.'

'Are you familiar with Nathaniel Hawthorne's book, *The Scarlet Letter*?'

Vail said to himself, *here she goes. She took the bait.*

'Yes, m'am, I know the book.'

'And does the phrase B32.156 mean anything to you?'

Stampler hesitated. He stared at her for several seconds without responding.

'Mister Stampler, do you understand the question?' Shoat asked.

'Uh, I believe those are the numbers that were on the back of the Bishop's head, in the pi'tures . . .'

'Is that the first time you ever saw them?'

'I reckon . . .'

'And you don't know what the numbers mean?'

'I'm not sure . . .' It was obvious to Venable that Aaron was getting fidgety and uncomfortable and she moved in closer, her voice turning hard and pushy.

'You mark passages in books that appeal to you, do you not?'

'Sometimes . . .'

'You marked passages in the books in the Bishop's library, didn't you?' she said, becoming even more aggressive.

'. . . sometimes . . .' Sweat began to form along the hair line high on Aaron's forehead. His lips appeared dry and he licked them several times. To a trained predator like Venable, it was the best of all signs. Stampler was showing signs of cracking. She went to her desk and picked up a book.

'Your Honour, I'd like this marked as State's exhibit thirty-two, please,' she said, showing the volume to Vail. It was the copy of Nathaniel Hawthorne's *The Scarlet Letter* from Rushman's library.

'No objection,' he said.

Venable walked to the witness box and handed the book to Aaron.

'Recognise this book, Mister Stampler?'

Aaron took it, looked at the cover and flipped through the pages.

'I reckon that's from the Bishop's libury,' he said thickly. She took the book back and turned to a page marked with a slip of paper.

'Mister Stampler,' she said, her voice becoming harsher. 'I ask you, did you or did you not mark a passage on page 156 of this copy of *The Scarlet Letter* – indexed by the number B32.156?'

Aaron looked at Vail but the lawyer was scribbling notes on his legal pad.

'. . . uh,' he said slowly.

'I'll be a little more direct, Mister Stampler, are you familiar with this quote from Nathaniel Hawthorne's *The Scarlet Letter*. "No man, for any considerable period, can wear one face to himself, and another to the multitude, without finally getting bewildered as to which may be true." Do you recognise that, Mister Stampler?'

'Uh . . .'

'Do you recognise it?' she demanded. 'B32.156 . . . doesn't that strike a bell, Mister Stampler?'

'I don't . . .'

'Mister Stampler, did you memorize that passage and print it on the back of the Bishop's head when you killed him?'

Vail leaped to his feet. 'Objection . . .' he started, but he never finished the sentence.

Aaron had slumped slightly as Venable's questioning turned to an attack. As Vail stood to object, Stampler suddenly looked up, his face distorted with hatred. His body seemed to change, his shoulders snapped back and his neck got thicker. His lips pulled back as he bared his teeth. With a growl like an animal in pain, he jumped up and leaped over the railing separating witness from examiner.

'You lyin' bitch!' he bellowed, 'Try to kill me . . .'

The jurors lurched back almost in unison, shocked by the sudden burst of violence.

Stampler moved so quickly that the guards and the bailiff were caught off guard.

Stampler landed two feet in front of Venable, reached out, grabbed her by the hair and twisted her around sharply as he pulled her to him. He wrapped one arm around her throat while his other hand grabbed her under the chin and twisted it. She shrieked with pain.

The court-room seemed to explode. Many of the spectators screamed, others rushed for the doors and tumbled out into the hall. The room was in pandemonium.

Shoat, startled and speechless, did not even bang his gavel.

Stampler backed away from the spectators, towards the bench, dragging Venable by the neck.

'Jesus,' Vail said half aloud and yelled, 'Roy, let her go!'

'I'll kill her,' he screamed. 'I'll break her fucking neck!'

Vail ran to within a few feet of him and stopped. Venable, her eyes bulging with fear, her tongue half out of her mouth, grabbed Stampler's arm with both hands. She looked at Vail with a combination of fear and pleading. Stampler twisted her neck slightly. 'Back off,' he ordered.

All traces of accent and humanity were gone. Only Roy's hate remained.

'Easy, Roy,' Vail said, holding both palms out towards him. 'Let her go, for God's sake. Let her go!'

'Why? So you can all kill me? Didn't even mention me, just gonna ignore me, were you? You were gonna let the bitch here crucify me!'

As Stampler backed away, a marshall stepped through a doorway behind him and, drawing his gun, crept towards him. The attention of everyone in the room was immediately drawn to this new player behind Stampler. Stampler whirled and lashed out with the hand that had been twisting Venable's neck. His elbow smacked into the marshall's face, shattered his nose, sent him reeling backwards. The gun roared and the bullet thunked harmlessly into a beam. The rest of the audience either bolted, screaming, towards the door, bursting out into the hallway or dropped to the floor. Vail continued his plea.

'Give it up, Roy. Nobody's trying to harm you.'

'You're all lying! You're the murderers, you're the ones who're gonna do the killing.'

Vail suddenly leaped forward and thrust an arm between Stampler's arm and Venable's throat. A second marshall and the bailiff bounded across the room and grabbed him from behind, snapping him sharply backwards as Vail broke his hold on Venable. She collapsed and scurried on her hands and knees away from the mêlée. Clutching her throat, she looked back astonished at the scene behind her. Stampler seemed superhuman. He tossed the bailiff away from him with one arm, sent the heavy-set man reeling across the prosecution's desk. The table crashed over with him. Papers, briefcases, notes, crashed to the floor or fluttered through the air.

Shoat regained his composure long enough to yell for order. His demand was lost in the chaos.

As the marshall and Vail struggled to subdue Stampler, another court officer led the jury hurriedly out of the room. Stampler was jerking back and forth, trying to throw Vail and the marshall off. Then a third officer jumped in, locking Stampler's arms behind him, pressing him forward as Vail lost his footing and fell to the floor. Above him he saw Aaron Stampler's face – Roy's face – contorted with rage, hissing down at him.

'*Aaron!*' Vail said. 'Aaron can you hear me?'

He scrambled to his feet and stood inches away from the struggling defendant. Then, almost as quickly as he had attacked them, Stampler's body went limp. He began to shake and then he collapsed as the bailiff and marshall rushed him from the room with Vail close behind.

'Order, order in this court-room!' Shoat demanded as the spectators turned into a babbling mob. Finally Shoat slammed down his gavel.

'This court is in recess,' he roared and headed for his chambers.

Thirty-Six

By the time the officers got Aaron handcuffed and back in the holding room adjacent to the court-room, he was completely subdued. He looked confused and frightened as they half-dragged him to a chair in one corner and sat him down. Vail knelt in front of him, taking Stampler's face in his hands and staring into his eyes.

'Aaron?' he said.

Stampler's eyes roved the room for a moment.

'I did it, didn't I? Oh, Lord, I did it right up thair in front of eve'ybody.'

'It's okay,' Vail said. 'Just take it easy.'

'What happened? What'd I do?'

'Don't worry about it,' Vail said. 'I sent for Molly, she'll be here in a minute.'

Stampler closed his eyes, let his head fall back and sighed. The door opened and Vail turned to face Venable.

'What the hell're you pulling?' she snapped.

Before he could answer, a court officer appeared behind her.

'Judge wants you both in chambers, pronto,' he said.

'Vail . . .' Venable started, but he stepped around her and smiled.

'Judge says pronto,' he said.

As they left the room, Molly Arrington rushed up.

'What happened?' she cried.

'Aaron was on the stand and he switched.'

'On the stand!' she said with surprise.

'I'll explain later. Just go in and talk to him. Calm him down. The judge wants to have a chat.'

As Venable and Vail entered Shoat's chambers, he was

pulling off his robe. He slammed it angrily into his desk chair.

'All right,' Shoat demanded, his face red in anger. 'Will somebody kindly tell me just what in hell is going on?'

'This is a scam, Your Honour,' Venable snarled. 'He rigged this whole scheme.'

'Your Honour, we had decided not to use this defence because we thought it would be too difficult for the jury to accept. I had no idea she'd trigger Roy to come out.'

'Roy! Oh God, that's outrageous. I didn't trigger *Roy* to do anything. Your Honour, it's tricks. Nobody puts the defendant on the stand right off the bat. That's suicide. It was all a set-up.'

'Who the hell is Roy?' Shoat demanded.

'Your Honour,' Vail said, 'we discovered recently – and this was after Ms Venable took Doctor Arrington's deposition – that Aaron Stampler is suffering from what is known as Dissociative Multiple Personality Disorder.'

'Explain, please,' Shoat said with a scowl.

'He has a split personality.'

'Oh for God's sake,' Shoat said, rolling his eyes. 'What next!'

'This is not a joke, Your Honour. Aaron Stampler is suffering from a severe form of dissociative behaviour. He enters a fugue state and adopts another personality. The other personality is psychopathic and commits acts of which Aaron is totally unaware. There is already testimony on record in this trial which identifies MPD as a mental disease.'

'That's bullshit,' Venable snarled.

'Easy, Miss Venable,' Shoat said.

'Judge,' Vail said, 'we have several tapes of Aaron switching personalities. No question about it, you can see it happen before your eyes, just like you did a few minutes ago in the court-room.'

'We asked for those tapes and you denied them to us,' Venable said.

'The tapes were not evidential because we had no plans to use them in trial – until now. Hell, we don't know when Roy is going to come out. Jane triggered him, not me. Besides, our tapes are privileged. These tapes constitute a privileged communication between the defendant and his psychiatrist. They are not public domain unless we choose to use them in court and Stampler agrees. Until now, our decision was not to introduce them.'

'Will you please explain to me who in hell Roy is?' Shoat said angrily.

'Aaron's alternate personality.'

'So you were aware of this, Counsellor?' Shoat asked with suspicion.

'Yes sir, but there was no way to prove it unless he actually made the switch, which, I repeat, I had nothing to do with.'

'It's tricks, Your Honour,' Venable pleaded. 'Nobody puts the defendant on the stand straight out of the barrel . . .'

'I beg to disagree,' said Vail with a smile.

Venable glared at him, her face red with humiliation. 'It was all a set-up,' she repeated.

'And this is all semantics,' Vail said. 'The point is, you introduced this line of questioning and I have a right to pursue it.'

The judge made a steeple with his fingers and stared across them at Venable with a raised eyebrow. 'Your turn, Ms Prosecutor. He's got a point. I'm not sure I'm going to buy this dual personality pitch, but we definitely must pursue it now.'

'I think he tricked me into turning Stampler around, Your Honour.'

'How?'

'I don't know,' she muttered. 'I have a right to at least *look* at this Goddamn tape if he's going to try and show it in court.'

'I have no problem with that,' Vail said. 'She can look at it as much as she wants. But we will object if she has some shrink come in and analyse my client from the television picture.'

'How come?' the judge asked.

'The best evidence in this case would be Aaron himself. We'll agree to let them examine him right on the stand.'

'Bullshit!' Venable snapped. 'That's a no-win situation. If we switch him around, you win. If we don't, you blame my psychiatrist.'

'Seems to me we have three choices,' said Vail. 'Our prosecutor can continue her cross-examination and I'll re-exam, or we can try to work out a settlement . . . or she can move for mis-trial . . .'

'Settlement! Not on your life,' Venable snapped.

'Excuse me, Judge, did I miss a meeting somewhere. *She* brought him out, I didn't.'

'You tricked the court,' she said.

'Not quite accurate,' Vail said.

'Just a minute,' Shoat said. 'I didn't come in here to listen to you two squabble. I want to know what the hell's going on?' He stroked his jaw and stared at Vail. It was true. Vail had not tricked the court, he had tricked *her*. But now the problem was about to fall in Shoat's lap.

'Your experts have qualified Stampler as sane, Madam Prosecutor,' Vail said. 'Did he look sane to you just now? Did it feel sane when he damn near broke your neck?'

'You want me to declare a mis-trial so you can go back in and have him re-examined, Madam Prosecutor, is that where you're heading at this point?' Shoat asked.

'I, uh . . .'

Vail said, 'Look, her contention is that Stampler is sane. We agree. It's Roy who's the killer. When she brought Roy out, she destroyed her own experts. I insist we finish this trial and let the jury decide whether he's sane or crazy as a jumping bean.'

'Why didn't you bring this up before, Counsellor?' the judge asked.

'I repeat: there was nothing to bring up. I didn't know the kid was going to lose it on the witness stand. This other character comes and goes. It would have been irresponsible of me to go in with that contention not knowing whether I could prove it or not.'

'So what's your plea now?'

'That Stampler didn't commit the crime, Roy did.'

'Oh sweet Jesus!' Venable cried.

'You want to fry him or cure him, Counsellor?' Vail asked.

'Cure him, my ass!'

'Now, now, Counsellor, control please,' Shoat said.

'I say we go on with it. She's had her day, now it's my turn,' Vail said.

Shoat was beginning to feel trapped by this development. What he had assumed would be a noisy but fairly cut and dried court case had turned into a bizarre headline maker. His safest stance would be to distance himself from them both.

'I have to go along with that, Miss Venable,' Shoat said finally. 'Seems to me you've got a whole new ballgame on your hands. In effect *you* introduced this new . . . person, whatever the hell you call him, Vail didn't. Anyway, you can't ask for a mis-trial – you created the problem.'

'I don't believe this,' she shrieked. 'I don't goddamn believe it. He's been contending all along that Stampler was insane. Now he says he's not!'

'No, what I'm saying is, Roy committed the murder, Stampler didn't. And Roy *is* nuts. Certifiable psychotic schizophrenic.'

'What do you want us to do,' she snarled sarcastically, 'let Stampler go and electrocute Roy?'

Vail shrugged. 'It's okay with me if you can figure out how to do it,' he said.

'Well, if Roy did do it, Aaron's an accomplice,' Venable said, trying to conceal her desperation.

'Wrong again,' Vail said. 'Stampler didn't even know what happened just now until Molly told him. He doesn't know for sure that Roy even exists.'

'Is Stampler capable of understanding the charges brought against him or not?' Shoat demanded.

'Stampler's as sane as Bascott says he is but Roy doesn't truly understand the concept of law because he doesn't accept the difference between good and evil. He's psychopathic, Judge. Totally amoral. He simply does not think the laws apply to him. That's part of his psychosis.'

'Can . . . whoever . . . be treated successfully?' Shoat asked.

'I can't answer that,' Vail said. 'Arrington or Bascott would be the best judge of that.'

'But you are saying he doesn't think murder is wrong?'

'I am saying that he doesn't think it is wrong for him to commit murder. In his mind, his only law is what he thinks and feels. He's judge, jury and executioner and he performs all three functions.'

'Stampler, you mean?' said Shoat.

'Well, physically, yes. But we aren't necessarily talking about Aaron Stampler. I've got some tapes here. I think if you look at them . . .'

'Not on your life,' Shoat sighed, slipping on his coat. 'This is your problem – both of you – and you can work it out. But let me make it clear, there will be no Goddamn mis-trial in my court. We're in it and we're going to finish it and if I hear another word about mis-trial, off comes somebody's head. Do I make myself clear?'

'Yes sir.'

'Perfectly, Your Honour.'

'It's almost noon. I'm going to lunch. I'll send my assistant in here to take your lunch orders. We'll reconvene at two. I trust you two will stay in this room and work something out by then. And I go with Vail on the interrogation. Stampler live on the stand or forget it. No TV analysis, understood?' He left the room.

Venable stood up and walked to the window where she stood with her back to Vail. 'You'll do anything to win, you son of a bitch.'

'Now wait a minute, Janie . . .'

She spun on him and said viciously, 'Do not call me Janie!'

'We can wrap this up very easily, Counsellor,' he said calmly.

'Oh, I'll bet.'

'Look Jane, Bascott sat up there under oath and testified that Stampler does not suffer from any dysfunctional mental disorder. Hell, now his whole testimony is dead in the water and you know it. He and his two pals screwed up.'

'You ambushed him.'

'No, he shot himself in the foot.'

Two marshalls entered the chambers carrying the TV set and the videotape deck.

'What the hell's this?' Venable growled.

'I think you better look at a couple of things.'

Vail and Venable ordered sandwiches while Vail plugged in the TV and connected the VCR. He put in the first tape of Aaron alternating with Roy. They watched as they ate lunch. Venable was at first angry and sceptical, then her scepticism turned to intense fascination, and finally, a look almost of horror. When the tape was finished, Vail pulled it out and put in his cross-examination – his practice tape – of Molly Arrington. Venable leaned back, puffing Bette Davis fashion on one cigarette after another as she listened to Molly explain, in medical terms and under Vail's questioning, exactly what had happened to Aaron Stampler.

'He's faking!' she said as he turned off the machine.

'Fine. Let's just go back inside and you prove that.'

'We've got a mis-trial here and you know it!'

'You brought him out, Counsellor. You can't move for a mis-trial and you know it.'

'Don't miss a trick, do you?' she said bitterly.

'I can't afford to, lady. Tough competition.'

'Goddamn it, you don't even have a case! If we do go into a new trial, I'll have twenty experts eat Stampler and Miss Freud alive.'

'Which you can't do – and even if you *can*, it'll take another year, year and a half. I don't think your new partners-in-law will like that.'

'Fuck you!' she spat, jerking to her feet, and turning her back on him again. She stared out the window.

'God *damn*,' she whispered.

'Y'know, you're also going to have to deal with Bishop Rushman's little hobby. And that's something *you'll* bring out in your cross.'

'What're you talking about?'

'C'mon, Jane,' Vail said, taking a chance. 'You found that altar boys tape and I know it. You're smart enough to know it's too hot to handle. Whoever introduces it is on dangerous ground because you can't prove it except by Roy's admission and right now you've opened that door.'

'Once it's out, it gives me a perfect motive,' she said.

'Except that Aaron's crazier than a waltzing mule. Whether he's motivated or not is moot. In the meantime, you're not only gonna bring down Rushman, you're gonna bring down the whole Foundation.'

'You're trying this case in chambers, you son of a bitch,' she snapped. 'That's why you were so loose with the jury selection. You *knew* this was going to happen.'

'You really think I'm that devious?'

'*Hah!* You invented the goddamn word.'

'Well, we can stop it right now,' said Vail. 'Let the prosecution agree to accept Roy's insanity plea. We'll agree that Aaron Stampler and Roy will be institutionalised and treated. If Roy is purged, cured, whatever you call it, then Aaron Stampler will be freed.'

'And go out and start carving people up again?'

'I said I have no problem with institutionalisation. But deal with the real murderer. *Roy*. It will be up to the doctors to determine the rest of it. You think the jury's going to send Aaron Stampler to the chair now? In fact, I'll even sweeten the pot for you.'

'Oh really, what're you going to do, have him come by at Christmas and sing carols outside my door?'

'We'll not only plead guilty to the Rushman kill, we'll plead to Peter and Billy Jordan.'

'You're admitting that?' she said.

'I said we'd cop to it. That way you get all three cases off the books. Otherwise, I'll insist we go all the way with this and that means I'll force you to establish the real motive for Rushman's murder.'

'And destroy the reputation of the victim!' Venable said. 'He's dead, he can't defend himself. The man was a saint.'

'Not according to Roy. Not according to the altar boys tape.'

'It could be anybody on that tape.'

'Except Roy will tell the whole story. He'll corroborate that Rushman was a paedophile.'

'You bastard!'

She sat quietly for several minutes. He had her and she knew it. But her inner rage would not permit her to submit.

'We're talking about truth here, Jane,' Vail said quietly. 'Let the state deal with him. Tuck him away at Daisyville, the public will forget all about him in a couple of months and we can all go home.'

She turned, her entire body rigid with anger, and stared out the window for a long minute.

'Forget it,' Vail shrugged. 'Couple of months from now we can have a drink some night and trade secrets.'

'You already know too many of my secrets,' she said, bitterly and turned back towards him. 'Right now why don't you tell me one of yours.'

'You want to know why I didn't blow the whistle on you in the Castillo case,' Vail said. 'Since you were sleeping with Miko Rodriguez.'

'That's a good guess. I don't understand why you didn't take me down.'

'I was surprised at your behaviour, Counsellor.'

She laughed harshly. 'You applying for a job as my mother?' When Vail didn't answer she sighed. 'Maybe I was in love.'

'Never fall in love with a client,' he said. 'It's unprofessional.'

'Don't you ever do anything unprofessional?' she asked.

'I never do anything that might stop me from winning.' He grinned at her. 'Been bugging you all these years, has it?'

'Just curious.'

'I had to get the tapes thrown out of your case, then admitted back into evidence in mine, so I gambled. I figured as long as you thought I wasn't going to drag you and Rodriguez into it, you wouldn't object – and you didn't. Once I nailed Rodriguez, it didn't matter anymore.'

'Just part of the strategy, right?'

Vail nodded. 'I didn't need you to win.'

'I'm glad,' she said with a sneer. 'I was afraid maybe you had a heart.'

'Not a chance,' Vail said and smiled. 'So? We got a deal?'

'You'll never get it past Shoat,' Venable said finally, weakly. 'He'll want to sentence him and have him serve out his time, if and when he is cured.'

'Let me worry about Shoat,' Vail said. 'Have we got a deal?'

When Shoat returned, the television set and tape recorder had been removed from the chambers as well as the residue from lunch. Venable was reading the plea bargain agreement which Vail had sketched out on a sheet of paper.

'Well,' Shoat said, 'have you worked anything out?'

'I think so,' Vail said. He took the sheet from Venable and slid it across the desk to the judge. Shoat put on his glasses and started to read the agreement. He stopped suddenly and looked up at Venable with surprise and shock.

'Have you agreed to this, Counsellor?' he said to Venable.

'Yes, Your Honour.'

'This isn't a compromise. It's exactly what he asked for going in!' Shoat said angrily. 'You're giving away the farm. No jail sentence? You going to let this killer plead to three brutal homicides and then walk out once he's pronounced cured?'

'He's sick, Your Honour,' Vail said. 'If he gets well what can possibly be served by putting him into a hard-time prison?'

Shoat stared across the desk at Vail.

'This was a shocking crime. A shocking crime demands retribution.'

'You mean revenge, don't you?' Vail said, edgily.

Shoat glared back. 'I won't approve this,' he said. 'I want him to do at least ten years after he's pronounced cured, if he ever is. He has to pay for his crime.'

'No,' said Vail.

'No?' Shoat said, raising his eyebrows.

'No way,' Vail said. 'Let's get on with the trial then. Only I think you should be aware, Judge, the Bishop is going to come under some serious scrutiny before it's over.'

'And just what's that supposed to mean?'

'We're going to raise some serious questions about

motive and we're going to have to scrutinise every facet of the Bishop's life. Look into his foundations . . .' Vail paused for a moment, and added, 'The Gudheim operation . . . everything.'

Shoat barely reacted. His eyes might have widened a hair, his jaw set a little firmer, but basically he was Mister Cool.

'You think that's necessary, eh?'

'Let me tell you how I feel about it, Judge,' Vail said. 'Ms Venable knows there's damaging evidence against the Bishop. She also knows if this goes on, it will be dragged into the trial. In the end, I think it would be foolish to destroy a dead man's good name, hurt the Church needlessly, raise doubts about the Rushman Foundation . . . for what? So we can exact another ten years out of a sick boy's life. He's already done his share of suffering, too.'

Shoat was not sure what they were talking about. What evidence? Obviously Vail knew about the Gudheim operation.

Was he willing to blow open the Foundation just to discredit Rushman?

The answer to that was obviously, 'Yes.'

Was there something else Shoat did not know about?

He pondered a little longer, staring at the scribbled agreement lying in front of him, as if it were lying on one side of the scales of justice. In the end, Hangin' Harry Shoat's decision was the practical one, it had nothing to do with the law or justice or retribution.

It was a simple answer to a simple question:

Why take a chance?

'All right,' Shoat said, with a shrug. 'In the interest of time and the taxpayer's money, I'll go along with it. Hopefully the little bastard'll never get out of Daisyland, anyway.'

'I applaud your compassion, Your Honour. Justice does have a heart after all,' Vail said, and laughed. 'And thank you too, Jane, for making a wise and prudent decision.'

'Go fuck yourself,' Jane Venable said.

Thirty-Seven

The decision caught everyone in the court-room by surprise.

'Your Honour,' Venable said rather brusquely, 'the State has determined that Mr Stampler is suffering from Dissociative Multiple Personality Disorder and Psychotic Schizophrenia and we have accepted his plea of guilty but insane in the murders of Archbishop Richard Rushman, Peter Holloway and Billy Jordan. The State therefore recommends that said defendant, Aaron Stampler, be committed to the state mental institute at Daisyland for an undetermined period and until such time as the State rules that he is capable of returning to society.'

Shoat did not waste time. 'The court accepts your recommendation. The defendant, Aaron Stampler, is hereby remanded to the custody of the Sheriff's Department for transfer to Daisyland. The court is in adjournment until nine a.m. tomorrow.'

Bang. He was a memory.

As soon as Shoat entered his chambers, the press charged the front of the room like a tidal wave. Pursued by radio, newspaper and TV reporters with their microphones thrust in front of them, Vail and the guards rushed Aaron out of the court-room, with reporters snapping at them as they fled to the holding room. One of the marshalls stood outside the door and kept the press at bay. A few minutes later, the Judge hustled Molly out through a back door into an empty office where they were joined by Vail. Naomi and Tom searched out an empty court-room and hastily set up a press conference for the young psychiatrist.

494

'I still don't understand what happened,' Molly said. 'All of a sudden it was over!'

'Marty sandbagged 'em,' said the Judge. 'Put Aaron on the stand and Venable brought Roy out. Next thing you know, Roy went over the railing and tried to strangle her.' The Judge chuckled and shook his head.

'Oh my God!' she said.

'The clincher was your testimony, Molly.' Vail said with a grin. 'Venable caved in when she realised what she'd be up against.'

'My testimony? I didn't even get to testify,' Molly complained.

'Of course you did,' Vail said, smiling. 'In the quiet of Shoat's chambers. And you were dynamite.'

'Excuse me,' she said. 'I thought we were a team. I thought this was about . . . about . . .'

'About what?' Vail said. 'It's about winning, Molly.'

'I remember all your talk about the majesty of the law and, and . . .'

'I also told you the only way to keep the law strong is to challenge it. We played by the rules and they had *all* the damn cards. Tell her, Judge.'

The Judge, true to his nature, raised his eyebrows and his hands. 'Excuse me,' he said. 'I have another engagement.' And he escaped from the room.

'You planned this all along,' Molly said, accusingly.

'That's right,' Vail answered. 'It *was* the strategy all along. Don't you get it, Molly, we never would have won if we'd played it straight up. There would've been a new trial. They would've brought in their big guns . . .'

'And I wasn't good enough to face them . . .'

'No, no, no. That's not the point . . .'

'What is the point!' she snapped back. 'Just winning?'

'That's right, winning,' Vail answered defensively. 'And Aaron Stampler's life was in the balance.'

The answer stopped the argument but not her disillusion.

'The court had a right to hear the whole story,' she said, finally. 'For Aaron's sake they needed to hear all the testimony.'

'Molly, welcome to the real world. This wasn't a popularity contest, it was a matter of life and death.'

Naomi popped her head around the door. She had arranged the press conference and moved the howling press minions out of the court-room and down the hall.

'Press conference?' Molly said.

'Your moment of glory,' said Vail. 'Now you can tell them the whole story. You'll have the media dancing at your feet.'

'I'm going back to my world,' she said. 'As soon as this dog-and-pony show for the press is over. But I want to say goodbye to Aaron first,' she said. 'Then I'm leaving.'

'Leaving?'

'I'm going back to my world. My rules. Goodbye, Martin,' she said.

'Just like that? Can't we even have a farewell dinner?'

She smiled sadly. 'I was in for the run of the trial, remember? Trial's over. I have patients waiting for me.'

'Molly . . .'

She turned back towards him at the door and said, 'We did save him, didn't we? We did do that.'

'Hey, maybe I'll call you sometime, come over to Winthrop for a big weekend.'

She looked up at him and smiled. 'No, you won't,' she said. And she left.

Aaron was sitting forlornly in a corner of the holding room, his hands and feet still shackled. The guards were seated in the opposite corner, joking quietly between themselves.

'I want to thank yuh, Miss Molly,' Aaron said awkwardly, as she entered the room. 'Uh . . . I reckon I owe yuh m' life and I . . .' he stammered, trying to find the right words to express his gratitude.

'You don't owe me anything,' she said. 'Just get well, okay?'

'Ah'll sure try.' He fell quiet for a few moments and then he said, quite pensively, Y' know the worst thaing of all?'

'What's that, Aaron?'

'Nothin' t'look forward to,' he said, sadly. 'I think 'bout thet a lot. Yairs n'yairs of nothin' t'look forward to.' He pondered a little longer before adding, 'But it's sure better'n bein' dead.'

She would think of that for years to come. Hopelessness was perhaps the worst of all plagues. And what could she say to Aaron, who was about to be sent off to an asylum, perhaps forever?

She went to him, leaned over and kissed him lightly on the cheek. 'I've got to go now,' she said. 'I'll come visit you, promise. Bring you Cokes and coconut cream pie.'

'Thainks,' he said, smiling as she went out the door.

Vail watched her as she hurried down the hall to the press conference. As the court-room door swung shut he felt a real sense of loss.

'That's real touching, Counsellor,' a voice said behind him. 'Run-of-the-trial romance?'

He turned around to see Shaughnessey standing in the doorway to Shoat's chambers.

'C'mon in,' the big man said. 'I'll buy you a drink. You deserve it after that show.'

Vail followed him into the room. Shaughnessey went to the sink, stopping to light a cigar.

'Shoat'll drop dead if he finds out you're smoking in this hallowed lair of his.'

'I could light a bonfire on his desk and all he'd say about it is "Thank you," ' Shaughnessey said as he slid back a panel over the sink to reveal a line of liquor bottles.

'You a bourbon man?' he asked.

'Yep,' Vail answered.

'Figures.'

He took down two pebbled highball glasses, dropped an ice cube in each, and poured each of them half full of whisky. Shaughnessey sat behind Shoat's desk and nodded to the chair facing him.

'Grab a seat, Counsellor.' Shaughnessey stared at him with a squinty, cautious look on his face as Vail sat down and swung his feet up on the corner of Shoat's desk.

'This resolution of the problem won't go down well with the public, I can tell you that,' Shaughnessey said.

'Why? Because they didn't get to strap the kid in the chair and throw the switch on him? In six months, Aaron Stampler will be forgotten.'

'You ambushed us, Martin. All that split personality crap. Then you sandbagged Shoat.'

'I didn't sandbag anybody.'

'I'm just saying the way this thing wound up, it leaves me wanting more. And the public'll feel the same way,' Shaughnessey said.

'Screw the public,' Vail said. 'We're talking about justice here, not appeasing a bunch of foaming-at-the-mouth closet psychos. The ones who want Aaron Stampler to fry are the same ones who'd like to see public executions. They'd sell hot dogs and T-shirts and let the highest bidder pull the switch.'

'The Bishop was a prince, Martin. He could charm the rattles off a diamondback and he never asked for anything for himself. He was a gift to this city.'

Vail laughed in the power broker's face. 'What a load of bullshit,' he said. 'Take off his mitre and robes and what've you got? A living stereotype of the cold-blooded, power-hungry, corporate scavenger. He was above the rules. He was an arrogant, mean, conniving, son of a bitch who used every trick in the trade to promote himself and his political itinerary.'

'Easy . . .'

'If this case had gone another day, Rushman's name would have been garbage,' said Vail, cutting him off. 'He would've been annihilated! And a lot of big balls in this town would have shrivelled up to the size of peanuts. Save me the hearts and flowers about Rushman and don't tell me about all the toes I stepped on. You're not going to believe this, but I did everybody a favour playing it the way I did.'

'Shoat says you ambushed him and Venable.'

'All I did was mention the Gudheim Foundation. You know all about that, Roy, you're on the board of trustees.'

'So?'

'So it's an illegal front. Everybody involved is a Goddamn felon and Shoat knows it.'

Shaughnessey scowled at him. 'What're you gonna do now? Run around town busting everybody's balls?'

'Not if it's stopped.'

'And how do you suggest doing that?'

'Simple. Reorganise, change your billing practices. Just get rid of it. I don't care how you do it, that's your problem.'

'Don't you understand? It's how things get done these days.'

'Not any more,' said Vail. 'A guy like Harry Shoat, he takes a fund-raiser from you or some big-shot lawyer and thinks he doesn't owe. Well, he owes all right. He's expected to say thanks in a very positive way – as you well know.'

'It's the way it's done, goddamn it,' Shaughnessey said gruffly. 'That's the way the country operates, in case you haven't been keeping up.'

'When you shake hands with the devil, Roy, you're already half-way to hell. You can never say no again.

You do what you're told because you're owned. Whether it's a million dollars or the key to the State House doesn't make any difference. All that does, that sets the price. It's like being in the Mafia. The only difference is, in your hustle, if you screw up, you die broke. In the mob, you die, period.'

Shaughnessey's lips curved into a reluctant smile. 'You are a hard-nosed bastard, all right.' His voice got hard and he speared the air with a forefinger. 'You want to get where you're goin' in this world, you got to know the routine.'

'I'm not sure where I'm going and I don't want to know the routine,' said Vail. 'I work for my clients, period. They get all I have to give. Somebody gets shot in the back in the process, tough shit. Now why don't we talk about what I'm really doing here.'

'Jesus, can't you ever be *nice*?' Shaughnessey said, changing his tone.

Vail flashed his crooked smile. 'And here I thought I was.'

'I got a firm offer for you,' said Shaughnessey.

'Oh? What are we talking about? Real estate? Used cars?'

Shaughnessey ignored the wisecrack. 'You go on as Chief Prosecutor and Assistant D.A. When Yancey moves up, you get the top spot. Then you move to Attorney General. Shit, you can be Governor before you turn forty-five. No strings attached.'

'No strings attached?'

'You heard me.'

Vail got up to leave. He finished his drink and put the glass in the sink.

'Hell, you don't want me to be Attorney General,' he said, walking to the door.

'Why not?' Shaughnessey said.

'Because if I am, you'll probably end up in jail,' Vail said with a chuckle, and left.

Jack Connerman was sitting on a bench outside the court-room drinking a cup of coffee when Vail came out. The reporter stood up and walked down the hall with him.

'Dynamite, Counsellor,' he said. 'Probably your best performance to date.' He motioned to a room with the hand holding the coffee. 'The rest of the press chased the doctor down there.'

'Why aren't you down there with them? She's got the story.'

'The story's right here, Martin. You're *always* the story. That was a hell of a long shot, putting the kid on the stand. How could you be sure Venable would turn him around?'

'Never give up, do you, Jack?' Vail said with a smile.

'I love to watch an artist at work.'

'Flattery doesn't work. You've tried it before.'

'And you never give up a thing, do you?'

'Hell, I don't have any secrets, Jack.' Vail smiled. 'I play every hand in public.'

'Sure you do, and this one is a classic. This perform-ance today? It's for the book! You were good in the Heyhey case, but that was a warm-up compared to this one. First-year law students'll be reading about this for years to come.'

'Second-year,' Vail said. 'Too advanced for beginners.'

They both laughed at his arrogance.

'You can get all the quotes you need from Dr Arring-ton,' Vail told him.

'I'm not interested in the mental jargon – I'm sure she's right on the button with whatever she says. I'm interested in how you manoeuvred this case into a plea settlement.'

'I didn't, the prosecutor did. She triggered Aaron.'

'How did you set her up?'

'What're you talking about?'

'C'mon, Marty, Christ, I've been following your career for six, seven years. You had everything riding on it – that Venable would turn him on the stand, I mean.'

'Who says?'

'It's obvious.'

'Circumstantial.'

'Yeah, well I'll read the testimony on that. I'll figure it out. Thing is, you could have revealed this thing about a split personality a couple of weeks ago but you figured it had to blow up in the court-room to have the impact, right?'

'It's your story, not mine.'

'You ambushed Venable,' Connerman said. 'I know it. When you two came outa Shoat's chambers she looked like she was just told she had to eat her own young. Before that, you had nothing . . . and you still ate her witnesses up.' He shook his head. 'You're the ultimate crowd pleaser, Marty. But you make me nervous.'

'Why's that?'

'Hell, it isn't as if this boy's some back-alley shooter, y'know. What he did makes my palms wet.'

'By the time they're through with ice cube baths and electric shock treatments, he'll be a pussycat.'

'You really think the kid's two different people?'

'Talk to Dr Arrington about that,' Vail said. 'She's free to say anything she wants.'

'Will she talk to me?'

'Ask her. Hell it's a free country.'

They stopped at the rotunda and stared down into the sprawling lobby of the court-house. Cigarette butts, discarded newspapers and trash from the mob littered the marble floors.

'Didn't get their pound of flesh today,' Vail muttered.

'Who?'

'The mob. You never write about the mob, Jack, and the mob's what it's all about. Justice is crowd pleasing. It's the freak show, the geek biting heads off live chickens. That crowd for the past few days wanted to see the madman who butchered the saint. Up close . . . so they could smell his breath. When he freaked out on the stand, it was like . . . like the Superbowl. They got to see madness up close, in person, got to wet their pants when he started tearing up the court-room. I don't please the crowd, Jack; the mob pleases itself. It comes to court to masturbate. Sometimes you have to manufacture the fantasy for it.'

'I'll quote you on that, whatever the hell it means. Do you think he'll ever get out?'

Vail started to say something and hesitated for a moment. 'Let's hope so,' he said. 'Be terrible to waste a mind like that.'

'But what do you *think*?'

Vail stared at him for a moment and said, 'I think I'm a lawyer, not a shrink.'

Connerman watched Vail stride down the hall towards the holding room, then threw his empty coffee cup into a crammed trash can and headed for the Arrington press conference.

Aaron would be leaving for Daisyland in a few minutes. He was sitting beside a table in a far corner of the room, hands cuffed and his legs shackled together by a short chain when Vail entered the small room.

'Could we have a moment in private?' Vail asked the two guards, who were smoking and joking between themselves near the door.

'Why not, Marty,' one of them answered. 'He ain't goin' nowheres.' They stepped into the hall. Vail sat down beside Aaron.

'Know what I heard the guards say?' Aaron said. 'Thet Miss Molly's gonna be faimous 'cause a all this.'

'Probably,' Vail told him. 'She certainly deserves to be.'

Aaron smiled at him and said in a low voice, 'Kin ah tell you sompin', Mistah Vail? Jest 'tween you n' me?'

'Sure.'

'You were a god-send t' me, y'know thet? You and Miss Molly.'

'Thanks, Aaron.'

'Thet night they found me in the confessional, I was scair't outa m' wits.'

'I'm sure you were. Must've been terrifying.'

'Yeah, but after ah met you, ah knew ev'thing'd be all right.'

'You have good instincts,' Vail said.

'Ah s'pose,' he said. 'Ah jes' knew from the first time I met yuh, we was gonna win, n' matter what.'

'How did you figure that?'

'Jes' the way ya talked.' He giggled and leaned towards Vail. 'Yuh had the right attitude.'

The comment surprised Vail.

'Right attitude?' he said.

'Y'know what I main,' he said, and winked.

'Look, she'll go over the tapes with Doctor Bascott and his staff. Brief them on what she knows about your condition.'

'They ain't as smart as she is.'

'They'll do okay by you, I'm sure. They're excellent in their field.'

'Didn't seem laik thet. You kinda made 'em look foolish.'

'That's how it goes sometimes. Doesn't work that way all the time.'

'Will I ever get t'see the taipes?'

'I'm sure you will, sooner or later. It will probably depend on how well your therapy goes.'

'Maybe they won't accept her opinion. Y'know, thet thair's two of me. Cain't she work with me?'

'I'd like that, too, Aaron. Unfortunately, you're now under the State's jurisdiction. It's their ballgame.'

'Kinda stupid, doncha thaink?'

'How come?'

'Well, her and me, we been workin' t'gether fer a while, you'd think they'd want t' take advantage of that experience . . .'

As Aaron spoke, something about him distracted Vail for a moment. What was it? Was it his eyes? An almost inperceptible shift in expression . . .

'. . . she knows Roy s'well . . .' he added.

Vail stared at Aaron for several seconds. He shook a cigarette from his pack, drew it out with his lips and lit it. Thinking.

'What about Roy?' he asked.

'Sometimes I annoyed myself,' he said.

He felt a sudden chill. An inner thing. Instinct. Something was happening here.

'I beg your pardon?' he said.

Suddenly all trace of his Appalachian twang vanished, replaced by Roy's flat mid-western accent. Vail smoked quietly, blowing the smoke towards the ceiling, waiting to see what was coming.

'Roy?' he said, finally.

'Thet depends,' he said in Aaron's voice. 'Who d'yuh railly wanna talk to? Me?' His body language changed suddenly. His eyes became dead, his tone harsh. 'Or do you want to talk to old Roy? Wanna hear a secret?' Once again his body language altered, his eyes brightened, Appalachia returned to his voice. 'Yuh'll get the saim answers either way.'

And he laughed at Vail.

This time the chill sliced through Vail. His mouth turned a little drier. He glared at the boy for several seconds, then he stood up suddenly and started towards the door.

'Hang on there, Marty. Don't be foolish.' The body language had changed again. 'Just relax and listen to me.' He stood up, stretched his arms out behind him and, without taking his eyes off Vail, shuffled to the end of the table and back. He stood a foot or so in front of the lawyer. Vail sat back down. When Stampler spoke, his demeanour and his accent changed. Back and forth. Roy to Aaron to Roy to Aaron . . . It was like watching a

505

surreal cartoon. Or an alien in a sci-fi movie. It was like watching mercury slithering back and forth in a test tube.

'Jest thaink about it, Marty. What'air ya' gonna tell 'em? That they screwed up? Christ, man, you ploughed up the court-room with their noses. You made that judge look like he just swallowed a fuckin' water melon.' He sat on the edge of the table, staring down at Vail through Aaron's soft eyes. 'Th' cain't try me n' more, that'd be d'ble jeopardy.' The eyes changed again, hardened. 'Besides, yuh tell 'em ah tricked yuh, you'll be the biggest fool in th' stait. And the Doc? hell, she'll be gone, man. She may get the word somewheres down the line.' Roy laughed. 'But you won't tell her, that'd be just plain stupid, right?' He laughed again. 'They'd thaink you two set up th' whole thaing. That might hurt you but it'd *ruin* her.' Vail glared at him with ball-bearing eyes. Anger boiled up inside him but he remained deadly calm. He finished the cigarette and leaned towards the ashtray.

'Here, lemme do that for yuh,' Roy said, twitching the butt from Vail's fingers. He took a deep drag and blew a perfect circle of smoke which wobbled across the room before it dissipated. 'Thaink 'bout it, Martin. Act'lly it weren't too hard . . . all I had to do was fool you and Molly and those jokers up at Daisyland for a few weeks. Just a few weeks is all. Plaiy it strai't fer th' thray stooges up at the nut farm . . . do the switch between me and Aaron for you and Molly . . . look good on yer taipes . . .' He laughed, a soft, mirthless, chuckle.

The hair on Vail's arms and the back of his neck was electrified as Stampler switched, suddenly and easily, in the middle of a sentence, merging Roy and Aaron before Vail's eyes.

'I gave her the lie, you maid it stick. I didn't know how lucky I was – until I heard the guards up at Daisyland talkin' about all her great work with splits . . . t'was thet background give me th' idea. I knew enough 'bout it, why shit I been readin' all them books 'bout it for yairs, even DSM 3 . . . so what'd I have to lose, anyway, right? I mean, they were gonna *burn* me, Marty!'

Vail looked up at Aaron – and Roy – and said harshly, 'Okay, what's the angle? Why the hell're you telling me this?'

'Ohhh, hell, I gotta tell somebody. Wouldn't you want to? Ah main, yuh cain't keep somethin' thet good t'yer-self. Who'm ah gonna tell, Harcourt Bascott? Shit, I'll bet he thinks he's gonna to be famous when he cures me. Y' know, he figgers he'll get ridda old Roy and then ah'll be jest fine. Well, let me give you a clue, Marty. Old Roy's gonna be around a while longer. See, somebody's gotta know. Or what'd be the point in doin' it?' Roy leaned forward, and whispered down at Vail. 'Look, they're gonna treat me the same way up at the nut farm no matter what the doc tells 'em, so why do something stupid now? You're a winner Marty. And you won. Don't throw away a victory over somethin' that don't make no difference to nobody.'

'Nobody except you and me,' Vail said.

'That's right,' Aaron said, 'you an' me,' and then he sat there, switching back and forth, laughing at Vail, laughing at all of them, until one of the guards stuck his head around the door. 'Time to go, son,' he said.

'So there never was a Roy,' Vail said flatly. 'That what you're telling me?'

He leaned back towards Vail.

'Well, thaink 'bout this, Mistuh Vail,' Aaron said, and Roy added a sentence, and then he started to laugh and he was still laughing as the marshall led him out the door. Vail could hear the laughter, muffled behind the door, echoing down the hall as they took Stampler away. And for years after that, in the silence of the night, he would remember that laugh. And hear Stampler's last words to him.

'Suppose there never was an Aaron.'

A Selected List of Fiction Available from Mandarin

While every effort is made to keep prices low, it is sometimes necessary to increase prices at short notice. Mandarin Paperbacks reserves the right to show new retail prices on covers which may differ from those previously advertised in the text or elsewhere.

The prices shown below were correct at the time of going to press.

☐	7493 0576 2	**Tandia**	Bryce Courtenay	£4.99
☐	7493 0122 8	**Power of One**	Bryce Courtenay	£4.99
☐	7493 0581 9	**Daddy's Girls**	Zoe Fairbairns	£4.99
☐	7493 0942 3	**Silence of the Lambs**	Thomas Harris	£4.99
☐	7493 0530 4	**Armalite Maiden**	Jonathan Kebbe	£4.99
☐	7493 0134 1	**To Kill a Mockingbird**	Harper Lee	£3.99
☐	7493 1017 0	**War in 2020**	Ralph Peters	£4.99
☐	7493 0946 6	**Godfather**	Mario Puzo	£4.99
☐	7493 0381 6	**Loves & Journeys of Revolving Jones**	Leslie Thomas	£4.99
☐	7493 0381 6	**Rush**	Kim Wozencraft	£4.99

All these books are available at your bookshop or newsagent, or can be ordered direct from the publisher. Just tick the titles you want and fill in the form below.

Mandarin Paperbacks, Cash Sales Department, PO Box 11, Falmouth, Cornwall TR10 9EN.

Please send cheque or postal order, no currency, for purchase price quoted and allow the following for postage and packing:

UK including BFPO — £1.00 for the first book, 50p for the second and 30p for each additional book ordered to a maximum charge of £3.00.

Overseas including Eire — £2 for the first book, £1.00 for the second and 50p for each additional book thereafter.

NAME (Block letters) ....

ADDRESS..

....

☐ I enclose my remittance for ....

☐ I wish to pay by Access/Visa Card Number ☐☐☐☐☐☐☐☐☐☐☐☐☐☐☐☐

Expiry Date ☐☐☐☐